Shadows of Fire

by

Clare Ritchie

First published in Great Britain in 2015
ISBN: 978-0-9928951-1-2

Published by The Wacky Wordshop
40 Emmerson Way, Hadleigh, Suffolk IP7 6DJ
http://thewackywordshop.co.uk

© 2015 Clare Ritchie

Cover illustration © Sarah Ritchie
Printed and bound by Amazon CreateSpace

Acknowledgements.
To Sarah, my Smarey and amazing sister, for
the awesome cover and for putting up with my stubborn
silence during those long hours when I was writing; to Janet
Tabinski for all the hours spent editing my work to shape
it into its final form; and to Brice Higgins for once
again publishing my book and continuing
to believe in me. Thank you.

Dedication
This book is dedicated to Granny and Grandad Ritchie and to Grandpa Hampshire for all the love they have shown me over the years, and is in remembrance of Granny Hampshire in Heaven.

The Pentelement Trilogy

BOOK 1

Shadows of Fire

by

Clare Ritchie

THE WACKY WORDSHOP

Hadleigh, Suffolk

Pronunciation Guide

Ahumaia Ah-hoo-*may*-a

Eishoxa Ee-*shoks*-a

Ewdicani Oo-dee-*kah*-nee

Düerasgörn Doo-er-*ras*-gorn

Dulcacohefen Dool-kah-ko-*hef*-en

Fiera Fee-*air*-a

Gresceva Gres-*sev*-a

Indocani In-doh-*kah*-nee

Maya *May*-a

Morika Mor-*ree*-ka

Rianox *Ry*-a-noks

Sicharenhafan Sik-ah-ren-*hah*-fen

PART 1

CHAPTER 1

THE GROUND BENEATH her was warm. Eishoxa smiled up at the sun, breathing deeply of the dry summer air. The bright rays of the desert sun were diffused by the wide fronds of the palm tree hanging over her.

Movement sounded near her. She looked up at the girl sitting opposite, whose face was creased in frustration as she surveyed the chessboard between them.

"I don't know where to move," the girl sighed, pouting in disappointment. "I think you've won again."

Eishoxa sat up and looked down at the board, set out on the low table between them. The white pieces were all cowering in one corner, hemmed in by Eishoxa's huge brown battalion. Her opponent's defeat looked imminent. She met the other girl's eyes mischievously.

"Well then," she grinned, "try doing this." And with one move she swept all the pieces off the board. They clattered onto the ground, rolling around their feet. Maya laughed and pushed the board away.

"I think that's considered cheating," Maya said, as she stopped a chess piece from rolling further away. She placed it on the table.

"You think a lot of things are cheating," Eishoxa shrugged, settling herself more comfortably on the hard ground. "But at least this way we draw."

"I suppose," Maya replied. The two girls were silent for a moment before Maya spoke again.

"I don't want the summer to end," she whispered mournfully. Eishoxa murmured in agreement. The end of summer meant the start of many things. Maya would go back to Cara, the neighbouring country, and Eishoxa would have to stay in Bareth, where there would be no one to talk to and nothing to do. At the end of summer, winter would settle in. Bareth was surrounded by countries on all sides, countries that were full of water and ice. For them, winter meant snow, making it difficult to transport the cartloads of food that kept Bareth alive. Winter was always harder to survive than summer.

"Why don't you ask whether you can stay here longer?" Eishoxa asked. Maya snorted. "That wouldn't work and you know it."

Eishoxa did know it, and had deliberately asked so that she could hear it from Maya's own lips. This particular winter would also see them both turn seventeen, and that meant the end of freedom for both. From then on, they would be confined to their respective castles until they were married.

Eishoxa loved Bareth with all her heart and wouldn't have lived anywhere else for anything in the world. When foreign dignitaries visited her father and mother, the King and Queen of Bareth, they would leave with a sympathetic, superior smile on their faces, looking down at her and saying, "What a hard life you have here. I'm sure, if you could, you would gladly give this up to live somewhere else." The answer every time, for Eishoxa at least, was a definite no. Bareth was

1

an unforgiving land, harsh and cruel, yielding only a meagre supply of crops, never enough to feed the people, but it was Eishoxa's world and she wouldn't have given it up for anything. However, to have to surrender her freedom – the one thing she cherished more than her country – to be what her society considered the perfect princess, seemed too hard. She shook her head abruptly, trying to rid it of the troublesome thoughts

"Let's go to the river," she suggested, jumping up and brushing down her dress. "Try to get our minds off all these things."

Bareth Castle towered above them as the girls ran down to the river. This river, the only supply of water for the whole country, had never run dry, not even during the many droughts. No one quite knew from where its source was, although some people believed it came from underground springs that started in the mountains. This belief had been mulled over and examined many times and was generally accepted, although some more sceptical minds pointed out that the nearest range was in Cara, and there were miles of desert between here and there.

The hill upon which Bareth Castle was built seemed nothing special because all the glorious gardens, fountains and beauties of the castle were hidden behind its high walls. Beyond the river were the few villages that still clung to existence, and beyond that lay scrubby wasteland. According to the elders of the village, there used to be fertile soil and bountiful harvests every year, but then many droughts and fires had come and their paradise had turned into a dry, barren desert, full of nothing but snakes and scorpions. This tale had been told many times in many different ways, and no one knew the truth anymore. Some said that they'd seen, with their own eyes, huge rivers dry up within moments; some said that they'd seen mountains tumble. One thing was clear though: Bareth hadn't always been like this. Its people waged a never-ending war against the elements, each opponent as stubborn as the other. The people would not submit and leave, and the droughts never failed to come every year.

The two girls ran laughing down the hill and to the edge of the river. They looked nothing alike and were as different from each other as they could possibly have been, and yet each relied on the other more than either would admit. Eishoxa was tall and slim; her skin was olive-brown from her natural desert heritage as well as many days spent in the sun, and her dark red hair hung loosely to her waist. Maya was from a very mountainous country, icy and wet, where the sun was rarely seen. Her pale skin looked out of place in this desert world, despite her also spending many days in the sun. She had straight, white-blonde hair, always pulled back from her face in a tight bun, and her eyes were the colour of the desert sky. She was also shorter than Eishoxa. But the biggest difference was in their demeanor. Eishoxa's face was almost always frowning, yet she radiated an aura of being loved and cared for, a feature that Maya lacked. Her face, although creased

2

with a hopeful smile, revealed the years of neglect she'd suffered at the hands of her selfish family.

At the riverside the two girls took off their shoes and splashed their way in. Despite the heat of the sun, the river was icy cold and the current very strong as they made their way out to a big crooked rock protruding bravely from the choppy water. It was one of five rocks known as the Giant's Fingers, which were spread out along the length of the river. Maya shivered as she wrung out the hem of her sopping dress and leaned back against the rock. Eishoxa clambered up beside her. The two girls surveyed the river in silence. The underwater current caused waves on the surface of the river to splash up onto the banks and over the desert sand. No creatures lived in this river, but on a calm day one could look down from these rocks through the clear water and see the river's bed, decorated brightly with strange-coloured stones. Eishoxa trailed her fingers in the water. Presently she asked, "Are things getting better at home?"

Maya clenched her teeth and shook her head. "The Queen is no better, and the King isn't helping. He still wants war with the rebels, despite everyone advising him against it. He's going to destroy everything. I think they're planning on getting rid of me, even before my confinement." Maya, for as long as Eishoxa could remember, had never called her parents anything but the King and Queen. Over the years, it had rubbed off onto Eishoxa as well. If they discussed them as the King and the Queen, then they could have been anyone. Maya too had never been called anything but Princess of Cara. It made the whole family impersonal to one another.

"Have they already decided that?" Eishoxa asked, picking at a piece of moss lodged in the rock.

"They'll find someone to marry me off to," Maya said quietly. "It's much easier to dump your daughter on someone else and claim the rewards that go with it than to have a long confinement." Her usually gentle voice sounded very bitter and her shoulders were hunched.

"We both have to get married sometime," Eishoxa reminded her softly. It was true. There hadn't yet been a Royal Family that hadn't married off their daughters within a year of their turning seventeen. As Eishoxa said it, she was reminded, with a sinking feeling, of the lack of freedom in her own life.

"Yes, but you'll have a choice. The King adores you and will surely take your preference into account. You probably won't even be confined. Unlike me," countered Maya, her expression twisted in resentment. She sighed. Eishoxa took her hand sympathetically.

"What's the point of thinking about it when you know it won't make anything better? I'll have to be confined as well. I don't get that much say, and the Queen won't give me my freedom. You know that."

Maya nodded, took a deep breath and tried to smile. "And there's the Masked Ball tonight to celebrate your sister Rosemarie's wedding anniversary, isn't there?" Eishoxa groaned. "You forgot, didn't you?" Maya smiled, her earlier thoughts almost gone. Eishoxa nod-

3

ded. "Everyone's been talking about it for weeks, and we saw most of the preparations, remember? How can you forget?"

"Because I don't listen to what they say, and you know it," Eishoxa snapped, and then she frowned. "I don't want to go," she complained, her face falling. "They make me dance when everyone knows that I can't."

"But it's the Masked Ball," Maya said. "It's one of the most famed events in the whole world." Her face had lit up. She loved to dance as much as Eishoxa loved to ride camels and climb trees and do things that were considered inappropriate for girls of her position and age to do. She rearranged her dress so that it didn't hang in the water.

"But it's always great fun, isn't it?" she teased, nudging Eishoxa in the shoulder.

Eishoxa playfully slapped her arm. "It isn't! How you can enjoy something like that always amazes me. It's full of formal conversations and unending meals that you have to eat very slowly, even if you're starving, and horrible dresses that are too tight. Rosemarie," she continued, "considering she only came back because it's specially for her this year, will be absolutely unbearable."

Maya giggled. "No, she won't be. She's much nicer than you make her out to be. And our dresses aren't that bad."

Eishoxa huffed. "Whatever you say, Maya." With that, she entered the river again and, despite the current, started to swim strongly out to the centre. Maya followed, slipping into the water like a fish, with barely a splash. She was happier in the water than anywhere else. She caught up with Eishoxa and overtook her easily. By the time they climbed out, dripping wet and cold, the sun was low in the sky and lights had been lit in the castle.

Maya looked down at her dress, ruined and soaked. "We're going to be in trouble," she warned as they picked up their shoes and began trooping up the hill.

"Let's say we fell in," Eishoxa suggested, leading the way to the gates. They got more than a few strange looks as they passed by the guards and headed towards the main body of the castle.

Bareth Castle had been built by nomads, people who had wandered from place to place and had decided that this was a good place to settle and make their home. At first the castle had just been a small thing, a house just slightly larger than those on the other side of the river. But soon it grew, and kept on growing. Its mud walls were replaced with wood, and then stone. Walls rose; towers and turrets erupted through the straw roofs. The place swelled, the grandeur too. The inhabitants built gardens within the walls of their castle, filling them with exotic rare flowers and imposing bronze fountains and statues. Flags now hung from turrets, carpets as thick and soft as lion's fur lined its many corridors, and the patriotic colours of yellow, orange and red adorned every room and hall.

The people of Bareth loved the sun and the day as much as the people of Cara loved the moon and the night. Two completely different nations, and yet they were allies of a sort, agreeing on some matters while disagreeing on others. The King of Cara was constantly warring against one neighbour or another, whether his allies approved or not; whereas, rather than shed blood, the King of Bareth preferred to negotiate treaties and agreements. It had been during one of these conflicts, when Maya's family had come to Bareth to discuss a treaty, that Eishoxa and Maya had met.

Maya followed Eishoxa into her room and went to the robes that lay on Eishoxa's bed. Teeth chattering, she pulled one on and sat on the floor, wringing out her loose hair.

Eishoxa took a little longer, going first to the window to open the shutters and look out over the courtyard. The sun was brimming with golden light, which seeped across the desert like water overflowing from a cup. The little courtyard below glowed in the light of the setting sun, and people there hurried to and fro, all preparing for the evening's festivities. At the sight of them, she winced again.

"I don't want to go," Eishoxa repeated, half-closing the shutters and thumping her fist against the wood.

Maya smiled, combing her hair. "You have to go; you won't be able to excuse yourself from this one," she grinned, struggling with a particularly stubborn knot.

Eishoxa turned and walked back towards her, removing the band that held back her long red curls. "You sound so satisfied about the situation," she grumbled, taking the comb from Maya's hand.

"It's funny when you don't like something. You make it so obvious. You sulk as though it's going to help," commented Maya, sweeping her hair over one shoulder to let Eishoxa comb it.

"But it's not fair that I should dance when I hate it. It's not that I can't – because I can," she snapped as Maya gave her a disbelieving look. "I just don't like it."

Maya turned her head and raised her eyebrows. "And I love it, but I'll never be asked to dance because I don't come from Bareth." It was, unfortunately, true. Maya's appearance was so different that she was rarely spoken to and certainly never asked to dance. It would be considered a humiliation.

"You know what we should do?" proposed Eishoxa, still engrossed in the task of combing her friend's hair. "We should swap dresses."

"What do you mean?"

"You go in one of mine and I'll go in one of yours. That will make tonight much more interesting, perhaps even bearable. Also, I won't be asked to dance and you will be. No one will ever find out because we'll have our masks and evening gloves on."

Maya laughed again, claiming the comb and starting on Eishoxa's hair. "You come up with the strangest ideas. It wouldn't work."

"But think about it," Eishoxa insisted, fidgeting with excitement. "It will make it fun for both of us. You get to dance, and I get to sit on the side and make the table manners of Cara look slightly more civilised than barbaric."

5

"Are you calling us barbaric?" Maya asked. Eishoxa turned around, grinning. "We can try," Maya said, sweeping the comb through the red locks for the last time. "But we'll look very strange in each other's things. And we'll be discovered."

"How? We'll have masks on and cover our hair."

"Someone will find out. But we can try."

It didn't take the two girls very long to get ready. Maya was right; they did look strange in each other's clothes, but Eishoxa liked the strangeness. It looked ethereal, as though they belonged to different worlds. Maya's pale skin looked ghostly in the dark wine red of Eishoxa's dress. Eishoxa tilted her head to one side, examining her friend's appearance. Maya wore the dress extremely well. It had a ruby skirt, which billowed alluringly as its wearer walked, but revealed the shape of the legs. The bodice was of a similar material and colour but fit tightly, and the neckline plunged in a seductive scoop. Upon Maya's head Eishoxa had fixed her own diadem. She'd insisted that Maya leave her long blonde hair loose and cover it with a hooded cloak fastened under her neck.

Eishoxa's attire was quite different. Maya's dress comprised many layers of blue and white silk under a dark blue skirt. It was decorated with the night sky: the moon and countless constellations. Eishoxa's dark shoulders were covered, but she too wore a light blue cloak that covered her red hair and dark skin.

"It looks much nicer on you," mused Maya, tilting her head to one side in thought as the two of them stood in front of the mirror.

"Nonsense," replied Eishoxa airily.

"We still look like ourselves though," Maya said.

Eishoxa picked up her mask. Maya had brought a simple one with her. Fashioned in the shape of a crescent moon, it was painted silver and covered in shimmery white glitter. She placed it on her face and secured it with two white ribbons at the back of her head, tucking them under her veil. "There! Now you wouldn't know the difference."

Maya fixed on Eishoxa's more elaborate mask. It was made of many sunbeams, painted in different shades of yellow and orange. The whole thing had been coated in gold dust, which gave the impression that the sun itself had come down and kissed the mask, covering it in sunlight.

Eishoxa seized Maya's hands and they spun around the room, laughing. For someone who hated dancing as much as Eishoxa, she was very graceful and fluid. "Promise me you'll dance with me tonight," Eishoxa begged as Maya hummed and continued to spin slowly.

"With you?" laughed Maya. "Why?"

"Because we do it so well together." Eishoxa brought her to a halt. "Promise me you'll give me at least one of your dances."

"If I'm not too busy," teased Maya.

A knock on the door interrupted them. "Come in," Eishoxa called, pulling down her mask.

It was Rosemarie. Eishoxa's older sister had the regal air of a princess and had treated Eishoxa, ever since she was born, as one might a novice who nevertheless had promise. She firmly believed that, with proper tutelage, Eishoxa had it in her to be the good daughter she herself was. When the two girls were younger, Rosemarie had been great to play with because she could always cover for them – no one would have suspected her of doing anything wrong. But since Rosemarie's marriage, Eishoxa thought she'd become a complete snob. Now, at the sight of the two girls' attire, her pretty brown eyes widened and she covered her mouth.

"What have you done?" she gasped, stepping into the room to get a better look at them. She looked radiant. Her thick dark-brown hair was barely held back by the richly embroidered red band adorning her forehead, and her long gown of red and orange satin swished around her legs as she walked.

Eishoxa grinned at her. "What do you think?" She spun round, making her dress flare out from her knees.

"You both look ridiculous," she declared firmly, putting her hands on her hips. "Eishoxa, what are you doing? This isn't the time to mess around!"

"Yes, we know," Eishoxa smiled, swaying to and fro as she approached her sister.

"You'll be discovered," Rosemarie continued, "and that would be embarrassing for our parents and Maya's parents too. Eishoxa, it's my celebration tonight. Don't ruin it, please!"

"No one will know."

"I knew immediately," Rosemarie pointed out. "Both of you need to change, this minute! You don't have much time left before you need to be in the Great Hall."

Maya self-consciously started to obey but Eishoxa stopped her. "Leave us alone, Rose, and go and bother someone else." She pushed her out and shut the door with a giggle.

"Eishoxa! You shouldn't do that! You should listen to your sister!"

"Not when she speaks nonsense, I shouldn't," countered Eishoxa, undeterred. Maya couldn't help it. She laughed too.

CHAPTER 2

THE MASKED BALL was the most celebrated festival in the whole of Bareth and one of the most famed events in the whole world. Eishoxa had seen more foreign dignitaries here than at any other celebration. The people had celebrated the Ball for as long as anyone could remember. The celebration of this event was more woven into their history than even their language. For them, this night was the annual climax of their existence. It was as much a part of the place as the name Bareth was. Everyone would come to the castle, dressed in their best clothes, from the lowliest peasant to the King and Queen themselves. The only compulsory thing was the mask. Everyone had to wear one. And this night the Great Hall was even more beautiful than Eishoxa could remember.

Transformed from its usual formal attire, the Hall had become a place of revelry and celebration with flickering fire and candlelight. Every inch of wall was covered with silk drapes in the patriotic Bareth colours of red, orange and yellow. The ceiling, made from a deep crimson wood, twinkled in the light from the fires roaring in the hearths. The mirrors reflected the many guests in their dresses of satin and silk. Candles were evenly spaced along the walls, dripping wax onto the tablecloths, and in the flickering shadows people laughed and danced with great jollity. Music was playing already, a slow dreamy tune, and in the centre of the Hall, couples revolved round and round. Set along the edge of the room, on little tables brought out only for this occasion, was an array of food and drink that was constantly replaced by stewards gliding amongst the many guests with platters of food and jugs of water and wine.

And the masks! Every man, woman and child was unknown behind their mask, sequined or sewn, bird-beaked or lion-snarling. The children had made their own from sticks and leaves. The nobility swirled in their ostentatious gowns, their faces covered with more beautiful pretence and made with great care from long ostrich feathers, jewels or silk. Here everything was hidden, everything was disguised. No one knew anyone else. All could attend without fear of being recognised.

Maya had been claimed by a stuttering young man, whom Eishoxa knew only by sight, and was now dancing elegantly on the dance floor. Both girls had kept their masks firmly in place, and Eishoxa felt perfectly safe and perfectly free.

At the top of the Hall Rosemarie was sitting at the table laid for the nobility and the Royal Family. Her husband was dancing with one of the ladies of the aristocracy and she sat there alone. Eishoxa watched her sipping wine from behind her mask. This ball was in particular honour of the anniversary of her wedding day, two years before. Rosemarie, who was three years older than Eishoxa, had been married off to a foreign Duke. The only time she came back to Bareth was when she celebrated events like this. Eishoxa didn't really know her sis-

ter anymore. It had been years since they'd done things together. In their childhood they'd been closer, but now they squabbled more than ever. After Eishoxa had met Maya, she'd withdrawn from her sister, who seemed only too happy to do the same, and left Eishoxa out of everything that she did or said. Eishoxa didn't miss her once she'd married and gone to live with her husband.

The dance ended and everyone clapped. Eishoxa hadn't yet been asked to dance and knew that she wouldn't be unless someone was forced to ask her, because the people of Bareth instinctively mistrusted foreigners, even their allies. It was a pity. Maya really was a superb dancer. The dance finished and Eishoxa watched her approach. She smiled at Maya and handed her a drink from a passing steward. Maya took it gratefully and fanned herself.

"Enjoying yourself?" Eishoxa asked, watching as Rosemarie left her table and joined the dance. Her eyes caught sight of the two friends, and Eishoxa could imagine her eyes narrowing in disapproval.

Maya nodded happily. "I had a great dance just then. Why don't you join in?"

"I can't dance the slow ones. Everyone notices if you don't know where to put your feet," Eishoxa explained. She left her empty glass on a table beside her and picked up another drink. Maya laughed and lifted her mask slightly to get some air on her face.

"Well, there's a fast one next. Will you dance that one?"

"If you dance it with me." There was only a brief interlude between the end of the present dance and the start of the next piece, a fast-paced, merry jig that attracted many more people. Soon the Great Hall was filled with the sounds of stamping feet and swishing dresses. Eishoxa seized Maya's hand and pulled her into the fray. Neither had taken dancing lessons – the former having no wish to and the latter having no need – so neither of them knew the steps, but regardless, when the music came to a finish, both were out of breath and their cheeks glowed. The Great Hall was now heaving with people but still the music played, faster and faster. The two girls spun and stamped and clapped, both of them gasping for breath. Maya gratefully agreed when Eishoxa suggested that they get some air and so they wriggled their way out through the crowds. If anyone saw them go, they said nothing.

The friends left the Great Hall and headed for one of the more private gardens. A dry wind blew, bringing the celebration's various smells of food and fragrances with it. Eishoxa removed her mask and wiped her face gently, smudging her makeup. "Hard work, all this dancing," she complained, kicking her shoes off.

Maya sat down gracefully on one of the stone benches and took off one of her shoes, setting her mask down beside her. "You danced one of them," she accused. "I, however, danced many – and my feet will suffer for it."

Eishoxa shrugged airily. "I have no need to dance."

Maya sighed and rubbed her heel. There was a fountain bubbling merrily in the centre of the garden, and Eishoxa approached it on bare feet. Removing a glove, she ran her fingers through the water and smiled to herself. "What are you thinking about?" her friend asked.

Eishoxa turned around. "Nothing really. Simply that I've got out of dancing at this Masked Ball as well," and she came and sat by Maya, replacing her shoes. She smoothed her dress over her knees and admired how the silver thread of the embroidered moon seemed to glow in the dark of the night. "See, my idea worked," she laughed.

"Yes, surprisingly well," Maya admitted. "I didn't think it would."

Eishoxa tutted, "You have no faith in me whatsoever."

"Of course not," replied Maya, facing her friend. "Your ideas …"

A sudden rustling in the bushes interrupted her. The leaves shook. "What was that?" Maya asked.

Eishoxa narrowed her eyes at the bush in question, but it was too dark to see anything. She felt the urge to investigate, but something held her back.

"Maybe we should go back inside?" Maya stood up. She sounded worried. Eishoxa walked towards the bush. Behind it the garden dropped away sharply, and beyond that was another, bigger garden that led to the palace. "Eishoxa —" her friend began.

Eishoxa again didn't answer. In the darkness she thought she saw something skulk out from behind a large statue in the next garden and slink towards the castle, but she couldn't be sure. She narrowed her eyes even further at it and then turned around.

"It's gone." She turned to her friend with a winning smile. "It was probably a dog, or maybe a gardener. Come on, let's go. It's time to eat."

On their return to the Great Hall, guests were starting to trickle out towards the Banqueting Hall. Eishoxa pulled Maya into their midst as she spotted Rosemarie exit the Hall and walk down the slope, surrounded by a group of laughing men and women.

"I don't know why you hate her so much. She's right about you most of the time," Maya commented, as she followed Eishoxa's glowering gaze.

"You wouldn't understand," grumbled Eishoxa. "If you'd lived with her when you were younger, you would've seen how much she's changed. And what do you mean she's right about me most of the time?"

Maya smiled and linked her arm through her friend's. It was possible to get to the Banqueting Hall through the inside of the castle, but there were so many people that the King had ordered everyone to enter through the outer doors that opened onto the grand Royal Gardens. The King and Queen wouldn't actually appear until the feast and Eishoxa hadn't seen them yet. She wondered if Rosemarie would tell them about their little charade that night, and was anxious – not for herself at all, but for Maya. The King would do nothing, but the Queen might tell Maya's father and Eishoxa didn't trust him to tell

Maya off gently. One had only to look at the film of fear that clouded Maya's eyes whenever anyone mentioned her family to understand what they were really like.

The doors were wide open now. The guests had to enter in two straight lines so that they could be announced. The peasants, villagers and the farmers had another hall to eat in, and the King and the Queen would feast with them first, as was the tradition. The aristocrats, nobility and higher-ranking people of Bareth all came to eat in the Banqueting Hall. It had always struck Eishoxa as strange that, on a night where there was meant to be no distinction between rich and poor, they were kept separate nonetheless.

Eishoxa pulled Maya behind her and made sure her mask was in place. They wouldn't even take them off to eat. The harbinger introduced them and then they filed away to their assigned places. They were both sitting at the High Table, but Eishoxa, taking Maya's place, had to sit further down the table. To Eishoxa's surprise, Maya took her role very seriously and swept gracefully into her chair, looking to the entire room as Eishoxa-like as possible. Eishoxa almost laughed when a seat was vacated beside Maya, who waved at her and called her over, even putting on Eishoxa's accent.

Eishoxa lowered her head and scurried over. Once she was perched next to Maya, Eishoxa muttered under her breath, "I don't really speak like that, do I?" Maya only nudged her and stuck her chin in the air. To their great relief, there were five chairs between them and Rosemarie, although this didn't stop her from leaning forward and watching them with suspicion. Many foreign dignitaries came to greet Rosemarie, and as they passed the two friends they would nod to Maya as well, ignoring Eishoxa completely. Rosemarie was watching the two of them out of the corner of her eye, and Eishoxa was delighted to see the look of utter bewilderment on her face as she watched Maya. Eishoxa covered her mouth with her hand and looked away. Indeed, the Masked Ball could hide many things. Who would have known Maya was such a good actress?

The arrival of the King and Queen was announced with a trumpet blast and a herald scurrying down the aisle calling loudly, "The King and Queen! The King and Queen!" There was a great scraping of chairs as everyone stood while the two of them proceeded through the room. The King's long embroidered gown swept the ground as he strode towards his seat, at the top of the Banqueting Hall. He'd abandoned his crown that day in favour of a mask shaped like the sun. It had been so exquisitely made that it looked as if sunbeams had been trailed delicately across his face. The Queen was wearing a dress made from many layers of different-coloured silk. Her long red hair hung loosely and her face was carefully disguised as a phoenix, cleverly made from different shades of red feathers. Once the Royal couple had sat down, the rest of the assembly followed.

Everyone looked expectantly at the King now, who was having a quick word with one of the servants standing behind him. The servant whispered something to him, bowed and stepped back. The King nodded and smiled. Then he stood, picked up his glass and, holding it high, boomed out, "Let the feast begin!" There was a round of applause as doors sprang open all around the Banqueting Hall, admitting many lines of servants, all bearing large platters. Even more stewards filed in after them, carrying jugs of red wine of every colour, from deep ruby to the lightest shade of pink. Eishoxa took a sip of her own and made a quick face. She'd never liked the taste of wine. Maya, on the other hand, drank hers with enthusiasm and Eishoxa raised her eyebrows at her friend. "What are you playing at?" she asked.

Maya grinned back. "I like wine," she explained. "But in Cara I never get to drink it because we very rarely have banquets like this."

Eishoxa laughed and picked up her knife. "I don't like it. Be my guest. Just watch how much you drink. You may find it's stronger than you think."

Maya laughed and took another sip. "I'll keep that in mind."

Eishoxa looked up as the traditional entertainment of fire-eaters and magicians came in through the side doors to perform between the rows of tables. She put down her fork and watched them with interest. Maya was watching as well. Her eyes opened wide as one of the fire-eaters swallowed burning match after burning match.

"How do they do that?" she asked Eishoxa quietly. Rosemarie was still watching. Eishoxa shrugged and swallowed a mouthful of food. "Magic, I guess."

"There's no such thing," Maya scoffed. Eishoxa grinned at her. "How do you know?" Maya cuffed her impishly around the head and Eishoxa gaped at her, rubbing the back of her head.

"What are you doing?"

"Being you is more fun than I'd expected," Maya admitted gleefully.

Eishoxa grimaced and turned back to her plate, lifting her eyes to watch the guests again. She knew a lot of them from the countless parties and aristocratic gatherings she'd been forced to attend. But as she swept her eyes up and down the rows of tables, she caught sight of two people she didn't recognise at all. They sat opposite each other at the table closest to the far wall. They didn't talk to their neighbours, but instead were leaning forward, speaking quietly to each other. In a crowd of animated people, they stood out, but to Eishoxa's confusion no one around them seemed to be paying them the least bit of attention. She couldn't see their faces because they both wore very elaborate masks, and their heads were covered with heavy, hooded robes. She nudged Maya. "Who are those people? Are they from Cara?"

Maya followed her gaze. "No. I've never seen them in my life. Why? What's wrong? They must have been invited if they're here."

"I know. But I don't know who they are."

"No one is meant to know anyone here." said Maya, sipping at yet another cup of wine.

Eishoxa nodded. "Yes, that's true, but I know everyone anyway, with or without masks."

12

Maya smirked. "Well done, you, but that's not the point."

Eishoxa shrugged and replied, "I suppose," before turning back to her meal. The courses kept coming and coming and wine flowed the whole night long. Although the night had taken hold of the outside world, it was forbidden to enter the fire-lit hall. Musicians played the traditional folk songs of Bareth, and the wild, fast-paced music pounded in Eishoxa's head and through her blood. Contentment blended with the aromas of good food and strong perfume to fill the air. Heat blasted from the fires, and shadows from the wavering candle flames chased each other over the walls. The two cloaked and masked figures in the corner of the room soon disappeared from Eishoxa's mind as, at Maya's request, she drank three cups of crimson wine one after the other, filling her head with a light, not unpleasant fuzzy feeling.

Towards the middle of the celebrations, the King stopped everyone again to pay tribute to Rosemarie and her husband. The two of them stood, hand in hand, and the Hall resounded with applause. The Queen kissed Rosemarie on both cheeks and the King shook the Duke's hand. The stewards then came forward with the various gifts that had the guests had brought. And as the seemingly endless line slowly dwindled away, Maya had to join the Royal Family as the Hall made a toast in their honour. Eishoxa, through a haze of wine and warm sleepiness, was happy.

Once the courses had started to slow down and the guests had eaten and drunk enough, everyone in the Banqueting Hall trooped outside, servants and aristocrats alike, laughing and merry, for the annual fireworks display. Even through her hazy mind, Eishoxa couldn't help but enjoy herself. The guests gathered at the top of the sloping garden, and the fireworks were lit at the end, near the castle wall. Maya half-screamed with delight as the sky filled with bright colours and loud bangs and whistles. Eishoxa turned her face to the night sky as golden sparkles rained down upon them, clapped loudly with the rest of them and joined in with the cheering. She was keeping an eye on Maya, who, she suspected, hadn't kept her promise in mind, and was laughing far too loudly for Eishoxa to believe she was reasonably sober. She turned her head to see Rosemarie standing in a great crowd of people, all congratulating her and shaking the hand of a tall man standing beside her, who Eishoxa imagined must be her husband, the Duke. The King and Queen were receiving just as many congratulations as Rosemarie and the Duke, and Eishoxa watched for a while before turning away. As she did so, she felt someone walk very close behind her and turned to see the two hooded figures walking by.

"Sorry," she muttered. One of them turned sharply to look at her, taking in the crescent moon mask and the blue dress. She couldn't make out the person's face, partly because of the darkness and partly because of the hood.

"My mistake," came a voice from deep within the large hood. Eishoxa nodded awkwardly and stepped back. They didn't move away; instead, looking past her towards Maya who had strayed a bit.

"That is the Princess of Bareth, yes?" the same one asked. The voice was low and accented, sounding similar to the Bareth accent but harsher and stronger. Eishoxa nodded quickly, tilting her head away. "And you? Where are you from?"

"Cara," Eishoxa replied without hesitation. The two of them glanced at each other and then nodded. They left without another word, walking away towards the castle.

When the fireworks had ended, people moved back into the Great Hall, warding off the typical chill that comes with a desert night. But Eishoxa didn't see the two hooded figures again.

Dawn was nearly breaking when the banquet finally ended and people staggered out, in tipsy pairs and groups of three and four, singing and laughing. Eishoxa followed Maya out into the pearly light, rubbing her tired eyes. They walked together to Maya's room, on the same corridor as Eishoxa's but further down. Eishoxa leant against the door frame and yawned.

"So what are we going to do later today?" Maya giggled. She'd drunk more wine than Eishoxa had ever imagined she could consume, drinking more when they'd returned to the Hall.

"Whatever we want," she laughed. "Would you like to ride the camels?"

"Of course," Maya laughed, and then crashed her way into her room. Eishoxa smiled and walked down the corridor to her room, feeling the world spin a little as she pushed open the door. As she lay down to sleep, the two cloaked figures rose in her mind again, but before she could worry about them too much, sleep pulled her into its warm, welcoming embrace.

CHAPTER 3

WHEN EISHOXA WOKE after a short sleep, she had the feeling that she'd had a dream of importance. Closing her eyes again, she turned over, trying to remember what it had been about. All she could summon to mind were three pairs of eyes: one black, one yellow and one blue. Sitting up, she groaned as the wine from the night before took its toll and her head throbbed.

"Who made me drink wine?" she complained to herself. She walked over to the window and threw open the shutters, taking a deep breath of the cool morning air. The dizziness in her head subsided somewhat as the air hit her lungs. The cold of the night still lingered, although the sun was starting to warm the cobbles. Already there was movement in the courtyard below: farmers bringing food to the gates of the castle, clattering hooves as a groom led three skittish young colts towards the castle entrance – the King would be selling them that day at the market – a pair of soldiers sitting by the gate playing cards. The aroma of freshly baked bread was wafting through the air, and Eishoxa breathed deeply again.

A tap on her door announced Maya, who entered wearing only her nightdress. Eishoxa shivered and pulled her blanket closer around her. "Aren't you cold?" she asked.

Maya shook her head. "No, I'm boiling. Someone kept the fire burning the whole time and I woke up almost roasted alive. You desert dwellers are so weird. You do know too much heat can kill you?"

Eishoxa laughed. "Yes, but so can too much cold."

Maya took a flying leap at Eishoxa's bed and settled herself right in the middle, crossing her legs. "That's why we wear so many layers of clothes," she muttered. Then she pressed her hands to her temples. "How much did I drink last night?"

Eishoxa laughed. "A lot. Definitely a lot."

"Your wine is a lot stronger than the stuff in Cara."

"That's because we make the best wine," boasted Eishoxa.

Maya gave her a look and rubbed her head again. "Well, how do I get rid of this?"

"Go and take some deep breaths of fresh air. It helped me."

"You drank hardly anything compared to me," grumbled Maya, going to stand by the window and doing as she was told. "What are we going to do today?" she asked.

Eishoxa grinned. "You said you'd like to ride the camels."

"When did I say that?"

Eishoxa gave her a triumphant little smile. "When we left the banquet."

"I was drunk," Maya whined.

Eishoxa shook her head. "No, you understood what I was saying."

Maya let out a grumbling noise of complaint. "You know I hate the beasts! They keep swaying and groaning at you."

Eishoxa chuckled. "That's just their way of saying hello."

"We get around by sleigh," called Maya as she left the room to get dressed. "And that's a much better way."

Although so much of Bareth was desert, camels were the least popular way to get around because not many people could afford them. However, the Royal Family had six camels in their possession and the King had a stable converted just for them. Eishoxa stood beside her camel, patting his neck. She loved her camel. The King had bought him for her some years back and Eishoxa had named him Helios. She stood next to his neck, feeding him dates and watching Maya choose her own mount. Finally, Maya decided on a small, shy-looking camel. It didn't belong to anyone, so Eishoxa didn't know its name. The groom holding Helios's bridle swung a blanket over the top of him for Eishoxa to sit on. She no longer needed help getting on and required no help to ride the beast, but, for safety and appearance, the King always insisted that someone should lead the camel whenever Eishoxa rode. Maya had less trouble than Eishoxa had anticipated, but once she was on she looked like all she wanted to do was to come down.

"Enjoying yourself, are you?" called Eishoxa, as Helios stood on his back legs, then his front legs, and began lumbering down the path towards the front of the castle. Maya didn't reply. Eishoxa laughed and rested her head against Helios's hump.

The two grooms led them through the gates and down the hill towards the village, beyond which the desert started. They crossed the river and trotted towards the cluster of houses. Eishoxa had asked to be on their own for a while there and the King had agreed, provided that the grooms took them to the desert and brought them home.

The village was dilapidated, to say the least. Although the houses nearest the castle were intact, those further out were crumbling, and by the end of the street only a few bricks remained standing. Few people lived here. At the sound of the camels' approach on the chipped cobbles, people came out of their houses to look at them. All the children wore a look of pinched hunger. All the mothers carried with them a sense of starved desperation. Not a lot could be done for them. They were all so riddled with disease that, if they were to be brought into the castle, there would be epidemics. The King never visited this village. There was another on the other side of the hill where slightly better people lived, so it was left to Eishoxa to show that the Royal Family hadn't completely forgotten these people.

She halted their procession to slide down from her camel momentarily. Staring up at her with hollow, hungry eyes was a little girl, clutching a dirty doll and holding the hand of an even smaller boy. They'd made their home out of boxes and leftover bricks. The occasional earthquake had caused many of the poorly made houses to collapse, crushing the inhabitants. Eishoxa reached into the wide pocket of her dress and took out a loaf of bread. The villagers watched as she handed it to the wide-eyed little girl.

"Be sure you share this with your brother," Eishoxa whispered. The little girl nodded, giving her doll to the boy so she could grip the loaf more tightly. Eishoxa turned back to her camel, who was kneeling for

16

her to mount. She swung her leg over his back and settled herself on top of the rich blanket. Helios groaned as he pulled himself to his feet and lumbered off, led by the groom. A scrawny dog ran between Helios's legs and he snorted in alarm, swaying slowly to a halt. The groom clucked his tongue and the camel moved on, his eyes darting from side to side. Maya, following behind, had been taking in the whole scene with big eyes. Eishoxa remembered that it was the first time she'd seen this village. Looking back at her friend, she saw, standing at the edge of the village, two figures covered in black cloaks. She recognised them from the Banqueting Hall: they'd been watching her for some time and, when she left, one nodded to the other and they started to walk towards the castle, talking quietly together.

The grooms had left them, as the King had permitted, and the two girls trotted close to a ridge of sand, blown by the wind to look like the spiny back of a dragon. The sky above was cloudless, the sun a burning white disk right in the centre of the sky. There was no vegetation here at all, unless one counted the rough grass sprouting harshly from the top of the dunes. Helios lifted his head high and led the way down the gently sloping ridge. Maya pulled her scarf higher over her head and turned wounded eyes on Eishoxa when her friend laughed.

"The sun isn't that strong, Maya. Take it down!"

"My skin is much paler than yours," protested Maya, "And I'm already very burnt."

Eishoxa laughed and urged Helios to move faster. Maya's mount followed suit.

"Eishoxa! Please slow down! I really don't like this!" Eishoxa turned around, laughing at the sight of Maya clutching on desperately as her camel jolted her up and down.

"Just pretend it's a sleigh," she suggested, throwing a date towards Helios, laughing at the sight of the camel lunging eagerly towards the sweet fruit. She threw another one towards Maya's camel and then giggled as her friend squealed when the camel lurched for the sweet fruit.

"Eishoxa! Stop it!" Eishoxa brought both camels to a halt and pushed on Helios's neck to make him kneel. Sliding gracefully down off his back, she held out her hand to help Maya dismount.

"It's not that bad, is it?" asked Eishoxa, brushing sand off Maya's scarf. Maya grumbled, pulling her scarf further up over her head. Eishoxa laughed and started running along the edge of the sand, kicking up little sprays of sand all around her. Maya followed more slowly. The ridge was quite low at first but then rose steadily. Eishoxa stopped running where sand had been blown away by the wind and a cool, shady cave had formed.

"Come and sit here!" Eishoxa called before flopping down onto the sand. Maya gratefully sat beside her. She pulled a water skin off her shoulder and took a long drink before offering it to Eishoxa.

"Do we just leave the camels there?" she enquired, wiping her mouth and peering around the edge of the sand cave to see them kneeling on the sand.

Eishoxa nodded. "We won't be very long. So, did you like it?"

"Once I stopped feeling like I was going to fall off, it was all right," Maya admitted grudgingly. Eishoxa started clapping her hands. "But I won't do it again the next time I come here," she said with finality.

"You might," Eishoxa teased, "You know you like it really."

"I don't!"

Maya received a laugh in return. She squinted out into the desert, shading her eyes. "How can you live here?" she wondered aloud. It was far too flat and dry for her. Everything was so harsh and barren. Although she hated her family, she would go back to Cara just to see the mountains and tall glaciers and lakes again.

Eishoxa shrugged. "I don't know. I suppose I just love the sun. Mountain people are too cold," she finished, her eyes twinkling.

Maya gasped in mock horror. "How dare you say that? They are much nicer than you desert people!"

"I don't think so," said Eishoxa, shaking her head. She clambered to her feet and ran out into the sun, to the top of the sand ridge. "Watch this, Maya!" and with that she turned a series of perfect cartwheels, right across the hot sand. Maya wrapped her scarf tighter around her head and shouted, "Showoff!" as Eishoxa started to somersault – once, twice, three times – spinning in the air with effortless grace. Eishoxa landed on her feet with a little jump, but then staggered and fell, turning on her back and rolling down the ridge on the other side.

"Come on, Maya!" she called, standing up and brushing the sand off the back of her dress.

"No! Stop messing around!" Maya shouted, standing at the top of the ridge. Sighing, she folded her arms, squinting against the glare of the sun. These hills were nothing compared to her mountains. There was a ridge of them outside her window at Cara, and their broad, flat faces were the kindest things she would see all day. She owed more than she could express to Eishoxa, who made her feel happy and looked after her all the time. But the summer was waning away and soon she would have to go back to Cara, to everyone she hated.

"Look out!" came a sudden yell, and then Eishoxa bundled into her from behind, rolling them both down the ridge, towards the cave again. Maya screamed as they picked up momentum, rolling faster and faster. Her scarf came loose and blew off, and gritty sand pricked her eyes. They landed in a crumpled heap at the bottom.

"Eishoxa! That's not funny!" But her friend had already charged back up the sand, picking up Maya's scarf on the way and wrapping it around her own head. Maya stood, feeling dizzy, and started to make her way back up the dune.

"Hey!" Maya said indignantly. "Give me back my scarf!" Eishoxa, very theatrically, swung the scarf around her head and then tumbled back down the hill, carrying Maya with her. When they reached the bottom this time, they were both laughing.

"Your Highness!" came another voice from the top of the ridge. Eishoxa looked up to see one of the grooms looking down at them. Eishoxa stood up, shaking the sand out of her hair. "Yes?"

"You must come back now. I've been sent by the King to fetch you."

Eishoxa groaned. "He always wants to speak to me whenever I'm enjoying myself, but never when something is boring. It's as if he wants to ruin the little fun I am allowed."

Maya smiled at the clear indignation in Eishoxa's voice. "It won't be very long," she soothed. Her friend never liked to obey anyone. It didn't matter who the person was. They struggled back up the dune, sand sliding away under their feet, and approached the two grooms who were holding the camels. Maya's smile slipped off her face. Whatever Eishoxa said, the Princess of Cara really didn't like camels.

On returning to the castle, Eishoxa was sent to speak to the King in his study. He had two studies, one private and the other for guests and more important meetings. Eishoxa was sent to the former, after she'd tidied herself up, brushed her hair and put on clean clothes. As she approached the study door, the two cloaked strangers she'd seen at the banquet emerged. She stepped back into the shadows to let them pass. She hadn't forgotten her strange encounter with them the night before. They were again wearing their long cloaks and she couldn't see their faces. When they passed her, they bowed low before walking off. Eishoxa jumped as a cloak brushed her bare arm. The fabric was scorching. She watched the two of them go down the corridor and turn out of sight. Pulling her scarf higher over her forehead to hide her hair, she knocked.

"Come in," came the familiar voice from inside. She pushed on the door, bowing as she entered. The King's private study was smaller than might have been expected, but she loved it anyway. It was one of her earliest memories, learning to crawl and walk in this room while her mother and father worked. As time moved on, the Queen had come into this room less and less, and it had grown messier and messier over the years. The King would let no one in to clean, but Eishoxa knew that he sometimes did it himself. Two large windows, covered in scarlet drapes, occupied one wall, and the other three – even the wall with the large door – were covered in the King's collection of maps and drawings. He loved collecting things, and he loved showing them all to Eishoxa, as Rosemarie had little interest in such things. An impressive globe stood in the corner, showing all the countries spread out around Bareth, and artefacts from all the known countries filled up any other available space.

The King sat behind his table, which looked like an island in the sea of clutter. He'd neglected his crown, which Eishoxa knew he hated wearing anyway, and clad himself in his most casual clothes. When Eishoxa stepped inside, he sat up from his work and smiled at her.

"Eishoxa! Come in, come in. Yes, yes, close the door behind you."

Eishoxa smiled back at him and pulled down her scarf. She'd only worn it in case anyone had been watching in the corridor, but she'd not had the time to deal properly with her wild, flyaway hair. Moving aside some of the papers on the King's desk, she perched on the edge, swinging her legs.

"Who were they?" she asked, nodding towards the door where the strangers had just left. "They were at the banquet last night."

"Oh, you saw them, did you?" the King asked. "They were some sort of foreign dignitaries sent here by someone who thought I could do with a visit."

"Magicians?" Eishoxa enquired, frowning.

The King sighed and smiled tiredly, "No, more like soothsayers. Trying to tell me something about my future and the future of my family. In fact, they were very interested in you in particular."

"Me? Why?" Eishoxa asked.

The King sighed and waved his hand dismissively. "You know, what with Rosemarie being married and that."

"Oh, that," Eishoxa snorted. She picked up a book off his table and leafed through it. Whenever she'd almost put her confinement out of her mind, something else came back to remind her about it.

"Yes, that," sighed the King.

Eishoxa raised her eyebrows. "So did the meeting go well? Did you enjoy yourself?"

"Not in the slightest. Their accent was so strong I didn't really understand a word of what they were saying, and they dismissed themselves before I could ask."

"Yes, they did come out looking angry," Eishoxa agreed.

"So what were you doing?" he asked.

Eishoxa frowned. "I was in the desert with Maya. I rode Helios because no one ever takes him out anymore."

"Did you have a good time?" the King enquired. She nodded. The King sighed. "I'm sorry to have to take you away from that, but as your mother reminded me, I want to have this discussion with you now so that it doesn't come as such a shock when it happens."

Eishoxa was suddenly apprehensive. Whenever the Queen was involved, there was never good news when it came to Eishoxa. The Queen had definite opinions when it came to things which made her a wonderful and just leader, but she was not the best of mothers. Eishoxa's wild ways exasperated her, and she was constantly pestering the King to do something about their younger daughter. As the months after her sixteenth birthday had ticked by, the pestering had increased and become more insistent.

The King stood and walked to the window, drawing back the curtain. Eishoxa slid off his table and watched him inquisitively. From this window the whole of the castle could be seen, as his study was in the highest tower.

"Look, Eishoxa. You know what this is, don't you?"

"Bareth?" asked Eishoxa, thoroughly confused.

The King nodded. "Yes. Bareth. Our kingdom, and one day maybe yours as well."

Eishoxa blinked. "Won't Rosemarie inherit it, being the elder?"

The King shook his head. "Rosemarie has her husband's lands. She's married her way out of freedom – and also the ownership of Bareth."

20

Eishoxa drew her brows together, wondering where this conversation was going. Had he called her here to talk to her about the politics of the monarchy?

"Therefore," the King continued, "this kingdom will be yours."

Eishoxa nodded.

The King sat down in his chair and folded his arms on the table. He took a deep breath, his expression becoming one of reluctance and unhappiness. "Now, you must understand that if it were up to me, I wouldn't do this. However, your mother strongly believes that, as you are to be the future ruler of Bareth, a little self-discipline would not go amiss. And so we've decided that, for the good of everyone, your confinement that will start at the end of the summer ..." He trailed off, biting his lip and looking anxiously up at Eishoxa. She smiled at him encouragingly, even though dread was drying her mouth. "We've decided it would be best for everyone if you went for your confinement to my family in Nasvasco."

Bareth had been a country fought over continually for many years. Many generations ago, the King's family, led by the King of Nasvasco, a country some hundreds of miles west, had conquered Bareth. On discovering it was a barren, next-to-useless country, he'd given it to a noble family whom he'd trusted and who had served him well for many years. Later on, royal families from other countries had come and taken over the leadership. The present King had descended from these people.

Eishoxa had never heard of her family in Nasvasco. This was a surprise, because the King talked often about his family. "Who are these people?" she asked. "I've never heard of them."

"They are part of our family, and you should get to know them."

"But why haven't you spoken of them before?"

The King paused for a moment before answering. "Well, we haven't needed to. If you need proof they exist, I can show you some pictures."

Eishoxa let the matter drop. Of course there were going to be members of the family she didn't know. Between the King and the Queen, their family was extensive, stretching over many countries.

"For how long?" she asked.

The King avoided her gaze. "The Queen and I haven't discussed this point very far, and I for one disagree about this, but sometimes I must listen to your mother because she's very clever—"

"For how long?" repeated Eishoxa, cutting impatiently through his babbling.

The King looked up at her. "A couple of years maybe. That's what your mother wants." He took in Eishoxa's look of pure horror and hurriedly continued. "This point does need to be discussed further ..."

"I won't go!" decided Eishoxa. "I will not give years of my life away to discipline! Especially not in a foreign country, in a foreign castle. If I need to behave, I can! When there are balls or banquets, I behave. I do! It's only when I'm allowed to have fun that I have fun, and I take myself far away from the palace." The King opened his mouth to say something but she interrupted again. "It's true! No one ever sees me."

"Eishoxa, you know that isn't the point." The King was practically pleading and she felt a rush of sympathy for him. Bareth was not autocratic, like Cara, and both the King and Queen had a say in what went on in the country. If the Queen wanted Eishoxa gone, then she would have to go. The King was not nearly strong enough to stand up against his wife. If Eishoxa was honest with herself, she took much of her personality from her mother, and not a lot from her father.

"You're almost seventeen," he continued, "and I know you don't want to get married. I understand this. So what other options do we have? You know the ways of the world."

"Let me stay here!" insisted Eishoxa, gesticulating. "If I had to work here, I wouldn't mind. But to send me away as if I've been badly behaved isn't fair!"

"I know," agreed the King sadly, putting his hands on her shoulders. "I know, but there are a lot of rumours circulating about the decorum of this Royal Family, and your mother won't stand for it."

"People lie!" fumed Eishoxa. "She lives her life guided by rumours!"

"That's not true, Eishoxa!" replied the King irritably.

"Then who? Who's been saying this?" she cried.

"Well, for one, the two who just left were talking about it to me."

"You're going to base my future on the word of soothsayers?"

"I hear that you roll down dunes with Princess Maya. Is this true?"

Eishoxa nodded and opened her mouth, but the King carried on speaking, walking away from her, his hands clasped behind his back. "And you enjoy running and riding and climbing trees and swimming in the river in your best clothes? The Queen simply will not have her sixteen-year-old daughter behaving like a tomboy. There is nothing more to be said on that point. It is true, and you must accept that. By your age Rosemarie was betrothed and set to marry almost the day she turned seventeen. With you turning out so differently, you must be able to see the Queen's predicament."

Eishoxa fell silent. "Well, if she wants it, I suppose it will happen," she spat bitterly. She then thought about Maya. "And Maya? Will she be able to visit me in Nasvasco?"

"Maya will be seventeen as well soon," the King reminded her gently. "And I believe her family has already made plans for her marriage. You must understand now that our countries are different, and your responsibilities come before your friends. You know how the people of Bareth think about foreigners."

Eishoxa bowed her head. Of course she'd known that their summer visits would come to an end. Of course she'd known that one day Maya would be put in Cara and as she herself would be in Bareth, and that they would only be able to write to each other. But so soon? She suddenly felt very, very miserable, as if all the anger had been leached out of her and replaced with a feeling of deadening gloom.

"Is there anything else?" she asked, looking up at her father. The King's face fell as he guessed what she was thinking. He hated making her upset and having to say this to her, but he'd agreed with his wife. Eishoxa was running wild, and a little taming wouldn't hurt her.

"I will talk to your mother about this. I'm sorry, Eishoxa, but there's nothing to be done."

CHAPTER 4

Eishoxa ran into her room and slammed the door as hard as she could. Maya jumped from where she was sitting on the bed. "Was it really that bad?"

"They're sending me away at the end of the summer to live with the King's family in Nasvasco," Eishoxa snapped acrimoniously, pacing the room.

"Why?" Maya asked, putting down the book she'd been reading and standing up. "What did you do?"

"It's not what I do. It's what I don't do," Eishoxa protested. "They think I'm running wild and that I need some discipline if I'm ever going to be a good ruler."

"Bareth is going to belong to you?" Maya, confused, sank back down onto the bed. The kingdom usually went to the oldest son or daughter unless he or she was considered completely inappropriate for the role, and Maya couldn't imagine a better ruler than Rosemarie. Yes, she was annoying and patronising, but she was also just and kind.

Eishoxa gave a grumpy nod and went to stand at the window. "Rosemarie married well enough to take her husband's lands. Apparently, she married her way out of the ownership of Bareth." Eishoxa had a face of outrage as she surveyed the scene outside. Then she sighed and sat next to Maya. "It's for a few years, Maya, and they say that I won't be able to see you. I don't want to go."

Maya absorbed this new piece of news in silence. She wasn't sure which to feel first: sadness, anger, acknowledgement of her own fate or sympathy for Eishoxa. She'd known for a long time, perhaps even longer than Eishoxa, that at the end of the summer she would have to give up the freedom she presently enjoyed. Cara was in every possible way a much stricter nation than Bareth, and she'd already seen the way her siblings had gone when they'd turned seventeen. Eishoxa had at least had some slack to do whatever she wanted for sixteen years. And Maya had also known that, at the end of this summer, they might not be able to see each other for many years. But even so, to be cut off so suddenly and with no chance of even writing letters to each other? It was hard. She put her hand on Eishoxa's arm. "What do you want me to say? We've known this to be coming. You said you knew they had something planned for you, and now it's happened."

Eishoxa turned her gaze on Maya. It was true. She'd known that something like this would be coming her way. Although it hadn't been all that clear, for the past two years the Queen had been hinting at sending her away – but she'd never imagined as far away as Nasvasco.

Maya carried on speaking slowly, as if choosing her words very carefully. "Even though we're far, we can write letters, and if you behave maybe you'll be out of there sooner."

Eishoxa brushed off Maya's hand and stood, striding to the window with a barbed retort. "It seems that you want me to go as well, to learn how to 'behave' myself!"

Maya stood up in horrified indignation. "I never said that, Eishoxa!

I'm simply saying that there's very little to be done about the situation, and if you go into it with a mind to work, then you may get out of it sooner!"

Eishoxa's shoulders sagged. "I don't want to leave Bareth," she mourned quietly, gazing over the courtyard. "I know it's a horrible place to live in but I love it, I really do. It's my whole world."

To Maya it was a country, and she knew that if she asked anyone else in Bareth, they would call it a country. But Eishoxa was attached to things, countries and animals in a way that Maya knew others weren't. It was when Eishoxa expressed it that Maya realised Eishoxa was as lonely as she was herself, and was finding consolation in the friendship of beasts like camels. "If you say no, they might relent."

"If the Queen says I must go, then I must go. The King will do nothing about it. He's a coward," she added in disgust.

Maya sighed. "Eishoxa, do you remember many years ago when we were lost in the desert?"

Eishoxa nodded. "Of course. It was during the night. We were both terrified."

"And we had no idea where we were. The only thing we did know was that we had to keep walking. That we had to keep going and we'd get home." Eishoxa nodded. "Well, this time, maybe it's the same thing. You and I have to keep going, no matter what."

"It's different this time, Maya. Now I have no choice." She turned around to face her friend.

Maya could see the shimmer of tears in her eyes. "I know you don't," she murmured, putting her arms around Eishoxa and resting her head on her friend's shoulder. "But what can you say? There's nothing to be done."

The morning of Maya's departure came far too quickly for Eishoxa. Not only did it mean her friend was going – it also meant the end of her own freedom. Before, her confinement had seemed a speck on the horizon, but now it was rearing its ugly head and there was no escape.

Together, the two friends stood just inside the castle gates, both wrapped in blankets, watching as three horses were saddled for the journey back to Cara. It was still very early. They could get through the desert before the sun became hot. The groom who was to go with Maya swung onto his mount and the last of Maya's things were loaded onto the back of the second horse. The third horse, which Maya was to ride, snorted and stamped its feet.

Maya turned to Eishoxa and smiled. This was the moment the girls had been dreading, maybe since Maya had arrived: saying goodbye. It was always the worst part. And this time it was not until next year; they couldn't be sure they would ever see each other again. But neither of them voiced the thought. Eishoxa gave her a sad smile in return. She kissed Maya's cheek and wiped away the tears that ran down her face.

"Be good, Eishoxa," whispered Maya. Every year previously, when she had to leave Bareth, she envied Eishoxa, who had such an easy life here. But seeing her friend's miserable face and knowing that they both went back to something equally awful, she felt nothing but sympathy.

"I will," agreed Eishoxa. "And whatever they say, make sure you at least try to write to me. They might not let you – but try."

Maya nodded, took the blanket from around her shoulder and handed it back to Eishoxa. "Goodbye," she said, mounting her horse. The dark blue cloak of Cara covered her shoulders and her white-blonde hair fanned out over her back. Eishoxa waved as the three horses trotted out of the gates, their hooves striking the cobbles loudly. She ran forward to watch Maya's horse canter down the hill and then, finally, out of sight.

Eishoxa was in her room at midday when there came a quiet knock on the door, and a timid-looking servant girl in clothes far too big for her poked her head around the door to say that she was wanted in the Great Hall immediately. Eishoxa, who had spent the past six hours haunting the castle and grounds like a ghost, wanted nothing more than to sleep. She threw a pillow at the terrified girl and said that she was not going to go. To the girl's credit, she didn't move, but said even more quietly that she must come at once.

"Fine! I'll come! Now just leave me be!" And the girl fled, slamming the door loudly behind her.

Rosemarie was already sitting in the Great Hall by the time Eishoxa had tidied herself up and forced herself out of her room. The remnants of the Masked Ball had all been whisked away and the long red carpet leading up to the two thrones had been replaced. Now they were occupied by the King and Queen of Bareth. Rosemarie was sitting in a small chair on one side of the Queen. When Eishoxa – never one for being on time – was admitted, her sister threw a little exasperated smile in her direction. Eishoxa glowered at her.

"You are late," called the King, sitting up in his throne in which he'd been slumping, but he was not cross. "We called you a long time ago."

"What have you been doing?" the Queen asked her daughter. Unlike her husband, she was sitting up very straight in her chair and, as was her custom, had covered her face with a translucent scarf.

Eishoxa shrugged. "Nothing."

The Queen sighed. "Why? Didn't you have something to do?"

"I didn't want to do anything. Maya left this morning."

The Queen leaned forward. "I was very much aware."

Eishoxa nodded. "Good." The Queen sat back in her chair.

The King leant forward. "I believe we should deal as quickly as possible with the matter we've brought you here for—"

"I understand that when Maya was here you were behaving badly in the desert," the Queen interrupted.

Eishoxa had to look away so as not to laugh out loud at the look on her father's face. She sighed. "Yes, we were rolling down the dunes, but there was no one there."

"That's not the point," the Queen hissed. "Your lack of propriety is disgraceful. Who knows what people must think."

"No one was there, so there was no one to think anything," Eishoxa retorted.

"Please, stop this," the King said.

Eishoxa clenched her fists inside the pockets of her dress. The King gave her a warning look and put a restraining hand on his wife's arm.

"I've already spoken to her about this. I don't believe that another lecture is necessary."

"I've heard," the Queen pressed, "that you swapped dresses with Maya at the Masked Ball."

Eishoxa froze and looked at her sister. The smug look on Rosemarie's face told her everything. She had no choice but to nod.

The King sighed. He hated telling Eishoxa off, and he hated it when his wife told her off. But it couldn't be avoided. "Did you really?" Eishoxa nodded again.

"You know that was wrong. Why did you do it?" he asked.

Eishoxa hurried to explain herself. "It was only a joke. It was just that I knew she wouldn't be asked to dance if she went as herself, and I didn't want to dance anyway so I gave my dress to her. That was all." The King's hand went to his mouth to conceal a smile. He hated dancing himself. That was Eishoxa's style – to overreact when confronted with a mundane problem. He made sure his features were appropriately stern before removing his hand.

"It just isn't the appropriate thing for someone in your position to do. If Maya's father hears about it, you're both going to be in a lot of trouble. If any of the foreign dignitaries had found out, the whole of Bareth would be ridiculed. It's not right, Eishoxa. No," he said, holding up his hand as Eishoxa opened her mouth in outrage, "I haven't told Maya's father yet."

"Yet," the Queen pointed out, "he ought to be told. You two should be ashamed of yourselves. The Masked Ball is a very important event, and it's not a time for pranks. Especially when it was such an important event for your sister – her anniversary. To think, we had a toast for the Royal Family made with a foreigner at our side!" Rosemarie was nodding behind her mother in agreement. Eishoxa glared at her.

The King put his hand on his wife's arm. "I think we'll discuss that later. I don't think that's fair on Maya either."

"She could have stopped it," the Queen said sharply.

Eishoxa raised her voice above that of her parents. "It was entirely my fault. You can ask her if you want. She won't lie to you."

"That's not necessary," the King said hurriedly before the Queen could reply. "I didn't ask you here to discuss the Masked Ball. Perhaps that can be done at another time."

Eishoxa sighed again. "So what did you ask me here to discuss?"

The King suddenly became grave, and even the Queen looked worried. The smug look slipped slowly from Rosemarie's face and she looked at her parents with a certain measure of trepidation. Eishoxa looked from one to the other, and the careless feeling she'd cloaked herself in since Maya had left suddenly disappeared.

The King and the Queen looked at one another. Rosemarie sat up straighter in her chair.

"We have something to tell you," the King began. "I understand this might come as a shock to you, but I assure you that this will change nothing in our family, and no one knows but the three of us."

"The three of us?" Eishoxa asked. The King nodded at Rosemarie. Eishoxa looked at her. "So this has nothing to do with her?"

"She has known about it for a few years perhaps. But no, this is to do with you."

"So …?" Eishoxa enquired. The fact that it had nothing to do with Rosemarie stirred mixed feelings in her. She waited.

"Eishoxa," the King said, "we are not your parents. "Rosemarie is not your sister. We don't know where you came from or to whom you belong."

Eishoxa didn't believe that she'd heard him correctly. What did the words mean? She couldn't have heard the King correctly.

"What?"

The King sighed. "You came in a little basket left by the windowsill. I wanted to give you to one of the farmers in the village because I was suspicious of the circumstances, but then the Queen lost a baby and, because you looked similar, we decided it was meant to be."

Eishoxa didn't know what to think or do. Something pounded in her head, very fast and very loud. Everyone seemed to be moving in slow motion, and the King's voice sounded like static in her ears.

"Eishoxa?"

"What … what … what do you mean, I don't belong to you? Who do I belong to then?" she demanded hoarsely, twisting her hands into knots.

The King replied nervously, "We don't know to whom you belong. You came in a basket to us, carried by eagles. That was why I wanted to leave you to someone else. I strongly suspected witchcraft. There was no note, no letter explaining anything. I couldn't make any sense of it, but the Queen insisted that we take you in. The rest of the country knows you only as our Princess."

"But I'm not," Eishoxa said in a hollow voice.

The King looked hopelessly at his wife. Standing, she removed the scarf from her face and left it on the chair. Taking Eishoxa's shoulders, she looked down at her. "This doesn't change anything, Eishoxa, I promise. To us … to me, you're the same person."

Eishoxa pushed her away. "But I'm not, am I?"

"Yes, you are. All that's changed is that you now know we're not your parents. What else has changed?"

Eishoxa gaped at her. Was she really going to pretend this was the only thing that could possibly have changed? She shoved the Queen's hands off her and looked up into the shocked brown eyes with hate. "Everything's changed! I don't know who I belong to; I'm not even a princess anymore. I could have been like any of the starving girls my age in the villages, and for some lucky reason I was chosen to be the one that landed at your window! I'm a nobody! I don't belong to anyone and I'm a stranger in this place! You think that changes nothing? How could you have kept something like that from me? How could you have pretended that I belonged to you, knowing something like that?"

"Because you do belong to us," the King interrupted, also standing up.

Eishoxa refused to look at either of them. "You told her," and she pointed a shaking hand at Rosemarie, "but you didn't tell me?"

"She was the one that we could trust," the Queen said in a placating voice. Eishoxa recoiled from her, scarcely believing her ears.

Just too late, the Queen realised what she'd said and hurried to explain herself, but Eishoxa cut her off. "You trusted her with my secret, but you didn't trust me. I'll never forget that!"

Eishoxa ran blindly down the centre of the hall and through the doors. When they crashed behind her, she knew something else had also closed, and it could never be opened again.

CHAPTER 5

SHE RAN THROUGH the palace, ignoring the stares. She ran, not towards her room but to the Star Tower, the one place she knew would be deserted. As the stars were not important to the people of Bareth, this tower was right at the back of the castle, hidden by the many other towers and turrets. She hurtled up hundreds of stairs, barely feeling the stitch in her side, a whirlwind howling through her.

Family was everything in Bareth. Your family gave you a place, a name, an existence. Not to belong to anyone scared Eishoxa more than she would admit. She'd had a family and now she was a nobody, blown to and fro by the winds of loneliness and non-acceptance. She felt she meant nothing to anyone anymore. She stared out across Bareth, across the small villages clinging desperately to the dry earth. Her vision blurred with tears as she surveyed her country. But it wasn't her country anymore. It didn't belong to her. She didn't belong anymore. All the patriotism she'd worn with pride now meant nothing.

The desert, in the distance, was hard and unyielding, but it was a beautiful, wild place. With all its imperfections, it made the world in which she lived. With all its flaws, it was the place that she'd known and had come to love. And now, she didn't know where she belonged, where she was. Why hadn't her family wanted her? Why did they not want her to stay with them? What was wrong with her? Across the whole world, family was important. Even in Cara, even in the terrible family Maya had had the misfortune of being born into, they would never have abandoned one of their children. They would have never given them away. Family was the rock every person wanted, every person needed. And she didn't have one.

Standing there, Eishoxa felt something inside her come loose and float away, a ship with no captain and no way of steering itself back into the harbour where it had rested in safety for so long.

Tears ran down her face, trembling for a moment on her collarbone before seeping into the shoulder of her dress. Looking across the gardens of the castle, Eishoxa saw the same two figures – still dressed in long black cloaks despite the hot weather – slowly making their way down the hill away from the main gates. They were the ones she'd seen leaving the King's study. Even with her tear-blurred vision and runny nose, the two strangers held her attention. She watched as they headed down towards the village until she couldn't see them anymore.

Pulling out the necklace she always wore around her neck, she looked at it. The sight of it brought fresh tears to her eyes. It was the crest of Bareth, stamped crudely into a bronze coin. She'd been given it for a birthday by Rosemarie. She'd had it for as long as she could remember. This was her oldest and most precious possession. Immediately, she yanked the chain to break it and stared down at the coin, twinkling in the sunlight. Along the bottom was engraved *Princess of Bareth*. My sister. That was a lie. She was not a princess of Bareth. She probably didn't have any royal blood at all. Had Rosemarie known the secret when giving this to Eishoxa?

Standing up again, she extended her arm over the wall running around the tower. The chain was clenched in her fist, looped once over her wrist with the coin dangling there. "I could drop it," she thought. The coin became a shiny brown blur as tears ran once again down her cheeks. But something stopped her. Instead she coiled up the chain and stuffed it in her pocket. Then she took off the red silk headband that showed that she was a princess and shook her hair loose. No more lies. It joined the coin in her pocket. Then, taking off all her jewellery, she put it in the other pocket, refusing to look down at it while doing so. She wouldn't live a lie any more.

Over the next few days Eishoxa drifted around in a daze, avoiding the King and Queen and especially Rosemarie. At one level she could understand the King and Queen keeping this secret from her. After all, a child with no family brought into the Royal Family was unthinkable. But Rosemarie? Until Eishoxa had met Maya, only three years earlier, they'd told each other everything, no matter what it was.

So deep was Eishoxa's level of misery that she'd taken to going to the library, researching every possible branch of the family to see if by some chance anything struck a chord. She looked at all the village censuses and all the books that used to record the old slave trade, but she found nothing. She spent more and more time in the village, becoming a familiar figure among the local farmers, streaking around dangerously on Helios.

She no longer took grooms with her everywhere, but if the King knew, he said nothing. The end of the summer was drawing near, and they still hadn't discussed her going to Nasvasco any further. Even if they weren't her parents, they were the King and Queen, and if they told her to go, she would have to go. So Eishoxa treated every remaining moment like a cool drink in the desert, clinging onto her freedom and trying to preserve her sanity. At least ten times a day, she had a mad urge to write to Maya and ask to come to Cara, or to just gallop off into the desert and start her own life. But these urges came to nothing, because she knew that in the end she would be found and brought home.

She couldn't get rid of Rosemarie's coin. She'd tried – standing in the middle of the desert and letting it fall, so that it would be covered by sand and lost forever – but she couldn't do it. Instead, she carried it around with her wherever she went but never wore it around her neck. She no longer donned the small artefacts marking her out as royal blood. If no one had known her, they may well have suspected she was the daughter of one of the aristocracy, but never a princess, and that is how she wanted it to be.

She made her feelings towards the rest of the Royal Family quite evident by refusing to show up for one of their private meals together. These took place regularly, especially when Rosemarie was visiting, and although Eishoxa had enjoyed them immensely, she now felt wrong joining in with them when she so clearly didn't belong. She didn't expect anyone to call for her so was surprised when there was a quiet knock at her door and someone came in. Eishoxa was lying on her bed and made no move to see who it was.

"What do you want?" she asked. When there was no reply, she looked up. Rosemarie stood by the door. "What are you doing here?" Eishoxa demanded. "You're meant to be with the King and Queen."

Rosemarie didn't meet Eishoxa's eyes. "I came to see how you were."

"I'm fine. Now leave me alone."

"I don't think you are. I haven't seen you in a while since ... after you were told ..."

"That's a nice way of putting it," Eishoxa said viciously, sitting up. "After I was told," she repeated, "and after they told me they didn't trust me, didn't think I could handle the truth. This is my life we're talking about here, and they tell you before they tell me! And you didn't think I would find that a bit annoying?"

She could tell her words had hurt Rosemarie, but was not expecting the simmering anger rippling across her face at those words. "You know, this is exactly why they didn't tell you before! Because you would have taken it like this! And when you were younger, you would have told other people and it would have affected everyone, not just you. Maya has returned to Cara and will be confined; you can't tell her. At least now you just sulk about it and no one else knows."

Eishoxa sat up straight, swinging her legs off the bed. "You think I'm sulking? Fine words, Rosemarie, for someone in your position. Do you know that Bareth is going to belong to me? I'm going to be the Queen of Bareth and I don't even know where I come from. The people of Bareth hate foreigners! And no one could be more foreign than I am!"

"It doesn't matter where you come from," Rosemarie insisted, "as long as you're loyal to Bareth."

"It matters to me! I thought I belonged here in this castle with you and the King and Queen! And I don't. Nor do I know where I come from or why I was abandoned. I don't know anything! You can say calm down from where you stand because you're safe! What if this gets out? What happens to me and your precious reputation then? When did you find out? Tell me that!"

Rosemarie's eyes showed no fear as she looked at Eishoxa. "I found out by accident, when I was about eleven," she answered.

"By accident?" scoffed Eishoxa.

Rosemarie nodded defiantly. "Yes, by accident. I overheard them speaking about it one day. I investigated and discovered the secret for myself. It didn't take long."

"So why didn't you tell me then?" Eishoxa cried.

"Would you have taken it any better than you are now? What would you have us do? Track down your family? Believe me, they've tried many times! Leave you out on the streets? I don't think so. Why didn't we tell you, Eishoxa? Because there was nothing to be done and the consequences would have been disastrous! You would have told Maya, who might have told someone else, and the secret would have leaked out. We would have been forced to give you away! Then what?"

The logic in her words hit Eishoxa and a shock of different emotions left her breathless. It was true what Rosemarie said. They couldn't have told her. She would have told Maya everything. But on the other hand, they had no need to keep it from her for so long.

"You told them about the Masked Ball."

"You shouldn't have done it," Rosemarie replied immediately.

Eishoxa glared at her. "Do you even remember what a joke is?"

"Don't say that," Rosemarie said accusingly. "I care about doing what's right, and you should as well."

Eishoxa pointed at the door, feeling overwhelmed. "Go back to your dinner, Rosemarie. The King and Queen will be missing their daughter. They'll be waiting for you."

The words were spiteful, but Rosemarie held her ground. "Believe me, Eishoxa, if I had thought it would help telling you earlier, I would have done so. But what would that have solved? Tell me that."

The door closed with a final click behind her. Eishoxa threw herself onto her bed and stuffed her face into her pillow, asking her real family what had she ever done to deserve this.

CHAPTER 6

THE MINUTE EISHOXA opened her eyes, she knew there was some-thing wrong. It took her a few seconds to work out what it was. Her head felt fuzzy and strange. Her room was dark and there was a figure bending over her. She could just make out the profile of another one standing by the door. The moon was hidden by the clouds, but even so Eishoxa could see that there were figures jumping off the glass, too dark to be shadows.

"Get up," someone above her hissed. "It's time to go." The voice was familiar but she couldn't remember where she'd heard it before. She scrambled out from under her blanket, numb with shock and trying to work out what was happening.

"Who are you? What do you want?"

"You don't remember me?" The voice came out of the darkness, but Eishoxa couldn't see to whom it belonged. She wondered whether this was all an elaborate joke. Cold sweat broke out across her hands. Was she dreaming?

There came a *tsk-tsk* from the dark. "And if I do this? You still don't remember me?" Eishoxa shielded her eyes against the flare of fire that suddenly erupted in his palm, illuminating the room and his face. Eishoxa jumped with fright and covered her mouth. For his face was different from any she'd ever seen in her life: half hidden in shadow, it looked like something from a nightmare. The skin was dark brown but covered with red and orange patterns that ringed the eye sockets and patterned the cheeks. The eyes were glowing, golden, angled slits. Long red braids hung down on either side of his face, and around his waist was tied a thick belt. His hand was alight with writhing flames but he was not burnt.

Eishoxa shook her head. "No," she squeaked. "No, I don't remember anything at all. What's going on?"

The fire was extinguished and the room went dark again. Eishoxa backed away.

"I suppose that doesn't matter right now. You need to come with us. Right now."

At that moment an explosion sounded from outside and the room shook. Eishoxa saw flashes of light at the window and backed away. As she did so, a picture fell off the wall behind her and smashed to the floor. She leapt away in shock. The person moved to grab her wrist and yanked her forward.

"Get moving!" he snarled, pulling her into the corridor. All the candles had been snuffed out and no light came in from the large windows. From deep within the castle, she could hear the sounds of running feet, confusion, shouting, smashing and screaming. Another boom shook the castle as if a giant were knocking to come in. A pane of glass shattered in front of them and Eishoxa instinctively dropped to the floor, but she was jerked up again.

"That won't help! Don't stop! Keep moving! We have to get out of here – now!"

"Ember!" shouted the other one. Ember, still holding onto Eishoxa, looked up in alarm. There was a soft chattering from up ahead in the corridor. Ember pushed her behind him and sent a quick succession of flames at what looked like a shadow swooping towards them. There was a shriek and then it was gone. Ember looked back at Eishoxa, his thin eyes even more narrowed.

"That's why we don't stop. That's why we keep moving, do you understand?"

She nodded numbly even though she didn't understand anything at all, and they pushed on. Her body was like a puppet and her senses had been dulled by shock. She made no resistance at all and felt nothing but terror and an insistent urge to flee. Ears ringing, she stumbled through the dark after the two of them, even though it went against every instinct of self-preservation.

They reached the castle's garden. Chaos reigned. The winged shadows screeched, sounding like metal on metal. They swarmed along the tower and tore up the plants. Clanging swords sounded up ahead, but nothing could be seen, as the moon was still hidden. As they rounded a corner, heading towards the main gate, Eishoxa froze with horror. Ahead of them, the once-ordered, peaceful courtyard was wrecked, its gates thrown wide open. The ground crawled with figures, some human, some not. Ember yanked again at Eishoxa, and she almost fell over.

"Come on, move!" he yelled. But Eishoxa couldn't, because at that moment she caught sight of something she recognised and her stomach contracted sharply with fear. Lying on the ground, caught between the bared teeth of one of the creatures, was a matt of blonde hair that Eishoxa knew so well. It was Maya.

She tore her hand out of Ember's grip. What was Maya doing here? She should have been in Cara now, far away from Bareth. She vaguely registered Ember shouting after her, but all she could see was that head of blonde hair flailing this way and that as Maya was shaken like a rag doll in the teeth of the beast.

Eishoxa barrelled into the side of the creature and was surprised to find it was very solid, despite looking like darkness and vapour. It hissed and turned on her, dropping to all fours, its teeth bared. Maya was flung aside. Then something else collided with the other side of the creature and fire licked up its flank. A hand locked itself around Eishoxa's arm and wrenched her backwards.

The beast, its side still on fire, made its escape upwards, at the last second hooking its claw around Maya. It took her with it, flying high into the sky. The last Eishoxa saw of her friend was her limp body, head flopping from side to side, being dropped by the creature. Maya was still falling towards the ground like a stone when Eishoxa felt another jerk and found herself being taken up into the sky, spinning around and around, like a boat on a wild sea.

The dizzy feeling stopped and Eishoxa hit the hard floor of a forest. Her legs collapsed under the impact and she landed on her hands and knees. Trees materialised in front of her and sunlight shone into her face. It took a moment to realise that she was no longer in Bareth and that it was daytime, when moments ago it had been the middle of the night. Her next thought was of Maya. Panic closed her throat and she gasped for air.

"We have to go back! We must go back!" She turned around wildly and saw Ember leaning against a tree, quite recovered. His posture was far more relaxed, now that they were away from the castle. His companion was on the other side of the clearing, watching her warily. All their skin was covered in the same designs, orange and red and yellow lines that crisscrossed all over their skin. They were both wearing dark red trousers but no shoes. Ember shook his head.

"No chance of that. You'll die. And our orders were to bring you back alive."

Eishoxa took a deep breath, trying to force her whirling brain to think rationally. "My friend. My friend is back there—"

Ember straightened up and interrupted her. "Your friend is dead. And if she isn't, then it's too late to save her now. Forget it. We're not going back."

Eishoxa gaped at him, her brain refusing to process this cruel indifference, which she was so unaccustomed to.

Ember shrugged. "We need to start moving. We don't have any time to lose. This is Coal, by the way," and he nodded towards his companion. He started to walk towards the trees, expecting them to follow him, but Eishoxa stayed where she was. "I want to go back anyway."

She watched as Ember stopped and turned around. He even looked mildly amused. "And do what exactly, Princess? Take down the entire army single-handedly? I'm sorry, but your friend is beyond reach now. If the drakon didn't kill her, then she died in that fall. Welcome to the way of the world. And now, as I said, it's time to move. There is far to go before we're safe."

Eishoxa shook her head, furious to find tears of desperation in her eyes. "Take me back – please!" Ember shook his head and moved towards her, but she stood her ground. Ember's face grew even more amused and not a little exasperated.

"If you want to fight this out, Princess, I assure you it will be quick and extremely humiliating for you. Think sensibly now. That army attacked your castle looking for you. The best thing you can do now is stay away, because they'll come after you and leave your people alone. Understand?"

"And what about Maya?"

"Your friend is dead! There's no point going back! Now, come on!"

"You're lying!" Eishoxa accused, stepping away from him.

Ember merely sighed. "I was afraid it would come to this." He swept her up over his shoulder, oblivious, it seemed, to her screams and flailing. Finally, the three of them started to move. When Eishoxa realised that nothing would stop him, she simply hung there, tears running down her face, her voice silent at last.

Ember, who still had Eishoxa thrown over his shoulder, along with his friend Coal, had walked for the whole day without even stopping for a drink. They seemed determined to put as much space between them and the castle as possible. They made hardly any noise as they moved through the undergrowth. Eishoxa, too distraught to notice the beauty around her, finally comprehended that she could be in danger as well, but such was the depth of raw grief for Maya and utter confusion that she barely had the energy to think about it.

When the sky above the trees was black once again, Ember deposited Eishoxa on the ground. She curled herself up into a ball and faced away from her captors. They were busy making a fire. Her throat felt parched and her head throbbed from the lack of water and the constant jolting of her journey, but her pride refused to let her ask for help. Instead she studied the bark of a nearby tree and said nothing. Maya was dead. She couldn't grasp it. She wouldn't grasp it. Whatever Ember said, Eishoxa felt sure that something inside her would tell her that Maya was dead, but all she could feel was a desperate fear for her dear friend. Why had she been in Bareth anyway? Eishoxa had seen her leave, had seen her go head back for Cara. Why had she come back?

She could hear Ember and Coal speaking quietly together. She felt a fine web of anger spread through her.

"Hey, Princess! Catch!" called Ember, and Eishoxa felt something thump her on the shoulder. It felt like a blanket. She made no move to take it, partly because she didn't want it and partly because she felt that any movement would result in her being sick.

"I wasn't trained to look after babies," Ember mocked and let out a deep breath of frustration. Coal murmured something and Ember made a sound of derision. "Well, I'm going hunting. You watch her." Eishoxa flinched at the coldness of his words. She heard him walk away, and then there was silence apart from the soft crackle of flames and the firewood breaking.

"You should take the blanket," came Coal's voice from next to the fire. Eishoxa didn't move. Although he sounded much gentler, she didn't want to speak to him. "It will be cold soon," he continued. When again she didn't reply, he sighed. "I'm sorry about your friend, I really am. There was no hope for her though. She was too badly injured to survive, even if we had brought her here." Eishoxa, for a third time, pretended that she hadn't heard him. Coal didn't speak to her again.

It was colder by the time Ember returned, but Eishoxa still refused to take the blanket and still refused to speak. She put her hands into her pockets to retain some warmth and, as she did so, she felt something familiar. Drawing out Rosemarie's coin, which was quite a lot dirtier now, she was hit by homesickness like a tsunami on a flat beach. Remorse overwhelmed her as she remembered her last conversation with Rosemarie. More likely than not, she was dead now and Eishoxa had never got to say goodbye. She rubbed her finger across the coin and the bronze dully shone through. Holding it tightly, she rocked gently back and forth, mourning Bareth as if she'd lost a limb. No, not a limb. Something more than a limb. One can live without a limb. Her captors didn't bother her again and instead spoke quietly together. Eishoxa tried to stay awake, but soon their voices faded into a soothing lullaby to which she fell asleep, the coin still safe in her hands.

The first feeling Eishoxa had when she woke up was one of delicious warmth and safety, and for a moment she thought it had all been a dream and she was back in Bareth, lying in the fire-lit room. Then she noticed that her pillow smelt of pine and there was a twig touching her face. She sat up and, as she did so, the blanket flew off her. She scrambled away from it. It was alight. Flames crackled around its edges, yet there was not a single mark on her.

Her sharp feeling of sickness and of thirst had ebbed away significantly overnight. Eishoxa hugged her knees and stared at the blanket in shock. The flames were slowly dying away now.

"You're awake then, I see," came a familiar voice from the other side of the clearing. Eishoxa snapped her head around. Ember had just come out from the trees. In his hand he held a sprig of leaves. Coal was stirring by the fire. Eishoxa nodded, watching Ember carefully. He approached the fire, poking Coal awake as he did so, and blew on the glowing wood. A tiny flame leapt up, closely followed by another and then another. Ember looked up at her and grinned.

"Are you never going to speak to me again, Princess?"

Eishoxa returned his gaze in confusion. "Why do you keep calling me Princess?"

"So you are going to speak to me? Good. I was beginning to worry."

Eishoxa simply looked at him, arranging her features into an expressionless mask. When he didn't answer her question, she repeated, "Why do you keep calling me Princess? I don't like it."

His grin widened. "That's what you are."

"Was," she corrected stiffly. "I'm not one anymore." He chuckled. "What?" she asked.

"Well, are you not a Princess of Bareth? Are you not a Princess of anything else?" he challenged, straightening up.

Eishoxa blinked. "How can I be when you've taken me away from Bareth and you won't take me back? Plus, they aren't my family anyway."

"Oh, aren't they? Then why are you so upset about leaving them?"

Eishoxa gaped at him. He shrugged and turned away, but Eishoxa felt no sense of triumph.

When Coal awoke, they prepared to go again. It seemed that they were going to head deeper into the forest that day, but when Eishoxa looked back the way they came, Ember asked immediately, "Are you going to walk, or do I have to carry you again?"

"I'll walk," Eishoxa said, not meeting his eyes.

"I thought you might want to," he chuckled, and followed her into the trees.

The forest closed in on them like a wave. One minute they were walking in dappled glades full of dancing spots of sunlight, and the next they were plunged into a dimness that surrounded them like well water. Deer leapt over branches ahead of them, and strange trees extended gnarled fingers through her hair. Sometimes Eishoxa thought she saw a figure slipping away between the trunks, but whenever she stopped to get a better look, they'd always disappeared.

Ember and Coal conjured fire to hold in their hands, but more often than not it was a weak and feeble flame and they didn't keep it alight for long. Eishoxa noticed that they avoided walking into water. Whenever they approached a little stream, they would leap gracefully over it, not once touching the water. Eishoxa moved straight through, but then Ember noticed that she was doing it and threatened to carry her again unless she picked her feet up. When she asked why, he simply pushed her ahead of him and told her to keep moving.

There was a lot she didn't understand about them. She caught them in the evening whispering strange words to the flames. The fire would leap higher and higher, its colour deepening, and they could make the flames writhe and dance. They never went anywhere in the dark without a fistful of fire, as if it were a comfort to them.

Eishoxa thought that some part of her subconscious had accepted that Bareth was, for the time being, a place that she had very little chance of seeing again, but the rest of her refused to accept it. She felt sick with worry for everyone there. Although the King and Queen had lied to her and weren't her family, she wished them no harm. And Maya? If Eishoxa had allowed herself to cry for her, she would have. But something held her back. It could have been pride; it could have been something else. Sometimes Eishoxa wondered whether that had really been Maya back at Bareth, since she'd seen her leave. But she would quickly dismiss that idea, refusing to give herself false hope. No one in Bareth had white-blonde hair like Maya's, and no one from Cara had come to pick her up. That had definitely been Maya, whether Eishoxa liked it or not. Day after day, Eishoxa would wake with the awful certainty that her best friend – perhaps her only friend in her lonely, lonely life – was gone forever. No matter what she did, she couldn't get rid of the feeling that suddenly something inside her was missing, a void that couldn't be filled. And at night, half-asleep, Eishoxa would notice that she slept engulfed by flames that did not burn her.

Ember and Coal told her that they were crossing the Black Forest to get to a place called Sicharenhafan and that was where the Indocani, their people, lived, but they wouldn't tell her any more than that. They walked and walked. Time didn't seem to exist anymore. Minutes slipped into hours, and hours into days. Had it been years since she'd been in Bareth? It seemed that the nights and days were far longer here. Eishoxa had tried to keep track of the nights, but that hadn't worked. What would it have proven anyway? She couldn't count on being rescued by anyone from Bareth. She'd tried to watch the phases of the moon, but trees hid it every night and, when they didn't, smoke from the fire Ember and Coal conjured obscured the night sky. It was as though they didn't want to see it and so hid it from themselves and Eishoxa.

The Black Forest ended as abruptly as it had started, and the glades full of sunlight were back. There were more rivers now, though, large ones bubbling under the huge roots of trees that sometimes curved higher than Eishoxa, thick, twisted arches from which moss hung. Days waxed and waned, just like the moon in the sky. Every day passed in the same way, and every night took on a uniform precision that both frustrated and calmed Eishoxa. In the evening she would sit apart from Coal and Ember, refusing to talk to them or respond to anything they said. Ember found this amusing most of the time, but Coal said nothing. Coal rarely said anything.

According to Ember, they'd made good progress across the forest, so for one morning he let them stay and rest where they were. Eishoxa sat by one of the rivers, looking out across the water. The stillness reminded her of the many mornings when she and Maya would swim in the icy river even before sunrise, where the same stillness had filled her with perfect tranquility. Trees trailed their roots in the water and a bird chirped in its nest in the high branches. The leaves still formed a canopy overhead, but there was more sun here than anywhere else. It felt good to feel some sun. This green forest was not what she was used to and she didn't like it. Maya wouldn't have liked it either. From the pictures she'd seen of Cara, it was much like Bareth, with wide plains and large spaces and, in the background, the towering mountains. Except that in Cara the wide spaces were covered with ice and water. They had as many problems with floods as Bareth had with droughts.

As she thought of Maya, a mother bird returned to her children, carrying a mouthful of worms. The bird landed on one of the branches and hopped along to her nest, disappearing inside. When she reappeared, her beak was empty. Eishoxa watched as she flew off again. That bird would never give up on her babies. She would keep on finding food for them, putting their lives before her own. Eishoxa had almost given up on Maya, but at the sight of that bird she was filled with new resolve. Sitting on the riverbank in the sun, she made an unspoken promise to her friend, wherever she was: I will find you, she vowed, and I will not stop looking until I do.

As she thought this, the wind whistled through the branches and lifted the hair on her neck. She took Rosemarie's coin out of her pocket and looked at it, rubbing her finger across the dull surface to bring back some of the shine. She smiled a little at the clumsily stamped letters. Rosemarie couldn't have been very old when she'd made this. She wondered where Rosemarie was now. Had they escaped perhaps? Were they trying to find her? Or had they taken Rosemarie and whatever else they could salvage and left her to her fate? She was not their daughter, after all. Just a girl in a basket carried by an eagle. Then she put her hand to her forehead, driving out those thoughts. Thoughts may be the last thing she had of them. She didn't what to mar those.

"Princess?" She turned at the sound of Ember's voice. "We're going hunting." She said nothing, hiding the coin behind her back. Neither of them had made any comment on it; perhaps they didn't know she had it. The coin was her last souvenir of Bareth and she didn't want it taken away. Ember paused. "Do you need someone to stay with you, or will you wait here?" She remained silent. Ember continued, with a bite of impatience in his voice, "If you run away, we'll find you. You'll never find your way out, trust me. So just wait here, all right?"

"I'll wait," she agreed, drawing her knees up to her chin and turning her back on him.

"Good girl." She listened to them go and then turned her eyes back to the river. It looked identical to many others they'd passed, and she wondered whether they all came from the same source. Wherever that was. This forest seemed to go on forever and ever. They were right: she would never find her way out of the forest. And even if she did, she had no idea where they were at this point. Bareth had no forest and neither did Cara.

A harsh caw sounded nearby and she looked up. A large, very ugly crow dropped down to the water's edge and took a sip of water. Eishoxa hadn't drunk since they entered the forest and, apart from the first night, she hadn't felt the effects at all. She had eaten, though not a lot. The crow cawed at her again and dipped its beak towards the water, drinking noisily. It then cocked its head and fixed her with its gaze for a moment before cawing for a third time and dipping its head towards the water.

"All right, I'll try it," she told the bird. It shrieked loudly and then flew off. Wiggling forward, she dipped her cupped hand into the water. Its icy coldness made her fingers ache and she withdrew them immediately. But it was a warm day. The water couldn't be that cold because the river was shallow and there was plenty of sunlight to warm it. Eishoxa scooped up a handful of water and took a cautious sip. A flash of sharp, white pain coursed through her as the water trickled down her throat. She keeled over, desperately grabbing her neck. As the black curtain of unconsciousness rose to embrace her, she prayed it would make the pain stop.

CHAPTER 7

WHEN EMBER AND COAL returned, they found her curled in a tight ball. Ember took one look at her fingers, blue and clawed with cold, and knew what had happened. He dropped to her side immediately and took her hand, ignoring the pain it caused him, and rubbed it between his own, trying to generate some warmth.

"She must have tried to drink the water," Coal murmured as he conjured a fire around her and covered her curled body with a blanket.

Ember didn't pause in his efforts. "Obviously – stupid girl. Why did we leave her? Will she live?"

Coal nodded. "Oh yes. It will take more water than that to kill her. No need to worry on that score."

"Why would she do that?" Ember puzzled out loud.

Coal lifted his head briefly. "Most likely she wasn't aware of the dangers. She claims she doesn't remember anything but being human."

"But she isn't …" pressed Ember. He wanted another reason aside from ignorance.

"She doesn't know that," reminded Coal gently, trailing fire over the blanket. The words were meant to be soft, but they hit hard.

Eishoxa's fingers were straightening under Ember's hand. He felt something hard and cold trapped in her palm and pulled it out. It was a circular bronze disk, very dirty and tarnished. Eishoxa had been clutching it so tightly that its shape was indented into her skin. It had some sort of crest stamped into it and the characters p-r-i-n-c-e-s-s-o-f-b-a-r-e-t-h ran along the bottom. Ember had never learnt how to read the human alphabet and so had no idea what that could mean, but he put it in his pocket anyway and turned his gaze back to Eishoxa. The pallor of her cheeks was lifting as the fire warmed her skin. Coal stepped back as her eyes suddenly opened. She gasped, pulling away from Ember. He rocked back on his heels, refusing to look at her. Eishoxa had done the same.

"What happened?" she rasped, and then coughed.

"You mustn't drink water," Coal explained. "You mustn't even touch it. It will hurt you now."

"But why?" The tears in her eyes shocked Ember. It had been so long since he'd seen anyone cry.

Coal's mouth quirked up into a pensive smile. "It just will. You mustn't ever touch it again."

"But I need water. I'm … human." But then she caught sight of the blanket, still burning brightly, and her eyes opened in fear – or was it wonder?

Ember suddenly couldn't bear it anymore. "Of course you aren't! Do you really think that would have happened to you if you were human?" Coal put a restraining hand on his arm, but he threw it off. Too long had he played games. Too long had he waited and watched. He wanted the truth. Her eyes were widening with disbelief and shock.

"If you're human, why are you not burning? You're like us! You're one of us! Don't you remember? You lived with us! Not so very long ago for you! Do you not remember?"

She shook her head wildly and looked at Coal as if for reassurance. But he said nothing. Her gaze travelled from the two of them to the river and then to the blanket, and finally back to them. He could see the facts finally dawning on her. She shook her head again.

"You're lying! You're both lying! Look at me and look at you! How can you say that we're the same? We don't look anything like each other!"

Ember seized her hand and plunged it into the flames. "Look!" he shouted, desperate to get her to see sense. "Look at your hand! Is it burning? No! Because your body welcomes fire! Like mine does and like Coal's does. You're one of us!"

He let go of her hand furiously and turned, showing her his right shoulder, where there was a brand of an eagle in full flight under the rays of the sun.

"An eagle? What does that mean to you, Princess? An eagle?"

She shook her head again and he could see tears welling up in her eyes.

"You were brought to Bareth Castle by an eagle!" he yelled. "I know you know that! Why would an eagle take you there if you weren't one of us? Why would an eagle care about a baby if you weren't one of us?"

"Ember, that's enough!" Coal pulled him backwards.

Ember stayed back from her. She still had her hand in the fire, turning it around in the flames. "Whether you like it or not, you have to believe it," he muttered. "Because it's true, and deep down you know it too."

Eishoxa could still feel the water inside her, a constant icy parasite eating away at her strength. They had to keep moving, as Ember repeatedly said, but she noticed the pace had been slowed for her sake. Coal was always fussing over her, and Ember insisted on carrying her across any water they happened to pass. She had the feeling that he was watching her to make sure she didn't do anything silly again. Another thing that had changed was how much he mocked her. Now he said nothing.

The revelation that she wasn't completely human hadn't quite sunk in yet. How could she not be human? And why hadn't water hurt her before?

It was not until a few days after the incident at the river that she noticed her coin was gone. She keenly missed its weight in her pocket. She made no comment about it, though, and neither Ember nor Coal mentioned anything about it. She must have lost it by the riverbank. Now all she had left of Bareth were the clothes she stood up in, and even these were getting dirty and frayed. It was as if the forest was slowly trying to persuade her to forget everything that had happened in Bareth.

According to Ember's reckoning, they were very close to Sicharenha-fan now. The forest had changed again, and water had completely disappeared. Unless Eishoxa was imagining it, the soil itself seemed a lot warmer, as if a fire were burning away underground.

That morning Ember and Coal seemed much more agitated than usual and they pushed the pace faster and faster during the day. Eishoxa, still recovering but refusing to be carried, concentrated on putting one foot in front of the other and forcing herself not to faint. The sun was touching the horizon when they finally saw it.

"Sicharenhafan," breathed Ember, raw longing palpable in his voice. They were at the top of a ridge. Eishoxa stepped forward beside them to look, curiosity getting the better of her. Down below, in a scoop of land, stood a colossal Tree. Even from here, Eishoxa could see that it was bigger than the whole of the castle at Bareth. Curved around the edge of the Tree was a large forest, and in the fading light of dusk it looked very much like the Black Forest they'd just left. Little fires could be seen burning in the branches near the centre of the big Tree, and a soft breeze carried the sound of shouting. Coal grinned at Eishoxa. "They're waiting for you, you know. All of them."

Ember muttered something but Eishoxa didn't catch it. She just nodded and looked straight ahead, refusing to meet either of their gazes.

The slope on the way down was covered in singed grass, charred from fire and smoking slightly. Ember and Coal walked beside her, not running on ahead. The grass crunched beneath her feet and little puffs of smoke irritated her nose. The Tree's branches stretched wide, and it was not long before Eishoxa was walking underneath them. She looked up and was greeted with grinning faces and clapping hands and joyful yelling. Petals fluttered down onto her head and, turning around, she saw children – smaller versions of Ember and Coal, but their faces were more carefree. Their skin was paler as well, very similar to Eishoxa's own dark olive colour, but already decorated with patterns. Standing by the great trunk of the Tree, someone was waiting for them. Even from far away, Eishoxa sensed an aura radiating off the figure that reminded her of fire itself: wild, intoxicating and dangerous.

"That's Vera," Coal whispered out of the corner of his mouth to her. "She's our leader, the Commander."

Vera towered over Ember and Coal and Eishoxa felt minute next to this monument of power. Her hair was plaited like theirs but around her neck hung many necklaces and her arms were covered with copper bangles. Her gaze was calculating as it swept over the three of them, but she nevertheless bowed low to Eishoxa, and when she straightened there was real respect in her eyes. The shouting had ceased. Eishoxa turned her eyes upwards and saw many pairs of golden eyes blinking down at her. People clung to the trunk or crouched on the branches. Every bough was lined with them. Eishoxa swallowed.

"Eishoxa, I did not think you would come back to us. It is good to see you," smiled Vera. She nodded at the other two. "Thank you, Coal and Ember," and they both inclined their heads. "I trust there was no trouble along the way."

Eishoxa clenched her fists slightly as she felt Ember's gaze sweep over her, but Coal answered, "No, everything was fine."

Vera smiled broadly this time. "Welcome, Eishoxa. I hope that you will find as much solace here as the last time, before you left us." Eishoxa made no reply. Vera blinked once at her – a slow, inquisitive blink – before raising her arms and exclaiming to the whole Tree, "Our Princess has returned!"

There was an almighty roar that echoed around the Tree and into the surrounding forest. Leaves dropped and branches shook as the people in the Tree stamped their feet or clapped their hands, shouting their approval. Vera, smiling, lowered her arms and the roar subsided slightly. She beckoned to someone in the shadow of the Tree who came forward. His skin was a much lighter brown than Ember's or Coal's, and a scar ran across his chest from shoulder to hip.

"This is Rianox," she explained, placing one slim hand on his shoulder. Rianox bowed to Eishoxa and nodded at both of her companions. Eishoxa distinctly felt Ember stiffen beside her as Rianox's gaze fell on her. She felt uncomfortable under it; his eyes were scrutinising. "I need to meet with Coal and Ember, so Rianox will show you around Sicharenhafan. I doubt you remember much from your last visit and things have changed since then." She laughed as if she found something funny, but no one else joined in. Eishoxa nodded once to show she'd understood and Vera gave her another smile. There was something strange about her smile, as if it weren't quite finished or quite meant. She lifted her head to the people above her and said something that Eishoxa couldn't understand. Her words were met with another cheer and they all started to move. Some disappeared into the side of the trunk, others ascended, jumping from branch to branch as nimbly as monkeys. Within moments they'd all gone, leaving just the five of them. Vera gave Eishoxa another bow and touched her cheek lightly. Eishoxa jumped at her touch.

"It is good to see you among us again." Her strange smile had returned. Eishoxa looked at the ground, not knowing what to say. Then Vera swept off, followed by Ember and Coal; the latter murmured a goodbye as he brushed past her. Eishoxa watched them go and then turned back to Rianox, who had his gaze firmly fixed upon her. They watched each other silently, each hoping the other would be the first to speak. Rianox seemed to be appraising her.

"Hello," he said at last. She quickly nodded back. "You look very different from the last time you were here. You don't look like you."

Eishoxa looked down at herself, at the torn and dirty trousers and long shirt. "I don't feel like myself either," she sighed.

Rianox looked her up and down. "We should probably start moving," he suggested. "We have a lot to see." He turned immediately for the Tree and started to scale the side of the trunk, waiting patiently for Eishoxa on the first bough. She was glad that she'd climbed so many trees in Bareth – it was second nature to her now.

Rianox started to speak, his voice a low hum that flowed over her like water. "So this is Sicharenhafan – the main city of the Indocani. There are a number of smaller settlements spread out in the forest, but mostly this is where we live, inside the trunk. A few rooms are built outside, and as our race has grown we've also dug underground. A few of us live there also."

Eishoxa looked around, nodding. Rianox grinned in encouragement. "You'll soon know your way around again."

They continued to climb slowly up the Tree. Rianox pointed things out to her that he thought she should know, and she acknowledged them with a nod. The Tree was even bigger than Eishoxa had imagined. Little stairs had been cut into the thick wood of the trunk or protruded slightly out of the wood, and every now and then a small doorway had been cut out of the side. Quaint little pennants and charms decorated each doorway, and stamped above each one was the image she'd seen on Ember's shoulder: an eagle in full flight underneath the sun. Much of the Tree was still being built and grown, Rianox explained, pointing to the weaker ends of branches.

"We keep getting bigger and bigger," he smiled. "Vera wants some of us to move to the smaller trees soon."

"Which trees do you mean?"

Rianox pointed towards the forest that Eishoxa had seen from the top of the ridge with Coal and Ember. "Most are hidden in there. For those who really like their isolation, there are even some in the Black Forest. But mostly we like to stay close to one another."

"I see."

Rianox moved swiftly up and down the Tree, never stopping long at one particular place but always moving on. Eishoxa noticed some of the Indocani – those who didn't mind her knowing they were staring.

"They're very impressed that you returned," Rianox explained. "We didn't expect to see you again so soon. Only Ember was convinced that you would return now. That's why he was the one to go and fetch you."

They arrived back at the bottom branch of the Tree, but on the other side. Rianox hadn't taken Eishoxa all the way to the top – there was nothing there, he'd said – but even so, Eishoxa's hands were chafed from the rough bark and her muscles ached. Now the two sat leaning against the trunk, swinging their legs over the branch.

"Do you really remember nothing?" Rianox enquired curiously. Eishoxa turned to look at him and shook her head. "I'd like to remember, really. It would stop me being so confused about all of this. But I don't. How long ago was I here, and for how much time?

Rianox squinted in concentration. "You were here for thousands of years. You were here when I was born. I remember you from stories that I was told as a child."

"Thousands of years?" Eishoxa squeaked.

Rianox nodded. "But our years are different from human years."

"I'm older than you?" Eishoxa asked.

He nodded vigorously. "Oh yes. Far older than me. You're as old as

Ember – and he's old." He chuckled. "But I believe Vera is older than both of you."

Eishoxa tilted her head. "As old as Ember?"

"Yes. There are many stories about the two of you. But most of them have been lost."

"Why? Where did they go?"

Rianox shrugged. "We thought that you'd taken them. But obviously not," he said quickly, as Eishoxa started to shake her head. "Maybe Ember took them then," Rianox concluded.

Eishoxa laughed. "Why would Ember take them?"

"Maybe he was embarrassed by them. It's the sort of thing that Ember would do," Rianox replied carelessly.

"Do you not like him very much, then?"

She'd been expecting Rianox to deny it, but he paused. "I think he's a noble warrior, but sometimes he lets his pride get in the way. Come, Eishoxa, we really must go."

They spent the rest of the afternoon climbing from bough to bough. Rianox leapt from branch to branch with practised grace. He put Eishoxa at ease as well. He was not silent and watchful like Coal, but neither was he brash and outspoken like Ember. He possessed a reserve that Eishoxa could sense beneath his teasing and playful exterior.

"Vera would like to speak with you," Rianox said presently.

Eishoxa sighed. "I suppose I should go then."

Rianox put his hand on her arm. "You don't have to go if you don't want to," he said seriously. "No one will make you do anything here. We're all glad that you're back home."

Home. The word sounded so right on his tongue, but so bitter on hers.

"I'll go." Eishoxa brushed off his hand. "Where do I need to go?"

Rianox stood up and led the way around the trunk. Cut into the side was a tall, narrow doorway. "Go in there," he instructed.

Eishoxa inclined her head in gratitude. "Thank you."

He bowed deeply in return. "My honour, Eishoxa. Goodbye."

She watched him leap away before facing the door again. Unlike the others, this was a solid wooden door, so she couldn't see or hear what was going on inside. The bark was smoother, as if sanded down, and ornate carving edged the door. However, like every other one, it was stamped with the eagle under the sun. Eishoxa gave it a curious glance before knocking.

"Come in," came a voice. Eishoxa pushed open the door and stepped through.

She was standing at the entrance of a large room, relatively bare except for a circular table in the middle. Eishoxa was surprised to see it there. It made the place look more like a room from the castle at Bareth. Vera sat behind it. Coal and Ember were at the back of the room, seated on a bench that ran around the edge of the whole room. Coal smiled encouragingly at Eishoxa, but Ember refused to meet her gaze, sprawling moodily on the cushions.

"Eishoxa," Vera began. "It's good to see you again. Would you like to sit down?"

Eishoxa took hold of the chair opposite and pulled it out. The legs scraped loudly in the silent room. Vera gave her a tight smile and began to speak. Eishoxa noticed that her eyes kept darting to where Ember and Coal sat, as if for confirmation.

"I suppose you already know why you're here—"

"Sorry, no," Eishoxa interrupted.

Vera blinked. "What do you mean?"

"I don't know why I'm here, no," Eishoxa repeated, feeling flustered already.

Vera sat back, relaxing visibly. "Well, I'll explain then. You must have been told that you've already been here, about fifty years ago in Ignorant years."

"Ignorant?"

"Human," came Ember's low voice.

Vera gave another tight smile and continued. "They're called that because they don't know how to tame fire."

Eishoxa nodded.

"The reason you left was because the Ewdicani – the Peacemakers – feared that you were becoming too ... how shall I put it? Influential? And some of them demanded that you leave. When you refused – and we refused to let you go, obviously – a pack of them ambushed you in the middle of the Black Forest and you were left very badly wounded. The only way for you to be saved was to live another life with the Ignorant. This you did, and now you've returned to us at what we believe is a critical point. We would like you to go to the Ewdicani and ask them to aid us in a war which at the moment we're currently ... losing."

It obviously pained her to say that. Eishoxa watched Coal and Ember out of the corner of her eye. Ember had definitely stopped fidgeting so much and was watching the pair of them very intently. Coal was leaning forward as well. Apparently, something Vera had said had caught their attention.

"Is that it?"

The corner of Vera's mouth twitched upwards attempting another smile. "We would like you to stay, of course, and make your home here again, but Ember has said that that idea does not sit well with you."

Eishoxa shook her head.

"And we would like you to help us in this war because just your presence there would be of enormous benefit."

Eishoxa again shook her head. She put her hand on the table as if to verify a steadiness somewhere in the world, because at present her mind was whirring with everything she'd heard.

"But I don't understand. Why me? Why am I so important?"

Vera glanced at Coal and Ember.

"We didn't explain that part to her," confessed Coal apologetically.

48

"She didn't even take well to the idea that she'd been here before. We thought that more explanations would be a bit too much."

Eishoxa looked from one to the other in confusion. "What?"

Vera merely looked at her, then stood and moved to the corner of the room. Eishoxa hadn't noticed before, but there was a pile of rolled-up pieces of paper. When Vera spread them out on the table, Eishoxa realised that they were not paper but very thin sheets of wood. Painted very carefully on top of the one of the sheets was a picture of someone.

"This is our Goddess, Fiera," Vera explained. "She has a sister, Wella, who is the Goddess the Ewdicani worship. Fiera is your mother."

Eishoxa took the picture and looked at it, her heart pounding suddenly. This was her mother? If Vera's voice hadn't been so serious, Eishoxa wouldn't have believed it. But a week ago she wouldn't have believed in the existence of any of this. Was her search for family so simple? Could she accept this and make another home here? She studied the picture of Fiera. In one hand she carried a burning torch and in the other a gleaming sword, held high above her head. Her face was intent and sharp and her eyes burned with passion. Red hair erupted from her head and blew around her face as if in a violent wind. Her skin was the colour of dark chocolate and her eyes exploded with golden flames. Eishoxa felt weakened just looking at them.

"This is my mother?"

"Yes, the Great Warrior," replied Vera with pride.

Eishoxa put down the picture and backed away from the table. "I think you're wrong. That doesn't look like my mother. I have a mother. I ... I don't want another one."

"Eishoxa, I know this is hard, but you must believe us. Much depends on your agreeing to believe us, even if you don't want to."

"But I don't know her! I don't know you and I don't know this place! How could she be my mother?"

"You do," contradicted Vera earnestly. "You really do. We have pictures—"

"No, I don't want to see them!" Eishoxa burst out.

Vera picked up again smoothly. "Then you must believe us. If you won't see proof, then you must."

Eishoxa blinked. It was all too much. "May I have some time to think about it?" she asked finally, looking up at Vera hopefully. Ember started forward, but Coal grabbed his arm and Eishoxa glared at him. She didn't need his words.

"Of course you may," Vera smiled graciously. "I will see you again soon to discuss this further."

Eishoxa nodded gratefully. She reached for the picture on the desk. "Please may I keep this for a while?"

"Of course. I will summon Rianox and ask him to take you to your room now." Vera swept to the door and pushed it open. Rianox was standing there as if conjured by her thoughts. His gaze swept over them, lingering slightly on the picture Eishoxa held. "Take Eishoxa to her room, would you?" Vera asked.

Rianox smiled kindly at Eishoxa and jerked his head towards the

49

outside. Eishoxa took the hint and followed him.

"Was it really that bad?" he asked, the moment the door was shut.

Eishoxa shrugged, holding the picture of Fiera out towards him like an offering. "This is my mother," she began tentatively. Rianox glanced at it.

"That's right. Fiera, the Great Warrior. Why? Didn't you know?" He took in Eishoxa's blank expression as she looked at the picture again. "Oh," he realised.

She looked up at him hopelessly. "I told you I didn't remember anything. Not even this."

She looked around, as though searching for an answer. "I don't know what to think anymore. I wish I could just remember something."

"Maybe you will once you're more settled here," Rianox suggested. "Come. I'll show you to your room. Give me the picture and I'll hold it while we climb."

The foliage grew mostly at the end of the branches, forming a natural cage around the edge of the Tree. Rianox had stopped showing Eishoxa around where the leaves had formed a natural ceiling. Now he led her to where more branches exploded out of the leaves, reaching for the sky that was dimming as night fell. On the other side of the trunk, which was now much slimmer, he indicated Eishoxa's room. It was made completely of coloured glass, which coiled to a point and formed the shape of a flame. The bottom was dark blue, almost black, but the colours slowly morphed into orange and yellow and red. In the setting sun, the effect was dazzling.

"Is this for me?" Eishoxa asked, stepping back hesitantly.

Rianox grinned. "It's incredible, isn't it? Yes, all for you. Here is your picture and this is where I leave you. Goodnight, Eishoxa."

Eishoxa walked in a daze to the glass room. The ornately carved door handle depicted the head of a phoenix. She ran her hand over it before opening the door. A blast of heat hit her from the fire that roared in the grate. The air was heavy with heat, but Eishoxa loved it. It reminded her of the desert climate of Bareth. The strong glass walls were carved on this side with elaborate decorations and calligraphy. In the middle of the room was a low-slung bed, a stretchy piece of orange cloth supported by two pieces of wood. A thick pillow made from folded leaves lay at the top. Lying neatly at the bottom of the bed was one of the blankets Coal had had in the forest. Eishoxa picked it up and rubbed her face against it, revelling in the soft feel of it against her skin. She left the picture of Fiera on the bed. In the light from the fire the intense look on Fiera's face looked evil. Looking up, she saw hanging from the ceiling were many little balls of fire, flickering dimly. In the corner of the room was a pile of clothes, all made out of light scarlet material. They were mostly cropped shirts and loose trousers, which tightened at the ankles. She ran her hand over the sleeve of the garment she was wearing now. She would have to get rid of this. But it was her last memento of Bareth. She had picked up one of the shirts when there was a light tap at the door.

"Come in," Eishoxa called.

The door opened slowly. Apart from Vera, this was the first female Indocani that she'd seen close up. The girl shut the door and bowed deeply. "Hello," Eishoxa said after a moment's pause. The girl raised her head and smiled. Her red hair was braided in two long plaits like everyone else's. However, she had flowers twisted into hers as well. Across her back was slung a quiver, and she carried a bow in her hand. She wore a pair of tight red trousers and a strip of red fabric across her chest. The fire illuminated her exposed skin and the decorative lines chasing each other across her back and stomach. Eishoxa stared at her. She was beautiful.

"Princess Eishoxa," the girl replied and made another deep bow.

Eishoxa waved her hand immediately. "Please call me Eishoxa," she corrected. "I … I would prefer that."

The girl smiled again. "I'm Amber. I've been sent by my brother, Ember, to see how you are."

Eishoxa bristled internally at the sound of Ember's name. "I'm fine," she said stiffly.

Amber laughed. "I told him you would be but he didn't believe me. He said that you had an accident in the forest."

"I didn't know that it was at all any of his business to keep checking up on me," began Eishoxa hotly, and then realised that Amber was laughing.

"You haven't changed, Eishoxa. Not at all." Eishoxa was warming to this girl despite herself. She carried with her a confidence that Eishoxa admired and an intense self-assurance that in Bareth had been frowned upon in girls. Amber placed her bow on the ground and unslung the quiver from her shoulder.

"I was hunting when you came. You definitely look different. Ember told me he was shocked when he saw you. You don't look like the Eishoxa he knew at all," and she chuckled. "What have they asked you to do?" she continued, throwing herself onto the bed and patting the space beside her. Eishoxa felt a bit taken aback. Was she supposed to know this girl? Amber took in her shocked expression and asked in concern, "Is there something wrong? Am I doing something wrong? Ember said you wouldn't remember anything, but I told him you'd remember me."

Eishoxa deliberately let fall the shirt she'd been holding and bent down to pick it up so that she wouldn't have to meet Amber's gaze. "I don't remember anything, sorry," and when she straightened, she didn't miss the puzzled look in Amber's eyes.

"So it's true what they're saying then," she murmured more to herself than to Eishoxa.

Eishoxa nodded, then quickly added, "But Rianox said that it might come back to me if I'm here for a while."

At that, Amber's face brightened. "Yes, probably. Rianox is usually right. Ah well, if that's the case, then I'll leave you for now. Goodnight, Eishoxa."

51

"Goodnight, Amber," replied Eishoxa.

Amber picked up her quiver and bow. "I'll come and see you in the morning," she called back over her shoulder. Eishoxa smiled and nodded. Amber closed the door behind her with a faint click.

The minute she'd gone, Eishoxa felt the smile slide off her face. How many more experiences like this would she have to go through? She couldn't remember anything or anyone yet, however hard she tried. She picked up the picture of Fiera, unrolled it and sat down on the bed, looking at it. The more she looked, the more Eishoxa could see similarities between herself and this woman. They had the same nose and the same shape of face and the same hair, but apart from that Eishoxa would never have guessed this was her mother. Her mother was a goddess? She was the daughter of a goddess? But she was the second daughter of a tiny country on the far edges of the world. Bareth was powerful, but it was insignificant compared to other countries. It didn't make any sense.

Eishoxa rolled up the picture and put it under her bed. She didn't want to look at it. She took the blanket off her bed and sat in front of the fire, letting the heat warm her face. She loved fire. She always had. But she didn't feel like one of the Indocani at all. It didn't take long for the blanket to ignite as well and the warm smell of smoke tickled her nose. The crackle of the fire was the lullaby that finally sent her to sleep.

Amber and Ember crouched beside the trunk of the Tree, keeping their gaze trained on Eishoxa's room. The two of them could feel the heat from the glass, even though they were so far away.

"The fire is glad to have her back. It dances beautifully now she's here," Ember whispered to his twin sister. "She is the same person. I'm sure of it."

"But she looks so different. I thought she would at least look like one of us. And the fire hasn't claimed her, has it?" mused Amber.

Ember hissed and shook his head in confusion. "I thought that, when she passed through the portal in the Black Forest, she would Change back into an Indocani. But I don't think her body is strong enough yet to complete the transformation safely. She's already rejected water, though. The rest will come."

Amber heard the hopefulness in her brother's voice and felt a rush of sympathy. Of course it was hard for him, maybe even harder than for her. "She doesn't remember you, does she?"

Ember turned his head away from his sister's searching gaze but shook his head all the same. "She claims to remember nothing."

"Maybe that's a good thing," Amber suggested wryly.

Ember snapped his head back. "Why? Do you believe the lies that filth of an Ewdicani spread about her?"

Amber hesitated but then pressed on with conviction. "I can't say what I believe. Maybe it's better for her to forget everything and make a new life here than to be constantly burdened with the mistakes of her old life – and she did make mistakes, Ember," she said as Ember opened his mouth.

"Of course she made mistakes!" he retorted. "But she did good things as well, and she's forgotten everything. Vera has given her over to Rianox to prove that we can trust him. Eishoxa doesn't even remember how much she used to hate him."

"We need to know who we can trust, Ember," Amber reminded him. "We can't do this alone."

"Of course we need to trust him," Ember snapped. "But there are other ways."

"Vera knows what she's doing," soothed Amber.

Ember turned his wounded gaze on her. "Eishoxa is the only one who has changed. Vera has not. Don't forget that."

"What was his name again? The name of the Ewdicani from before?"

"Rush," Ember hissed, a quiet hiss like the last sound the fire makes before it dies. And he sprang forward, landing cat-like on the next branch before letting the darkness swallow him.

CHAPTER 8

"EISHOXA! WAKE UP!" There was a sharp rapping at the door. Eishoxa grunted and rolled over, hitting her head on the grate. "What is it?" she groaned, sitting up and rubbing her forehead, wincing. Amber pushed open the door, bounding through. She grinned when she saw Eishoxa sitting on the floor. She had her bow again, slung over one shoulder, and she carried her quiver in her hand.

"You know, Eishoxa, here at the Tree we sleep on beds. Did you sleep on the floor?"

Eishoxa nodded and yawned. Amber shut the door behind her. "Well, isn't it warm in here? It's freezing outside," and she shivered.

Eishoxa shrugged off her blanket and stood up. "Why are you here, Amber?"

Amber looked mildly exasperated. "I have to take you to Rianox. You're to receive simple tutorage apparently," and she yawned. "Vera's doing – I don't know why, though. I said that you'd prefer to go exploring and hunting with me, but Ember agrees that you need lessons," and she frowned.

Eishoxa smiled. "Lessons in what?"

"Everything that you've forgotten or missed," Amber supplied, still frowning. "He thinks he knows everything," she grumbled.

Eishoxa didn't take long to get dressed. She put on the clothes that she'd been given and tied a belt around her waist. Although Amber offered to plait her hair, Eishoxa declined. She'd never tied her hair up in Bareth unless she was required to, and this felt more like her. She noticed that Amber didn't wear shoes and so she stayed barefoot herself.

Ember was waiting for them. He too was wearing a quiver and bow over his shoulder. He stood one branch down, leaning against the trunk. When Eishoxa and Amber came into sight, he addressed his sister, "You're late. Where have you been?"

"She was asleep," Amber retorted. "Don't order me around, Ember!"

Seeing the two of them together, Eishoxa could easily see that they were siblings. They had almost identical faces, they were the same height and they carried themselves with the same concentrated confidence.

Ember turned to Eishoxa. "I'm not sure whether Amber has told you what we're going to do now—"

"She has. I know," Eishoxa cut across him.

Ember nodded curtly. "Good. Then let's go."

The two girls followed him down almost to the bottom of the Tree. In the side there was a little door, smaller than the other doors. Amber grinned at Eishoxa, slung the bow off her back and held it in her hands. Then she sat on the branch, pushed on the door with her feet, which swung backwards like a trapdoor, and pushed herself through. There was a whoosh of air and Amber had gone. The trapdoor swung back into place.

"You next, Princess," Ember said. Eishoxa sat on the branch and pushed the trapdoor open with her feet. A blast of air hit her in the face and suction dragged her forward. She hurtled down, round and round, tossed from side to side, her hair lashing her face. It was relatively dark, but she could make out other tunnels branching off. Just when she was sure she was going to be sick, her feet hit something hard and she was pushed out. Amber offered her a hand and pulled Eishoxa to her feet.

Her head swimming, she gasped and looked around. She was standing in a huge hall, bigger than the Great Hall in Bareth. High above her, the roots of the Tree dangled through the ceiling, twisting and still growing to form the natural walls of the hall. The floor was covered with dried rushes and leaves, and a faint smell of herbs filled the air. There was no natural light, but fires burnt all along the walls. Indocani were crossing the hall at the other end, holding big chunks of metal and wood in their arms. On a large platform ahead of her was a table set for many people, though it was empty.

Eishoxa's voice echoed through the space. "What is this place?"

"This is our Great Hall," Amber informed her. "We don't use it very often because it's too dark for us and not close enough to the sun, but in times of danger it's very useful because the only way people can enter is by the trapdoors which can be blocked and the side rooms which can be collapsed." She seemed amused at the blatant awe written all over Eishoxa's face.

Ember shot out of the trapdoor at that moment and landed deftly on his feet. "We're to go over there," he said, pointing to the far side of the hall. Eishoxa followed and Amber brought up the rear, the sound of their feet loud and hollow in the large room. Spread unevenly along the walls were small rounded doorways, also formed by the roots of the Tree. Ember marched through one and the two girls followed.

Rianox leant against the wall and by his feet was a small pile of scrolls. Ember nodded to him and he did the same back, but when the girls entered, he bowed.

Ember turned to Eishoxa. "Rianox will teach you the basic history of our people, as well as our language, Düerasgörn. Listen well, because I guarantee that you'll need it." And he swept out.

Eishoxa looked curiously around. The ceiling sagged slightly and small shoots with pale green leaves sprouted here and there from the walls. There was no furniture or ornament in this room at all.

"He still hasn't gained a sense of humour, has he?" Rianox asked Amber, chuckling slightly.

"Ember? No, not at all. He thinks that every problem we have is resting personally on his shoulders," and she laughed. Amber put her bow back on her shoulder. The tip pressed into the ceiling. "Well, I'll leave you two to your work. I'm off hunting. Have fun," and Amber brushed her hand along Eishoxa's arm and left, smiling at Rianox as she did so.

The two of them were all alone now. "Did you sleep well?" he asked. Eishoxa nodded. He picked up the scrolls on the floor. "I chose these from the library to help you learn the alphabet of Düerasgörn." He opened it. "You will notice that our alphabet is very different from the one you know now."

Eishoxa looked at the spiky, defined script and sighed. She'd hated learning languages back in Bareth, and this one looked even more difficult. Rianox grinned. "Don't worry. This is the language you were born to speak, no matter how much you remember. Trust me. You'll soon understand it again."

They sat next to each other on the floor, and Rianox laid the scroll over their knees. He handed Eishoxa a stick of charcoal and a board made from a very thin sheet of wood.

"You write down the characters as I tell you and then we'll look at them in more detail." Eishoxa nodded and held the charcoal more tightly, disregarding the soot that smudged her hand.

"There are actually three hundred different characters in our language," Rianox started, and then hurried to explain as Eishoxa looked at him in horror. "But we only really use about fifty of them."

"That's so many," she said hopelessly.

To her surprise, Rianox laughed again. "You may not be so far from the Eishoxa we knew after all. She never liked to sit down and work. 'That's for the Ewdicani,' you used to say." His eyes softened with the memory.

"Who are the Ewdicani?" Eishoxa asked. "Vera mentioned them yesterday but I wasn't really listening."

Rianox took another of the scrolls and unrolled it, after moving the other carefully off their knees. He put his finger on a small drawing that spread over the centre of the page. She could see a sea and a glorious golden sunset and a small person standing on the sand, arms outstretched. Underneath was some more of that script that Eishoxa couldn't begin to decipher. She leant forward to scrutinise the picture, trying to decipher it, but the figure was too small. All she could make out was that the person had the palest of skin.

"They are our opponent race, so to speak. They worship Wella, the Goddess of water, just as we worship Fiera. The Ewdicani are a much calmer race, it's said," and he smiled wryly as if remembering something.

Eishoxa thought for a moment. "So these are the people I must go to and convince to join you in your war?"

Rianox paused for a moment before nodding. "We would be very grateful."

Eishoxa didn't answer. Rianox cleared his throat. "Maybe we should get back to our characters," he suggested, taking the second scroll away and replacing it with the first.

Eishoxa picked up her charcoal stick and smiled. "Of course," she agreed.

Rianox pointed at the first line of characters. "Copy that row down first. As you can see, the lines are simple, although there are many of them."

He took the stick of charcoal and the wooden board and expertly sketched the first character. "You see? Very easy to draw. This means

Fiera," he supplied. Eishoxa took a deep breath as Rianox handed her the charcoal again. "Try it," Rianox urged. "It's not as difficult as it seems."

They stayed in silence as Eishoxa copied down the characters. Then she asked curiously, pausing for a moment in her work, "And are they a calmer race, the Ewdicani?"

Rianox gave a short unamused snort of laughter. "I wouldn't say so and neither would Ember. We've had dealings with them in the past. But you may think differently."

Eishoxa didn't respond but focused on her task. Her hand ached by the time she'd finished copying down the alphabet, and she had a smudge of charcoal on one cheek. Rianox, however, was very pleased with her work.

"That is well done," he complimented, examining it closely. "I think we're done here for today. Would you like to finish?"

Eishoxa nodded tiredly, massaging her cramped fingers.

Rianox took the board from her and carefully rolled up the scrolls. "Do you have any questions at the end of our first lesson?"

"Just one," Eishoxa admitted. "How is it that Ember and Coal can speak to fire and conjure it? And make it do what they want?"

He smiled at her, as if pleased that she'd asked this question. "Düerasgörn is the language that Fiera gave us. It's the language that the fire knows and understands, and if you can master the tongue, then the fire may listen to you and do as you say."

"So is the language magic?" she asked. In Bareth there had been many magicians who'd come to the castle to show their talents, and many fire-eaters who'd devoured flame upon flame in front of her eyes. But the control that these Indocani had over it made their magic seem like fraud.

"No, not magic." He shook his head. "Although magic is what the Ignorant call it. This is just a language that fire understands. If I speak to you in the Base Tongue, the language that we're speaking now, and ask you to open a door, you'll understand. If I ask you in Düerasgörn to open a door, you won't understand and you won't do it. We don't control fire. Only Fiera can do that. We may ask it to dance and play with us, but if it doesn't want to, it won't."

"I don't think I'll ever be able to do that," Eishoxa laughed in frustration. Her last characters had been smudged and messy and she'd already forgotten most of what Rianox had told her. She would never master this language, no matter what he said.

Amber was waiting for them in the Great Hall. She stood up when she saw them and came over. "Have you had a good morning?" she asked. She smelt like wood smoke. Eishoxa shrugged, which made the two of them laugh.

Rianox spoke for her. "She hated it, but she's too polite to say so."

"Well, Vera said I can have her now, so it's time to go away!" Amber retorted, taking Eishoxa's arm possessively.

Rianox inclined his head. "Take her then, my lady, and with my blessing!" A teasing light glinted in his eyes as he left, waving good-bye to Eishoxa.

Amber grabbed her hand. "Now we can go outside and I'll show you the forest," she exclaimed, dragging Eishoxa back towards the trapdoor. The wind inside the tunnel sucked Eishoxa right back up the tube and expelled her, wind-swept, onto the branch, much higher above the hall. Amber emerged moments later, shaking her hair out of her face. Being with Amber was like Eishoxa imagined Maya had felt when they were together. Maya was always the quieter of the pair, more pensive and thoughtful, less reckless and wild.

Amber grinned at Eishoxa and pointed down towards the lower boughs. "We'll go to the forest. Not the one you came through, but on the other side. You used to love it." There it was again, that little stab at her pride. A reminder that everyone here would expect her to be the same person she'd been when she supposedly left this place, although she herself could remember nothing.

The forest they entered was the one Eishoxa had seen on the ridge with Ember and Coal. The first feeling Eishoxa got of the place was one of destruction. Here there were no green plants, no soft damp leaves covering the forest floor. Here the sticks lay burnt and harsh against the dry ground, and few trees retained any leaves. The tops of them showed a little sign of life, but even so, those leaves were limp and pale.

"What happened here?" Eishoxa asked, avoiding a scorched log and looking up through the burnt branches to the clear sky.

Amber gave her a quick look over her shoulder. "Nothing. We use this forest for target practice sometimes." She said this as if it were normal. Eishoxa thought that it looked very sad and bare, with ash blowing through the air and black twisted stumps decorating the place mournfully.

"Yes," continued Amber. "When we practise with fire, we come here. It just never grows back because obviously we have no rain."

"Why not?" Eishoxa asked. That seemed strange. If there was no rain, then how did the trees and foliage on the other side stay alive?

"Well, we don't want it," Amber said, as if it were evident.

"But the other forest ..." Eishoxa trailed off in confusion.

Amber gave her a swift look. "It doesn't belong to us, remember? It belongs to the Ewdicani ... and other people." She said the name as if it were a disease. "They took that forest from us ages ago. I think some here believe that you will get it back for us."

Eishoxa thought that forests were much nicer when things actually grew in them, but she didn't voice her thoughts. "Why don't you like the Ewdicani?" she asked, quickening her pace to catch up.

Amber didn't look at her when she answered. Her eyes were careful-ly scanning the trunks ahead of them. One arrow was already held in her bow. "Why do you think?" she replied.

"I don't know."

Amber gave her another quick look. Her eyes were puzzled. "You'll work it out before long." She stiffened suddenly and grabbed Eishoxa's arm, pointing between the trees. "Can you see it? Look, just there."

"What? What am I looking for?" Eishoxa could see nothing.

Amber pointed impatiently again before taking aim and setting loose the arrow. It whistled through the air and there was a satisfying thunk, joined by a small squeak, as the arrow found its mark. Amber smiled and ran forward. Eishoxa followed more slowly. Lying on the ground was a little raccoon-like creature, its muzzle covered in ash and its yellow eyes still open. The arrow had pierced it right through the middle. With one swift movement, Amber freed her arrow and picked up the animal by its short, fluffy tail. She swung it gently and its head flopped around pathetically. Smiling, she looked up at Eishoxa, but her smile stopped at the look on the other girl's face.

"What's wrong, Eishoxa?"

Her face cleared. "Nothing."

Amber dropped the animal into the ash. "It clearly isn't."

Eishoxa closed her eyes briefly but that didn't help. All she could think about was another limp head flopping from side to side as it was carried away from her.

"Eishoxa?" Amber asked again cautiously. "What's wrong?"

"Nothing," she repeated more firmly. "I was just remembering something."

Amber looked from her to the animal and back to her. "Didn't you hunt when you were with the Ignorant?"

Eishoxa shook her head. She could use a bow and she knew how to shoot, but she never dreamed that she'd need to use it in another situation. The casual way that Amber wielded her weapons, the casual way she killed, somehow sickened Eishoxa.

"Do you not enjoy it? It's just hunting. We eat everything we kill ..."

Eishoxa heard the dismay in her voice and shook her head, lowering her eyes so she wouldn't have to see Amber's reaction.

The other swung the bow back onto her shoulder. "Well, then, we won't hunt," she said. "Come on. It's no fun if you don't like it anymore." She led the way out of the woods. Eishoxa followed, feeling like a failure once again.

CHAPTER 9

WHEN THEY RETURNED to Eishoxa's room, Amber gave her some news. "We're having a feast tonight to celebrate your coming home," she announced. Eishoxa looked at her in horror.

"What is it this time?" Amber asked worriedly. Eishoxa sat on her bed, thinking hard.

"What do you do at your feasts?" she enquired, looking up at Amber. The other one grinned, happy that at least Eishoxa wasn't refusing outright to go. "We eat and dance and have a good time," she shrugged. "It's been such a long time since we've had one, so everyone is really excited."

Eishoxa had frozen at the word *dance*. "You dance?" she asked.

Amber nodded vigorously, "Oh yes, lots and lots. It's always great fun."

Eishoxa flinched, feeling a bittersweet rush of *déjà vu*. Maya had said that to her before the Masked Ball.

Amber looked at her anxiously. "Are you all right, Eishoxa?"

Eishoxa forced a smile onto her face and pushed Maya to the very back of her mind. "Yes, fine."

"So you'll come?" pressed Amber uneasily.

Eishoxa nodded tiredly. "Yes, I'll come. But I won't dance. I can't."

Amber frowned. "Fair enough. Maybe you'll change your mind later on."

Amber insisted that Eishoxa let her braid her hair with flowers and ribbons and Eishoxa finally agreed just to stop Amber's pestering. The sky was dark by the time Amber finally proclaimed them both to be fine. Eishoxa stood in front of the glass wall and looked at her reflection. She didn't look like herself, but she supposed that was deliberate. The dress was red like the dresses from Bareth but shorter, stopping at her knees, and underneath she wore a pair of very tight red trousers. Her hair stopped at her waist, brushed and fought into two long braids, and Amber had lined her eyes with a stick of charcoal, making them look bright and exotic. She compared her attire to what she would have worn in Bareth, and then reminded herself that she was not in Bareth anymore.

"You see?" Amber smiled. "You could pass for one of us now."

Amber took them downstairs. They used the tunnel to enter the Great Hall. The place had completely changed. Many long tables were now set out in the large space, all laid with plates for many people. The ceiling was burning brightly with flames that licked down the blazing walls, and the room was packed with people and alive with the hum of conversation. Every Indocani looked different: some had lined their eyes as she and Amber had done, others had tattooed themselves with little flames, and others had covered themselves from head to toe in a glittery powder that caught the light whenever they moved.

Amber was positively trembling with excitement. Eishoxa could only gape. Standing where she was, she had the impression that she'd walked into a kaleidoscope. None of the Masked Balls at Bareth had equalled the grandeur this place displayed with such ease. Flitting swiftly above them were little sprite-like creatures, clothed in minute dresses of sparks held together with flame-red ribbons. Amber took in Eishoxa's overwhelmed face with a grin. "Like it?" she asked, and Eishoxa nodded, still in a daze.

They were joined by another familiar figure. "Coal!" exclaimed Amber. "Where have you been hiding? I never see you anymore."

Coal dipped his head at Amber and bowed to Eishoxa. He too had lined his eyes heavily with kohl but hadn't dressed up like the others in the Hall. He cleared his throat seriously. "There are many things to do now, Amber. We can no longer pretend that we're not in a war."

Amber waved her hand. "Oh, that. Please don't bother me with things like that now. For tonight, we enjoy ourselves and forget about the war!"

Coal smiled. "Forgetting about it won't make it go away, Amber. And, as to my purpose here, I've been asked by Vera to bring Eishoxa up to the High Table."

"Oh, she gets to sit up there, does she?" Amber grumbled. "And I suppose you're allowed to as well – and my brother."

Coal gave her one of his little smiles. "Yes, of course she's allowed. And we're allowed because we're now part of the War Council. You know that, Amber."

"Yes, of course I do. Ember won't stop going on about it."

Coal laughed. "He takes it very seriously."

"He's no fun anymore," she complained and, waving off Eishoxa, pushed her way into the crowd.

Coal led the way up to the High Table. Eishoxa could already see Ember sitting there, talking very passionately to his neighbour, a wizened old Indocani whose braids were going yellow with age.

"That's the Lord he's going to take over from," whispered Coal. Eishoxa turned to him. "You have Lords as well?"

Coal blinked. "Of course."

"What is he taking over?"

"He's the one in charge of the whole army. Ember now has a great responsibility."

His voice was carefully neutral and immediately Eishoxa suspected that she and Rianox weren't the only ones who disliked Ember. Coal led her over to the table. She was seated between Coal and Vera, whose seat was empty still. Eishoxa pretended not to notice the many eyes that had suddenly turned to her and watched Ember instead.

"Why is he taking over from that Lord?"

Coal leaned forward to look at the talking pair and sighed. "Vera says that Lord Swoth is too old to continue doing his work to the best of his ability. She says that she needs someone she can rely on."

Eishoxa guessed that Coal was not happy about this arrangement. "So she chose Ember?"

"Ember is a fine warrior," said Coal carefully.

"Could she have chosen anyone?"

Coal turned his searching eyes on her. "Why so many questions, Eishoxa?"

She blushed. "I'm just curious," she replied.

He smiled. "Yes, she could have chosen any warrior. I'm more of a healer, so I wouldn't have been chosen. I think that Amber had a chance of being chosen, and that's why she's very annoyed that he was the one chosen."

Eishoxa looked through the crowd as they took their places at the tables and picked Amber out from among them. She was laughing at something said by Rianox, who sat opposite her. No wonder she'd looked angry when talking to her brother. "Why wasn't she chosen?"

"It's a tradition that I think Vera was unwilling to break. Traditionally, the Commander, or the leader, is a female but the Lords of the War Council are all male."

"Oh, I see."

"Personally, I don't see the point," Coal confided. "There are plenty of males who would make great Commanders, but the Indocani wouldn't have any of it if such a decision was made."

Eishoxa laughed. "What's a healer?" she asked, but Coal didn't have time to answer before there was a loud bang at the other end of the hall and Vera strode into the room, apparently through the wall. Everyone rose to their feet. Eishoxa was reminded so forcefully of Bareth that she almost choked on a ball of memories that rose up in her throat.

Coal looked down at her in concern as Eishoxa coughed a few times and asked out of the corner of his mouth, "Are you all right?"

Eishoxa nodded and straightened, turning to look again as Vera walked between the tables. Following her were seven other Indocani, each wearing a large golden bracelet.

"Those are the other Lords," Coal whispered. "They all have charge of different aspects."

"Of what?"

"Of life here at Sicharenhafan. They were elected by Fiera, just as Vera herself was."

"Fiera chose them?" she enquired.

Coal nodded imperceptibly. "To a certain extent, yes. Vera was chosen, and then she chose the Lords according to what she believed Fiera would have wanted."

Eishoxa snorted quietly. "So she chooses them?"

Coal shushed her as Vera went to her chair. She pulled it back and sat down. Eishoxa was once again reminded of Bareth and had such a strong feeling of homesickness that she didn't notice that everyone else around her had sat down as well. Coal tugged on her sleeve and Eishoxa hurriedly sat, sliding ungracefully into her chair. Sitting this close to Vera, Eishoxa could feel her power but, unlike before, this aura felt slimy and cold. She shuddered slightly.

Vera didn't notice. She raised her arms and called something out to the silent hall in the strange, detached language that Eishoxa knew was Düerasgörn. There was a round of applause, with which Eishoxa hurriedly joined in, and then food appeared out of nowhere on platters. A hum started across the hall, slowly increasing in dynamic as Indocani loaded their plates and began to eat. Vera turned away from Eishoxa and started to talk to the person sitting on her other side.

Coal nudged her. "Are you sure you're all right? You look very pale."

Eishoxa nodded and, in order to excuse herself from answering, took one of the biscuits lying on her plate and put it in her mouth. From the moment it touched her lips, she could tell straight away that nothing here would have a drop of water or liquid of any kind in it. The biscuit exploded into powder once in her mouth and Eishoxa felt it drift slowly down her throat. She looked in her cup and took a sip of the thick soup-like substance glowing faintly in the bottom. A coarse, spicy concoction oozed over her tongue. Eishoxa put down the cup. Coal looked at her.

"What's the matter? Don't you like it?" Unlike her, he was eating everything in front of him with relish. He took one look at her face and chuckled.

"I can see why you don't eat much food generally," she said crossly. "It's because it isn't very nice, is it?"

Coal put down his food and dusted his fingers clean of any crumbs. "Well, maybe for some people, but for most it's because we don't need to eat. All we need to feel satisfied is to have a good fire burning inside of us and that doesn't require much."

"You have fire inside of you?" Eishoxa asked incredulously.

Coal nodded, smiling at the look on her face. "Yes, of course. It's Fiera's gift to us. It's so precious that even we cannot take it away, unless …" He trailed away, a shadow passing suddenly over his face.

Eishoxa prompted him, "Unless …?"

"It doesn't matter," he smiled. But Eishoxa saw right through it.

The noise in the hall gradually rose to a din. Unlike the Masked Ball, there was no order to this feast whatsoever and no entertainers came in. Instead, Indocani at the tables provided their own entertainment.

Eishoxa was swallowing down another biscuit when there was a shout from one side of the hall and a young Indocani jumped up onto the table, scattering dishes with his feet. From the other side of the hall, large, bright yellow flames shot high into the air from the palm of an Indocani and spurted towards the opposite side of the hall in the form of a hissing serpent, only to be stopped halfway by another snake of vivid orange flames attached to the palm of another sitting opposite. There were general shouts of encouragement and booing, and Eishoxa saw Amber laughing as the two fiery snakes battled violently, urged on by the two Indocani that controlled them. Coal laughed quietly to himself as he watched. Vera was sipping from her goblet, her eyes trained in amusement on the scuffling pair. Finally, the first Indocani stood up, pulling sharply on his snake, and his opponent was lifted up into the air and dashed quickly against the wall. Stunned, he slid down to the floor, his fiery snake slowly fizzling out to ash beside him. The victor bowed to the High Table, to Vera and to Eishoxa and then sat down amidst many cheers and yells.

After that, good-natured chaos took over the hall. Crowds of Indocani leapt up onto the tables, dancing and shouting. The dishes, so carefully placed on the tables, went flying and the cheering, yelling crowd of Indocani moved as one heaving body. They stamped their feet to a fast, wild beat, and from somewhere in their midst a harsh-sounding pipe began to play. It was a feral tune, a song that had never known control or restraint.

As Eishoxa listened, pictures formed in her mind, images of running through forests and leaping over fallen trees. Elation coursed through her as she ran, faster and faster, revelling in the strength of her legs and arms. She could see the ground flying away underneath her, as if she were being carried at a huge height by some great beast and fire engulfed the ground, turning the green forest into a black, burnt desert. In any other circumstances, it would have looked like devastation, but Eishoxa saw the fire as a beautiful thing, taking control, being in control.

The tempo quickened and quickened and Eishoxa could feel her head spinning, the hall and the people around her fading into a blur as she listened. Then there was an explosion and Eishoxa was shocked back into reality. Out of the centre of the hall rose the moving figure of a bird, a phoenix. As Eishoxa's vision cleared, she could see that the bird was actually made up of many Indocani. They'd set themselves on fire, and the contrasting colours of the flames, smoke and shadows formed the image of the bird. Eishoxa could feel the heat from where she was sitting. It rose higher and higher above the crowd of stunned Indocani surrounding it. The piper – Eishoxa couldn't see who it was – changed the melody slightly, but it was just as fast and just as riveting. By now all Eishoxa could think was: fly! She wanted the phoenix to fly. She didn't want it to stop. She could hear Coal clapping his hands from beside her and she clapped as well, her eyes glued to the scene unfolding in front of her.

But before anything could happen, Vera stood up and waved her hand, calling for silence. The minute she did, everyone was on their feet, shouting angrily and protesting, Eishoxa with them. She didn't want it to stop. She wanted the phoenix to fly, to keep living. The fire around the Indocani forming the phoenix had dimmed, and Eishoxa felt the loss of the heat and pure vibrancy as if it had been a limb on her own body. Vera, undaunted by the shouts, waved her hand again.

"There's something I must do with Eishoxa now. I will take the Lords with me and please, Rianox, if you could come too."

Coal sat down, but Vera turned to him. "Coal, you may come too. Eishoxa?"

Eishoxa stood slowly, wondering what was going on. Had she done something wrong? Why was this so important? From across the hall, she could see Amber looking worried and caught some of the other Indocani with apprehensive expressions on their faces. She jumped when Vera put her hand on her shoulder.

"This way, please, Eishoxa." Eishoxa rose but stumbled slightly, her head still full of the music that she longed to hear again.

CHAPTER 10

S<small>HE FOLLOWED THE REST</small> of the Indocani into the side chamber. Inside there was a long, large table, completely bare apart from a lit candle, standing right in the middle of the fire. The flame was burning low but flared up, swaying regally as the Lords, Eishoxa and Vera filed in. Vera motioned Eishoxa to sit down at the bottom of the table, closest to the door, and she herself took the seat at the other end of the table. Ember slid into the seat beside her. Rianox and Coal flanked Eishoxa. Everyone looked expectantly at Vera. She sat forward, speaking to no one but Eishoxa.

"Now, as you're new here, Eishoxa, I don't expect you to know about what we're going to try to do."

Eishoxa clasped her hands in her lap, painfully aware of the many intense stares she was now being subjected to. Obviously, they all knew what was going to happen.

"Now, as I've already said, we hope that you will go to the Ewdicani, to persuade them to join us in our war. I stress again the vital importance of that treaty. Therefore, because of that, you must Change."

Eishoxa stared at her blankly.

Vera gave an almost inaudible sigh. "When anyone joins the world of the Ignorant, the barriers that are placed around every individual from birth, which enable them to live in our world unharmed, are broken and cannot be restored, with only two exceptions. The first is when the person in the world of the Ignorant is a fully grown Indocani with a great deal of strength. The second exception is when an Indocani has been granted special permission, and given special protection, to go into the world of the Ignorant and not lose his or her barriers. When Coal and Ember came to collect you, that is what I gave them so that they could go and get you without harming themselves. But you, Eishoxa, having taken on an Ignorant body, couldn't regain or hold onto your barriers and so they've been lost. We know that you are not completely human because an ordinary Ignorant body wouldn't be able to survive for very long here. But this protection won't last forever, so we're going to attempt to Change you and make you into an Indocani again."

Eishoxa cleared her throat nervously. "And what if I don't want to be an Indocani? What if I wanted to be completely human?"

Her words were met with a horrified silence. A few of the Lords actually stood up to get a better look at Eishoxa, perhaps to see if she was being serious or not. Eishoxa kept her eyes trained on Vera, who had suddenly clenched her fists. Ember's thunderous face was like stone.

"Well, if you don't want to, then we won't try," Vera said carefully.

Eishoxa glanced around at the other Indocani and was met with glares. Even Rianox didn't look comfortable. Eishoxa looked back at Vera. "I don't think it will work but I suppose you can try."

Vera shoulders sagged with relief and she carried on as smoothly as possible. "Thank you. Perhaps you will be surprised."

At these words, all the others stood up and joined hands. Eishoxa, on Coal's command, stayed sitting. They now formed a chain running all around the table, all around Eishoxa. Her eyes were drawn to the candle flame, which was burning higher and higher. Vera started to speak in the curious monotone of the Düerasgörn language. The words swam around Eishoxa like fish in clear water.

She watched the candle flame burn even higher as Vera continued speaking. Then everyone in the room dropped hands and the flame in the centre split and engulfed all the people in the room, leaving out Eishoxa once again. Now she could feel something moving and twisting in the room – not Vera, not anyone that she could see, but a presence, at once foreign and familiar, alien but also known. And then, just as Eishoxa thought she could work out what it was, the fire left all the others and moved for her, covering her with yellow flames that licked up and down her arms and across her face.

Through the fire in front of her eyes she could still see Vera and all the Lords standing there, but could hear nothing save for the fire humming quietly in her ears. It was the oddest feeling, as if she were completely in control but also subject to a force much older and more powerful than herself. Compelled and too dazed to resist, she pushed back her chair and stood up, the fire dancing around her, smoke hiding her from view. Eishoxa felt as if the flames were penetrating her deepest, most private being, going into places of her mind that even she herself didn't know existed. She felt a deep joy within her, a loud rejoicing, and a huge happiness.

Heat built up where the fire now was, spreading right through her. Her body trembled with the raw power of it and her feet spun her around and around. A roaring pounded in her ears and hammered through her bones, a sound so loud it almost lifted her off the ground.

Just as she was sure her body would explode with the energy inside it, a cold feeling of regret entered her, slipping down her throat like cold water. Resignation filled her, not from herself but from the fire: it was not ready. She was not ready. Not yet.

The fire died out around her body and her arms fell to her sides. She was standing in the room with the Indocani again, a few paces away from her chair. Vera looked at her expectantly and a little fearfully. "What happened?"

"It didn't work," Eishoxa said, and was surprised to hear how calm her voice was. "It wasn't ready."

One of the Lords slammed his fist down on the table and the noise reverberated around the room. "What do you mean, girl? What do you mean, it wasn't ready? Fire is always ready. It's you who are not ready!"

A murmur of agreement ran through the room. Vera looked around, avoiding Eishoxa's gaze.

The Lord continued, encouraged by the others' concurrence. "And when will you be ready? We don't know. You don't know. Are you even the Eishoxa that we know, that we want? Are you even the right person? Vera, send Ember and Coal back to the Ignorant world to find the right person."

This was met with cries of outrage from Rianox and Ember and a whisper of furious condemnation from Coal. Vera said nothing. She simply looked around, pondering what had happened.

Ember spoke up angrily. "She is the right person. I would like to point out, Orious, that if you were in her situation right now, there might have been a similar result. Vera," he insisted, turning to his leader with wide, urgent eyes, "give her more time. She'll change, she'll adapt, and in a few days, when she's lived with us and learnt our ways more thoroughly, we can try again. This was too early."

"And if she doesn't?" Orious demanded.

Vera set her hands on the table and everyone pretended not to see that they were shaking, ever so slightly. "If she doesn't, then we'll think of another plan. Rest assured, Orious." The Lord glared at Eishoxa, as though all of this were her fault, and sat back down.

Vera nodded slowly and clasped her hands together. The candle in the middle of the room had gone out, leaving a pool of wax. "This Council is over," she declared. "We will discuss these events at a later time. Let us all go and rejoin the feast."

Everyone stood up to go but Vera called out, "Eishoxa! Wait a moment. And you, Rianox." Ember opened his mouth and Vera nodded at him. "You may also stay, Ember."

Eishoxa didn't miss the piercing look that Coal shot Ember, but her mind was too clouded to think much about it. There were a lot of strange things going on.

Rianox stood by the door while Ember and Eishoxa remained in their places. Vera took a deep breath. "How did you know that the fire wasn't ready?"

Eishoxa shrugged. "I don't know. I just know it wasn't. There was something about me that it didn't like."

Ember started to speak, but Vera held up her hand sharply. "You may have been given a high position that you're not used to, Ember," she snapped, "but that doesn't mean you can speak whenever you want." Chastised, Ember hung his head for a moment.

"This is a good sign. Perhaps all you need is to spend more time with us and then you'll learn."

Eishoxa's head shot up. "You speak as if I've decided to stay for good. I don't want to stay here. I don't want to learn to be one of you. All I want is to go back to Bareth."

Vera glanced swiftly at Rianox before turning back to Eishoxa and hitching the smile back onto her face. "Of course. If you decide to stay. But if you do, then maybe this is a good sign. Now I suggest that you go back and join the feast. Rianox and Ember, I would like to have a word with you."

Eishoxa stood up brusquely and walked out angrily. Whatever she said, whatever she did, she couldn't go anywhere unless they let her. She would die in the forest; she hated being at their mercy.

When she returned to the Great Hall, the tables had been pushed against the walls, and in the centre of the room the Indocani were dancing again – in pairs, in threes, in tangled groups, writhing and stamping their feet. There was no order, there was no dance to learn, everyone danced to the tune in their heads. They hadn't a clue about what had happened in the little side room.

The Lords hadn't joined the dance and had instead returned to the High Table. They gave Eishoxa a cold glare when she emerged, but she ignored them. She knew what she'd felt and she knew that she was right. No matter what they did, they couldn't change that.

She spotted Coal leaning against the wall, drinking something from a little cup, and was relieved when he beckoned to her. "What did they want?" he asked.

Eishoxa wrinkled her nose at the sharp scent coming from his cup. "They wanted to know how I knew the fire wasn't ready," she said. Despite the fact that Coal had also taken her from Bareth, Eishoxa trusted him a lot more than she did Ember. He nodded, as though it were to be expected, and took another sip of his drink. "And what did you say?"

Eishoxa was saved from answering by a shout from Amber. She was stumbling and laughing loudly. "Eishoxa! Come and join us!" Her kohl eyeliner had smudged, giving her a slightly manic look, but her eyes were alive with excitement. She'd joined a circle of Indocani who were laughing and clapping their hands as they spun in circles and shook little golden bells on their anklets.

Coal gave her a smile and said, "It looks like you're wanted," before walking off into the crowds. Amber was kicking out in a very exuberant dance and Eishoxa was pulled in to join them. Once in the ranks of dancing Indocani, she could hear faint traces of the music they were dancing to: strange and fast-paced, completely different from the earlier tunes. She found her feet moving uncontrollably as the people around her carried her with them. Although each person in the circle was dancing independently, all of them came together in some weird and wonderful way to form a beautiful pattern. The frenzied energy that thrummed through the air was infectious, and Eishoxa soon found that her feet took flight by themselves, dancing faster and faster, until she too was laughing and clapping along with everyone else.

The feast went on into the night and early hours of the morning, but still they danced. No matter how numb her feet felt, Eishoxa didn't want to stop. She'd never danced this long before but she couldn't remember any of the balls at Bareth being half as much fun as this. Her hair had come undone and the flowers and ribbons floated around her feet. The Indocani gradually got more and more drunk, some of them finally slumping against the wall in defeat – Amber included – but Eishoxa kept dancing, her mind blissfully clear of any troublesome thoughts as the feast went on.

At some point she registered the curious looks she was getting from people around her, but before she could address them, another dance started or another group pulled her into their ranks. She couldn't work out where the music came from because the tunes were different as she moved into different areas of the hall, but she didn't care. She couldn't remember having so much fun before in her whole life and, for the moment, she just revelled in it, all worry at last put out of her head.

CHAPTER 11

THE DAY AFTER the feast was a drowsy day. When Eishoxa left her room that morning, there was an unfamiliar calmness over the Tree and the air was hot and heavy. Swinging gently from branch to branch, she slowly climbed down to the bottom. As she rounded the trunk she almost crashed into Rianox, who had just emerged from around the side of the Tree.

"Eishoxa!" he said with a smile. "I was just coming to look for you. Do we not have a lesson today?"

Eishoxa shrugged. "If you want one."

Rianox's smile widened. "Do you not want one?"

"I don't mind. I'm trying to find something to do. Where is everyone?"

Rianox laughed. "Well, most of them are sleeping off the effects of last night, including Amber."

Eishoxa smiled. "Yes, well, she did have a good time."

Rianox chuckled and then asked, "Would you like a lesson today? Apparently Vera would like us to continue them, based on what happened last night."

Eishoxa immediately bristled. "What I said was true! The fire wasn't ready to accept me. No amount of lessons is going to change that."

Rianox's face was carefully guarded but his voice, when he spoke, was open and soothing. "I believe you, Eishoxa."

Eishoxa relaxed. Rianox had done nothing to offend her, and his wide, honest eyes put her at ease. "All right," she agreed.

Rianox's smile returned. "I thought we could have one in the open air. It's very stuffy down there in the hall." Eishoxa nodded. Rianox led the way back further up the Tree, but instead of going all the way to the top and through the foliage, he swerved off and headed down a long bough. Eishoxa had noticed before that this bough didn't grow out straight but instead curved around almost the whole of the Tree. Ropes had been tied to it every so often, so tightly that they'd cut into the wood, and they swayed in the breeze. Rianox balanced gracefully along the bough and walked out to the edge. Eishoxa followed more carefully, crouching slightly. They were some way off the ground, and if she fell from here, she wouldn't survive. Cautiously, she sat next to Rianox and let her legs dangle.

He watched her, slightly amused. "Why are you so frightened? It's only a tree."

Eishoxa looked down nervously. "Yes, but if I fall, I'll die."

"If you fall, you'll be caught before you hit the ground," he contradicted.

Eishoxa looked up, confused. "Caught? By what?"

Rianox grinned mischievously. "Do you want to fall now and see?" Eishoxa shook her head vigorously. "Well then, you'll never know."

Eishoxa peeked once again over the side but saw nothing that could catch her. It was a straight drop from there to the ground.

Rianox cleared his throat and she looked up. "Well, what do you want to learn today? I have no books with me, so we can't learn the alphabet. I'm sure you're glad to hear that."

Eishoxa smiled. "It isn't that difficult, I suppose. There's just a lot to learn."

Rianox inclined his head, agreeing with her. "Yes, there is. And that isn't even half the language."

"Does anyone know the whole language?"

"Oh yes. Vera, for one, has had to learn it. I know most of it, and I believe your friend Coal is very close to knowing it all as well. When you're born here, it's not so difficult. But for a lot of people, learning the whole language isn't necessary. They just learn the words and phrases they need."

"I see. And do you know all my language as well?" She'd noticed that Rianox spoke it without any accent, unlike Ember and Coal, whose pronunciation had a slight sibilance.

"The Base Tongue. Most Indocani know it, although very few know how to write it. Ember, for one, doesn't know a single character."

"Well, Ember doesn't like a lot about us," Eishoxa grumbled quietly.

"So what do you want to learn then?" Rianox repeated.

Eishoxa shrugged. "Just tell me a bit more about your people."

"My people?" he asked, and then crossed his legs, leaning precariously to one side. "Very well." He didn't say anything for a moment and then began. "Well, we're the opposite of the Ewdicani. Everything that they think is important, we don't; and everything that we think is important, they hold in disdain. For instance, they spend a lot of time making sculptures and statues, but there would be no point of that here when they would be destroyed very easily. On the other hand, they don't know how to fight very well, while that's one of our main priorities."

"What do you fight with?"

"Some like to use swords and some bows. Most, I believe, prefer bows. A few of the Ewdicani may know how to shoot a bow, but not very well, and they are by no means masters."

"Where do they live?"

"I've never been to their dwelling, in Dulcacohefen, and most of the books about it were destroyed soon after you left. But I've heard that it's a beautiful place. They love their art and their beauty, and it's made entirely out of ice. They have many mountains there as well. Do you know what a mountain is?"

"Of course I do. They had them in Cara. I've never seen one in real life though."

"Where's Cara?" Rianox asked curiously.

Eishoxa looked down and picked at the bark. "It was the country next to Bareth. My best friend came from there but she's not there anymore."

"Ah," said Rianox very quietly.

To break the silence, she looked up again and asked, "Do you want to visit the Ewdicani's land ... Dulcacohefen?" The word sounded strange in her mouth.

"I've always wanted to see as many places as possible," he said carefully. "And maybe one day I will see their dwelling."

"Where is it?"

"You must first cross the desert. After the desert comes the Forest of No Flame, and once you've crossed that, you come to the Cursed Marshes. Then you are very close."

"How long does it take?"

"It depends how you travel," he answered.

"What if you walked?"

He frowned. "Maybe a hundred days."

"A hundred days," Eishoxa echoed. One hundred from here to the mountains. If Maya were here, would she have wanted Eishoxa to go? To go and see the mountains? She was always speaking about them whenever she came to Bareth. She turned back to Rianox. "What was Vera trying to do yesterday?"

A shadow passed over Rianox's face. "She tried to Change you. Inside every one of us is a flame, a flame that Fiera gives us. If we look after it, it will grow, but if we don't, then it will die. You no longer have your flame because it can't be sustained in the Ignorant world, but there's a place for it in you. Living for a prolonged period of time at the Tree without a flame inside you can upset the balance between your body and the environment you're now living in. Eventually, your body would combust. Yesterday, Vera tried to rekindle it because it would help you start to talk to fire and protect you. It would also turn you into a fully-fledged Indocani, with all of your powers and with the same ideologies and beliefs as us."

"She was trying to change me that much?" Eishoxa asked in disbelief. Rianox met her gaze steadily. "It would have been easier to convince you to go to the Ewdicani. But, as you said, the fire wasn't ready."

"Do you believe me then?" she asked, looking up at him hopefully.

"Of course I believe you."

Eishoxa nodded happily and turned her head away, shifting slightly on the branch. "So what about this war?"

Rianox looked up sharply. "What do you mean?"

"Well, can you tell me about it? About what's happening?"

He looked at her shrewdly. "Why do you want to know?"

"Well, I've been told to ask the Ewdicani to join us. I'd like to know why."

Rianox nodded slowly. "That's a good reason. We're fighting on a plain many days' journey from here, known as the Plain of Despair, and have been fighting this war on and off for many, many years. You were here when it started, and it's carried on all the while you weren't with us. We can see that we're slowly being forced back towards the Tree. And if the war were to come here, we would be destroyed. It's hard to defend a tree, even one like this. But between us and the war are the Ewdicani. So far they won't let us pass through their lands, even to protect them. But if they do let us cross their lands, then we'll be able to attack the enemy on both sides, not just one as we're doing now."

"Why won't they let us pass?" Eishoxa asked.

"There are a few reasons. For one, since you left we're not allies with them anymore. Also, their lands would be completely destroyed by our crossing, and the Ewdicani won't allow this."

Eishoxa thought for a moment. It made sense, of course. "And who are we fighting?"

"The Empty," Rianox said. His voice sounded very hollow, as if something about this word horrified him.

"Who are they?"

"They are another race who live in the Sorrowful Mountains. It's with the greatest shame that we must admit we're losing to them."

"Why with shame?"

"We Indocani were born to fight, Eishoxa. That is the purpose of our existence. And to know that for the first time in all of our history we're being defeated is one of the greatest shames for us to admit. And it's taken us many years – and cost many lives – to admit it." He stopped and swallowed as if fighting something in himself. Then he said, in a tight voice, "All my family included."

"I'm sorry."

"They died for their people – it's a very good death. But that's why they need someone to go. Ember is known by the people to be very ruthless and cruel, and would only speak for himself. And Vera is the leader, and it's obvious that she would speak only for her people. We need someone who is clearly not biased towards any side and can show the Ewdicani the benefits for them."

"And that's me," Eishoxa finished. She had the uncomfortable feeling that Rianox was hiding something from her.

He smiled sadly. "Vera would have done anything not to admit it, but there was nothing to be done. They want you to go to the Ewdicani because, unless you do, we'll be destroyed."

After the lesson, because Amber was nowhere to be seen, Rianox took her back to her room. He'd said, very apologetically, that he was expected elsewhere after their lessons. Having waited in her room for some time, she became restless. Her mind was full with what Rianox had said: *They want you to go to the Ewdicani because, unless you do, we'll be destroyed.* They were willing to sacrifice the Ewdicani's lands but not their own.

She left her room and found her feet taking her back to the Great Hall. She was glad that all signs of the previous night's revelry had been cleared away. Even so, the sight of the room sent familiar prickles of guilt running through her. She had enjoyed herself yesterday, something that she couldn't afford to do. She had made a promise to Maya. She couldn't forget that. And going to the Ewdicani would delay her return to Bareth to find her friend.

But whatever her feelings, she did like the Great Hall. There'd been nothing like it in Bareth. She liked the dark and the earthy smell of it and the tangled roots high above. Walking around its edge, she dragged her fingers across the roots of the walls. Some were still burnt

74

and blackened from the night before. She picked at one of them and it came away, revealing more layers of roots underneath. How thick were these walls? Looking up, she pressed her palm against it and, although the soft, newly grown roots yielded, she could feel older, harder roots underneath.

An Indocani appeared from one of the rooms at the other end of the Great Hall, crossed over and disappeared through a different door. The Hall was empty now. She walked to the very corner of the room and pressed against the wall again. To her surprise, this time it gave way, falling back to reveal a long, winding tunnel, dark apart from regular pools of light from flaming torches. The passage was relatively narrow but wide enough to walk down. Eishoxa took one of the torches and walked forward apprehensively.

The tunnel twisted and turned but never branched off, and Eishoxa wondered where it led. After walking some distance and not finding an end, she looked at the walls more closely. They were covered in carvings. Bringing the torch closer, she examined them with interest. Here was a picture of a girl leading many troops into the desert, and there another of the same girl flying a dragon-like creature high above a forest. Further on, she was shooting a bow, and swinging a sword, and kneeling beside a snare with a long thin knife in her hand.

Eishoxa continued down the tunnel, looking at the carvings. Here and there other people were depicted, but the girl was always there, the same girl all the time. Every so often there was a carving with the girl just staring into space – at the sky, at the ground, at one of the trees in the forest. One showed her sitting in a room, head down on her folded arms. Eishoxa put her hand on the carving, feeling the work of many years under her fingertips. When she moved her hand away, the strangest thing happened: the carving started to move. They all did. Eishoxa gasped and stepped away, wondering what was going on. The girl in the room sat up and started pacing; the dragon carrying the girl was flying; the troops were marching across the plain. The girl fired the arrow; she swung the sword; she sat back from the snare she was setting.

Little tongues of fire now licked up the wall and brought out every line in the carvings. Eishoxa held her torch higher, looking to either side. None of the carvings had faces, not even the girl. Then came a blank area, which the little flames didn't cover. But beyond that there were more carvings lit by the flames, and she hurried down to look.

Something turned in her stomach. The same girl was now in a place Eishoxa recognised: Bareth Castle. There she was learning to ride a horse and practising archery. The figure lacked the energy of the previous carvings, but it was the same girl. Then she was embracing another girl, a girl dressed in flowing blue robes and combing her white-blonde hair.

The realisation of what she was seeing hit Eishoxa in the stomach like a hammer and she dropped the torch, feeling winded. The girl was Eishoxa. It was her life, written in this hidden tunnel deep underground – both the life she could remember and the life she couldn't remember.

They weren't lying. She had been here before.

As if in a dream, Eishoxa returned to the other set of carvings and ran her fingers over them. This was her? Really? If Eishoxa hadn't seen the carvings of herself in Bareth, she would never have believed it. But she'd come across them by accident. No one had led her to the tunnel.

Her brain kept questioning. Was that why they hadn't shown it to her? Was that why they'd left her alone, so that she'd find these carvings and realise they were telling the truth? She *had* lived here before. Whether she belonged here was up to her, but she had been here. Any last doubts were driven away.

She walked back down the tunnel, trailing her fingers over the wall and watching in awe as the flames wrapped themselves around her fingers and whispered and crackled at her. In the back of her mind she could hear the first song played at the previous night's feast. It started very slowly as Eishoxa looked at the burning walls. The fire was burning down now, but the wall was still warm under her fingers. And then it burnt out.

Eishoxa left the tunnel in a daze. The wall grew back over the entrance, hiding it again. Eishoxa watched the roots merge together and then left, wondering whether anything here would ever make sense.

CHAPTER 12

SHE FOUND AMBER waiting for her in her room. She looked completely recovered from the feast, although, the last time Eishoxa had seen her, she was being carried from the hall by several others.

"There you are," her friend called as Eishoxa closed the door behind her. "Where have you been?"

"In the Great Hall," she said. Eishoxa was thankful that Amber didn't pursue the question. She didn't want to tell her about the tunnel.

"Rianox sent me here," Amber said, by way of explaining her presence.

Eishoxa smiled and sat in front of the empty fire grate. "Yes, he said he had to go and do something."

"Vera wants to see you again," Amber recalled suddenly. "Coal told me."

Eishoxa stopped. She knew what Vera would want to talk to her about, but she didn't know that it would come so soon.

"Are you in trouble?" teased Amber. "Vera wants to see you an awful lot recently."

Eishoxa gave her a half-hearted smile. "She wants me to go to the Ewdicani. To persuade them to join the war." To her surprise, Amber looked shocked for a second before covering it up with an interested smile. Eishoxa responded to the worry on her face. "What's the matter with that?" she asked.

Amber bit her lip.

"Amber?" Eishoxa prompted again.

Amber attempted a careless smile but didn't pull it off. "Nothing's the matter ... It will be difficult to persuade them to join the war; I'm surprised Vera's sending you so soon."

She was lying. Eishoxa could see it, but she didn't say so. There was no point. The Indocani never gave up a secret they wanted to keep. Instead, she played along. "I think she wants them to join the war as soon as possible, or something like that. But I wasn't claimed by the fire yesterday, so she's worried."

Amber nodded, obviously glad that the conversation had swung away from the subject she clearly didn't want to discuss. "Well, no one except Vera and the Lords – and of course Ember – expected you to Change. You're still full of your old life. Even I know that."

"My old life?"

"All the Ignorant stuff," Amber replied, gesturing vaguely at Eishoxa.

"Stuff?" Amber snapped her fingers, a habit she had when she was frustrated. "You know – their way of thinking, their way of looking at things, their way of doing things ..."

Eishoxa was baffled. "How on earth am I meant to change that?"

Amber hesitated. "You're not. That's why no one except Vera, Ember and the Lords expect you to Change."

This confused Eishoxa even more, but she didn't press the matter. Instead, she concluded slowly, "So they expect more than I'm capable of?"

Amber nodded. "Oh, yes. But they do that with everyone. It's not just you. Anyway, we should go and see Vera. She's not one who likes to be kept waiting."

Eishoxa stopped her. "All I promised to do was to listen to her," she said. "And if I don't want to go the Ewdicani, then they can't force me to go, can they?"

"No one will make you do anything, Eishoxa. Rest assured of that."

Eishoxa wasn't sure that she agreed, but she didn't argue.

Eishoxa pushed through the vines slowly, wondering what she would see. She was a little apprehensive about this meeting. Although Vera had made it quite clear at the feast that accepting the task was entirely Eishoxa's choice and Vera would hold no grudge if she refused, Eishoxa couldn't see her giving up so easily. If Vera wanted something, she would get it, whether Eishoxa co-operated or not.

She had never been in this room before. It had a more casual exterior design. Instead of a door, a barrier of vines obscured the room as if less privacy were needed. She stepped inside, looking around. The room was round, like most of the rooms here, cut elegantly out of the Tree. Vera sat at the back of the room behind a table, her arms and hands forming a steeple on which she rested her chin. Ember paced behind her, talking quietly but passionately. His hand kept jumping to the sword he carried at his waist. A sentry stood nearby, arms folded and eyes fixed firmly on the ceiling. As usual, fire glimmered around the room. The three of them turned their gaze on her as she let the vines fall back into place.

"Eishoxa. At last. I'm glad you've come." Vera stood up and gave a little bow to her, gesturing towards an empty chair in front of the table. Eishoxa slipped into the chair as instructed and looked anywhere but at Ember, who was now leaning on the back of Vera's chair and glowering down at Eishoxa.

Vera smiled and took a deep breath. "Well, you already know why you're here and what I'm going to ask you, so I won't go through that again."

Eishoxa nodded curtly. She slid her hands into her trouser pockets and clenched them. All she'd promised to do was listen. She didn't have to do anything. Vera smiled in what Eishoxa presumed she thought was a reassuring way.

"During the last few days, I've realised that it's been difficult for you. Therefore I have a proposition to make to you. You will help us by going to the Ewdicani and persuading them to join us in the war, and then we will let you go back to Bareth." Eishoxa couldn't help herself. She gasped.

So did Ember. "Vera, that's not—"

Vera held up her hand and Ember fell silent, looking now at Eishoxa. Vera seemed to think that Eishoxa was going to say something, but when she didn't, Vera pressed on. "I know you don't want to be here. Therefore, if you give us this help, you may go back to Bareth and I promise we'll leave you alone after that."

Eishoxa looked into Vera's golden slit eyes. She didn't trust one word the woman was saying. "You're telling me that if I go to the Ewdicani and persuade them to fight on your side and to help you in your war, you'll let me go back to Bareth and you'll leave me alone?"

Vera nodded. Ember suddenly spoke up, his hand gripping the pommel of his sword. "But that's ridiculous! She belongs here!" Vera looked at him as if willing him to be silent. Ember instead addressed Eishoxa. "You belong here! How will you ever live among the Ignorant again when you can't touch water? You'll be labelled a witch and burnt! What is left back there for you that we don't have here?"

Long enough had Eishoxa borne Ember's insults. Now it was time to fight back. "Bareth is my home!" she retorted. "That is the place I know as home! Think about it, Ember. If you were taken away from here and put into Bareth Castle with thousands of humans and told that you belonged there, would you believe them?"

"Of course not!" he scoffed.

Eishoxa jumped on his reply. "Well, then, you know how I feel. Told to do this and that, everything out of place, told I belong here and belong there, I must do this and must do that! Why don't you stop being so selfish?"

Ember slammed his hands down on the table. "Our people are dying out there in their hundreds and you're telling me to stop being so selfish? Why don't you grow up first?" Vera tried to break into the conversation, but he waved her off. "I told you in the forest, Eishoxa. The life that you had before is over! Now you live here – now you have to learn to live here! Because this is where you belong! You want to go back to save your friend. I know! But she's dead, and you can't bring her back!"

"Ember!" shouted Vera. "That is enough! How dare you speak like that?"

Ember didn't even look at his leader. "She's playing games with us! She knows she belongs here! I saw you today down in the tunnel underground, looking at the carvings."

Eishoxa looked up sharply. How could he know that?

"You see?" he said triumphantly. "You know as well as I do what you saw down there. I know you remember. You just won't remember your duty anymore."

Vera looked at her and cut in. "You went to the tunnel today?" Eishoxa nodded reluctantly. Ember looked as if he wanted to speak again, but Vera got there first. "You saw your life written on the wall, did you not?" Eishoxa had to nod agreement. Vera sighed. "Then why will you not go?"

"Because I don't remember that life!" Eishoxa cried. "I cannot remember a life before the one I have now, so how am I meant to be the person I can't remember?"

Vera opened her mouth again to speak, but Ember cut in. "Indocani are dying in that war! Indocani you used to call your friends! Indocani whom you promised you would do anything to save! And they went out there because you said before you left that you would come back and help us!" he accused. "And now you sit here and refuse to do anything because you're mourning the loss of one insignificant Ignorant whose death will do nothing but cause more bloodshed for our people!"

Eishoxa knocked her chair over as she jumped up, the blood pounding in her ears. "Don't you dare speak that way about Maya! Don't you dare say anything like that about her! You and your people are nothing compared to her! It was you who let her die, and don't think for one minute that I'm going to forget it!"

"Ember and Eishoxa! Will you sit down!" Vera's voice resounded in Eishoxa's ears, but although she stopped shouting, she wouldn't sit down. Vera gave Ember a hard look. He turned on his heel and returned to his pacing. Vera forced a smile and looked at Eishoxa.

"Eishoxa, I know this is hard on you, but you must listen to us and understand. This is what you were made for. This is why you were put on this earth. To do this. You cannot hide from it."

"I'll think about it," Eishoxa muttered.

Vera's smile started sliding, but then she hitched it back up. "Thank you. You may go now."

Eishoxa left without another word.

When she'd gone, Vera sighed, smiled contentedly to herself and sat back in her chair. Ember glowered at her shoulder.

"What have you done, Vera? A promise like that she won't forget. We need her to stay here. She would be useless in Bareth."

She raised her eyebrows at him, tilting her head back. "You want her to stay here," she pointed out. "I need her for one purpose only. And when she's fulfilled that, I don't particularly need her anymore, although admittedly it would help to have her."

"But you've let her go!" he exploded, flinging his hands into the air.

Vera sat forward and smiled. "I've said she may go back to the Ignorant through the portal in the Black Forest. But, hypothetically speaking, *if* her friend is dead as you say, and *if* Bareth has been destroyed … what would there be for her to go back to?"

Ember stopped in his tracks, catching her meaning "That's wrong, Vera. We can't destroy an innocent city and kill an innocent girl. There are limits you must respect!"

"Well, then," she sighed, poking her quill at one of the pieces of wood on her desk, "say goodbye to your little sweetheart, because between staying here with you and going back to Bareth, we both know which one she'll choose." She heard him leave and sat back again in her chair, a calculating smile on her face.

CHAPTER 13

THAT NIGHT EISHOXA WOKE while it was still dark. The fire was down to a few glowing embers and the room was colder than usual. She snuggled deeper under her blanket and sighed, looking up at the ceiling. She wanted to go outside. She wanted to see the night sky. It was kept away here, kept away by fire and light and celebration. She wanted the calm and peacefulness the night brought, and for which the Indocani hated it. Yes, they were a wild people. She could see the wildness now, never tiring, never stopping, just like the fire they came from.

She opened the door of her room, inhaling a deep breath of cold night air. The fire in the grate flared momentarily as the wind hit it, then died back down as Eishoxa closed the door firmly behind her. She walked to the very edge of the branch and sat down. Out there, where the fire no longer tainted the forest, it was pitch black. She held onto the branch with both hands, looking over the trees. She was swinging her legs aimlessly when she heard footfalls behind her. Turning, she saw Rianox approach, his face half hidden by shadow and a ball of fire glimmering in his hand. She turned away when she saw it.

"Can't sleep?" he asked, sinking down beside her.

Eishoxa shook her head, correcting him. "Didn't want to."

"Ah," he nodded. They sat in silence. The sky ahead of them was a bruise of purple and blue, and the moon was nowhere to be seen. "Doesn't the night bother you?" Rianox asked.

Eishoxa started to shake her head, then stopped. "I'm meant to nod, aren't I?" she sighed.

Rianox frowned. "Tell the truth?"

Eishoxa shook her head firmly now. "No, it doesn't. And that's another thing. I'm too human to ever properly belong to this place, to this people. I can't. And now I'm meant to go and tell these Ewdicani to join a war I know next to nothing about. Ember's right: I'm just playing around. I'm a fraud."

"That's not true," Rianox replied quietly. "You're not used to us yet, but it's still early days. You can't see it, Eishoxa – and I know you probably don't want to – but you do belong here. The Ewdicani are more like the humans than we are, so when you see them it may help you to realise how much you're suited to life here at the Tree. We're not asking you to forget the life you had before. We're asking you to remember this one."

"Ember wants me to forget that life," countered Eishoxa bitterly.

Rianox scratched the back of his head in thought. "Ember has the ability to shut down all emotion when it comes to duty. And his duty to his people will always come before the needs of his own heart. He's not the majority, though, and few people share his radical views."

"Is that really so?" questioned Eishoxa hopefully.

"Absolutely."

"I feel that I should go because afterwards I can go back home – back to Bareth, I mean – and that's where I belong."

81

Rianox nodded. "No one will force you to stay, after you've persuaded the Ewdicani to join us. But we need you to ask them. It's only if you go that they'll come."

"But I'm not the same person I was before. They won't believe me if I go now."

"Maybe it's a good thing that you're not the same person," he suggested quietly. He stood up. "In the end, Eishoxa, it's your decision. Just remember that."

She put the conversation with Vera and Ember out of her mind and focused on her lessons with Rianox. They were the only thing in Sicharenhafan that kept to a steady rhythm. Rianox was right. It was not long before she could recognise many of the characters, and Rianox was delighted when she haltingly read a short passage.

"That's it!" he exclaimed. "Just master this and it won't be long before you can speak to fire."

That was what Eishoxa really wanted to do. Amber could do it and so could Rianox. She saw them whispering to the flames and felt a prickle of envy, as if she weren't allowed to do something she wanted to do, as if the fire wanted to talk to her but someone had forbidden it.

During one lesson Rianox wanted to speak to her about the history of the Indocani and also of the Ewdicani. "It's important that you know all you can about both races," he explained, opening a large scroll. "If you do decide to go and see them, it will be more respectful if you at least know their history, even if you can't speak their language."

"Why? Can you speak their language?" Eishoxa was surprised. Rianox had said that the two races kept apart and didn't share information.

Rianox didn't meet her gaze but busied himself with opening the scroll. "Yes, some parts of it I can speak. I'm by no means fluent but, being who I am," – he paused and smiled wryly – "it's important that I know as many languages as I can."

He passed her one end of the scroll and pointed to the end closest to her. "If you look there, you'll see the start of the world. Now you'll note that there was originally only one god. His name was Pentelemence and he had control over all five elements. With the Elements themselves he created three daughters: Fiera was the oldest, Wella was second, and finally Nezrax. For a while they were happy. But then the three daughters decided that Pentelemence was running the world very badly and would destroy it completely, so they fought him in a battle and banished him to the far corners of the universe. The battle destroyed the world, so they set about creating it again, but in a better fashion. They made Fire, Water and Rock, the three main elements. They built the mountains for Rock; they made the rivers and seas and lakes and streams for Water; and they made the sun to sit in the sky – and of course all the deserts – for Fire. The other elements came later." Eishoxa followed his finger along the characters as he read them. "Each daughter became a Goddess and claimed an element. Fiera, the Goddess of Fire and War; Wella, the Goddess of Water and Peace; and Nezrax, the Goddess of Rock and Darkness."

"Darkness?"

"Yes. Without darkness there can't be light, can there? How could one recognise either light or darkness unless there was something to compare it to? But the story has variations. One is that Nezrax took Darkness after strong persuasion from her sisters, and another is that her sisters gave it to her without thinking. She was doted upon and they wanted her to share in their success. But it doesn't matter now. They created our world. Fiera and Wella made two races, one to be made of fire and the other of water. They would be different but they would live in harmony with each other. Fiera, who loved to hunt and fight, named her race the Warriors, and Wella, who loved to play music and look after animals, named her race the Peacemakers. They lived together in a special place called Pellimeth, which means the Perfect Union of Different Souls.

"But they didn't tell Nezrax they were doing this. Darkness, and hence evil, is usually stronger than good for some time because it's deceptive and cunning. No matter how strongly a fire burns, it can be put out, and no matter how fast and powerful a river flows, it can be dammed. The two Goddesses knew this. Needless to say, Nezrax found out. She was much cleverer than her sisters thought. But instead of making her own race, she was so angry with her sisters that she took revenge on them by destroying the work they'd made.

"We are made from fire, Eishoxa, and this is very important to understand. We hold fire in us because we *are* fire. The Ewdicani *are* water – that's what they're made of. But Nezrax was so angry that she stole the inner element of fire or water from many of the people. That's why they're called the Empty, because their element has been stolen from them."

"And you're fighting against the Empty now, aren't you?"

"Yes, we are. But originally they were *only* empty. The ones we're fighting now have been filled with evil. You see, before, Nezrax simply took their element and abandoned them. But after a while she realised they would make perfect soldiers for her. They have nothing left. So she took them for her own. Fiera and Wella – in their pride, I presume – let her take them."

"Why?" Eishoxa said.

"The Goddesses have changed. Unlike, I believe, the Gods and Goddesses the Ignorant worship, ours are not perfect. They have their faults. But they were very young when this happened. They'd got rid of their father and so had no one to advise them. I believe that they didn't want spoiled goods, so to speak. So they let their little sister take the Empty, and by the time they realised the full extent of what was happening, it was too late.

"Nezrax also tricked each race into thinking that this disaster was happening because of the other race. She turned her two sisters against each other, took the race that she'd fashioned – the Empty – and went to live in the Sorrowful Mountains. Fiera and Wella each took their own race and put them on different sides of the world. And now we live in Sicharenhafan and the Ewdicani live in Dulcacohefen."

"So do the Goddesses still hate each other?" Eishoxa questioned.

"No one knows what they feel," Rianox said heavily. "If they indeed still hate each other, then the Ewdicani will know about it and they won't help us. Fiera made it clear that she wanted us to live for ourselves and to protect and learn to defend ourselves. On the other hand, Wella takes a lot more interest in her people, conversing with them and sharing her thoughts and wishes."

"Did Wella have a child like me?"

"No, she didn't. Maybe that's why she takes more care of her people. Maybe Fiera gave you to us to watch over us in a way that she won't."

"So we're all meant to be warriors then?" she asked.

He sighed. "Yes, that's what Fiera meant us to be, but sometimes a baby is born with different qualities. Coal, for instance, is more of a healer than a warrior. Ember is a warrior."

"Yes, I can see that," she laughed. "What are you, Rianox?"

His face broke into a mischievous smile. "Has Amber not showed you yet?"

"Showed me what?"

His smile widened. "Come on. I'll show you."

They left the Tree and headed towards the forest where Amber had taken her hunting, but they moved deeper into it. The trees were even more sparsely spread and the ground was burnt black. Rianox led the way through the trees, guiding Eishoxa around great piles of uprooted trees.

She examined the slashed bark of a tree closest to her. "Was this done with more target practice?" she asked, picking at the torn tree.

Rianox gave it a quick glance. "Amber told you that we use this forest for target practice?"

"Yes. Why? What is it used for?"

Rianox helped her over a fallen tree. "It is used for target practice, but I don't think she meant the same target practice you were thinking of."

"So what made those marks?"

Rianox smiled secretively and took her hand. "I'll show you. Now, close your eyes." She gave him a suspicious look. "Trust me. Just close your eyes. It's a surprise."

Eishoxa did so reluctantly. With only Rianox's hand to guide her, she continued through the forest. She'd abandoned wearing shoes soon after she arrived because no one else wore them, and her feet had got used to the sharp stones and sticks. She could smell smoke now and the unfamiliar scent of something else … something animalistic and earthy.

"All right, open your eyes," Rianox whispered in her ear. Eishoxa opened them slowly and was greeted with a blast of fire. When it cleared, she gasped. Directly in front of her was a huge pit, deep and wide and containing with a sort of creature she'd never seen before. The very ground was heaving with them. The creatures were large though of varying sizes, and covered in smooth scales like snakeskin. Their heads tapered to a point and fangs curved over their bottom lip. They were a variety of colours: red and orange, yellow and black and orange, yellow and smoky grey. A fringe of spikes ran along their backs all the way to the tips of their tails. Every now and then one would let out a snort and fire would erupt from its nose.

Rianox grinned. "This is what I do. I look after these. Do you like them?" Eishoxa, speechless, nodded fervently. "These are real dragons, not the ones the Ignorant draw. An Indocani may ride a lot of dragons, but one particular dragon will be special to each Indocani. That dragon is like a missing half. An Indocani and his or her dragon can speak together in their minds, and they both know when the other is hurt – they exist always in each other's awareness.

"Dragons are very intelligent and wise. Each one is connected to the others in a vast web of consciousness. Everything a dragon has ever seen or heard or done in the history of the world is stored in this web. And they are a way of connecting with Fiera. She calls them her 'stepping stones' because they are in between her and us. But Nezrax can also pollute a dragon's mind. She takes them to be the mounts for her Empty. We call them drakons."

"Drakons attacked Bareth Castle," Eishoxa remembered quietly.

Rianox nodded. "Yes, with the Empty … My dragon is called Navaz, which means Dancing Smoke. Come. She's down here."

Eishoxa scrambled down into the pit after him. Before them, the dragons moved back and hissed. "They won't hurt you," reassured Rianox as Eishoxa moved closer to him. "Each one has been chosen by an Indocani and will only attack the enemies of that particular Indocani. There's Navaz, over there." He walked up to her.

Navaz was shredding a piece of wood with her teeth. Behind her a massive hole gaped in the wall of the pit. Its edges were charred, and lumps of burnt mud lay on the ground around it.

"That's where all the young are born," grinned Rianox. He ran his hand over Navaz's nose. She snorted and rubbed her big head against his chest, eyeing Eishoxa as she came closer.

"She won't hurt you." Rianox took her hand and put it on the scaly back. Eishoxa smiled and rubbed the smooth skin. "Would you like to ride her?" Rianox asked, patting Navaz's back. Eishoxa drew back dubiously. She'd ridden a camel in Bareth, but a dragon was a very different proposition.

Rianox laughed. "She won't hurt you, I promise." Eishoxa took his hand, letting him help her climb onto Navaz's back. "Hold tight with your knees," Rianox instructed. "Can you do that?" Eishoxa looked nervously at the ground. Navaz's wings were rippling, preparing for flight. "Trust yourself, and trust her. She's never once dropped me, I promise."

Eishoxa rested her hands on Navaz's back. The dragon's muscles coiled beneath warm skin. Rianox grinned and stepped back. Navaz's wings unfurled and stretched out. She nosed her way forward. He could see Eishoxa bite her lip in concentration. She will learn, he thought as he smiled to himself. Opening his mind to his dragon, he whispered "Fly!" and felt her purr in amusement as she agreed. Air buffeted Rianox as the dragon took off, smoke billowing from her nose.

At first, in the backflow of smoke, Eishoxa could see nothing. But soon the air cleared and she saw that the trees were very much taller here. To clear the trees Navaz had to fly through them. Eishoxa could hear her snorting and feel the dragon's mighty muscles stretching and contracting, lifting them ever higher. The trees moved past them faster and faster, the air felt cooler, leaves whipped against Eishoxa's face. Then, as the trees tapered at the top, they burst into the sky and the full light and warmth of the sun.

Navaz's warm skin rippled as she snorted and rode the wind. Below them lay a world so very different from what Eishoxa had known, yet it seemed achingly familiar. The forest hadn't gone on forever, as it seemed to on the ground. They had soared above a desert as dry and barren as the one she'd left in Bareth. The heat of the sun was fierce, the air hot and heavy. The smell of burning wood reached Eishoxa's nose, golden grains of sand blew around her gently, and for the first time since her arrival here she felt truly happy.

Suddenly, she felt the same tickling in her subconscious that she'd felt after the feast, when she'd tried to be claimed by the fire. She recalled what Vera had said – *"Open your mind. Let it in."* And now she did.

For the first time she felt it: a low, soft hum in the back of her mind, a sign that something else was there, that she was not completely alone. The hum turned into a pressure, which turned into a presence.

"Like it?" The voice came more as a thought than actual words. Navaz turned her head, and in the dragon's eye Eishoxa could see a glimmer of amusement.

"Navaz?" she asked.

"Just speak to me here. It's easier."

"What's happening? How can you do this?"

"They tried to force the fire to claim you too early. But now your body is starting to remember things that happened before, and sooner or later it will remember fire too."

"Are you sure?" Eishoxa didn't know whether she was imagining the conversation in her head or whether it was really happening.

"I am a dragon. I know many things that Vera will never know." Eishoxa could tell by her voice that she didn't think very highly of the leader. *"Now hold on."*

Suddenly Navaz pulled in her wings and plummeted in a well-executed dive. As they neared the trees, she rolled dangerously and Eishoxa yelped and tightened the grip of her knees. She heard the dragon chuckling. Navaz skimmed the tops of the trees, then soared upwards again, spinning this way and that, moving towards the desert again. On and on they sped, high above the ground. As the desert spread out below them, Navaz roared and dived again, heading for the sand. Fire streamed in a golden ribbon from the dragon's mouth and engulfed Eishoxa in heat and flames. She tried to keep her eyes open, but sand flew into them and she squinted instead. Just as they were about to hit the ground, Navaz pulled up, brushing the sand with her claws. She rose again and flew more slowly this time, circling the desert.

"I hear they want you to see the Peacemakers."

"Yes," Eishoxa replied, stroking Navaz's neck thoughtfully.

"I hear that you don't want to go," continued the dragon carefully.

Eishoxa looked at her hands. *"No. I don't think they'll listen to me."*

The sides of the dragon shook as a great rumble ensued from her throat. *"Now listen to me, Eishoxa, and listen well. We dragons know more about the Great Goddess than you, Vera or anyone else does. And the Great Goddess would want you to go. This I know."*

"But how?" Eishoxa asked desperately. *"How do you know? How do you know that they'll listen to me? I look nothing like one of the Indocani."*

"The Peacemakers do not judge by race. They are great sticklers for judging by individual merit. Many dragons and people are dying in this war, this fact cannot be denied. And if this is what can stop it, then I'm greatly in favour of your going. You are not Vera's pawn. You can do the easy thing or you can do the right thing. Those who do the right thing have the power. Vera is doing the easy thing, I'll be honest with you. She's placing upon you too much pressure so that if anything goes wrong she can blame it on your youth and inexperience and both of you are relatively safe. But you must decide which path is which and choose the one to take. Be who your mother would have wanted you to be. Be yourself. Be Eishoxa."

Eishoxa listened to the low voice in her head and clenched her hands so hard that crescent moons marked her skin where her nails had dug in. "But that's the thing," she said out loud. "I don't know who I am." She stared out across the sandy expanse of the desert. Dunes swelled like golden waves, and bizarre-looking cacti were dotted across the land. It was a wild and harsh landscape, and Eishoxa could find no answer in it.

"You may find your answers there," Navaz rumbled. *"Answers were never found by those who did not go looking for them."*

Eishoxa made no reply. There was nothing to say. The dragon was right.

Navaz gave another deep bellow and rose once more high into the sky, flying even faster than before back for the forest and the dragons' pit. She didn't speak again, and for this Eishoxa was glad. She knew not what her mother would have wanted. She hardly believed in goddesses, let alone the fact that she was the child of one.

The wind forced Eishoxa's eyes shut and she held tight with her knees. When at length they dived for the trees, Eishoxa was sure Navaz would crash, but at the last second the dragon angled her body so that neither of them even brushed a twig. Rianox was standing in the dragons' pit, waving his arms. The other dragons greeted Navaz as she landed, roars and dust rising equally around them. Eishoxa slid off Navaz's back and patted the dragon's neck. Navaz, snorting and snuffling, moved back to her log of wood and began once again to tear at it with her teeth.

Rianox was giving her a strange look.

"What?" Eishoxa asked.

He shook his head quickly, as if warding off an unpleasant thought. "Nothing. Did you enjoy the ride? You look all wind-swept." He brushed a strand of hair off her face, smiling. "You still won't let Amber braid your hair? She keeps complaining, you know."

Eishoxa smoothed her hair and swept it back over one shoulder. "I don't need it braided. I never did it like that in Bareth. I know how to keep it out of my way."

"So you did enjoy yourself then?"

Eishoxa nodded vigorously. "Oh yes. Very much."

"See? What did I tell you?"

"You mentioned that every Indocani has a dragon," she said. "Does that mean that I have one as well?"

Rianox's face fell. "Your dragon disappeared when you left, Eishoxa," he said sadly. "No one knows where she went."

Eishoxa knew that she shouldn't feel anything. After all, she'd never met this creature. But even so, at Rianox's words she felt tears prick the back of her eyes.

"But now that you've come back, she may come back also," he consoled her. "You may ride any dragon here," he offered, "including Navaz. Yours is not lost forever, I'm sure of it."

Eishoxa was saved from responding by the sound of a voice calling her name. "I think Ember wants you," smiled Rianox, looking up to the pit's edge as Ember came into view. He looked very annoyed as he caught sight of Eishoxa and Rianox standing in the hollow together.

"Eishoxa! Where have you been?" and he jumped down into the pit in one athletic move, causing the dragons to scatter.

"Rianox!" shouted Ember. "You were meant to keep her at the Tree. That's the safest place for her. Vera has called another meeting and you both must come."

Rianox bristled beside her. "There are other people capable of taking care of her."

Ember shot him a look of disgust and stalked back towards the wall of the pit.

"We should go now as well," Rianox sighed.

As he trailed after Ember, Eishoxa quickly turned her head to look at Navaz. She hadn't told Rianox that she could feel the hum of many minds, thrumming in the back of her own. The dragon raised her head to look at Eishoxa and blinked slowly. "*Be yourself.*"

Eishoxa ran to catch up with the other two. *Be myself*, she thought.

CHAPTER 14

THEY WERE IN the Council Room again, just off the Great Hall. Ember and Rianox had gone in first, telling Eishoxa to wait outside until her name was called. Now she entered. Seated at the head of the table was Vera, at that moment deep in discussion with Ember, who sat on her right. Coal occupied the seat on her left. Further down the table sat Rianox, laughing quietly at something his neighbour had said. Three very old-looking men had their heads together, and every now and then one of them would draw deeply on a heavily smoking pipe.

When Eishoxa entered, everyone stood, including Vera. Eishoxa took her seat at the other end of the table and everyone else followed her example, apart from Vera, who stayed standing. Looking around, Eishoxa could recognise very few people from the first Council meeting. Vera braced her hands against the table and the bangles on her arms twinkled in the light. She cleared her throat and everyone's gaze focused on her.

Vera picked up a little orange glass pot which lay in front of her and blew into it gently. Smoke billowed out to form a large oval, which then cleared to reveal a moving picture. It showed a large plain with many troops marching across it. On the standards that they carried, Eishoxa could see the symbol of a flying eagle. So these were the Indocani.

From behind the smoke came Vera's voice: "This is the plain that borders the smallest of the Sorrowful Mountains. We've had few victories of late, which has allowed the Empty to get much closer." She waved her hand through the smoke and the picture changed. The image showed another battalion, but this one was in disarray, moving like a colossal, deformed bug towards the plain from the other side. "The Empty march closer and closer to us."

Suddenly the scene in the smoke started to move very fast, speeding along the ground, past great rivers and ravines, past desolate moors and towering mountains. Then the Tree came in view, alight with little fires.

"We haven't fallen yet to the Empty," Vera said. "But our defeat is their greatest goal. The Ewdicani mean nothing to them, and they are too weak to put up much of a fight." Her dislike was obvious in her voice, and a few others around her joined in agreement.

"Be that as it may, if the Ewdicani let us cross their lands, we can protect them as well as ourselves. There are many things that they control and we have no power over. If they block the path of the Empty for even a little while, then it buys us much-needed time."

There was another murmur of agreement. Eishoxa felt Rianox's eyes turn on her and she lowered her head. She hadn't forgotten what Rianox had said: if the Indocani were given entrance to the Ewdicani's land, it would be destroyed.

Vera took a deep breath. "But they haven't yet agreed to join our cause."

All eyes turned to Eishoxa. Ember stood up and whispered something in Vera's ear. She nodded slowly, considering it. Then she beckoned to Rianox. "Rianox, a word with you in private."

"Yes, Vera." Rianox followed her as she swept out of the room. A tense silence ensued. Eishoxa could hear the sound of Vera's voice but couldn't make out any words. Then came Rianox's voice and Eishoxa fidgeted uncomfortably. They would want their answer soon, that much she knew: yes … or no.

The two of them entered the room again and Rianox returned to his seat. He didn't look at Eishoxa but instead kept his gaze trained on his leader. Vera seemed to be considering something very deeply. Ember stood up again as if to say something else to her but she waved him away. "Thank you, Ember, but I do not need your consultation on every thought that passes through my head." Eishoxa bent her head to hide her smile. Ember sat down again, chastened.

"Eishoxa, I require a private word with you as well." Eishoxa stood up and her mouth suddenly felt very dry. She swallowed nervously and followed Vera out of the room, twisting her hands together in apprehension. Vera led her away from the room towards the Great Hall so that they wouldn't be overheard.

"Eishoxa, I must have an honest answer from you now. Will you go where I send you, or will you not?"

Eishoxa bent her head. She could feel the power reverberating in the air around Vera, but she could also feel her desperation. Even Vera, in all her might, leader of the Indocani and with more power than Eishoxa had ever dreamt of having, was desperate for an answer from Eishoxa. Eishoxa had the power now, and Vera knew it.

She continued: "I know these past few weeks haven't been so fair to you. You've lost much and been told to do things for people whom you apparently cannot remember. I know this is hard. But I must tell you now that things are worse in this war than I let on. The Ewdicani are our only hope now, and if you don't convince them to join us, I fear for this people, Eishoxa, I fear for them."

Vera put her hand on Eishoxa's shoulder. Eishoxa didn't like it there, just as she didn't like Vera trying to be kind and sympathetic, but politeness kept her still. In all honesty, she didn't care about the Ewdicani or the Empty. She could have seen a thousand carvings on the wall, but they didn't persuade her that she belonged here. They simply showed that she'd been here before. Be yourself, the dragon had said. And make your own choices, uninfluenced by others. What did Eishoxa want to do? She wanted to go home. And this was not her home.

"I shall go," she said. Vera visibly relaxed. Eishoxa continued. "But on one condition: that you promise me now that, when I return, I may leave straight away for Bareth and you and your people won't bother me again."

Vera looked slightly taken aback. "Are you sure, Eishoxa?"

Eishoxa nodded. "I don't belong here. Whatever anyone says, I don't. I've made promises to people which I intend to keep, and therefore I hope that you'll honour your promise. Do you promise?"

Vera nodded slowly. "I promise, Eishoxa. You may go back if you persuade the Ewdicani to join the war."

They went back into the room together. Everyone looked up. Vera gestured for Eishoxa to return to her chair and walked around the table to sit facing her. The Lords looked towards Vera and then towards Eishoxa. No one spoke.

"Eishoxa has agreed to go," Vera said finally. A cheer rose around the room. Rianox clapped his hands and most of the Lords grinned broadly. Ember was the only one who looked slightly suspicious. He leaned forward to try to talk to Vera, but she waved him away.

"To make this official, Eishoxa, I must ask you again so that everyone here can know that you are going of your own free will and I am not forcing you." Silence fell for the second time.

"Eishoxa, do you promise to go to the Ewdicani, the Peacemakers, and persuade them to join the war that we're fighting against the Empty?"

Eishoxa let the words hang in the air for a moment. It was upon her answer that their war depended. She could choose. And she did.

PART 2

CHAPTER 1

THE ARROW WHISTLED through the air and hit the white mark on the tree exactly in the middle. Eishoxa put down the bow, shielding her eyes against the sun to see the arrow better.

"Perfect!" called Rianox from where he'd been crouching to sharpen his own arrows. Eishoxa ran to the tree, pulled out the arrow and returned to Rianox. He smiled up at her.

"You've really got the hang of it now."

"Yes, well, I suppose it will be helpful for when I go."

A few days had passed since Eishoxa had agreed to go to the Ewdicani, the race that lived in Dulcacohefen, and try to persuade them to join the war against the Empty. From that moment, Vera had said that Rianox needed to teach her how to use a bow and a sword, as these skills would be necessary.

"We must prove to them that we are not weak," Vera had said. As Eishoxa now looked down at her bow, she agreed. She must not be weak. She must prove that she was different, different from how she had been before. The only reason Eishoxa had agreed was because Vera had promised that, if the Ewdicani joined the war, Eishoxa could return to Bareth and find Maya.

Amber straightened from where she'd been leaning against a tree and took her own bow off her shoulder. Eishoxa and Amber had been spending more and more time together recently because she was helping Rianox remodel Eishoxa into a more realistic Indocani.

"Your stance could be a bit neater though," Amber observed critically, taking aim and firing. "It won't make much of a difference because your bow is so perfect, but if you were given a worse bow it might. And it just looks better."

Eishoxa nodded and pulled her bowstring back again, squinting slightly along the shaft of her arrow at the white smudge on the tree. Opening her fingers, she let the arrow go and, once again, it embedded itself in the tree. They were practicing on the stretch of scuffled grass that lay between the Tree and the burnt forest where the dragons lay. Rianox had said she mustn't let on that she knew about them, but he wouldn't tell her why, and because of this she wasn't allowed to see them again. Eishoxa had seen Rianox's dragon, Navaz, several days earlier and already missed her. The dragon was so wise and Eishoxa wanted to know whether Navaz thought she'd done the right thing.

As she collected her arrow from the tree again, she heard Amber shout a greeting and turned around. Ember, Amber's twin brother, was approaching them from the Tree. He caught sight of the bow in Eishoxa's hand, and she noted the slightly raised eyebrows as he saw where her arrow had hit the tree.

He's constantly waiting for me to fail, isn't he, she remarked to herself. Rianox came to stand by her shoulder. He didn't seem to like Ember either. She suspected that Ember liked her even less than she liked him, but he was one of the Indocani who'd been chosen by Vera to take her to the Ewdicani. They were going to hear any day now who else was coming.

"Are you practising, then?" he asked.

"I can already hit the target," she replied hotly.

He raised his eyebrows again. "That's good."

"It's true, Ember," Amber snapped. "Now either tell us what you want or go away."

"Vera wants to see Eishoxa, that's all." Ember had interpreted Eishoxa's decision to go as his own personal victory, and he'd made sure the whole Tree thought so too. Eishoxa sighed. At the latest War Council, Vera had said they would leave soon. That was vital because time was running out for the soldiers on the battlefield.

"Coming!" she called, handing the arrows back to Amber and swinging her bow over her shoulder. Amber gave Ember a look of intense dislike. "Why does he constantly think he has to order everyone around in order for them to live their life?"

Rianox laughed and put an arm around Amber's shoulders. "Because he grew up having to do the same to you and Eishoxa." Amber playfully shoved him away and adjusted her bow. Eishoxa laughed, a little tensely, pretending not to hear her own name mentioned. Her life beforehand was a sensitive subject. Amber glanced back at Ember, still walking away, and turned back again quickly to Rianox. "I don't like it," she said.

Eishoxa looked up, slightly confused. "Don't like what?" Amber didn't answer and instead said something quietly to Rianox. Eishoxa couldn't understand because they were speaking in their native tongue, Düerasgörn, the language of fire that Rianox was teaching her, very slowly and painfully.

"What is it?" Eishoxa asked curiously. Amber gave her a worried look. She opened her mouth but Ember interrupted them, calling back, "Please can we go now? It's not as if we have all the time in the world."

"We do when it's to your advantage to have it," muttered Amber. Eishoxa swung her bow onto her back and followed Amber as she started to walk towards Ember and the Tree. Rianox brought up the rear, holding his bow in his hand. She'd noticed that something had been bothering Amber ever since Eishoxa had announced her decision to go to the Ewdicani. Not just Amber, but Rianox too, and Eishoxa had seen some other Indocani giving her strange looks as she passed them. Getting no information out of Rianox, Eishoxa had given up, knowing the stubborn attitude of this race.

The four of them approached the base of the Tree. Eishoxa put her bow more firmly on her shoulder and put her hands to the bark, feeling for the familiar footholds. Ember swarmed up it like a monkey, but Eishoxa followed more slowly. "Where are we going?" she asked Ember as they waited for Rianox and Amber to catch up.

"To Vera's rooms," he replied shortly. When Amber and Rianox were standing beside them, he said they weren't needed and excused them. To Eishoxa's dismay they nodded and left, although Amber did it with a lot of complaining. Then it was just her and Ember, standing on the tree bough together. He leapt up to the next branch, giving Eishoxa no time to catch up. He was already standing by the entrance to the little room in the side of the tree when she scaled up to stand beside him.

"Ready?" he asked curtly and she nodded once, straightening her bow on her shoulder. He knocked twice on the door and then entered. Vera was sitting there at the table with Coal standing behind her, looking down at the piece of paper she had in front of her. Coal was frowning at something. Eishoxa smiled when she saw him. Ember and Coal had both taken her out of Bareth, but Eishoxa had warmed to him more. He was a lot older than her and Ember and reminded her of an older version of Rianox. She hoped that he might be accompanying them. As Ember and Eishoxa approached, Vera moved the paper out of sight with a glance at Eishoxa. Two other Indocani standing at the back of the room bowed when they saw Eishoxa, but she only nodded at them.

"Hello, Eishoxa," Vera said, standing. Eishoxa turned her gaze on her. "I thought that you could leave tomorrow," she explained. "Ember will go with you, of course, as you already know. And," she motioned towards the two Indocani at the back of the room, "I thought that Ash and Smoke would be good companions also." Eishoxa's eyes trailed slowly over them. They looked like brothers, with the same face and eyes, and although they carried themselves with the same pride she'd seen in all the Indocani, they did not stick their chins out with arrogance like Ember. She noticed that Vera was watching her carefully. "Is that to your liking?"

"Yes," Eishoxa replied and then asked, "Could Rianox come too?" She felt Ember stiffen and glance swiftly at Vera.

Vera, however, shook her head. "I'm sorry, but Rianox is needed here. He is very clever and we need him in our War Council while Ember is away. I hope you understand."

Eishoxa sighed. He was clever and that's why she wanted him with her, for his familiarity and good sense. Vera pointed at Ash and Smoke. "These two are very good companions and they know what they must do."

Eishoxa nodded. "That's good. I understand." Vera inclined her head and opened her mouth as if to dismiss her, but Eishoxa had one more question. "And our deal still stands, doesn't it? If I get the Ewdicani to join your war, I may go back to Bareth?"

Vera's hand slowly drifted, as if unconsciously, towards the piece of paper she'd been writing on when Eishoxa had entered. Eishoxa adjusted her bow and repeated her question. "That was our agreement? And I won't go unless it still stands."

Vera nodded and smiled. The tense atmosphere eased slightly, but out of the corner of her eye Eishoxa could see Ember shifting restlessly. "Of course you may go back to Bareth after that. That is what we agreed," she said.

"And right away? Not when you decide?"

"Right away," Vera supplied. Eishoxa glanced at Ember, who was looking anywhere but at her. She felt a rush of mistrust

"You must keep your word," Eishoxa stipulated. Vera rested her chin on her folded hands, leaning on her elbows. "Eishoxa, do you not trust anyone, or do you just lack belief in my honour? I have promised that you will go back to Bareth and I keep my promises."

"I don't trust anyone here," Eishoxa answered bluntly. "I have no reason to."

Vera sat back in her chair. "Thank you, Eishoxa. You may go now."

CHAPTER 2

T HEY WERE READY to leave at dawn on the next day. Eishoxa had her things in a small leather bag: all the clothes she'd been given, as well as two long curved knives given to her by Rianox shortly after she'd chosen to go. She carried her new bow over her shoulder with a full quiver of sharpened arrows in her bag and another one slung over her back. The spare quiver had been a gift from Amber. She and Rianox had come to see Eishoxa the night before to say their own good-byes, and Eishoxa had wondered whether she'd see them again before she left.

As she stepped out of her room and closed the beautiful glass door behind her, she heard someone call her name. One of the twins stepped forward from where he'd been leaning against a branch. "Hello," she said awkwardly. He bowed. "I'm Ash, if you didn't remember. Ember has asked us to meet by the Dragon Forest. We'll be taking the dragons to the Ewdicani."

Eishoxa felt a little leap of excitement. She loved the dragons, especially Navaz. But that was Rianox's dragon, and as this thought crossed her mind, she remembered what he'd said about her own dragon, which had disappeared when she'd left. Which dragon would she be taking then? Ash led the way down to the ground and hurried across the beaten grass towards the burnt forest. The morning light was dim and the dew still lingered on the ground. Eishoxa was surprised to find her feet stinging a little as they brushed against the damp grass.

Drawing closer to the trees, Eishoxa could see Ember standing there with Smoke and Vera. With a rush of surprise and delight, Eishoxa recognised Rianox and Amber on the other side of Vera. When Eishoxa and Ash stood before the little group, Ember made a little sound of impatience. "Why did you take so long?"

Eishoxa simply looked at him, refusing to give an answer. She had been told to arrive at dawn and it was dawn. Ember glared at her and then cleared his throat.

"We will be taking the drag—"

"I know," Eishoxa interrupted. "You aren't the only one who can give instructions." She noticed that Smoke was looking at the two argue with a very strange expression on his face: part shock and part disbelief, as if he couldn't quite believe what he was witnessing.

"Good," growled Ember. "Then I hope you were listening." Vera held up her hand and the bangles on her wrist glimmered in the early sun. "Please, no arguing. Let us go and get the dragons and you can start on your journey. Rianox, lead the way."

Eishoxa had only been here once before, but Rianox had made her close her eyes for some of the journey, so it came as a surprise to her that, no matter how far they went into the woods, the trees stayed burnt and black and there was nothing on the ground but broken, charred sticks and dry, cracked earth. As they approached the dragons, Eishoxa sniffed the air and breathed in again the earthy animal smell that surrounded the pit. When they stood at the top, Eishoxa looked down into a nearly empty pit. Most of the dragons had retreated to sleep in the dens that burrowed underground. Several lay outside, covering themselves completely with their wings. The only signs of life were the regular snorts of smoke that issued from their noses. Rianox made his way down first and held out his hand to help Vera climb down. Ember followed and then Ash and Smoke. Finally Eishoxa and Amber scrambled down into the pit. Ember, Ash and Smoke seemed to know where to go and headed for the far corner of the hollow where a group of dragons nestled together. Eishoxa looked around at Amber.

"Aren't you going to go and see your dragon?" she asked curiously. Amber shook her head. "No, I'll see him when you lot leave. It will be quieter then. Which dragon will you ride?"

Eishoxa shrugged and looked around for Rianox. He was standing with Vera and the two of them were whispering intently, Rianox gesticulating. Vera shook her head. Finally Rianox nodded and bowed, although his face didn't look happy. He beckoned to Eishoxa. "You will ride Zeexa," he said, leading her to the opposite side of the hollow. A lithe, small dragon crept out of one of the tunnels and breathed out a little snort of fire. She was not unlike a cat, stretching in the sun, her sharp claws scrabbling at the ground. She was about the height of a horse and had a long barbed tail, viciously pointed at one end. She yawned and her curved teeth flashed.

"She's a good dragon and she will bear you well," Rianox said, stroking Zeexa's nose gently. She was black – not a solid black, but black like the night is black – with small scales of orange and gold spread out across her body. She was not like Navaz but she was a beautiful animal nonetheless. Eishoxa pressed her hand against the scaly skin and Zeexa gave a little shiver. Eishoxa opened her mind and tried to sense Zeexa's so that she could talk to her. The dragon's mind was like a little flower, opening and closing. She was very shy and very different from Navaz.

"*Will you ride me?*" came the little, wispy voice in Eishoxa's head. She smiled and rubbed Zeexa's back. "*Yes, I'll ride you.*"

"*I am honoured to bear the daughter of the Great Goddess,*" Zeexa replied, turning her wedge-shaped head towards Eishoxa and lowering her snout as if to bow. Rianox helped her up onto the dragon's back and Eishoxa settled herself, tightening the straps of her bow and bag so they wouldn't fall. The other three were already mounted and ready, waiting for her. Rianox stood by Zeexa, shifting restlessly as though he wanted to say something.

"What is it?" Eishoxa asked quietly. Rianox put his hand on the dragon's side, not looking up at her deliberately.

"Rianox!" came Ember's voice. "What's taking so long? We need to go." Eishoxa looked towards the other three and then back down to Rianox. He clasped his hands together very tightly and then looked up at her, saying very quickly, "Others would not want me to tell you this. But I must, because if I don't, I know you will blame yourself. No matter what you hear and what you see with the Ewdicani, know that people change and it is not *your* fault. Do you understand?" Eishoxa nodded. Rianox put his hand on her ankle to stop her going. "Do you promise me? That you will not blame yourself if you hear anything about your past life?" he asked, looking up at her intently.

Ember was riding a huge black beast, even blacker than Zeexa. A huge crest of black spikes ran from the top of his head to the end of his tail. His claws were razor sharp and very long and his legs were ridged with muscle. His bright green eyes swept over Eishoxa and Zeexa haughtily. Eishoxa could see at once why this dragon had chosen Ember. Ash and Smoke were riding two dragons that could have been twins as well. They were identical down to the very tips of their tails, but one had orange eyes and the other yellow. Zeexa was the smallest, but Eishoxa could sense the other dragons' awe of her, and then realised it was because she was carrying Eishoxa.

Vera came to stand beside them and looked up at Ember. Something unsaid passed between them and he nodded. Eishoxa realised they were talking in their minds, as she could do with dragons but not yet with people. Then Vera stood next to Zeexa. Even though the dragon was small, Vera had to look up to see her.

"I hope it goes well," she said. "For all of us." Rianox stood on the other side and Amber stood beside him. "Make sure you come back safely and soon," she said. Eishoxa smiled down at her. "Of course." Rianox held something up to her. "These are a few scrolls that you could read on your journey. Carry on practicing Düerasgörn and you'll master it soon enough." Eishoxa hastily brought out her pack and put the scrolls inside. She looked back down at the two of them. "Remember your promise," Rianox said to her and Amber nodded as though she knew what he was talking about. Eishoxa nodded. "I'll remember," she said.

Ember's dragon raked the ground impatiently with his huge claws. "Time to go!" his rider called. Amber, Rianox and Vera watched as Ember guided the group into the centre of the pit. He took off first, followed by Smoke and then Eishoxa. Ash was the last. The four dragons gave a great bellowing cry as they rose and fire streamed from their mouths. Eishoxa could feel the joy vibrating through Zeexa's skin as her wings moved powerfully. Eishoxa was bathed in the beautiful warmth that fire brought. When she looked back to see Rianox and Amber again, the flames and smoke hid her view.

By the time the smoke cleared, the four of them were already up in the sky and the people on the ground were too far away to make out. Ember circled slightly, waiting for everyone to catch up. Eishoxa looked around. She could just see the desert beyond the trees. Remembering what Rianox had said about the journey to Dulcacohefen, she squinted but could not even catch a glimpse of the Forest of No Flame. The desert was too vast. Zeexa snorted excitedly, her wings beating with an urge to fly. They all hovered in a circle and Ember started to speak.

"We all know why we're here. And we all know that Eishoxa is the one who must get to the Ewdicani. She is therefore the one we must protect. She will fly in the middle with Zeexa and we will circle her at all times. I will take the front to begin with, then it will be Smoke and then Ash. Agreed?"

Eishoxa rested her bow on Zeexa's back and spoke to the dragon in her mind. *"Do you think we'll actually start to fly today?"*

"He thinks I am not capable of taking care of myself," came the angry reply. Eishoxa looked towards Ember. *"Who, Ember?"*

"No, Ferac, his dragon. He thinks I am weak and that I am not worthy to carry you. He thinks that it should be he who carries you." Eishoxa stroked Zeexa's shoulder soothingly. *"Just ignore him."* she replied. *"We'll show him that you are more than capable."* And with an agreeing growl, Zeexa fell silent.

Ferac swung his massive head from side to side, his teeth snapping. Ember turned him around and directed him towards the desert. "We head this way. Everyone stay close together and remember to protect Eishoxa." Then they started to fly. Eishoxa had the same euphoric feeling she'd had when riding Navaz, but even more so because Navaz would never belong to her. Zeexa was her own and had not belonged to anyone else before. The pride the dragon felt at carrying her infiltrated Eishoxa's mind, as if they were not just sharing words but emotions too. She smiled slightly; it was strange to know almost nothing about this place or these people, and yet be so well known. She looked down as the wind sucked at her feet and watched the Dragon Forest sweep away under her. Resting her feet in the hollows of Zeexa's shoulders, she looked around. On her left, Ash scoured the land below them and around them. She noticed that he crouched on his dragon, rather than sat as she was doing. He had braced his feet against the bones that ran halfway along the edge of the wings. Zeexa had two pairs of wings but his dragon had three.

"Do different dragons have different numbers of wings?" Eishoxa asked Zeexa.

"Oh yes. Wings grow as we grow. Jerath and Kereth over there have three, but Ferac is growing his sixth or seventh. I cannot remember." Eishoxa examined Zeexa's wings. The one on top was black and firm, with the same scaly look as her skin. It was ribbed with fingers of bone like bat wings and only beat once or twice. The softer wings underneath were a pale orange and in a constant state of flapping. As Eishoxa thought about it, they were nothing like the pictures she had seen of dragons in Bareth. These were more like insects and lizards than the huge big-boned animals that burnt down silk forests on the walls of the cavernous dancing halls.

The desert swept out below them and before them, like an endless sea, and the dry wind whipped up the gritty sand into frenzies so that the ground was simply a blur. Eishoxa looked back over her shoulder to watch the Tree fade completely out of sight and then faced the unknown horizon. This had to be done. And then, after that, she could go home, home to Bareth and home to Maya.

CHAPTER 3

EMBER WAS THE self-appointed leader of the group, and although Ash and Smoke looked surprised when he started to issue orders, Eishoxa said nothing about it. She didn't want to fight over it. As Navaz had said, Ember could order everyone about, but the final decision rested with her. If she wanted to, she could go back and they would all have to follow her. Let him tell them what to do if it made him happy. It didn't give him any authority over her.

The day was long and, as the sun rose higher and higher, the heat of the day increased. By midday the sun was burning down so fiercely that the blinding rays distorted Eishoxa's vision whenever she looked up towards the horizon. She spent those hours lying on Zeexa's neck, listening to the comforting vibration of the dragon's breathing and watching the desert streak by beneath them. Ember decided that the first night they would sleep on the ground, but when they crossed the Forest of No Flame they would have to fly through the whole night. Zeexa did not seem at all apprehensive about this idea, though Eishoxa knew she was small and not the strongest of the group.

"I love to fly," Zeexa purred into Eishoxa's head. "Flying does not make me tired; I was made to fly as you were made to walk."

"Walking makes me tired, if I do a lot of it."

"Well, maybe you were made to run then. I know that Navaz's rider never gets tired when he runs; he has often said that he could go on forever."

"Rianox?" Eishoxa smiled at that. She could very easily imagine Rianox running through the woods at full speed, with nothing but Navaz for company flying high above her. As soon as she thought this, she shook her head. Why did she imagine that? In fact, how did she imagine that? She had never seen Rianox run through the woods, nor been with Navaz except for when she had been first introduced. Disconcerted, she looked around as Smoke and Ash swapped positions.

"We will descend now," Ember's shout came from ahead of them. Eishoxa straightened and looked down. The wind had dropped with the approach of nightfall, and below them stretched an untouched blanket of sand, perfectly formed and without a mark of any kind. But as the sun set, all shades of purple spilled onto the desert, from the palest lilac to the deepest indigo, staining the far corners of the land. Ash and Smoke pulled their dragons into a steep dive and Eishoxa watched as they raced towards the ground, pulling up at only the last second so that the claws of their dragons barely brushed the sand. Ember was keeping a careful eye on her.

"Well, are you going, Princess?" he asked, and Eishoxa, ignoring his scathing tone, urged Zeexa forward. The dragon paused for a fragment of a second and then dropped like a rock through water, falling faster and faster as she tucked all her wings in and pinned her ears against her head. Eishoxa's eyes watered furiously, but she didn't want to blink and didn't dare let go to wipe them. Like Navaz, Eishoxa was sure that Zeexa would crash, but then – leaving it even later then Navaz did, so late that Eishoxa could see Ash and Smoke standing there – her wings extended, there was a buffet of air as she was caught, and they touched gently down. Sliding off Zeexa's back, Eishoxa rubbed her dragon's head fondly and said, *"What were you doing?"*

"How can you get tired of that?" the other crowed, sweeping her tail from side to side and nuzzling Eishoxa's hand with her nose. Ember landed, and Eishoxa and Zeexa noticed with a satisfied nod that he didn't land as gracefully as they did. Ferac's claws scrambled for a landing on the slippery sand.

Eishoxa took her bow off her shoulder and looked around. They were standing in a little hollow, carved out by the wind and framed by four dunes, which weren't very big or tall but gave shelter. On one side a cave, big enough for all four dragons to fit comfortably, gaped like a huge black mouth in the side of the east dune.

Ember immediately took charge again. "We'll make a fire and Ash and Smoke can go hunting." The twins looked at each other, then at Eishoxa and then at Ember. He noticed their confusion and said irritably, "What?"

Ash stepped forward. "Isn't Eishoxa supposed to be in charge? That's what Vera told me. She didn't know the way and so you should lead in the air, but on land, we don't follow you, Ember. We follow her." He then added something else quietly in Düerasgörn and Ember scowled, his face darkening. Ferac growled. Eishoxa, who'd been looking around curiously and paying no attention to what Ember had been saying, had suddenly frozen at Ash's words. She raised her eyebrows at Zeexa and turned around. Ember was looking thunderous but she ignored him. Instead, she smiled sweetly at Ash. "Don't worry, he can take charge. I don't mind."

Ash bowed to her but then continued. "With all due respect, Eishoxa, Ember is not a Lord yet and therefore neither does he hold any authority over me or Smoke. You're the one in charge." Eishoxa looked back at his serious face foolishly. She could feel Zeexa keeping quiet in her mind and deliberately not offering advice. She looked at the three of them and then said, "Well, why don't I tell you to do what Ember says now and I'll watch, and tomorrow I'll know what to do and I'll take charge."

Ash seemed to be satisfied with this answer, and in a few moments Ash and Smoke had disappeared over the side of the dune, their bows on their shoulders. Eishoxa and Ember avoided looking at each other, and instead the two of them went to stand by their dragons. Zeexa had stretched out on one side of the hollow, closest to the cave, surrounded by a little oval of her own fire to keep warm. Eishoxa sat down gratefully beside it and warmed herself.

"Will you not stay in the cave?" Eishoxa asked Zeexa, motioning with her chin. She heard Ember snort derisively behind her.

"Princess, if you are going to ask questions like that, I suggest you speak them in your mind, so that no one else can hear them."

Eishoxa turned to Zeexa in confusion. She could feel the dragon's amusement flicker through her head. *"What is wrong with what I said?"*

"We hate the dark," Zeexa explained. *"It would be madness for an Indo-*

102

cani to sleep in there when we could sleep out here and conjure fires for light and warmth."

"I didn't know that."

Zeexa snuffled, a sound she made when she was laughing. "Now you do."

Eishoxa opened her pack and stowed her bow inside. The end protruded out of the top.

"Did you understand what Ash said?" Zeexa asked. Eishoxa looked up briefly.

"No. He spoke too fast and I don't know the language fluently yet."

"He said, 'And you're not Fiera's son yet'."

Eishoxa's head shot up at that. "Fiera's son?" she said, unaware that she was speaking out loud until the dragon's horror spread through her head. "Be quiet!" the dragon warned. Eishoxa turned to look at Ember. Luckily, he didn't seem to have heard. He was sitting on the opposite side of Ferac, sharpening his arrows, but Eishoxa noticed Ferac's ear had pricked slightly.

"Sorry. I don't think he heard. But Fiera doesn't have a son."

The dragon blinked at her slowly. "I suppose you have not been told this story yet. No, she does not have a proper son, but it is said that when you fall in love – and you can only do so once – that person will be Fiera's son. I wonder why Ash said that to Ember."

"I don't know," Eishoxa murmured. Her mind was suddenly whirring. Why had Ash said that to Ember?

"I can only fall in love once?" she asked and Zeexa nodded. "Some call it a curse. Some call it a blessing."

"Princess?" Ember had stood up from where he was sitting behind Ferac. "We need to make the fire, if you're ready."

She dusted off her hands and stood, saying, "I won't be very useful because I can't make fire yet." His face didn't change but she thought she heard a faint sigh. "I'm learning," she said defensively. He blinked at her from across the hollow and muttered something that Eishoxa couldn't catch. "What was that?"

"I said I thought you didn't want to learn our ways. That's what you said in the Black Forest, wasn't it?" He crouched down and clenched his fist over the ground. Flames curled up and around his fingers. As he withdrew his hand, he looked up at her as if expecting her to say something. Luckily, she was saved from answering by the return of Smoke and Ash. They had each caught one of the raccoon-like creatures that Amber had shot on the first day in the Dragon Forest.

"Were they hard to find?" Ember asked, standing up and ignoring Eishoxa again.

Smoke shook his head. "Prey is not used to being hunted with arrows. The desert is swarming with it."

Eishoxa went back to Zeexa and sat down beside her, leaning back against her warm scales. The dragon coiled her tail around Eishoxa's legs and tucked her wings in more firmly to make it more comfortable for her. As the two of them watched Ash and Smoke skinning the animals and cooking them over the little fire Ember had made, they said nothing to each other but Eishoxa could sense Zeexa's comforting presence in the back of her agitated mind. She wasn't quite sure why she felt so agitated; it was as if there were ants running around inside her head. When their food was ready, Eishoxa came to sit beside the fire and Zeexa crawled up behind her so she could rest once again against her stomach. The meat, like all the food at the feast, was dry and tasteless and crumbled to ash in her mouth. When Eishoxa put her share down in her lap, unable to eat anymore, Zeexa snaked her head over and gobbled it up. Eishoxa stroked her nose. *"You already had your share."*

Zeexa's tongue darted in and out of her mouth and her eyes twinkled. *"Well, we couldn't let it go to waste, could we?"*

"I don't see how you can eat that," Eishoxa replied, swallowing a few times to get the dust off her tongue.

"It's delicious," Zeexa purred.

That night, Ember and Smoke blew the fire up very high so that it would burn the whole night long. Eishoxa lay next to Zeexa on the sand and the dragon covered her with one of her lower wings. Smoke took the first watch, sitting on top of the dune with his dragon. He had conjured a fire to keep warm, and he and his dragon crouched close together. Ash and Ember lay close to the fire but Eishoxa kept to one side of the hollow. Zeexa's warmth was all she needed. The sand was a soft pillow under her head and the sound of Zeexa's breathing right next to her was the lullaby that sent her off to sleep.

Ember didn't sleep that night. He closed his eyes but sleep wouldn't come. In the end, he sat up and leaned back against Ferac. The black dragon grumbled in his sleep and drowsily opened one eye. When he sensed Ember's unrest, he blinked his huge green eyes open. *"What is it? I can't sleep with all your problems running around my head."*

Ember rubbed the back of his neck distractedly and nodded towards the other side of the hollow where Eishoxa lay sleeping. Through Zeexa's translucent wing, Ember could see that some of her red hair, which she refused to plait like everyone else did, had fallen over her face and fluttered rhythmically as she breathed.

Ferac lifted his huge head off the ground and growled wistfully in agreement. *"She no longer belongs to us though, does she?"*

Ember was surprised at the loss that Ferac felt. It poured through both their minds, a great mutual pain. *"No. We lost her and Fiera,"* he replied bitterly, thinking of Eishoxa's lost dragon. Ferac agreed again, thinking as well of the golden dragon that he had loved.

"And now Rianox has taken her and that pathetic excuse for a dragon, Navaz." If Ember had been in another mood, he would have reprimanded Ferac for speaking in such a way about them, but he couldn't help but share the sentiments. He looked up at the night sky. There was no moon tonight and no stars. The night went on and on. He looked back at the fire and raised it a little because it was dying down. Ash stirred slightly and moved towards the heat a bit more. Ember sighed.

"She will remember. We only have to wait." And then he realised he wasn't stating a certainty but rather praying that it would come about.

The following day, Eishoxa woke to the warmth only a sleeping dragon could provide. Although she had brought no blanket with her, the heat emanating from Zeexa's wings was like being wrapped in several of them. Without waking Zeexa, she stretched and carefully wriggled out from underneath the wing. The plummet in temperature made Eishoxa want to wriggle right back under, but the sight of the sunrise drove all thoughts from her mind. She had seen many sunrises from Bareth, but this was nothing like those. In the land of fire and heat, every sunrise and sunset was the epitome of perfection. The rays of the sun streaked across the sky, as if painted with an impatient brush. The oranges and yellows of dawn drove back the purples and indigoes of night in glowing chariots of light, and the cloak of night took itself to the far corner of the sky, fleeing from the glowing orb of beauty and warmth that rose in a dignified ascent into the sky. The colours seemed brighter and bolder than any Eishoxa had seen in Bareth, and the whole desert seemed enthralled by the sheer brilliance of what it was witnessing.

She heard a rustle behind her and turned to see Zeexa stretching luxuriously, her claws leaving long gashes in the sand. Eishoxa smiled. *"Sleep well?"*

"As well as can be expected," replied the dragon, giving a huge yawn and flicking her tongue in and out of her mouth. The others were waking now, stretching and yawning and grumbling at the cold. Eishoxa rubbed Zeexa's nose and waited for them to rouse themselves.

"Have you been looking at the sunrise?" Zeexa asked, and Eishoxa nodded, turning her head to look back at the sky. *"I've never seen anything like it."*

"And you never will," finished Zeexa with satisfaction. *"Nowhere in the whole world will you see sunrises compared to the ones you see in the desert, here in the Land of the Sun."*

With that, Eishoxa had to agree wholeheartedly. The Land of the Sun. It definitely looked like that as the shadows were chased away by the light. She saw Ash, Ember and Smoke pause for a moment as they took it in, as if they too were surprised, but then Eishoxa saw a faint hint of pride on their faces and knew they had seen it before, probably many, many times. This was their country and it was their great joy to watch the sun rise.

It didn't take them very long to be ready. Eishoxa swung her bow onto her back, put one knife into her belt and checked that everything was safely in her bag, which she added to the load on her back. She could tell Zeexa wanted to be off. Her wings kept rising with impatience and her claws were scrabbling against the sand. She, for one, agreed. Riding camels was all very well, but nothing compared with riding a dragon. Ember was the last to be ready.

Through the impatience that Zeexa felt, Eishoxa could sense a small measure of pride. *"You don't have to beat Ferac at everything, you know,"*

Eishoxa said in her mind, stroking Zeexa's shoulder comfortingly. Zeexa turned her head slightly to look at Eishoxa. *"There will be many things that he will beat me in. I need to win in everything I can."*

Eishoxa gave a small snort of amusement. *"Well, you're perfect to me,"* she smiled and Zeexa purred.

Ember led the way into the sky. As they rose, Eishoxa looked at the back of Ferac's tail, coiling slightly with the effort of lifting himself into the air, and remembered that although she told Zeexa not to constantly compare herself to Ferac, was she not herself competing with Ember?

The desert took them four days to cross, four days of hard flying towards the Forest of No Flame. Eishoxa tried to read the scrolls Rianox had given her, but she got so frustrated at the little pointy scratches in the parchment that she was tempted to throw them down to the sand below. This desert had at first reminded Eishoxa of Bareth, but as they continued their journey she realised that this desert was a lion, while the land covered with sand and dunes outside Bareth Castle was a newborn kitten.

Every evening, every night, as they advanced into wilder and wilder country, there would be another predator, another pack of animals that thought four dragons and four armed riders would be an easy meal to take down. It was at these times that Zeexa, small though she was, proved she had teeth and claws, quite capable of protecting Eishoxa from anything that came her way. Strange cat-like shadows would attack, with long teeth that protruded at odd angles and legs that would grow back. When one tried to hit them, they would merge into the shadows and reappear moments later.

In Bareth, Eishoxa had played mock sword-fighting with Maya, but the grace and ease with which Ember, Ash and Smoke handled their weapons diminished any skill she had down to nothing. They moved with twice the speed and strength and skill of any attack that presented itself, leaping and jumping and slashing with their sword or knife, which seemed a metallic blur cutting through the air. Eishoxa tried her best, whenever she was allowed, but she could tell her greatest effort was poor stuff compared to the effortless moves of any one of her companions.

She'd never appreciated what Rianox had said about the Indocani being warriors and soldiers who, like fire, would give their last breath fighting an enemy. She had not yet appreciated, until that moment, the shame that this nation carried from encountering an enemy they not only couldn't beat but to whom they were losing.

She looked at the fierce concentration of both dragon and man and knew that she would never understand them, neither the dragons nor the Indocani. She couldn't understand the deep pride they wore like a second skin, a pride they could not get rid of, a pride that had turned to arrogance. They didn't give in because losing was too much of a shame. But despite that, when the smudge of dirt on the horizon told all of them the Forest of No Flame was approaching, Eishoxa knew she would miss the desert and everything in it. In the short time she had spent with the Indocani, she had realised maybe only one thing about them: that they were loyal to themselves and to their people, fiercely so. They would kill a thousand innocent people if it meant saving one of their own.

CHAPTER 4

UNLIKE THE DESERT that had approached gradually, the Forest came upon them before any of them were expecting it. One minute they were soaring above sandy slopes and curves, and the next the scenery beneath changed into trees sprouting up from damp earth. Two opposite worlds. Co-existing. Eishoxa voiced these thoughts to Zeexa.

"*And they do it so peacefully, don't you think?*" Eishoxa asked, leaning over Zeexa's back precariously.

"*Peacefully?*" Zeexa snorted. "*I don't think so. There used to be a river running between the two of them, keeping them apart, but not anymore. No, there's tension between them, not peacefulness.*"

Eishoxa looked ahead and could see the beginnings of thick fog clouding their view. "*Look at that fog,*" and she pointed to it. Zeexa huffed through her nose and a cloud of smoke erupted from her left nostril. "*I hope we avoid it. It doesn't look very good.*"

By the time night had fallen, none of them could see a thing. Eishoxa could sense all the dragons flying close to each other; if she looked to her left, the wingtip of Smoke's dragon, Kereth, occasionally brushed Zeexa's. She swiped again at the water drops beading on Zeexa's skin. Ember had cast shields around them all to protect them from the worst of the water, but she could still feel its chill pervading her body. Beneath them, the fog hid the trees, and around them it formed a cage of dense, wet wool.

"Ember!" she shouted and felt Ash and Smoke look towards her from their mounts. Zeexa slowed to a halt and Eishoxa could just make out Ferac's shape hovering in the air. The fire in Ember's hand glowed dully, sometimes disappearing before relighting and flickering feebly.

"What, Princess?"

"Is this really necessary? Can we not stay on the ground?" The fog seemed to swallow her words before she had spoken them, and she had to shout very loudly to make herself heard.

"The ground is too dangerous," Ember called back. "Too wet for the dragons and for us."

Eishoxa sighed. "Then where are we going? Can you see, because I can't. I say we go to the ground. The fog may be less thick there."

"It doesn't stand to reason," came the patronising reply. "Fog thins as it rises."

"This isn't normal fog," she called. A wind whistled in her ear and she spun her bow around, trying to catch a glimpse of something to train her arrow on. Ash's voice came out of the fog from her right. "She's right, Ember. We could be going around in circles. Our shields won't hold out forever. Our best chance is to go to the ground."

Eishoxa could sense Ember weighing the possibilities. "All right!" she heard him shout at last. "But go carefully and don't break formation." Eishoxa immediately felt Zeexa dip beneath her and start to slowly sink to the ground. She kept the arrow in her bow swinging from side to side, squinting through the fog at anything that might appear. As

Eishoxa had predicted, the fog started to thin considerably as they sank; at times Eishoxa could glimpse the tip of Ferac's tail. She grinned and turned to her left. Smoke smiled at her briefly and mouthed the words "Smart thinking" before turning away and checking around him. As they moved very slowly towards the ground, Eishoxa felt a definite rise in the temperature, slight but enough to be noticed. She said nothing about it, though she knew the others would have sensed it much sooner than she had.

Huge fingers of trees loomed suddenly out of the fog, and Zeexa had to swerve to avoid them. Yet when Eishoxa looked down, she could see no sign of them. *"Be careful,"* she said tensely to Zeexa and felt Zeexa's acknowledgment in return. *"It's thinning out but not quickly enough."*

Zeexa dropped slowly, following the twitching tip of Ferac's tail that would appear out of the fog now and then. It was so close that Eishoxa could have touched it, but Ferac was such a big dragon that Ember was too far away to be seen. The ground, when it came, came very quickly, just like the desert had started and ended. One minute they were surrounded by the fog, and the next it had all disappeared and they were hemmed in by huge tree trunks that towered around them. Eishoxa made to slide off Zeexa as they touched the ground, but Ember stopped her.

"Let's first check the ground is safe, shall we, Princess? Before you go sliding into something you don't really want to be touching."

He pointed to a large thick patch of ferns that she was about to land in and raised his eyebrows. Eishoxa nodded and repositioned herself on Zeexa's back. She heard a bird cry from somewhere above them and pointed her arrow towards the sky. The fog hung above them, however, and she couldn't make out anything.

As the fog cleared and visibility improved, Eishoxa lowered her bow slightly. Ember was throwing little balls of fire down towards the ground. Wherever they touched, they fizzled out in a puff of smoke. "We'll go further in. It's too wet here," Ember called, guiding Ferac around a tree and speeding up slightly. Eishoxa looked around curiously. She had never been in a forest that felt quite like this. The forest that Ember and Coal had taken her to had a light and gentle atmosphere, while the Black Forest had had an oppressive, hostile ambience. This place, however, felt like neither of them. An alien feeling, as if the forest knew they were there and would tolerate them as long as they played by its rules and its rules only. In every strange coiling tendril that brushed Eishoxa's face and in every branch coated in thick, soggy moss, she felt the forest was watching them, judging them, assessing them, working out whether they were dangerous or not. She kept her gaze trained ahead of her, but, as Rianox had taught her, spread out her senses, checking and rechecking for any sign of danger whatsoever.

After some time, Ember called back to the rest of them, "This place is as safe as we'll find. Let's stop here."

Zeexa lowered herself to the ground slowly and rested gently on her claws as if she didn't want to touch the ground. Eishoxa slid off her back and patted her neck. *"What's wrong?"*

"I don't like it here," Zeexa whined. *"Something seems familiar about it, but also unfamiliar."*

Eishoxa rubbed her dragon's nose soothingly. *"We'll be fine,"* she replied. *"You'll see."* Zeexa whined again and nuzzled Eishoxa's arm with her head. Eishoxa smiled and patted her shoulder. They were standing in the centre of a close circle of trees. There weren't clearings here; the trees grew too closely together. No sunlight penetrated the canopy of leaves and branches above her – nature and the fog had made sure of that – and no light came through the trunks because moss had filled in any chinks. The only light here was a strange, green, glowing light that seemed to come from the air around them. This was the only explanation Eishoxa could come up with because she could see perfectly clearly, but it wasn't thanks to the sun.

"We should light a fire," Ember decided. "That will stop anything unwanted coming after us. They don't like fire here." He had been quieter than usual, as if the forest scared him. Ferac's ears and tail were drooping slightly, and everyone else also seemed more subdued.

"Then maybe we shouldn't light one," Eishoxa cut in. All eyes turned to look at her. "This isn't a normal forest. Maybe we shouldn't do something we know they don't like."

Ember didn't even look mildly annoyed; the patronising, exasperated look he wore was even worse. "Eishoxa, do you want to die of cold here? Or would you like to get to our destination intact?"

Eishoxa bristled. "Just because you have a head big enough for both of us, it doesn't mean that there a lot of sense inside it! Look around you. You don't know this place and neither do I. Just bear it for one night."

Ash and Smoke silently watched the two of them speak. Smoke had his arms folded and kept his gaze trained more on the ground than on the pair, but Ash was watching them very intently, his eyebrows raised. Eishoxa pretended she didn't care about their presence, but their attention caused a blush to creep onto her cheeks.

"Do you remember what happened the last time you had an encounter with water?" Ember asked.

Eishoxa stamped on the ground hard. It didn't yield. "There's no water here. The ground is bone dry. It will be cold, but our dragons can keep us warm."

"Then where do the trees get their water from?"

"Why don't you start digging and find out?" she retaliated. Eishoxa didn't know why, but the more Ember refused to agree with her plan, the more agitated she got to keep him from lighting a fire. She heard Zeexa hiss a warning in her mind, and Ember's eyes had narrowed even more. Ferac had bared his teeth and was snarling at her furiously from behind Ember. Ash and Smoke still said nothing. "We do not use our dragons to keep warm! That is what our fire is for," Ember spat forcefully. "You have a choice, Princess. Walk off by yourself and endure the humiliation of being dragged back because we need you

alive for Dulcacohefen, continue arguing with me until it attracts some kind of wild animal we don't want to face, or be quiet and let us light our fire."

Ash started to speak at this point but Ember held his hand up for silence. Eishoxa could feel her cheeks flaming. Ember raised his eyebrows at her. "Your answer?"

"Light your fire," she said through clenched teeth, and turned away from him, returning her arrow to the quiver and slinging her bow over her back. She felt Ember's triumphant gaze stay on her a little longer before he turned away. "Ash, will you find dry wood? We need to keep it going for some time."

Eishoxa fidgeted in annoyance. Did Ember really always think that he was right? She looked around at the trees nervously. A rustling sounded all around them as leaves blew gently in the wind. The approach of anything would be hidden by this sound. She sighed again and walked away from the rest of them, climbing up a little ridge of moss between two huge trees.

Zeexa touched her hand gently. *"Don't worry. It will be fine."*

"It won't be. We can't just light a fire in the middle of a forest and expect everything to be fine. And why can't you dragons keep us warm?"

Zeexa blinked. *"We are wild animals, Eishoxa, not used to curling up and being of use. We fight for ourselves and if, at a certain point in our lives, we respect one of you more than another, then we may choose to speak with you. Mostly, we keep ourselves to ourselves."*

"Well, I don't understand it."

"You would if you were from here."

If Zeexa's words had come from anyone else, Eishoxa would have been immediately insulted. But when she looked at the dragon, she could feel nothing but waves of compassion rolling off her, and she managed a smile. *"That's just the point. How am I meant to convince these Ewdicani if I'm not from here? How many more wrong things will I say?"*

Zeexa simply snorted at her. *"You'll work it out, and there will be people to help you."* And the little dragon slunk off to sit beside Kereth.

Ember was still giving orders in his loud, angry voice. Eishoxa forced down a wave of anger and anxiety and turned to listen. "Smoke, will you go with Ash to collect wood? Eishoxa—"

"I'll go with Ash," interrupted Eishoxa, standing up immediately. She was not staying here with Ember to watch him make his fire, knowing that she didn't want him to light it. She would go where it was safe. The three of them just stared at her. She stepped forward off the little ridge. "I'm in charge, remember? Come on, Ash." The words came out more aggressively than she'd intended, and Smoke and Ash looked taken aback. Ember, on the other hand, simply resumed his natural arrogant mask.

Adjusting her quiver on her shoulder, she crossed over to the other trees and took off into another part of the woods. Ash followed her. Pausing to let him to catch up, Eishoxa looked around. Away from Ember's voice and the worry she felt at lighting a fire in this place, she noticed that the forest really was quite beautiful. There was no pattern to it, not even a similarity between one tree and the next. The forest grew as it wanted to grow. The trees wore long garments of moss and thick belts and necklaces of ivy. But unlike forests elsewhere, here everything was green. The flowers were green, the trees were covered in green moss, the ground was covered in grass and dark green rotting leaves. Even the light was green – light which she noticed hadn't changed even though some time had passed since they'd entered the forest.

Ash's light tread made no sound against the ground as he came after her. He carried his bow and an arrow in one hand, leaving his other free to collect wood. He gave Eishoxa a small smile, which she did not return.

"So where should we look, do you think?" she asked, refusing to meet his gaze. At this moment, all of them reminded her of Ember. She couldn't understand his stubbornness and his refusal to accept the advice of others. He was going to get them all killed.

"I'm not sure. Should we just head in this direction and have a look at what's there?"

"That's strange," Eishoxa bit back before she could stop herself. "I thought Ember would have told you where to look, as he knows everything."

"Eishoxa, I know you may not understand, but fire in a place like this is very important to us. I agree with Ember."

Eishoxa sighed, apologising quietly. She didn't need to take her anger out on Ash. He hadn't done anything to her. They didn't have to walk far to find wood. Under the huge, twisting, knarled roots of a tree, there was a small pile, laid there neatly as if it had been made for taking. Ash said nothing until they were picking up the pieces of wood. "I'm sorry as well, Eishoxa. I didn't mean to make you angry."

She nodded brusquely, accepting his apology, and then burst out, "Why doesn't he listen to anyone when they say anything? He isn't always right. He should know that." As her voice echoed through the strange forest, the leaves seemed to rustle more loudly. Jumping slightly, she trained her arrow on the forest around them, but there was nothing there.

"Don't worry. I'll hear anything before it's close enough to hurt us," Ash said. Eishoxa put down her bow, feeling rather foolish and replied, "Well, that's reassuring." Ash sat down on the ground and Eishoxa crouched next to him, wondering why he had suddenly stopped collecting wood.

"Don't we need to hurry up?" she asked. When she looked up, he had a very strange look on his face as he stared back at her. "What is it?" she said.

"What do you think?"

"I don't know."

He sighed. "Then it's nothing."

Eishoxa looked at him. "It obviously is … "

He met her gaze evenly. "All I'll say is that you weren't always like that with Ember."

Eishoxa felt another ripple of anger. She picked up a piece of wood and snapped it in half. "Oh, you mean in my 'other' life?"

"Why are you angry?"

"Because you're all so closed! You expect me to know all these things, and then no one will tell me anything about it. And when I don't know anything about it – because I don't – then you all get angry because I make mistakes."

"That is our nature, Eishoxa," he reminded her gently. "We expect a lot."

"Why doesn't he listen?" Eishoxa repeated.

"It is not in his nature to listen," Ash said.

Eishoxa picked up another piece of wood from the ground and stood up. "Let's go back," she snapped. Through her haze of anger she felt a pang of sympathy for Ash, who stood there so humbly, but she was too angry to apologise for her outbursts. Why did Ember treat her like a child? Why was he so patronising? According to all the dragons, she was the most important person living in this strange world. So why did he do it? Her mind drifted unwillingly to what she'd heard Ash say in the desert, but then she wrenched her thoughts back to the present. That was neither here nor now.

She could hear Ash's light tread even more clearly than her own loud steps. How did he keep his temper so well? The more time Eishoxa spent with the Indocani, the more she realised something: Ember was the image of a perfect Indocani – impulsive, arrogant, strong and brave. But others had aspects of serenity and calmness about them, like Ash and Rianox. Some could keep their temper and some couldn't. It was ironic, she reflected bitterly, that at this moment in time, she was acting more like an Indocani than Ash.

Arriving back at the clearing, Eishoxa dropped the wood next to Ember, who was crouching in the middle, and stalked over to Zeexa. The dragon rubbed her head soothingly against Eishoxa's arm. "*It will be all right*," she repeated.

Ember, relaxed and confident, was feeding the fire in the centre, but Ash and Smoke were less so. Eishoxa could see them looking around nervously as they unpacked their belongings and sorted out their packs. Ember straightened.

"Will you stop looking so scared?" he drawled. "Nothing is here."

"Are you blind as well as stupid?" Eishoxa snapped. Zeexa growled warningly as Ferac's head jerked around, his teeth bared. Ember glared at her. "Look around you," she continued. "The rest of us can tell that we shouldn't be here. There's something here that doesn't want us in this forest."

"We are warriors," he hissed back. "We've decided to stay here and we will, and anything that comes to try to move us we will fight."

"Have you ever tried to turn back the tide?" she retorted. "You can't fight everything, Ember. You don't always get enemies like that."

"What are you suggesting?" he asked.

"I'm saying that the forest might not want us here." A wind stirred through the trees. Ember turned his back on her. "That's ridiculous.

There's no one here."

Eishoxa was still prepared to fight, but Ash laid a hand on her arm. "Enough now, Eishoxa. You aren't going to make him change his mind."

She brushed him off. "Yes, that's what I'm afraid of. He's going to get everyone killed. Even if he's right about this, one day he'll regret it."

That evening, Eishoxa only picked at her food. She no longer had the same urge to eat as before. The Indocani ate very little. Rianox had said it was because they were fuelled by the fire that grew within them. Food didn't matter to them, and they couldn't drink any liquid except the one they brewed themselves. Water, of course, was out of the question.

"Ember is still watching you," Zeexa said, shuffling over to Eishoxa. She looked up and caught Ember's eye. He looked away first. *"Just stop provoking him,"* Zeexa offered. *"You're constantly looking for a fight."*

Eishoxa stiffened with indignation. *"No, I'm not!"* she protested. *"Can't you sense it? A fire in this place is lethal, for all of us."*

"That is what it looks like to everyone else. And that is what everyone else is thinking. Ignore him. He's trying to make you angry and you're the one who's suffering. As for the forest, there is something strange about it," admitted the dragon. *"But at times like this, we need fire more than ever. Look."* And she lifted her nose in the direction of their companions. The dragons were snorting sparks into the growing dark. Ash was sharpening his arrows with a glowing stone, Smoke was lying on his back, watching as flames grew around his arms, and Ember was crouching by the fire in the centre. *"They all need their fire. They need to know that they're safe."*

"If they got rid of it, we would all be safer."

"Sometimes," the dragon reflected wisely, *"mistakes are the best way to learn. They cannot learn if they do not see them. Have no fear, Eishoxa. I will give my life to protect you. You're the daughter of the Great Goddess, and you're one of my friends."*

The sincerity in Zeexa's voice calmed Eishoxa somewhat. She rested her head against Zeexa's warm neck and smiled. *"And I yours, Zeexa. And I yours."*

CHAPTER 5

"WHO WILL TAKE the first watch?" Ember's voice startled Eishoxa out of her reverie. She struggled to sit up and awakened Zeexa in the process.

"I will," she said. Ember looked around. "No, Princess, not you."

"Yes, I will," she said. "I would like to, actually."

"Just because you would like to, it doesn't mean you can do it."

Eishoxa remembered what Zeexa had said, but the words tripped off her tongue before she could stop them. "Who is in charge again, Ember?" Her tone was light but he caught the meaning behind it. She picked up her bow and took a station next to the tree. "I'll wake you if anything comes."

"You might hear it too late," argued Ember. Smoke cut in. "Let her be, Ember. If she wants to take it, she can take it. Let the rest of us sleep."

"Fine," Ember said. "Wake me up when you want to sleep." He lay down next to Ferac who was already asleep.

"*Goodnight, Eishoxa,*" muttered Zeexa sleepily. Eishoxa smiled fondly. "*Goodnight, Zeexa.*"

The forest was quieter at night, but the wind blew just as loudly. Eishoxa stood next to the tree until her legs ached and then she sat down and rested her head against the trunk instead. Her bow was ready if trouble should arise. She glanced at Ember from across the clearing. His face was so different when he slept. The lines on his forehead and around his mouth faded almost completely and made his face look softer and more likeable. In the soft glow of the fire, he looked like he could be someone different. The proud look, though still on his face, was unblemished by anger or annoyance. It looked noble rather than arrogant. Ash had suggested that she and Ember had been in love once. Although Eishoxa could never see herself falling in love with anyone, looking at Ember in the fire, she almost changed her mind. He stirred and turned over so that all Eishoxa could see now were black shadows flickering across his tattooed skin.

Eishoxa turned her attention to the fire. It was dying down and the embers were casting strange shadows on the ground around them. She looked down at her palm. In the light, her pale brown skin looked a different shade entirely. The flames that Smoke had made still danced over his body, but more slowly now, a more stately dance.

Eishoxa stretched out her fingers. There was no harm in trying, and no one would know if nothing happened. But she had to know. She had to know whether she could be like them as well and control fire with a look or a thought or a gesture. She remembered the night of the banquet when the fire had failed to recognise her, when it had told her in its own way that she was not ready for it yet. Was she ready now? Would she ever be ready?

Concentrating on the flames, her eyes tightly shut, she asked it to blaze up, to rise. She opened her eyes. Nothing had happened. It wasn't working. She turned her attention to her hand. Could she make the fire blaze on her hand, as she'd seen Ember do? Taking a deep breath, she closed her eyes and concentrated once again. This time she tried a different approach. She pictured the flames rolling up over her wrist and her hand and her fingers, long tongues of fiery heat and light, burning hot to start with but then cooling and disappearing. And then other thoughts filled her head, thoughts of fire blooming like dangerous wildflowers, thoughts of the trees surrounded by fire, like wreaths on their heads and feet. She imagined the flames circling the trunks in a deadly embrace and saw how the bark charred and burned, coiling off in flaming curls. In the back of her head, she heard the music that she'd heard at the banquet, the fast-paced wild music, the music that the phoenix had risen to, had appeared to.

She opened her eyes just a slit and saw another hand connected to her wrist, a hand clothed in blazing lights. She had done it. She could do it. But then she felt something dragging her back. The images disappeared as quickly as they'd come. And a firm voice said, '*No, not yet*'.

And then a cold wind blew and Eishoxa lost it. She was crouching on the ground as though poised for flight, and her hand was extended towards the fire that had almost gone out. The sky was much darker than she remembered. How long had she been crouching there? It felt like a matter of minutes. She shook her head to clear her thoughts and then stood up. It was no use. She wasn't ready. A great tiredness hit her all of a sudden and she reeled backwards, almost falling over flat. Stumbling across to Ember, she bent down and shook him.

"Ember, wake up," she whispered. He rolled back towards her and she stood again. But before she could move away, he grabbed her hand. "Are you going away again?"

Eishoxa jumped. "What do you mean?"

"Stay a little longer," he said quietly. "You can wait. You promised me, remember?" Eishoxa tried to pull her hand out of his. His eyes opened but it took him a moment to register where he was. She stared down at him, shocked. Trying to understand why she was staring at him, he noticed his hand and let go immediately. "I'm sorry. I was dreaming." Eishoxa nodded. He jumped to his feet. "Do you want to sleep now?" She nodded again but didn't move. "All right, then go."

"You asked me whether I going away again," Eishoxa said slowly. "Where did I go before?"

He sighed and looked away.

"Where was I going, Ember?"

"To Bareth."

"Oh." Eishoxa swallowed.

Ember smiled wryly. "I didn't want you to go, but you didn't listen to me. I don't think you ever have listened to me." His mouth curled up in a smile, but it wasn't directed at her. He was reminiscing about the past, the past that had been and the present that could have been. The present that should have been.

"Well, nothing happened," she said. "Out in the forest, I mean."

He left his reverie behind. "Quite," he nodded stiffly. "Well, goodnight, Eishoxa."

"Goodnight." She settled herself across the fire next to Zeexa, then said, "Ember?" He looked over at her. In this light he still looked as he had when he was sleeping. Or maybe it was because it was just the two of them.

"Yes?"

"Why did I go to Bareth?"

He smiled sadly. "Go to sleep, Eishoxa. We'll cross the Cursed Marshes tomorrow. You need your strength."

She was too tired to argue. Sleep felt like a huge warm blanket falling gently over her eyelids and absorbing her into its depths.

CHAPTER 6

Eishoxa looked down at the Cursed Marshes. They had earned their name: there was a reek of death about them and no sign of life anywhere. Rivers flowed sluggishly and the air was hard to breathe in because it was so cold and wet. Eishoxa shuddered violently and called out to Ember, "Can we not fly higher?"

He looked over at her. "No. The air gets even colder higher up, and thinner. We can't risk it."

Eishoxa patted Zeexa in concern. "But I think Zeexa is suffering." Ember gave the dragon a once-over before meeting Eishoxa's gaze again. "It won't be long. She'll survive." He urged Ferac on a little faster and Eishoxa fell behind.

"*I don't like the smell and the damp,*" Zeexa's wispy voice sounded in Eishoxa's mind.

Eishoxa looked at her anxiously. The dragon's eyes were half-closing and her breathing was shallow and weak. She could barely manage to keep her wings flapping and they were steadily losing height. "*Zeexa! Come on! Just a bit further!*"

A shout came from up ahead. "Eishoxa! Hurry up! Get back up here!" It was Ember. Eishoxa turned her head and yelled furiously, "Zeexa's struggling. She's younger than the rest of your dragons!"

Then came another shout from Ash, more urgent this time. "No! Eishoxa! Look out!"

She caught a glimpse of the three dragons pelting towards her before something hard hit Eishoxa on the back and she lost her seat, tumbling off Zeexa's back and plummeting towards the water below. Zeexa wailed as her rider fell. Then something caught the neck of Eishoxa's shirt and shook her fiercely, like a cat with a mouse. Teeth snapped at her, breaking the skin on her neck and slashing at her arms. Her bow was no protection. Vaguely she heard screams and yells from above her, but all she could focus on were two facts: she was still falling, and she was being attacked. There was a sudden blast of fire and beside her something screeched, like metal on metal and so loud that it set Eishoxa's ears ringing. The teeth let go of her but still she fell, down, down, down. The water was coming closer and closer, and the stench of the marsh seemed minor compared to the pain in her neck and ears. Then something else seized her around the waist and dumped her on a scaly surface.

"For goodness' sake, Princess, are you incapable of doing anything by yourself?"

Eishoxa could have cried with relief on hearing Ember's irritable voice behind her. One of his arms was wrapped tightly around her and in his other hand he carried his bow. They soared back up into the sky, where Ash and Smoke were protecting the still weak Zeexa and warding off the attacks of four or five strange beasts, half insect, half snake, which hissed and spat and swung long tails at them. They had gigantic wings and disproportionately small bodies, but every inch of them was covered in long, thin spikes which could kill a dragon and its rider with one well-placed blow. The twins, working as a team, were defending themselves with fire and weapon. Ash slashed viciously at the noses and eyes while Smoke circled, crouching high on his dragon, Kereth, and shot arrows into their sides.

"We've got Eishoxa! Clear out! Clear out!"

Smoke looked up at the sound of Ember's voice and sat lower on Kereth, urging her forward. She engulfed another of the beasts in a blast of fire and it dropped like a stone, half its side on fire and the other wings burnt and useless.

"Come on! Clear out!"

Smoke drew Kereth up to Ferac's neck and, taking Eishoxa's hand, pulled her off Ferac, flipped her over Kereth and landed her safely on Zeexa. Somehow all her belongings had survived, but most of her arrows had been lost in the first tumble. Hooking her feet into the hollows of Zeexa's shoulders for support, she turned and took aim at one of the beast's eyes. Her arrow took out its left eye, and Smoke's arrow, following on from hers, embedded itself in the right eye. Blinded and in agony, the creature took off lopsidedly towards the forest. The remaining three lost courage and backed off.

Ash wheeled Jerath around, heading back to his companions. He flew on the other side of Zeexa, so that Eishoxa was flanked on both sides. Ash stowed his sword and swung his bow off his shoulder, keeping it trained behind them in case the beasts came back. Eishoxa did the same.

After a while, Ember called for a stop and the three circled him. He turned on Eishoxa furiously. "What was that? A great lot of good it does us if we get you this far and you die within sight of the place!"

"It wasn't her fault, Ember," said Ash, putting his hand on Ember's shoulder, but it was shrugged off.

"Of course it was. You fell behind. You couldn't keep up. We can't keep our eyes on you every second of the day. You have to do some work."

"It wasn't my fault," retorted Eishoxa. "The air made Zeexa sick! In case you haven't noticed, she's the youngest of the four dragons here and doing a great job of keeping up." Ember opened his mouth to reply, but Eishoxa cut across him again. "Just because you believe something, Ember, it doesn't make it true." Ember looked as if he wanted to say a lot more, but he swallowed it down. Wheeling Ferac sharply around, he flew off again. Smoke and Ash took their positions and the whole party started to move.

"The Cursed Marshes are behind us," shouted Ember from where he sat on Ferac. "Keep together and protect Eishoxa! Those things might come back! Head on to Dulcacohefen!" Their three pursuers shrieked furiously in the distance and flapped their huge wings. Their hoarse screams sounded like crows. She patted Zeexa's shoulder.

"Are you all right?"

"Yes, of course. I wasn't even touched."

There was a faint trace of bitterness in Zeexa's voice, and when Eishoxa looked to her right she saw why. Ferac was bleeding slightly from a wound on his flank, but that wasn't what caught Eishoxa's attention. He was looking very superior and aloof, and when Eishoxa looked at him he gave her a little mocking look. Eishoxa met his gaze and patted Zeexa comfortingly. *"We'll have our chance. He didn't do anything really. Jerath and Kereth did most of the work and Smoke and Ash did the rest. Ignore him, Zeexa. It's none of your fault."*

She felt Zeexa's guilt at dropping her like a headache in her temples. As she patted Zeexa's shoulder, she tried to sooth her. *"It hit me from behind! There was nothing you could have done!"*

"I dropped you," she wailed. *"And Ferac picked you up. I'm useless!"*

"You're not!" she said firmly. *"Ember picked me up. He was the one that caught me. It just so happened that Ferac was his dragon – it had nothing to do with him. Don't worry, Zeexa; you haven't let yourself or me down at all."*

She spurred Zeexa forward slightly and Ferac and Ember fell in behind them. Ash and Smoke had joined Ember to form an arrowhead behind Eishoxa so she was in front. She wanted to see Dulcacohefen first. Because of the attack, they had lost altitude and the wind blew hard, making it hard for them to rise. But having cleared the Cursed Marshes, Zeexa seemed much improved and flew with her previous strength. Ahead of them, the ground rose steeply in a massive hill, but beyond that, Ember had said, lay Dulcacohefen. The two of them, dragon and rider, rose and rose and rose, with the other three falling further and further behind as Zeexa flew even faster. The smell of death and rot had gone and instead a cold, clean, clear smell filled the air. Eishoxa sniffed, sensing what it was, yet unable to put a finger on it. Just as they cleared the ridge she identified it and breathed it in awe as her eyes took in what she was seeing.

It was ice. Not far below them was an open water lily made entirely out of transparent ice. Each of its petals was intricately carved, with holes and little platforms protruding gracefully from the sides. The lily sat on a huge lake, off which ran roaring rivers and thundering waterfalls. Far away, beyond the lily, Eishoxa could see mountains – beautiful, dignified mountains, older than anything she had seen before, even in Bareth. Eishoxa took another deep breath of the cold air, so clean and so free from any scent of smoke or dust. It seared through her, but not as the water had done. It hurt in a good way.

"Dulcacohefen," she whispered and for some reason she felt as if … as if she had come home. This place was beautiful.

An unearthly quiet hung over this land. She could see no one at all. There was no great shouting and clapping to welcome her here. There was nobody. And Eishoxa shivered with excitement; she loved it already.

"Isn't it beautiful?" she murmured to Zeexa and felt a faint plse of amusement. *"Well, I prefer our woods to this place of cold and wet, but … if you say so."*

"But it's so pretty, isn't it?"

She hadn't realised she was speaking out loud. So enthralled was she by the sight ahead of her that, when Ember spoke sharply, she jumped. "We are not here for the beauty. We are here on war business.

And remember, their haven may look beautiful, but the people do not reflect the glory of their home." He took over the lead and the others followed. Looking back over his shoulder, Ember called, "I've alerted them to our presence. You should see movement soon."

Sure enough, several seconds later a tiny figure, arms waving, appeared on the tip of petal closest to them. Ember pointed. "There! Head for over there!" Eishoxa wheeled Zeexa round and they streamed through the air. The cold wind, although not comfortable, was not painful to endure and she breathed it in deeply, grateful to be away from the stench of the Cursed Marshes. As they prepared for a dive, circling about the little figure, Eishoxa tried to get a better glimpse of him, but he was too small and was blocked from view by Zeexa's wings.

"Ready?" the dragon asked, and Eishoxa nodded. Zeexa dived, pursued closely by Ferac. Jerath and Kereth followed behind, and the whole party landed one after another. Eishoxa dismounted and turned. The Ewdicani was standing back slightly and, judging by the anxious look on his face, he didn't like the dragons much. Rianox had said that the Ewdicani were completely different, and now Eishoxa realised he hadn't been exaggerating. He was tall for a human, but still shorter than Ember. His skin was white, and tinged with the palest possible shade of blue around the edges of his face. His blue eyes were as dark as midnight and his hair cerulean, like the sky on a clear day. It was far shorter than that of the Indocani and slicked back against his skull. He had very thin limbs and very small hands and bare feet. Zeexa gave him a quick glance and said to Eishoxa, *"I don't like him. He smells weird."* Eishoxa had to hide a laugh.

Ember jumped down from Ferac and strode over to the Ewdicani. "Ember," he announced, bowing. The Ewdicani pressed his hands together and pushed them towards Ember, bending his knees and head as he did so. Eishoxa thought he looked very funny and had to smother another giggle. Ash gave her a little smile and then folded his lips and shook his head, telling her not to laugh.

"Greetings." The Ewdicani spoke with a very distinctive accent, quite different from the Indocani. Eishoxa likened it to Maya's, although her friend's accent wasn't as strong. "My name is Leap, and I'm honoured to welcome you to Dulcacohefen." He made the same welcoming gesture to Ash and Smoke and then to Eishoxa, although he paused before doing so and gave her a hard glance. Eishoxa, surprised, had the feeling he didn't like her very much. Leap gestured to Ember.

"I will take you to the Lily Hall. Lady Gresceva will be there and will like to meet you." He gave the dragons another glance. "Your dragons may come with us, but I ask, for the duration of your time here, that they be stationed outside."

Ember nodded but then said, "The idea was that they would return until we had finished business here." Leap nodded and shrugged, gave Eishoxa another glare and led the way down the petal.

"He doesn't like you at all," Zeexa warned. *"I can sense mistrust in him."* Eishoxa started at this. *"Why? Can you tell?"*

"No. His thoughts are carefully guarded, but his emotions hang around him."

The two of them were the last of the group. As Eishoxa stepped onto the ice, she winced slightly. The cold bit at her feet, but the others were walking perfectly fine and so Eishoxa stepped after them. Looking down through the ice, she could see another layer of petals underneath, distorted slightly. "Do you really have to go?" she asked Zeexa.

The dragon gave a little sigh. "I don't want to, but apparently we must. The Ewdicani don't like you, and it's just too much to have four dragons around who are in constant danger of burning and defacing all this stuff," and she tapped the ice with a claw. "We're trying to get them to like us, remember?"

Eishoxa sighed sadly. "I don't want you to go." Zeexa nuzzled her shoulder. "I don't want to go either. But if you concentrate and get this done quickly, then you will be home soon."

"Hurry up, you two," shouted Ember irritably from ahead of them. "You're always so slow." The others were disappearing into the side of the petal, and Eishoxa could just see the tip of Ferac's tail whisk out of sight down a long tunnel. Ember waited a moment and then stepped inside. Zeexa and Eishoxa followed suit. The ice tunnel echoed mournfully with every step they took. The result was a strange vibrating noise that filled the space. Eishoxa ran her hand over the wall and shuddered at the strange cold. The tunnel sloped slowly downwards, not enough to make them slide but enough for Eishoxa to take each step carefully.

Ember looked behind. "Are you all right?"

Eishoxa nodded curtly. "I'm fine," she replied without thinking. Ember's slightly softened demeanour hardened again and he turned away from her. Eishoxa sighed. Ever since the incident in the Forest of No Flame, she'd found it even hard to look at him, let alone speak to him. This just made everything so much worse. Zeexa touched her hand with her nose, and Eishoxa smiled at her gratefully. She had told the dragon, but Zeexa had no advice to give Eishoxa. What had happened had happened, was all she could say.

The tunnel widened slowly to open into a circular cave made entirely of very faint-blue ice. Eishoxa could only think how pretty it was. All around, tunnels entered into the cave, and in its centre was a small pool fed by two trickling streams of clear water. Leap led them around the pool to take the tunnel opposite. This one was much shorter; after a couple of minutes' walking it opened into a hall, about the same size as the Great Hall under the Tree. Eishoxa could only stop and gape. Never had she seen a room more beautiful than this one. Above them was the centre of the ice lily. The ice of the ceiling was palest blue like the previous cave, but the colour darkened down the fluted columns until, at floor level, the ice was indigo. Green streaks ran through the floor and walls like the iridescence of fish scales.

They entered at the end of the hall, through massive double doors At the far end, on a dais, Eishoxa could make out a chair shaped like an open shell, made completely from mother-of-pearl; she couldn't see who was sitting in it because the chair faced away. Leap meanwhile led the way towards the centre of the room and then up the hall towards the chair. Apart from them and two Ewdicani stationed on either side of the chair, the hall was empty. Eishoxa was painfully aware of the loud noise their steps made against the ice floor. As they approached the stairs of the dais, the two guards turned the chair slowly around to face the visitors.

Eishoxa shivered at the iciness that surrounded the woman. She sat upon the chair as if it were a throne, and when she stood it was with the grace and elegance of a queen. Eishoxa was strongly reminded of Vera, but this woman looked nothing like Vera. She was dressed from head to foot in a long, light, many-layered dress of blue and white. Covering her shoulders and hanging all around her were various shawls, all different lengths and colours. Around her forehead she wore a white band on which glowed a large white stone, and as she made her way down the stairs Eishoxa could see that her light blue hair tumbled down her back in a wavy waterfall, far longer than Leap's. She looked very gentle and kind, but her eyes, once fixed on Eishoxa, became cold and unforgiving. Eishoxa held her gaze but felt nervous. What she had done she couldn't begin to guess. Ember followed the woman's gaze and gave Eishoxa a warning look as if telling her not to speak. Leap pressed his hands together and moved them towards the woman, bending his knees deeply. She nodded to him, gave a little smile and waved him away.

"Greetings," said Gresceva, stopping a few paces in front of them and clasping her hands together loosely. She let her gaze travel over them all and nodded to Ember. "I remember you from the last time we were here. Tell me, do you bring news from my sister, Vera?"

Eishoxa blinked in surprise. She had not realised they were sisters.

"They're not blood sisters," Zeexa explained quickly, sensing Eishoxa's puzzlement. *"They both interpret the will of a Goddess and they're sisters like that. She is known as the Protector."*

On closer scrutiny, Eishoxa could see Gresceva was wearing a tiny flame pin on one of the shawls swung over her shoulder, and she smiled wryly. Vera would never wear anything that reminded her of the Ewdicani. Her disgust for them was very clear. Ember bowed to her. "I do indeed bring news, my Lady, if you remember our message."

She smiled. "Ah yes, I remember. Well, we will consider it and I will gather my Assembly to discuss it with you further."

Leap stepped forward at that and pointed to Ash and Smoke. "And these are Sires Ash and Smoke."

She barely glanced at them, but trained her cold gaze on Eishoxa, who forced herself not to look away. Zeexa shrank back from her. *"I don't like her. She smells so strange. And there is hate in her."*

"For me?"

"Yes, and for others. It is so strong."

Eishoxa said nothing. Gresceva's smile widened slightly. "And of course we have our Princess Eishoxa back in our midst." Eishoxa nod-

123

ded but made no move to bow to her.

"Tell me, Eishoxa, did you enjoy your time with the Oblivious?"

"She means the Ignorant," Zeexa butted in quickly, and Eishoxa nodded slowly, wondering where on earth this conversation was going. She saw Leap smile slightly and had the feeling they were laughing at her.

Ember gave her a quick glance and stepped forward, cutting through. Eishoxa looked at him gratefully. "My Lady. Although this is very strange – and we do not understand it either – Eishoxa has no recollection of the last time she was here. She does not remember what she said or did, and on her behalf we are here to make amends."

Gresceva's expression did not alter, but her piercing gaze turned to Ember. She looked around at Leap, who nodded once to her, and then she turned back to Ember. "That is strange. I can sense no lie in your words and neither can Leap, which means you must be telling the truth. But I can sense the Princess Eishoxa that we know inside this person." She gestured at Eishoxa.

"I'm sorry," Eishoxa broke in, and all eyes turned towards her. Glancing around at everyone, she saw mostly hostility in their stares and swallowed nervously. She looked back at Gresceva. "But what did I do?"

Ash winced and Smoke looked down at the ground. Even Ember looked uncomfortable. Gresceva, however, gave a little tinkling laugh. "If you cannot remember, then we will save it until you do. It will make an enjoyable story. Now," she said, noticing that Eishoxa was going to protest, "Leap will show you to your rooms. We will have to have you put in the petals because you can't stay in the water, can you? Leap?"

But they hadn't taken three steps when she said, "And where will your dragons stay?"

"We will send them home, my Lady," Ember answered quickly. "They will be gone before nightfall." She nodded and returned to her chair to watch them leave the hall.

CHAPTER 7

They exited the hall through the double doors. The minute they were outside, Eishoxa looked around curiously. Three tunnels faced them: one straight ahead, one to the left, one to the right, and they undulated here and there to fit the shape of the lily. The walls were covered in paintings and drapes, the floor was strewn with lily leaves, and the whole place was rather dim.

Leap led them along the right tunnel, moving briskly, and Eishoxa thought this was a shame because she wanted to look around more carefully. A harp was playing somewhere and the Ewdicani they met moved silently, with their heads bowed. The atmosphere was one of absolute calm and peacefulness. After the wild weeks with the Indocani, Eishoxa couldn't imagine anything more soothing. Leap stopped rather abruptly in front of a pair of double doors. They were made of intricately carved wood and the handles were shaped like two leaping dolphins. He pointed to them.

"Sires Ember, Ash and Smoke, this room is for you. Lady Eishoxa, please could you follow me." Eishoxa noticed Ember watching rather suspiciously as they walked away, but he looked a little happier when Zeexa followed. He doesn't trust them, she realised, probably because of what I did when I was last here.

"*Ember thinks they'll punish you,*" Zeexa muttered.

Eishoxa drew closer to her. "*How did you know that?*"

"*He's thinking so loudly I could've heard it from the Tree,*" was the reply. "*Yes,*" Zeexa continued as Eishoxa put her hand on the dragon's neck, "*stay very close to me. I'll protect you.*"

They followed Leap much further along the tunnel, and Eishoxa was just plucking up the courage to ask him more about what had happened the last time she was there when he stopped in front of another set of double doors.

"And my Lady, this is for you." He glanced at Zeexa, then continued. "There is a balcony where your dragon can stay until she leaves." He bent his knees to her and then headed back down the corridor.

"Thank you," Eishoxa called after him, but he had disappeared. She gave Zeexa a nervous glance and then stepped through the double doors. They opened very smoothly and made no sound. Zeexa followed through. The minute they were inside, Eishoxa shivered. In the far corner of the room, another set of double doors were open and white curtains flapped in the icy breeze. She closed the doors immediately and drew the thin curtains across the windows.

"It's very cold," she remarked. But that was the only complaint she could make about the place. It wasn't a large room, about the same size as her room at the Tree. The ceiling curved slightly to the right – because she was in the top of the petal – and was decorated with all the constellations of the night sky. Eishoxa looked up at them with wonder and turned in a circle. There were many that she recognised from the desert sky in Bareth – a lion, a warrior, a bull – but others were unfamiliar: fish and birds and strange creatures with forked tails.

A crescent moon arched over them protectively. The floor was covered in blue material, as thin and gauzy as the curtains, and the walls were decorated similarly with a green material. It was very simply furnished with nothing but a cloth hammock, strung from the ceiling and covered with a thick, dark green blanket, and a little basin in the corner. Propped up against one wall was a large wooden flute; Eishoxa wondered when it had last been played.

Zeexa stood by the door, looking around with interest. Eishoxa couldn't help but notice how very strange Zeexa looked with her bright orange and black amongst the cool, plain colours. Eishoxa swung her bag off her shoulder and took out the scrolls that Rianox had given her. Looking down at them, she wondered what Rianox was doing now and whether he was missing her as she was missing him and Amber. Sighing, she put them on the hammock, took her bow off her shoulder and stowed it away in her pack. So far, she'd seen nothing to suggest the Ewdicani even knew what war was, let alone that there was one being fought. She said this to Zeexa who blinked thoughtfully.

"*Well, as you can see,*" she replied, turning her head from side to side, "*they don't care for much but art and beauty.*"

"*It is beautiful,*" Eishoxa protested, and Zeexa chuckled. "*Yes, Eishoxa, it is beautiful, but it's said that the Sorrowful Mountains had their own kind of beauty, and look what happened to them. I've heard from many of the older dragons that this place doesn't care for defence or attack of any kind, and what use is that? If the Empty come here, then this race will be wiped out.*"

"*Which is why we are here,*" Eishoxa said determinedly, taking all her clothes out of the bag and folding them again. "*We'll make them see that they need to help us, for their good just as much as ours.*"

Zeexa's tongue darted in and out of her mouth with amusement. "*Wise words, little one, but not here. Don't say things like that too loudly. I doubt Gresceva would be much impressed.*"

Eishoxa picked up her folded clothes and put them on top of the scrolls on the hammock. Then she took the pile and placed it all back in her bag, dropping it to the floor. "I don't like Gresceva," she said out loud, and Zeexa growled in agreement.

"*Very few people do. Her general state of mind is very strange.*"

"She's meant to be a gentle leader, according to Rianox," Eishoxa grumbled aloud.

Zeexa made a little sound of amusement. "*Vera is meant to be a noble leader.*"

Eishoxa turned around in amazement. "*I thought you were meant to respect her.*"

Zeexa snorted. "*Respect is a very different thing from liking. Very few of the dragons actually like her. She has changed from the fine leader she once was. I don't know what it is, but there is a strange dishonesty in her now, as if she's holding a great secret that she shouldn't have.*"

Eishoxa turned this over in her head for a while and then shrugged. "I have my secrets; you have yours."

"*Not like Vera. She holds bad secrets. And as leader, her actions affect all of us.*"

Eishoxa laughed at the little dragon's intensity. *"Well, I don't think I can worry about her now. I have enough to do."* She leaned against Zeexa's shoulder and absentmindedly stroked her head. *"And anyway, what will you do now?"* She could feel the start of a purr gathering in Zeexa's throat, but when she spoke, the purr disappeared.

"We dragons have been speaking. We must leave before the night comes. I, for one, don't want to cross the Cursed Marshes in the night. They may not belong to the Ewdicani, but these Peacemakers are not fond of us, no matter what they say, and I wouldn't put it past them to try to injure us in some way as we cross them."

Eishoxa laughed. *"You don't think very highly of many people, do you?"*

Zeexa turned her head so her large, snake-like eye was fixed on Eishoxa. *"Very few. But then again, it's in the nature of a dragon to be suspicious. It's how we survive."*

"Are you suspicious of me then?"

Zeexa laughed and it came out as a faint rumble in her throat. *"No. I've been your dragon for some time now, and I can sense no dishonesty coming from you or any attempts to hide anything."*

Eishoxa nodded. *"So when will you go?"*

"When the other dragons are ready."

"I don't want you to go, Zeexa. Without you, I'll only have Ember to speak to."

"Maybe that's a good thing," and Eishoxa could see a little mischievous hint in her eye. She playfully slapped Zeexa on the neck. *"Stop it now. You know that that's not what will happen. And that time is past – as you said, if you remember."*

"It is past, but there's no reason why it can't come again."

Eishoxa graced the comment with a small smile and then sighed. No matter what she did, she couldn't get the image of Leap out of her mind and how much he had openly disliked her. *"Zeexa … do you know what I was meant to have done the last time I was here?"*

Zeexa gave another thoughtful growl. *"No. None of the dragons talk about it, and I can't discover it from any of these Peacemakers."*

"You don't like them very much, do you?" smiled Eishoxa.

Zeexa gave a small hiss. *"I don't like anything I don't understand, like the Forest of No Flame, and the creatures that attacked us in the Cursed Marshes."*

"The Forest of No Flame?" said Eishoxa, and Zeexa growled in agreement. *"I don't understand it either. But that doesn't matter. You don't have to be scared of it because of that."*

Zeexa looked up at her, surprised. *"Strange words, Eishoxa. You should be careful of what you say – and what you don't say as well. A lot rests on that here."*

Eishoxa didn't say anything. She looked once more around the room, at all the beauty in which her dragon looked so out of place, and knew that Zeexa was warning her: that although Eishoxa had been given this, it was all for show. For some reason, these people hated her, and it was in her best interest to remember that.

127

Once again, just as with Maya, Eishoxa felt that the time for Zeexa's departure came far too quickly. The two of them had decided to part on the balcony of her room, instead of going to meet the others. Eishoxa shivered in the cold air that blew and looked over the land of ice and cold, a land she had never belonged to, not in Bareth and not here. A land that was filled with hostility towards fire and everything that she held dear, yet it was this country that she had to make peace with.

"*Fly fast and fly safely. Good luck!*" she said to Zeexa, rubbing her nose.

The dragon blinked her orange eyes. "*And you,*" she replied. "*Come back home soon, Eishoxa.*"

Home. Where was that? Eishoxa nodded, but she felt a rush of unease at the dragon's assumption that she was going to stay. As if everything she wanted was right there. Pushing these thoughts away, Eishoxa smiled at her and stepped back to give the dragon room to spread her wings. And although Eishoxa felt sad that she was not riding with Zeexa, she realised that Zeexa did not belong here, that this creature of fire and heat and destruction did not belong amidst the beauty and tranquillity of this place.

Zeexa was rising slowly, beating her wings against the cold and wind. "*Take care!*" Eishoxa shouted, waving her arm above her head.

Zeexa, unable to breathe fire here, lashed her tail from side to side and called back to Eishoxa, "*And you! Be careful! Come back soon!*" And then she whisked around, flying back towards the Tree, flying back towards her home. As Eishoxa watched, she saw the three other dragons rise to join her, flying together towards the dying sun.

CHAPTER 8

With Zeexa and the other dragons gone, Eishoxa felt lonelier than ever. She wandered back inside her room and closed the doors against the icy draught. Not only was she trapped in this strange place, but everyone here hated her for something she couldn't even remember. She swung lithely into her hammock and rocked from side to side; the sensation was oddly soothing, and she briefly closed her eyes. Then, sitting up again, she opened her bag and took out the scrolls Rianox had given her. Carefully opening one, she stared down at the strange, sharp edges of the letters on the page and sighed. She would never understand it, even if she had improved.

She returned the scrolls to her bag and took out her bow and quiver. Laying it on the green blanket, she reflected on the fact that it looked so strange, lying there on the cool, even colour. The quiver was decorated in harsh lines, as if an unskilled craftsman had hacked at the wood. She laid her own hand on the covers and looked at it. Her skin was olive-coloured, not quite white and not quite brown, but a balanced mix. But it looked better lying on the sea-green gauzy cover than on the thick, garish orange one she had in her pack. She took out the little black cloth she used to clean her arrows and polished them until they were so shiny she could see her reflection in them. Then she did the same with her three knives. Looking into the shiny metal, she remembered how Smoke, Ash and Ember had so casually handled them, had so casually dealt with prey.

There was a quiet knock on the door. Eishoxa scrambled out of the hammock, tumbling gracelessly to the floor. "Come in," she called, straightening her clothing.

Leap pushed open the door, giving Eishoxa a suspicious glance before briefly bending his knees to her. Then he caught sight of her weapons lying in full view on the hammock. His eyes widened in horror. "Lady Eishoxa, I hope you do not intend to use those here," he said.

Eishoxa followed his eyes and gave a small intake of breath. "Oh no," she replied with what she hoped was a reassuring air. "No, I was just cleaning them."

He glared at her. Taking one more step into her room, he closed the door slightly, as if to tell her something in confidence. "My Lady, you would not have to clean them if you did not use them," he answered.

She nodded. "I'll put them away."

"Right now, if you would. No weapons are permitted here." Eishoxa glanced at him to see whether he was serious and he was nodding at her expectantly. She stuffed the things pell-mell back into the bag and tied the straps down. The corner of her bow poked conspicuously out of the top. Leap's gaze lingered on it for a moment longer before he turned to face Eishoxa. "Lady Eishoxa, you have been asked by Lady Gresceva to come and join her in the Lily Hall," he proclaimed formally.

"Right," Eishoxa answered.

"This is a great honour," Leap added. He paused. "My Lady does not usually give up this much time for guests." He paused again. He had a strange way of speaking, as though each slimy word slipped over his tongue and out of his mouth like some creature emerging slowly from its hole. "But of course you, my Lady, are a special guest." He waited again and then said finally, "When it is time to go, someone else will come and get you."

"Thank you," she said. Leap nodded. He glanced again at her hammock. "And, my Lady, remember – no weapons. If you cannot follow this rule, they will be confiscated and destroyed. We are not the warring race, remember." His last words hinted faintly that he knew why they had come.

Eishoxa nodded once more. "All right, I understand," she replied. He bent his knees to her and left the room.

It wasn't long before there was another knock at the door and Ember came in. He hadn't abandoned his weapons as Eishoxa had been told to, and his large sword hung at his waist in full view. Eishoxa strongly suspected he'd also been told about the rule but had deliberately not followed it to prove a point.

"What do you want?" she asked before he could say anything.

"We have to go to the Lily Hall," he said. "Gresceva is expecting us. She's not used to being kept waiting, so I suggest you hurry."

Eishoxa stopped what she was doing, put the scrolls back into the bag and set it on the floor. She smoothed her hair back behind her ears, then scrambled down to the ground. "All right, let's go then," she said. She could feel the tension heighten but tried to keep her voice light and casual.

"Wait. May I say something first?" Ember asked in a much different tone of voice. Eishoxa bit the inside of her lip and nodded. He looked very awkward and Eishoxa could feel the awkwardness reverberating around her.

"What it is? Can we walk?" She started towards the door.

"No. Just wait a moment – please?"

And Eishoxa stopped and turned back towards him. "What is it?" she repeated.

He looked like he was steeling himself for something, but at the last minute couldn't find the nerve. "Nothing," he said and led the way out of the door.

Ash and Smoke weren't there when Ember and Eishoxa arrived at the Lily Hall, but Gresceva was, along with her two guards. Leap was standing in the corner, his hands behind his back and a look of deep mistrust on his face. Eishoxa walked behind Ember, focusing on him rather than anything else. Gresceva stood as they approached. Ember bowed but Eishoxa didn't. Gresceva said and did nothing. Then she took a deep breath.

"Ember and Eishoxa, come with me." She descended the steps gracefully and beckoned to them to follow her. The guards didn't move, but Leap followed at a distance. Gresceva led them behind her chair to a small room hidden by a screen. Leap stayed outside. Gresceva seated herself in an elegant chair and looked at both of them. "Please explain what you wanted to tell me," she said, gesturing at them to begin. Eishoxa waited for Ember to speak.

"Lady Gresceva," he began, "you understand that there is now a war raging across this land of ours. The Empty draw ever closer to you, closer to Dulcacohefen than to us. If you let Indocani come into your land and fight them from here, then I believe it will be beneficial to both our races and not just one."

Gresceva nodded. "But my people are not a warring race."

"With all due respect, this is not about what your people are or are not. There is no time for hesitation. I must have an answer to take back to my leader."

Gresceva pointed at Eishoxa. "Is she not your leader now?"

"No," Ember said. "Our leader is still Vera."

Gresceva looked bemused. "Then why have you brought her?" Ember said nothing. Gresceva widened her eyes slowly. "Maybe that matter is for neither here nor now."

"What matter?" Eishoxa interrupted. Gresceva and Ember looked at her. She glanced once at Ember in confusion and then turned back to Gresceva. "Ember told me why I've come here. I'm here to negotiate a treaty. What other reason is there?"

Ember and Gresceva exchanged a glance. "Perhaps we should discuss this," Gresceva offered, but Ember answered before Eishoxa could.

"I will speak to Eishoxa myself later," he assured her. "Lady Gresceva, I know that war goes against your people's wishes, but I ask you to consider this very carefully. If the Empty were to come here, they would destroy all of this, all the beauty that you have attempted to preserve here. All razed to the ground, just like Pellimeth."

The beauty of Pellimeth, remembered, hung in the air for a moment. "I know that," Gresceva said slowly. Standing, she sighed and rearranged her shawls. "You put forward a persuasive argument, Ember, and it is true what you say. I will discuss this with my Assembly. I expect you both to be there as well." Ember nodded. Gresceva folded her arms. "These are strange and dangerous times," she reflected.

"And we must be ready to meet them," Ember added.

Gresceva looked at him. "Indeed," she said, "we must be ready." Eishoxa looked from one to the other. Gresceva shook herself. "But it would be helpful if you showed me something." Gresceva rustled to one side of the room and brought back a scroll. She sat in her chair and unrolled it. "This is our land," she said. Eishoxa leaned forward slightly to get a better look at the map, but Ember blocked her view. "So tell me, where are the Empty now?"

Ember immediately stepped forward and pointed. "So far we've held them back at the Plain of Despair, but they may have discovered a way across the Cursed Marshes and therefore will come towards you on two fronts. Here is one: the Plain of Despair, along the sea's edge down towards Dulcacohefen. They would also double around, across the Cursed Marshes and through the rivers."

Gresceva sighed. "They do not rest, do they?"

"And they will not, until all the world is in submission to them," Ember replied solemnly.

Gresceva nodded, almost dismissively. "Yes, all of the world, or what is left of it."

She rolled up the map again and stood. Ember took a step away from her and Gresceva put the map back again. "Ember will take you back to your room, Eishoxa. I expect you're very tired. We will meet with the Assembly tomorrow, and may the guidance of all Goddesses be with us."

Ember bowed to her and led Eishoxa out from behind the screen. As she followed him from the Lily Hall, Eishoxa realised that things were going to be a lot more difficult than she'd expected.

When Eishoxa woke in the early hours of the morning, the cold had penetrated her bones and her hands were stiff and icy. She'd left the balcony doors open and now a frosty wind was blowing through the room. Rocking the hammock soothingly, she took deep breaths, then swung out of the hammock. She wrapped herself in a blanket and stepped onto the balcony. Night still hung dreamily over Dulcacohefen, a calm night on which a cold wind gusted every now and then. At night, the place seemed even more beautiful. By the Tree, the night seemed to dampen the fires, a thick oppressive blanket. But here the night was like gossamer, adorning the world and adding to its beauty. Eishoxa had never stood in a night so beautiful and yet so foreign.

She sighed, and her breath billowed out like a big-bellied sail. Her thoughts were pacing and circling like a restless wolf inside her. Gresceva had subtly implied that she was here for another reason besides that given by Ember and Vera. Eishoxa thought back. She didn't trust Vera but that was because she didn't believe Vera would let her return to Bareth. But now that Eishoxa thought about it, there was something not right about Vera, something that didn't sit well with Eishoxa, as if two sides of Vera were clashing fiercely and one was overcoming the other. She thought of Leap's cold green eyes and shuddered. Whatever she'd done, it was something bad.

The water looked like liquid silver. Eishoxa had never seen a more glorious moon. Like the sun at the Tree, this orb of crystal and silver lit up the sky and the ground beneath it in a softly glowing, pearly light. Far below her, Eishoxa could see the quiet figures of the Ewdicani, slipping in and out of the water. These were a nocturnal people, but Eishoxa had never heard of anyone who could be so active and yet so quiet. She held onto the cold metal of the railing and leaned over the edge. Maya had been a great swimmer, Eishoxa recalled. She would have loved it here. Cara was in the mountains, focused on the cold and the ice and the moon, just as Bareth was focused on the desert and the hot summer sun. But Bareth possessed a gentleness that Cara opposed with ferocity. Here ferocity belonged to the fire people and gentleness to the water.

Eishoxa looked down again at the Ewdicani leaping in and out of the water, silver droplets flying in all directions. It was beautiful. And in her opinion, at a level of beauty the Tree would never achieve. But according to everyone else, she didn't belong here.

CHAPTER 9

THE FIRST MEETING with the Assembly was to be the next day. Eishoxa had been dressed for hours but no one had come to collect her. She could easily get lost in the Ice Lily and, as Leap had said with a slight smirk, that would not be very good. But there had been no sound from outside her door. Stepping into the corridor, Eishoxa padded softly towards the room where Ember and the others were staying. Leap and Ember had navigated the twisting passages so adeptly that Eishoxa had supposed it to be easy, but it took a lot longer she than expected to find her way. The door handle of their room had been tied with a bright crimson ribbon, and Eishoxa wondered why hers had not been similarly decorated. She knocked on the door several times and waited, but there was no sound from within. Again Eishoxa knocked, frowning, but again there was nothing. She tried the door but it was locked.

Then it hit her: they weren't going to take her to the Assembly. That had been the plan all along. Of course they weren't. A strange girl, who didn't look anything like an Indocani in the first place, claiming to have returned from the Ignorant and trying to get the Peacemakers to join a war. Thumping her head against the wood of the door, she cursed her stupidity. Ember was going to speak in her place. Of course he was. And Eishoxa was to be left in her room so that she couldn't cause any trouble.

The brazenness of the plan and its utter effectiveness made Eishoxa suspect that this had been the intention from the very beginning. Resisting a strong urge to kick something, Eishoxa started back towards her room fuming. Stupid little girl, they must have thought. She was here as a prop, not as a person. A façade, that was all she was.

Eishoxa paid no attention to where her feet were going and, when she finally looked up, found herself in a different place from the one she had left. Hanging from ceiling to floor were many soft blue cloths, smelling of something fresh and cold, which rippled as she passed through them. She heard music playing somewhere in the distance, such a sweet tune that Eishoxa ventured further through the drapes to follow the sound. The drapes carried on for some time and so did the music, swelling in dynamic and tone until, passing one final drape, Eishoxa found herself staring into a little room where a young Ewdicani was playing a flute. Eishoxa recognised him immediately: he was one of the guards who had stood in the Lily Hall with Gresceva. Eishoxa watched, fascinated, as his fingers flew over the instrument. With his eyes closed, he was creating a tune without written music or accompaniment.

Suddenly he stopped and opened his eyes. The music still held him in a sort of trance, it seemed, and it took a moment for him to realise that Eishoxa was standing there. He lowered his flute immediately. As if he'd been caught doing something he shouldn't have been, he stood, bent his knees hastily to Eishoxa and put the instrument behind his back.

"What are you doing here? You aren't supposed to be here." He put down his instrument and started towards her.

Eishoxa took a step back. "I heard the music," she muttered, "and it sounded so beautiful that I followed it. I'm sorry." He looked her up and down and something about his face relaxed. The strange haunted look disappeared from his eyes, which Eishoxa hadn't even noticed until it was gone. He seemed much more at ease now, and his closed face softened.

"Eishoxa, isn't it?"

"How do you know my name?"

He laughed quietly. Everything any Ewdicani did was quiet – quiet and controlled. "Everyone knows your name. Daughter of the Fire Goddess."

Eishoxa shifted awkwardly. She knew that was what everyone called her, but she didn't see the point of the title. She was not extraordinary in any way; in fact, with the exception of Rianox and possibly Amber, everyone thought she was a failure. "It's just Eishoxa actually."

"Really? That's changed as well, has it? The last time you came here, you demanded that everyone call you by your proper title and nothing else."

This made the situation worse, if anything. "Oh, I was that kind of a person?" Eishoxa asked bitterly. Although his voice was much gentler than anyone else's she'd heard in this place – except maybe Rianox's – it still stung.

He looked surprised. "You don't remember?"

"Not a bit," she bit sharply. He was tall, tall for the Ewdicani anyway, and taller than Eishoxa. His skin possessed the same ethereal quality as Leap's, white with a faint tinge of blue but his hair was paler and not as gaudy as Leap's. She pulled herself up slightly. None of these people had the right to judge her if they didn't tell her what she had done.

"Oh." He looked slightly chastened. "I'm sorry then. My name is Rush." He bent his knees to her again and bowed his head. Eishoxa inclined her head as well, feeling awkward. "Why aren't you with the Assembly?" he asked.

Eishoxa shrugged. "They didn't want me there. No one came to get me."

"So you decided to do some exploring by yourself, I see?" He laughed quietly to himself. "It isn't the politest thing to do."

"Yes." Eishoxa rubbed the bridge of her nose uncomfortably. "I've never seen a place like this before," she stuttered as she attempted to explain.

Rush looked around him and then looked at her, dressed in bright orange and yellow, with her electric-red hair floating behind her shoulders. "No, I don't suppose you have. But, strictly speaking, you're not really allowed to go looking around this place. Some of the people here guard the secrets of the Ice Lily jealously."

She smiled stiffly and nodded. "Well, if I'm not allowed to look around, I'll go back to my room," and she started for the drapes.

"No, it's all right," he replied quickly, stopping her. He grinned. "You may not be allowed to look around by yourself, but if I'm with you, you would be."

She paused and shook her head. "No, that's fine. I'll go back."

"Please?" he asked. "It would really be my pleasure."

Eishoxa thought of all the places she hadn't seen yet here and then she thought of her small room, the inside of which she already knew like the back of her hand. "If it doesn't inconvenience you in any way."

He grinned at her again. "Not at all." He gestured for her to lead the way out of the room and Eishoxa stepped back into the cool, fragrant drapes. As she walked back through the corridor, she heard him murmur again. "Not at all."

As they walked back through the blue cloths, Eishoxa ran her fingers over them, watching them sway gently as if moved by a breeze. "Why are these here?" she asked.

Rush pointed to the ceiling. "Above us, you will see a mural of birds. The drapes, when they move, give the illusion of the birds flying. One of the great wonders of your people is that you can fly without having wings. Alas, we aren't able to do that."

"Oh, you mean by dragon?" she asked, and he nodded.

When they reached the corridor, he pointed down a side passage. "Down this way. I'll show you some of the more beautiful pieces of craftsmanship that we have here."

Eishoxa smiled. Although the Assembly meeting weighed heavily on her mind, she could not help but enjoy herself. It was nice to be with someone who didn't look on her with contempt or sympathy. As they walked along, the twisted passage narrowed slightly, and Eishoxa put her hand on the cool, white wall. "This is all ice, isn't it?"

Rush smiled. "Yes. But there are barriers constructed around it so that it doesn't melt."

"It's so different from what I thought it would look like," Eishoxa murmured.

"How? What do you mean?" Rush asked. Eishoxa turned. "Well, I've never seen ice before in my life. In Bareth I lived in a desert." She swallowed. Thinking about Bareth was painful. Rush nodded slowly. "Bareth? I suppose that's where you lived before coming back here?"

Eishoxa nodded. "Yes. I'm supposed to be returning there after my work here is done." Rush paused for a moment, thinking something through. Then he gestured ahead and Eishoxa started walking again, looking at him curiously. "What is it?" she asked.

He pursed his lips but then shrugged and shook his head. "It's none of my business, but I would be surprised if the Indocani let you go."

"Vera made me a promise," Eishoxa provided.

"I suppose being you has its advantages," Rush finished.

He led the way for a little longer before turning to Eishoxa. "This is the Peace Corridor. If you start to look at the walls, you'll see a mural that shows the Great Days, the days when there was peace across the whole land and both races lived in harmony together." Eishoxa approached the painting slowly, and she recalled the tunnel she'd come across in the Tree, where the moving pictures in the stone had revealed her past to her. This time, however, she was nowhere to be seen. Although the mural was dominated by Ewdicani, Eishoxa could see the brown-skinned Indocani weaving their way amongst them. The scene showed feasting and dancing. A table was suspended in the middle of a cool lake. Ewdicani swam around the edge, floated on the water, or rested on the backs of satin-smooth dolphins and huge humpback whales. The sky above them was full of stars, and a full moon bathed the land.

Eishoxa put her finger on one of the Indocani. "It's strange that you have them here. In all the Indocani books there's no sign in any drawing that another race even exists."

Rush came to stand at her shoulder. "Well, that's because the Indocani are much prouder than we are." He looked down at her. "They don't accept us. This picture, Eishoxa, is a picture of peace. See how the animals and both the races are connected? We're together under a full moon, which signifies the never-waning sun, and the stars, which signify the night. There are subtle things that connect us that we cannot escape from, no matter how hard we try to get rid of them or deny them." His last two words carried a hint of bitterness.

"What do you mean we're connected?"

"We're not warring, we're not arguing. We're co-existing. We're standing beside each other without complaint," Rush explained. Eishoxa nodded and walked further down the corridor, still looking at the mural. As they followed a turn, they met another set of billowing drapes. These were green, and the ceiling above depicted many swimming fish.

"What are we going to look at now?"

Rush smiled and walked a little faster along the corridor. "I'm going to take you outside. We have a beautiful place inside, but it's the outside, I think, that's the most beautiful." Eishoxa followed him as he took another turn and opened a small door to reveal a beautiful little garden.

"Oh! It's so pretty," she exclaimed, and walked through. They were now at the very bottom of the ice flower, and one of the lily's petals loomed above them.

"This is one of the few gardens that aren't open to everyone. Only Gresceva and her guards may come here. Your room is in the petal above us," Rush said, pointing.

Eishoxa craned her neck and looked up. "Up there?" He nodded.

The garden they stood in was slightly heart-shaped and kept in perfect order. Along the borders were many species of flowers, some Eishoxa could name and some she could not. Their scent filled the air. The sea-green grass she walked on was well grown, and she could feel through her shoes the softness that only watered grass could bring. She had missed that feeling. By the Tree, the grass was hard and burnt, a stiff stubble that pushed its way through the cracked earth.

The garden was open to the sky, but the dark shadow cast over it by the petal was cold as well water. In the middle of the garden, surrounded by perfectly round white rocks, was a fountain in which a regal-looking woman poured water from a shell onto a laughing dolphin.

"Who is that?" Eishoxa enquired, stepping towards the fountain. Rush followed her. "Wella. Our Goddess." Wella's kind face looked down at the dolphin in a loving way but, Eishoxa noticed, the sculptor had made her eyes seem unfocused, as if she didn't care about the dolphin at all. The tall, slim body ended in a large fish tail that coiled in a tight circle on which the figure balanced.

"I have to say, she looks a lot nicer than Fiera," Eishoxa said, laughing slightly.

"Your mother?" Rush asked.

Eishoxa gave a tight smile and turned to look at Rush. "I don't think of her as my mother."

"Can I ask why?"

Eishoxa paused and looked back at Wella, a faraway look in her eyes. "A mother shouldn't give her child away."

"Maybe she didn't want to. Maybe she had to."

"She gave me away to the Indocani instead of keeping me with her."

"Yes, I know. I'm saying that maybe she didn't have a choice."

"She's a Goddess," Eishoxa replied quietly. "She is worshipped by thousands of Indocani. She shouldn't have to do anything."

"That should be true, but sometimes they have no choice. Wella and Fiera must work together to a certain extent, and for that to happen, sometimes sacrifices must be made on either side."

Eishoxa pointed to the fountain. "She didn't have a child to give away."

"I know," Rush reasoned. "But that doesn't mean she doesn't have to make sacrifices."

Eishoxa shrugged. "I don't think Fiera had to."

Rush sighed. "Well, if that's what you believe, I don't think I'm going to be able to change your mind."

Eishoxa turned around and grinned. "Other people would try to."

He smiled back. "Well, I'm not going to try to."

Eishoxa's eyes followed the sound of the bubbling water. "Is that a river?" she asked, more to change the subject than to know the answer. She could tell it was a river.

Rush followed her gaze and nodded. "Yes." He glanced at her again. "Do you want to see?"

"Can I?" she asked eagerly.

"As long as you don't tell anyone that you've seen it."

"I don't have anyone here to tell."

Rush stopped and faced her again. "What about the people you came with? Ember? The last time you were here, I remember you went everywhere with him."

"Oh. Well, it's not the same as last time," she said.

The river ran at the back of the garden. It wasn't as wide as Eishoxa had expected, smaller than the river at Bareth. On the other side there was a grassy slope that ended in a copse of young trees. Attached to one of them was a rope swing for getting from one side of the river to the other. On their side of the river, a boat was resting lightly on the water.

"I've never seen a boat in real life before," said Eishoxa. "Only in pictures." She started to walk towards the river, but Rush held her back. "No – be careful! The ground is very weak. You may fall through."

She looked at him sceptically. "Fall through? Really?"

"Yes," he said earnestly. "Yes, indeed."

"And what would happen if I did?"

"You would die," he said simply.

"Just like that?"

"Almost. You're too much a part of the Indocani to survive, but too human to die instantly."

"So I don't want to fall in."

He shook his head vigorously. "Definitely not. But I can take you on the boat if you want."

She turned to him, eyes sparkling. "Would you?"

"Of course." He put his hand out towards the boat and it rose up out of the water and came to rest at their feet. "Climb in," he invited, holding his hand out to help her.

She took it hesitantly and put one foot over the side of the boat. "This won't break, will it?

Rush looked affronted. "No. I made this boat with my own hands and it's foolproof."

Eishoxa stepped inside. The boat was made out of reeds, folded many times, and was shaped like a very narrow almond. There were two seats, one near the front and one at the back. She sat on the front one, following Rush's directions. "Ready?" he asked, and she nodded excitedly. He smiled. "Hold on." She gripped the sides of the boat as it rose up again and floated to the water. It was so light Eishoxa could almost feel the pressure of the river pushing up from underneath.

She turned to Rush. "Is it really safe?"

"Yes," he nodded. "It really is." He took a long stick from the bank and pushed them off from the bank, and the boat glided out towards the centre of the river. The water beneath them looked very cold and very dangerous, as if daring someone to touch it, to disturb its rippling mass. They barely made any noise as they floated down the river. The water creamed beneath them but did not splash. Rush was rowing them down with long, steady strokes of his stick. He was standing at the back but the boat did not rock at all.

"The balance is perfect," Rush reassured her. "I'm lower in the water so you'll be higher. Not one drop of water will touch you, I promise." He sounded so confident in his declaration, so confident of his little reed boat, that Eishoxa found herself trusting him.

The river broadened ever more. Tall green reeds framed it on either side, and the water that they nosed through was covered in white and pink water lilies. A snow-white bird followed by little grey ones moved smoothly and regally up the water, their strong legs paddling underneath the water.

"What is that bird?"

"It's called a swan," Rush explained. "It's the symbol of Wella. She lives in every swan."

"And Fiera's symbol is an eagle?" Eishoxa asked.

"Yes," Rush replied. "Yes, her symbol is an eagle in full flight." Eishoxa thought about the fierce bird striking from above, high up where the sun was, and knew that no bird could better describe Fiera.

"Whose symbol is the phoenix?" Eishoxa asked, thinking back to the banquet on her first night.

"Your own symbol, Eishoxa. That's the bird you chose to be your own. If I recall, you had a pennant that you took into battle with you." Eishoxa looked at her reflection over the side of the boat again. She could barely make out her face, so dark was the water. But her red hair stood out around her head, a great cloud of colour.

"Is it strange not to remember a thing of what happened before?" she asked, wondering immediately if she wanted to hear the answer.

"Yes," Rush said honestly. "But I suppose in some ways that's a good thing as well as a bad thing."

"In what ways?" Eishoxa asked, turning back to look at him.

"You're not hindered by any of the mistakes you might have made," Rush explained. "You can start again. You can have a fresh beginning."

"But everyone sees me as that girl," Eishoxa replied hopelessly. "How can I make a new name for myself?"

"I didn't say you had to make a new name. You can just be yourself and have a new life."

"When you say it like that, it doesn't sound so bad," Eishoxa realised, turning back to the water.

"Maybe you just have to look at it like that," Rush said. "If you look at things in a bad way, things will look bad. If you look in a good way, things will look good."

"Are you an optimist?" Eishoxa asked puckishly.

Rush shrugged. "It's a character trait. The world is full of bad things, but if you're an optimist you can make them seem better. If you're a pessimist, then what's the point of even venturing into the world?"

"I've never thought of it like that," Eishoxa murmured.

"You're a pessimist, aren't you?" Rush asked.

Eishoxa shrugged. "No, I'm a realist."

"What's the difference?" Rush asked. "If something bad is happening and you look at it like that, it seems bad."

Eishoxa disagreed. "No, you see it how it really is. Thinking everything is better than it actually is isn't good either."

"I don't see things as better than they are," Rush contradicted. "I see things as they could be and try to get there."

Eishoxa raised her eyebrows at him. "People must think you're strange, mustn't they?"

"Strange?"

"Very. But in a good way."

"Well then, I suppose I'll take that as a compliment. And no, compared to most, my way of thinking is quite normal."

A fish jumped out of the water ahead of them and landed back in the river with a splash. Rush laughed. "Look at them. They know that something is bad for them and could kill them, but still they do it because they want to see the world."

"Are they pessimists or realists then?" Eishoxa asked, turning again to look at him. She was surprised to see that his eyes were deadly serious.

"They're optimists – and that's what I'm trying to be."

CHAPTER 10

"WHERE HAVE YOU BEEN?" Ember shouted when she returned to her room that evening. He had been waiting in the corridor when she had returned and with one glance, Eishoxa could tell he was furious. The smile on her face disappeared. Her hair, still flyaway from the wind on the river, refused to lie flat as she tried to smooth it.

"I might ask you the same thing," she said coldly. "I know you were with the Assembly and that I was deliberately not taken to attend. Why was that?"

"You didn't answer my question," he accused. She folded her arms. "Answer mine first."

"You weren't there when we came to get you."

His deception like a slap across the face. "You liar," she spat. "I waited here for a long time and then went to your room to see where you were. I may look like an Ignorant but I'm not stupid."

"Oh really?" he mocked. "Well then, tell me why we didn't invite you along."

"That was my question," she retorted.

"You didn't come because we didn't need you," he said. "Because trying to organise an alliance with you would be next to impossible."

"And why is that?"

"You don't know about the war. You don't know about our country. You barely know who you are. You act like a baby, and as a baby you need to sit in your room and wait. Because everything will be much quicker if you aren't involved."

"Then why did I come to this place?" she cried, throwing her hands into the air. "Why ask me here?"

"That's between me and other people, and is none of your business."

"It involves me. That makes it my business," she said sharply.

"You're wrong," he repeated.

"Vera sent me!" Eishoxa contradicted. Ember put his head on one side and looked at her. "And what have you done so far? Not much to help."

"Because you won't let me do anything!"

"Because you can't. Because in your head the only thing that matters is getting back to your beloved Bareth as quickly as possible. You don't care about any of us!"

Eishoxa trembled with anger. "I care about people too! And if you're too blind to see that, then I refuse to continue this conversation." She stalked into her room and slammed the door.

The minute Eishoxa left, Ember made his way to see Gresceva. He walked briskly, ignoring the Ewdicani who greeted him in the corridor. Leap had asked that they put away all weapons and Ash and Smoke had complied. Ember had not. He didn't trust these people, no matter what Vera had told him. As he approached the Lily Hall, the two Ewdicani guarding the doors bent their knees, pushed their clasped hands towards him and opened the doors. He nodded to both. Gresceva was nowhere to be seen, but her two guards were there. Ember walked up to the raised platform.

"Where is the Lady Gresceva?" he asked them. "I must speak with her as a matter of urgency."

"The Lady Gresceva is resting," came another voice. Ember turned around to see Leap coming out of a side door. Of all the Ewdicani, Ember disliked Leap the most. His loyalty lay with Gresceva but with his own belief first – that Ember knew – which meant he was thoroughly against the alliance. He believed in peace and that peace would be achieved only if they didn't go to war.

"Leap," Ember said, bowing to him. Leap's eyes trailed down to Ember's hand, which rested on his sword.

"Sir Ember, didn't I say no weapons?" Leap asked, clasping his hands in front of him. "You must understand that, here in the heart of the Peacemakers' dwelling, weapons should not be tolerated. I hope you understand."

"And I have already given you my answer, Leap," replied Ember. "I will keep my sword on me at all times."

Leap opened his mouth but was interrupted by another cool voice: "A trait that should both be admired and discouraged, I think."

Gresceva appeared in the frame of the side door that Leap had just come through. Leap greeted her in the Ewdicani manner. Ember bowed.

"Ember," Gresceva said in mild surprise, "is there something you wish to tell me?"

"Indeed, my Lady," Ember said. He watched her walk to her chair and sit down. An excellent actress, he observed. With her graceful, flowing steps she seemed to glide along the floor. She looked, to everyone, the perfect leader. If he didn't know the things he did about her, he would have believed her as well. As it was, he just admired the lengths she would go to.

"Speak," Gresceva invited.

Ember cleared his throat and took a step towards the little dais. "In private, please, my Lady." One of the guards looked at him then. Ember looked back with intense dislike. Here was one of his enemies from the past, one of the reasons Eishoxa had left to go to Bareth. Knowing that people like him were still here had made him seriously consider whether Eishoxa should be allowed back. His hand tightened on his sword. As he'd said, he didn't trust any of them.

Gresceva put her hands on the arms of her chair and stood. "Come with me, Ember. Leap, you may go."

"My Lady," began Leap, "is it entirely—"

"Leap, I said you may go," Gresceva repeated, and with a final bow Leap left through the side door. Gresceva slid her arm through Ember's and guided him towards the back of the Lily Hall, where a screen hung from the ceiling. Pulling one side of it away, Gresceva motioned for him to go first and then followed.

"So. What is it?" Gresceva asked. Ember noticed immediately that she'd lost most of the dreamy tone that infused her voice. "Ember, you must be more careful. I know Vera has told you of the plans, and if you keep asking to speak with me in private, people will start to get suspicious."

"Have you told Leap?" Ember asked.

Gresceva laughed and shook her head. "No, and I don't plan on doing so. He's a very slimy and untrustworthy person. If it weren't for public appearances, I'd have him banished without hesitation."

Ember laughed stiffly. "It's Eishoxa," he said.

"Ah, and what has your little princess done this time? Started to chase another one of my guards across the country?"

Ember shook his head. "Not quite. She's a lot cleverer than you've given her credit for, and she knows that something's not right."

"She is perfectly correct."

"If she starts to speak to the Ewdicani, or even to Smoke and Ash, she'll work out something she shouldn't. Vera is most adamant that this mustn't happen."

Gresceva turned on her heel and sat down in the only chair behind the screen. She rested her chin on her hand thoughtfully. "How long will it take to stage this alliance?"

"A month," Ember said without hesitation. "At least. The fact still remains that we are in the land of the Peacemakers, and if it takes any less time than that, people will suspect something. Especially here, where they think over everything again and again."

Gresceva nodded and rolled her eyes. "I know. One of the more annoying traits."

Ember agreed with a nod. "And a month is a long time. Enough time for her to figure everything out. She already suspects me and Vera. She knows we're not telling her everything. You saw her. And she's spent sixteen human years with the Ignorant, and they've taught her to be questioning and careful."

Gresceva contemplated Ember's words. "Well, there's nothing to be done then. She must stay in her room and have no contact with anyone."

"That may not be possible," Ember said.

Gresceva looked up. "Why not?"

"She left her room today. She knows how to get around rules and she's not scared of anything – not you, not me." Ember immediately quenched a small flame of pride that flared up at his words. Here, now, that fearlessness was not to be commended but eliminated.

"You say that she remembers very little from her last time here?" Gresceva asked.

"Very little indeed. In fact, almost nothing."

"Good, good. That will work in our favour."

"How?"

"I will talk to her," Gresceva said. Ember raised his eyebrows.

"With all due respect, Gresceva, I don't think you'll be able to do anything."

Gresceva looked up at Ember. "I think you'll find, my dear Ember, that I can be very persuasive. More than you've given me credit for. Now you must go. We've spent long enough behind here."

"Yes."

Gresceva adjusted one of the shawls over her arm and stood up. "And, remind me," she added, as Ember started to leave, "which one of the guards was it, from before?"

"I think you remember, Gresceva."

She smiled at him. "Of course I remember. That wasn't why I asked."

CHAPTER 11

WHEN EISHOXA HEARD a knock on her door the next day, she assumed it would be Ember. It was. She'd been trying to read more of the parchments that Rianox had given her and was also cleaning her weapons, despite Leap telling her not to take them out of her bag. They were growing dull because she'd not used them for some days.

"You're to stay in your room," he announced. "You're not to leave here."

"And if I do?"

He glared at her. "I wouldn't advise it. Or would you like me to ask Gresceva to post guards at your door?"

"You wouldn't do that," Eishoxa said, knowing full well he would.

"Try me," he replied. "Take one step outside and there will be consequences." He left the room, closing the door loudly behind him. Eishoxa made a face at the door and polished extra hard at one of the arrow heads.

She'd woken up in a surprisingly good mood that morning, and even Ember couldn't dampen it. She looked at her distorted reflection in the polished metal and whispered to it, "I wonder if it means something good is going to happen today?"

She left the books on the table and looked around her room. It was a very beautiful room, although still a prison. She opened the balcony doors and a breeze soared though the room. Eishoxa walked onto the balcony and looked down over the edge. The petal curved so she couldn't see the garden at the bottom, but she knew that was where she'd been with Rush the day before. To her surprise, she wasn't as angry as she had suspected about not being allowed into the Assembly meeting. After all, Ember was probably correct. She wouldn't have been much help at all. All she wanted to know was why she wasn't allowed into the meetings. And, if she was honest with herself, she would find that out a lot more easily if she wasn't closeted in a room with Gresceva, Ember and the members of the Assembly. Except that, at the moment, she wasn't allowed out of her room.

Sighing, she went back inside and closed the doors. Walking over to the large flute she'd seen her first day there, she picked it up and rubbed the dust off its wooden surface. Along the back of it there seemed to be a long scratch, and as Eishoxa looked closer, she saw that the scratch was a join. The flute had been broken in half and then put together again. Her finger traced the mark.

On a whim she placed her fingers over the holes along one side of the flute and held it up to her mouth. It made a very low, rich sound when she blew across it. Then, without her fingers moving, a sad tune came forth, as though the flute were remembering something. Eishoxa looked down in wonder at the instrument in her lap. As she listened, she heard another flute join in, a much higher flute, peeping and piping all around the strong, low notes. Eishoxa took the flute off her lap and rested it once again by the wall. Once it was off her lap, the music slowed and finally stopped.

A quiet, rapid tap-tapping sounded on the glass of her balcony door. Eishoxa walked towards it.

"Can my Lady Eishoxa come out again today?"

Eishoxa opened the door and saw Rush clinging mischievously to the side of the balcony. Somehow he'd managed to climb up. "Rush," she asked, "were you playing the flute?"

"Of course. I heard the music coming from your room and had to join in on my little flute."

"No," Eishoxa protested, laughing slightly. "The big flute that I had. Were you playing that one?"

Rush looked confused. "How can I play a flute if I'm not even present in the room?"

"It just started playing."

"If you'd let me in, I could come and examine this self-playing flute more closely," he suggested, and Eishoxa stepped back. Rush walked inside and closed the door behind him. He looked around. "Hmm, I haven't been in this room for a while. Nothing has changed at all."

"When was the last time you were in here?"

"When my Lady was here last," Rush replied with a flourishing bow in her direction. Eishoxa laughed. Rush stood again and put his flute down on Eishoxa's hammock. "So, can you come out again? I heard you were to be abandoned here again."

"I can't, Rush. Ember said that if I did, he'd ask Gresceva to post guards at my door."

"Oh," Rush said, his face falling. Then it brightened again. "Well, maybe you can't go out, but I can come in."

"You'll get into trouble, I'm sure," Eishoxa said.

Rush shrugged. "That means I'm already in trouble. I might as well get something out of it."

Eishoxa laughed. Rush picked up his flute again. "We could play duets," he offered.

She looked back at the large flute. "I don't know how to play," she admitted.

Rush put down his flute. "What do you mean?"

"Well, I was just holding it and it started to play itself."

"My dear Little Flame, it will only play itself if you play it first. I thought you were joking before."

"Little Flame?" Eishoxa queried. Rush picked up the large flute from the wall. "Yes –that's what your name means."

"I didn't know that."

"No? Oh well, you do now. Now, pick up your instrument."

Eishoxa picked up the flute again. "Now play anything you want." He adjusted his own and danced his fingers over the holes so that a peal of sound ran around the room. She blew tentatively down her own and sound warbled out, but with none of the grace and skill of Rush's.

"Good!" he encouraged. "You've got to feel music in order to make it sound beautiful. It's got to come from somewhere deep inside of you. It wants to play and sound beautiful. Just listen to it. Think about what

147

you want it to sound like and then just try it. It may be easier than you think."

"That sounds too easy," Eishoxa said in a slightly scoffing tone.

Rush laughed. "Well, maybe you're making it too difficult."

Eishoxa closed her eyes. She thought about the clear piping of a bird that had woken her that morning. She thought about the sweet sounds that Rush had made on his flute, and about the bubbling sounds of the river. Then she thought of the flute she held and the deep, low sounds it had made, like a bell deep underground. She thought of the sound the boat had made as it coursed through the water, and the wind as it had whistled through the trees in the Forest of No Flame. And as she thought, a tune formed in her head, a tune she'd never heard before, a tune full of patterns and rhythms that were strange to her. And as her fingers moved over the instrument, she heard the tune ripple through the air, one note following another. And as the music filled the room, she heard Rush's high notes join in. They were like fish swimming in and out of a current, and when she opened her eyes, she could almost see them weaving in and out of the water. She stopped playing and looked at Rush.

He grinned at her. "See?"

"I didn't know I could do that," Eishoxa smiled.

Rush nodded. "Music is not a tool, it's a living thing – that's what we Ewdicani are taught. The only way it can express itself is if it's played, and here you can hear its joy when it sings."

"Music is *alive*?" Eishoxa asked, fascinated.

Rush nodded vigorously. "Oh yes. It has no boundaries, no limitations. It follows no rules and has no answers. It's the most beautiful of all living things." Eishoxa kept her eyes on him as he paused mid-flow and then continued, almost shyly. "They say that before Ewdicani die, they each hear their Soul Song, the song that was written especially for them. But you have to be worthy of hearing it. I only hope I'll prove myself to be worthy." Eishoxa put the flute down gently. Rush smiled to himself briefly and then stood up. "And now that we have played the most beautiful tune together, I must show you something."

He stood and looked around. Making his way towards the basin, he pulled it out to reveal a small stack of books behind it. He brushed the dust off them, handed them to her, then took them again after he put the basin back. He offered her one. "Here. This one is in Düerasgörn." He looked at another and gave it to her as well. "And this one is in the Common Language."

"The Common Language?" Eishoxa asked.

"Yes. The language that the Ignorant and Oblivious speak," Rush explained. "That's how you can understand what I say. Plus, speaking in the tongue of water or fire, as the case might be, would be like doing magic all the time. Very tiring."

Eishoxa opened the book. "What are they?" she asked.

"Children's stories. Very amusing. If you have to spend a lot of time in here, amuse yourself by reading," Rush answered.

"Reading?"

"Yes. You're in a part of the world where learning things is almost as enjoyable as going to war is for Indocani."

"I didn't think anyone could enjoy going to war," Eishoxa replied.

Rush shrugged. "My opinion entirely. But the Indocani do." Rush was looking through the other books. Then he snapped them shut. "I saw Ember speaking to Gresceva in private yesterday."

Eishoxa closed the book. "When?"

"Soon after we left each other."

"So that would be after he spoke to me."

"What did he say?" Rush asked quite sharply.

"Simply to stay in my room," Eishoxa said, climbing up onto her hammock. "And to stop being a silly little girl."

"Why are you talking like that?" Rush asked.

She swung her legs over one side. "I don't want to be here. They made me come here and they won't let me do anything."

"They must have their reasons," Rush offered.

Eishoxa nodded. "Yes, I know their reasons: I don't know anything, I'm new here, I can't remember anything from my last life. They think I'll slow the proceedings down and they're not prepared to let me do that."

"There is a war going on, Eishoxa," Rush reminded her. "Haste is the key weapon here. They can't sit around teaching you the alphabet while their comrades are dying on the battlefield. That's what Ember would say, anyway, to justify his action."

"I know," Eishoxa sighed. "I know, but I'd like to help. I feel so useless sitting here. I'm just a pawn in their game."

"Why do you say that?"

"It's the truth, isn't it? They don't let me hear what they're saying. They don't tell me anything. I'm here probably because Vera thought I'd make a good peace offering."

"She was right, though," Rush reflected. "The last time you came, the Ewdicani didn't like you – and that's an understatement. And now that you've come of your own free will, it's a big sign to people. You said you'd never set foot on this place again."

"But why? Why did I say that? It's infuriating! I can't remember it!"

He looked at her. "Eishoxa, believe me when I say I want to tell you. But you're of a different race and I must keep the secrets of the Ewdicani."

She turned away. "Ah yes," she said bitterly. "The famed secrets."

"Hey," he replied indignantly. "Don't be like that."

She turned back to him. "But this is all so ridiculous. Everything is just a game. They don't care about me; all they care about is the stupid war. And I'm not even staying here."

"You aren't?" he asked.

Eishoxa turned to look at him and shook her head. "No, I told you yesterday. First, I go back to the Tree and then I'm allowed to go back to Bareth. I made a deal with Vera."

"I thought you were joking," he admitted. "But you would leave your people whilst they're at war?" he enquired in disbelief.

Eishoxa turned her gaze away from him and looked at her feet. "They aren't my people. I feel no loyalty to them. I was forced to leave my people in Bareth. That's where I belong, and anyone who says anything different is wrong."

"I don't want to argue with you, Eishoxa," Rush sighed. "But that sounds like you're running away."

Her head jerked sharply up. "What do you mean?"

"Exactly what I say. I can't help but think it. You take all this injustice upon yourself, you do everything that you're told to do, and then when it matters you return to the Oblivious. I don't understand it."

"They aren't just Oblivious. They're my people. That's my home," she argued.

He opened his mouth as if to say something, then closed it and shrugged. "I cannot say anything. I'm not part of your race."

Eishoxa nodded curtly and turned away again. Then she turned back. "And Oblivious of what? Why are they called that? Why are they called Ignorant? That's so rude."

"They're oblivious or ignorant of the joy of knowing what it's like to devote your entire being to an element," Rush explained calmly, laying the books on the table beside him and clasping his hands.

Eishoxa scoffed. "That's ridiculous."

"Only for those who've never experienced it," Rush replied coolly.

Eishoxa, knowing she'd been beaten, smiled ruefully. "Is that a fair thing to say?"

"It's the truth."

Eishoxa smiled properly. Rush took up the books again. "Here. You can read them." he joked. He bowed to her. "I must go now, my Lady Little Flame," he said. "I have duties to be getting on with."

"What sort of duties?" Eishoxa asked curiously.

"Oh, many," Rush said with a mock sigh of exhaustion. "Too many to count." He opened the doors to the balcony and climbed onto the rail. "But I'll see you again tomorrow, Eishoxa. And don't worry. They can't punish me." And he was gone.

Eishoxa smiled and then looked back into the room. He'd left his flute. "Rush!" she called. He looked up from the side of the ice petal. "Your flute?" she said, holding it out to him.

"Count it as a present – and practice!" he called back. "I shall expect many more duets," he warned her, before grinning once more and climbing down out of sight.

CHAPTER 12

MUCH LATER THERE was another tap on the door, and when she called "Come in" it opened to reveal Leap. Eishoxa had been looking at the books Rush had left her, some of them in the Common Language and some of them in Düerasgörn. Reading had never been one of her great passions, as it had been with Maya, but she enjoyed it and the stories were really quite funny. Leap entered and bent his knees to her. "Lady Eishoxa." He then glanced around quickly as though to make sure that there were no weapons lurking anyway around the room. He will never trust me, Eishoxa thought as she sat back in her chair. "Is there a particular reason you've come?" she asked.

Leap nodded. "Lady Gresceva asks that, if it is not too much inconvenience, my Lady would be willing to see her in her rooms now."

"Oh, of course," Eishoxa said, closing the scroll and standing up.

Leap looked at the scrolls with suspicion. "Where did you get those?" he asked. "They belong to our library and you're not allowed outside your room."

Eishoxa hesitated. If she said that Rush had given them to her, Leap would tell Gresceva, but she could think of no other explanation. Leap narrowed his eyes even more, guessing at the truth. "Come," he said finally. "We must go." He opened the door for Eishoxa and closed it behind them. "This way, Lady Eishoxa," he said, gesturing down the corridor.

They walked back to the Lily Hall together. Gresceva was seated in her chair up on the platform. Rush and the other guard were standing on either side of the chair, looking straight ahead. As Eishoxa and Leap approached, Rush showed no sign at all of recognition.

Gresceva stood. "Eishoxa, you accepted my invitation. Come with me." She took Eishoxa's arm, linking it through her own, and drew her to the back of the hall where a screen hid a section of it from view. Gresceva let Eishoxa precede her. Then, taking her arm again, she guided her to a small door that opened into a delightful little rounded room. The walls were decorated with all sorts of murals, as Eishoxa suspected was a custom here, and the blue and green colours used by the artist gave the paintings a muted look, as though they could just fade into the walls. In the centre of the room was a small glass table whose feet were crafted like the feet of a bird Eishoxa now recognised as a swan. Around the room lay curious artefacts that Eishoxa could not name even if she wanted to.

Gresceva stood by the table. "Do you like what you see here, Eishoxa? Do you like my kingdom?"

"I've never seen a more beautiful place," Eishoxa replied honestly. Gresceva nodded, as though Eishoxa's answer was satisfactory. Gresceva gestured to her to sit, and sat down herself. The glass table was very cold against Eishoxa's legs, and she repressed the urge to shiver.

"And you never will see a more beautiful place," she said smugly. "No place can match the beauty of Dulcacohefen."

"I agree," Eishoxa answered, wondering where this conversation was going. Gresceva rearranged her shawls about her. As she put her hand on the table, Eishoxa saw her wrist. Never had she seen such white skin. Not even Maya had white skin like this.

"Are you hungry?" Gresceva asked. "I can call for food to be sent here."

"Not very hungry," Eishoxa answered.

Gresceva sighed. "Never mind, then. We will simply talk."

"Talk about what?" Eishoxa asked, before she could stop herself.

"You and your Indocani," Gresceva replied softly, with a quiet laugh in her voice. "You are all very impatient, are you not? You never have time to wait and think." Eishoxa said nothing. Gresceva nodded. "You're learning. I wanted to talk to you about a problem that you yourself have brought up. You're not allowed into the Assembly meetings to discuss with the rest of us why we should have this alliance."

"Yes," Eishoxa said. "If I'm not allowed in, then what is the point of my being here?"

Gresceva held up her hand. "Eishoxa, you must learn not to interrupt. Hardly anyone will get to say what they want to say to you if you do. Another fault of your people, I presume." Eishoxa again repressed the urge to speak. She wanted to know what Gresceva had to say about the Assembly. "Now, you're not allowed in. This is not just the wish of Ember, but it is my wish too."

As she paused, Eishoxa took that moment to say quickly, "You know, someone might think you have something to hide."

Gresceva's eyes narrowed, but she continued smoothly, "Of course, which is why you will be staying in your room for the duration of your stay here. I trust that you find it adequate enough to spend some time in there."

"But why may I not join? What am I doing here if I can't?"

"Alliances are not made in minutes, Eishoxa," Gresceva said. "You, as you have proven, remember little of your time here. If you were to upset the extremely delicate proceedings, then we all might suffer for it. And it would be courteous of you to respect my wishes when we are in my kingdom."

Eishoxa looked down at her hands, resting her lap. "That's not a good enough answer for me, actually. Why couldn't I sit in and not say anything?"

"That is the answer you are being given," Gresceva said with finality. "There is no more to be said."

After a moment of silence Eishoxa spoke. "Why might we all suffer for it?" she asked.

Gresceva looked at her. "Excuse me?" she asked finally.

Eishoxa repeated the question. "What do you mean?"

"Well, you're the Peacemakers," Eishoxa replied, just as smoothly as Gresceva had spoken before. "If there is no alliance – which means you don't have to go to war – then that is good for you, isn't it?"

Gresceva put her hands on the table and leaned forward, very close to Eishoxa's face. "I'm not as selfish as that, Eishoxa. As you cannot remember, we Peacemakers desire peace across the world. Unlike you Indocani, who wish to fight and fight and fight. Sometimes peace requires war." She sat back and the two of them looked at each other. Eishoxa had nothing to say. Gresceva clapped her hands. "Now we will eat," she said.

"I'm not hungry," Eishoxa reminded her.

"We will eat," repeated Gresceva, more sharply. She clapped her hands again and through the door entered three Ewdicani, each bearing a different type of food. Gresceva stood gracefully and walked to the other side of the room, coming back with two clear glass plates, two clear glass forks and two clear glass cups. She set one of each of them in front of Eishoxa and the others in front of herself. When the Ewdicani had set the food down in front of them, they each bent their knees, once to Gresceva and once to Eishoxa, and then left the room.

"Eat, Eishoxa," said the other. It sounded more like a command than an invitation. On one of the platters there was a large fish, on the other a wrinkled plant with large bulbous air pockets, and on the last a large crab.

"This is seaweed," Gresceva explained, pointing to the plant. "And some of the fruits of the sea – fish and crab." A large jug of pale blue liquid had been placed on the table as well, and Gresceva poured each of them a glass. It did not look like water, but Eishoxa doubted it would do her much good.

"Why aren't you eating?" Gresceva said.

"I can't eat anything that has water in it," Eishoxa said, pushing the food around her plate. Gresceva nodded. "This food cannot hurt you. I would never dream of hurting a guest. Eat. It is rude not to."

Eishoxa picked up her fork and speared one of the pieces of fish. The food was slimy in her mouth at first, but then tasted a lot like what she'd eaten in Bareth. The drink was very salty and Eishoxa wasn't sure that she liked it. Gresceva was eating everything on her plate, but Eishoxa noticed that she kept glancing up at her. When both of them had finished, in complete silence, Gresceva clapped her hands again and the Ewdicani entered and cleared the table. When they'd gone, Gresceva sat back in her chair again for a moment, then leant forward again saying, "I know that you've already left your room in the company of one of my guards. I warn you, I'm not someone to be trifled with."

"So you're spying on me as well," Eishoxa countered. "Does that count as politeness?"

Gresceva made no reply but abruptly stood up and went to the room's only window. Opening it, she called something out, and in a moment Eishoxa heard the sound of beating wings. Gresceva put her hand outside and, when she drew it back inside, seated on her arm was a beautiful bird: a swan, but bigger than the one Eishoxa had seen on the river with Rush.

"This bird is mine," Gresceva said, carrying it over to Eishoxa. Its sleek feathers looked like snow, and its graceful curving neck ended in a large orange beak, with two small black eyes sparkling above.

Eishoxa drew back slightly. The swan was beautiful, but Eishoxa felt fearful. She did not believe that it could do her no harm.

"It looks very peaceful, doesn't it? Very beautiful and very peaceful. Maybe this is how you see Dulcacohefen."

Eishoxa said nothing. Gresceva was speaking in a dreamy voice, but Eishoxa was not fooled for a minute.

"But ..." Gresceva whispered. Without warning, the bird struck out with one of its strong feet and a long scratch appeared on Eishoxa's hand. "But we are not like that at all." The bird flapped its huge wings and suddenly it seemed so much bigger. Eishoxa could feel blood welling up in the scratch on her hand. Still she said nothing. Gresceva held out her arm and the bird flew to the windowsill and then flew out of the room.

"Do as I tell you, Eishoxa, or there will be consequences."

Rush came to Eishoxa's balcony the next day as promised. She let him in and he went immediately sat down on the little stool. "That climb is not one I do often," he said, a bit breathless. "It's more tiring than you'd think."

"I can imagine," said Eishoxa. Rush looked up at her. "You still look very strange dressed in your red and orange clothes. You should switch to something blue and green."

"I don't have anything like that, and they'd feel very strange on me," Eishoxa responded.

Rush stood, recovered from his climb. "I think they'd look lovely. Anyway, how was Gresceva?"

"Awful. I hate things like that," Eishoxa said, twitching her hand to put the scratch out of sight. She'd spent most of the previous night trying to decide what Gresceva had meant by setting the swan on her. Had the swan been a warning? Was Gresceva trying to tell her something? Or perhaps Gresceva had unintentionally given something away, something that gave Eishoxa an insight into what they were doing. Whatever it meant, she couldn't explain it, but she wasn't ready to share it with anyone yet, not even Rush.

"Really?" Rush asked, putting his head on one side.

"I can't stand her," Eishoxa admitted, and then realised she probably shouldn't say such a thing in the hearing of an Ewdicani. Rush was so easy to talk to that sometimes she forgot he was Gresceva's guard. He seemed just like Maya, a friend in that sense, to whom she could say whatever she wanted.

"I think you may find that many people share your feelings."

"Then how did she become leader? How does she stay leader?"

"Wella trusts us to choose our own leader. Although Gresceva isn't liked by many people, she has a way of speaking that makes people believe she's right, or at least making sense."

"Dangerous," Eishoxa reflected.

Rush nodded. "I agree. But all the more reason to keep her there. If she's thrown down, she could start a civil war within the Ewdicani and then, with that added chaos, we'd really be destroyed. No, at this time of conflict, it's better to leave her there and simply keep a watch on her. So what have you decided for today?" Rush asked. "More duets?"

"I suppose that's all that's left to us," Eishoxa sighed, looking wistfully at the door.

Rush shook his head. "No matter how tempting that sounds, I have something to show you. Something that I think you'll enjoy."

"Rush, I can't leave this room. Gresceva made that very clear."

"And since when did you start following rules?" Rush asked.

Eishoxa looked at him. "You're not at all like the other Ewdicani."

"Is that a good thing?" he asked, as though he couldn't quite decide.

"No! You're meant to follow the rules and convince me to follow them as well."

"Why do you think that?"

"Because Indocani are more rebellious, and so far every Indocani I've met in this place has told me to follow the rules."

"More rebellious than the Warriors," Rush mused. "That's something that hasn't happened yet."

"It's not a good thing," Eishoxa replied.

"But I want to show you something," Rush said. "And no one will see us and you did as you were told yesterday and so you can have a day off today."

"I thought you jealously guarded the secrets of the Ice Lily," Eishoxa said, hands on hips in mock accusation. Rush shrugged. "I do. But with some people, it's useless trying to guard things when they're going to find them out anyway. Now come on, let's go."

Eishoxa hesitated only a moment. "All right, I'll come. But you know it's Ember we must answer to if we're caught."

"We call this the Mother's Nest," Rush grinned. "But to you it's just a library."

He opened the door for her and she smiled her thanks. "Well, I hope it lives up to my expectations."

"It won't disappoint," Rush promised.

Eishoxa entered the room and was speechless. "Like it?" he asked. Like couldn't begin to describe it. It was shaped like a lotus flower, made totally from ice. The place shimmered with a strange blue light, cast from iridescent sapphires resting in the middle of a silver nest, impeccably crafted. A cool breeze blew gently. All around the room, set into white stone, were clear basins of still water. The walls were lined with layer upon layer of shelves, all made from mother-of-pearl, its mottled colours proudly on show.

"It's beautiful," Eishoxa breathed. Rush beamed. "I thought you'd like it. Come on, I want to show you something." He walked her towards the back of the room. Eishoxa followed slowly, looking at everything around her in awe. Rush stood before a plinth on which were painted statues of three women.

"The three Goddesses," Eishoxa guessed aloud as she came up behind Rush.

"Yes," he said. "Fiera, Wella and Nezrax. Fire, water and rock."

Eishoxa approached the statues. Fiera's skin was dark brown, a warm, dark, desert brown, and she stood almost at the very front. She was looking up and her sword was drawn and held high above her head. On the other arm perched an eagle with outstretched wings. Her red hair, loose and explosive, surrounded her head in a halo of colour. She was dressed for battle and the expression on her face was fierce, brave and arrogant. On her back hung a huge bow along with a curved quiver of arrows.

"I wonder how the arrows fit in that thing," Eishoxa remarked dryly.

Rush laughed. "Yes, well, the sculptor was going for what it looked like, rather than the truth of it."

Wella was sitting down, looking very like her depiction in the fountain, but here she was looking at Fiera with something like jealously, or at least awe. Twisted strands of seaweed made up her corset, and her long plait fell down her back. Her skin was palest blue, and on her left shoulder was a tattoo of a swan in full flight down a river. Where legs should have been, she had a tail, a long beautiful tail made for swimming through the depths of the sea.

Eishoxa turned to Nezrax. She had never seen this Goddess before. The sculptor had placed her right at the back, and seen from a certain angle the other two blocked her out entirely. The first thing Eishoxa noticed was that Nezrax looked so young, perhaps even younger than Eishoxa. Her skin was white like Wella's, but a strange white, as if all the colour had been drained from it. Eishoxa was reminded of something, but couldn't quite remember what. In contrast, the Goddess's hair was black and straight as pokers. Her feet hovered on a cloud.

"What is that?" Eishoxa asked.

Rush looked at what she was pointing at. "That's the roof of Hell. It's said that she stands upon it. Of the three Goddesses, she's the only one who can fly without assistance. Even Fiera must use a dragon. You see around her neck, she carries the key to Hell, where she's said to lock away all her enemies."

Eishoxa stepped closer. The eyes of Fiera and Wella were looking away from her, but no matter where she moved, the eyes of Nezrax were trained on her.

"What's that on her arm?" Eishoxa asked, pointing at a strange symbol that adorned her right shoulder.

"That is the symbol of the Pentelement. Haven't you heard of it?"

"No," Eishoxa said.

Rush looked slightly surprised but didn't falter. "I heard that Rianox gave you some history lessons. I'm surprised he didn't mention it. So of course you know about how the world was once ruled by a single God, named Pentelemence?"

Eishoxa nodded. "Rianox mentioned that. He also said that the Goddesses defeated him and destroyed the old, corrupt world by going to war. They created a new world."

Rush nodded. "Correct. The world that we live in today. And they grew forests for Earth and filled the world with wind for Air. After

156

that, they divided the three remaining elements between them: fire, water and rock. Wella and Fiera tried to work together, but Nezrax took her powers and left the other two. She formed a cult, you might say, and called it the Pentelement. She wanted mastery over all elements, instead of restricting herself to just one."

"And did that work?"

"She's the Goddess of sorcery as well. Did you know that?" Eishoxa shook her head. "Of course," Rush corrected himself, "Fiera and Wella have their own magic, magic that they've passed on to those who follow them. But the magic of the world, the sorcery that hides in the world, belongs to Nezrax. And she used her magic and the knowledge she'd retained about Pentelemence and has gained mastery over all five."

"Really?" Eishoxa said.

"Really," Rush nodded. "And she teaches her followers how to do the same. Fire, Water, Earth, Rock and Air. There's hardly any substance in this world that they don't control."

"Why don't the Ewdicani and Indocani do the same then?"

"We've been chosen by our element, Eishoxa. They're strange things, living within us but allowing us to control them and do what we want with them. When you've been chosen by one, it would be sacrilege to try to take more upon yourself. And it's very dangerous. It can lead to one going mad, as has happened to so many of the Empty. Their minds are filled with impulsive, reckless thoughts that they regret after. The elements are so different, you see."

Eishoxa nodded. "Why does Nezrax look so young?"

"It's to unnerve people," Rush explained. "All three Goddesses can take many forms, but these are their preferred ones. Nezrax looks so young because it makes her look very different. It's a trick. Nezrax has sorcery under her command. She can invade dreams and minds much more easily than the others can. She can befuddle sane thoughts and make insane ones seem perfectly rational. She is the most dangerous because she can get everywhere, and there's very little anyone can do to stop her."

"Why is she blocked from view if you look a certain way?"

"This is the image of an Ewdicani's mind. No matter what we do or think, a part of us admires the wild way of the Indocani, no matter how wild they are. They live without reservation, without apology, without thinking. There's a reckless, dangerous freedom in them that a part of us can't help but look kindly upon. That's why Wella is looking up at Fiera like that. And most of the time, we block darkness out of us because we don't want to see that it's there. If we acknowledge it, then we acknowledge that we're doing something wrong. But Nezrax is always watching us, waiting for the best moment to strike." Rush looked again at the sculpture. "Everything we make has a symbolic meaning."

"So beauty is not there just for the sake of beauty?"

"That depends on what you call beauty. For me, this image is beautiful because it captures so perfectly something that a lot of us refuse to admit."

"And do you think that you should only control one element, despite it putting you at a disadvantage?" Eishoxa enquired.

"I believe that the elements have chosen us. I know that if one has control over all elements, they're more powerful certainly, but what would that do to a person? To have so much power? Our nations refuse to believe that any good can come from having more than one element inside you. I think it would destroy us."

"So you agree?"

"I don't agree exactly … I think that denying that it's all bad is a bad thing. It cannot be denied that five elements will make you more powerful, and that fact is what both our nations refuse to accept. They think total control of a single element is better – but then again, they were made to think that way."

"And you weren't?" Eishoxa asked.

Rush smiled at her, seeing her point. "I was made to think, and to think of new ideas and new alternatives, and that is what I delight in doing."

"So the Indocani and Ewdicani lie to themselves?"

"They withdraw information, or refuse to accept it," Rush said.

"So they lie," Eishoxa concluded.

"You would call withdrawing information lying?" Rush asked, his thoughts stopped in their tracks.

"Not being honest," Eishoxa offered. "Maybe not all the way to lying."

Rush nodded. "Interesting," he said. "Interesting."

"What's so interesting?" Eishoxa asked.

"The Indocani are masters of battle strategy and defence. When they're young, they're trained to lie convincingly so that, if they're caught by the enemy, they can give false information. It's interesting that you believe lying is wrong when, for many of your kin, lying is part of their lives."

Eishoxa turned this over in her mind. She thought she could tell when Ember was lying. Was that something she'd learnt to detect the last time she was here? Or was he creating an elaborate pretence, a mix of deception and truth? She would never know.

CHAPTER 13

THE DAYS TOOK on a steady rhythm, as they had at the Tree. Every morning Ember would come in and check on her, remind her that she was to stay in her room, and leave to go to the Assembly. Rush would then arrive to take her away to see the delights of the Ice Lily. He showed her strange instruments, shaped like flowers and animals and birds, instruments with strings and without them, with hollow bodies and made from reed or made solidly from wood. He would take her out on his boat and show her all the weird and wonderful creatures that lived up and down the river. He would take her around the whole of Dulcacohefen, showing her the lakes and streams and great rivers that roared down their courses. They would spend long hours on the riverbank, talking about everything they could think of and debating back and forth. He would take her again and again to the library and was teaching her how to read simple pieces of his own language. And all the while, the Assembly was debating and discussing, and Eishoxa heard nothing more about what was going on inside.

She would have enjoyed herself a lot more if she hadn't felt so guilty. She was not meant to be enjoying herself, she told herself time and again. I need to finish here and get back home, home to Bareth. That was all that mattered. But the longer she stayed, the more Bareth seemed to stray from her mind. This place was so beautiful, much more beautiful than the Tree. But here was the one place she couldn't stay.

Eishoxa was sitting with Rush by one of the lakes. He'd brought some of the Ewdicani's fruit with him and was eating it, throwing the seeds into the lake. She'd noticed that the Ewdicani ate a lot more than the Indocani. In all her time here, she hadn't been hungry once, and had only eaten when she had arrived with Gresceva and a few times when Rush had brought her new things to try.

The sun was shining and Rush was sitting in the shade of a tree, out of the sun's glaring rays. Eishoxa was skimming stones along the surface of the water. Rush had taught her how to do this and she was getting better and better at it. As she did so, she noticed that the water was bubbling and frothing slightly by the bank. She stopped to watch it. It bubbled for a few more seconds before a jet erupted from the surface and bounced along the surface, just like her stones had been doing a minute before. She turned and saw Rush grinning at her. Tossing the rest of the stones into the lake, she sat by him, still in the sunlight.

"I wish I knew what they were saying," Eishoxa revealed suddenly.

Rush sat up. "What who were saying?"

"The Assembly. I want to know what they're saying."

"Why?" Rush asked. He sat up straighter and shrugged. "You're leaving here. Whether they secure an alliance or not, whether they go to war or not, it doesn't bother you."

"Do you always speak in that way?"

"You're a very confusing person, Eishoxa," Rush said, standing and walking out a bit towards the lake. "You want to leave here, but you want to make sure there's peace. In other words, you care about something that you think you shouldn't care about."

"No, I don't!" Eishoxa denied. "To want peace somewhere, that's just common morality and decency."

"Not what the Indocani would say," Rush pointed out.

"No. That's not what Indocani would say," Eishoxa agreed, hearing a hint of sarcasm acidify her words. "But I don't consider myself one of them, as I keep telling you."

"But you let them tell you what to do." Rush's words were provoking but his voice was as calm, as though talking about the size of the lake or the colour of the sky.

"They know how to get back to Bareth, and that is where I want to go! I have no choice!"

Rush sighed. "Eishoxa, you need to remember that there are times when things seem unfair, but you have to take them as they come."

"That sounds like you're encouraging me to give up," Eishoxa accused.

Rush nodded. "Maybe I am. But you take the all too dangerous path of wanting things that are almost impossible to have."

"How can you say that?" Eishoxa asked in disbelief.

"Long ago, I too lost people I loved," Rush explained. "I lost them in an unprovoked ambush to one whom I started to hate with all my strength. Every minute of my day was consumed with thoughts of revenge. I did terrible things, and I thought them brilliant. All it did was bring me misery. Sometimes you must follow your head."

Eishoxa didn't reply. She couldn't argue with Rush, whose arguments were so true and presented so calmly. Instead, she picked up a stone and chucked it towards the lake angrily. It disappeared with a huge splash.

Rush sat back down beside her. "As it happens," he began slowly, "I know a way into the Assembly Hall. If you really want to listen, I could take you there."

"Really?" Eishoxa asked.

He nodded. "But we have to be quick, and at the first sign of trouble we have to leave. The penalty for doing this is probably greater than you think."

He took her back to the Ice Lily. They entered through Gresceva's garden door and walked hurriedly through the corridors. "Now, we must not be seen," Rush told her. "You're meant to be in your room. If anyone sees us, we'll both be in trouble."

They walked in the direction of the Lily Hall, but before they reached the double doors Rush pressed his hand against the wall and pulled Eishoxa into a small passage, so narrow that she had to walk through it sideways.

"This takes us to the small balcony over the Assembly Hall," Rush said softly. "We must be quick and quiet now." He closed the door, throwing them into complete darkness. For a moment Eishoxa panicked, then she took a deep breath. "Right, let's go," Rush said. They walked crab-like down the slim space, which twisted and turned like all the passages here, and then the ground started to climb upwards. Rush stopped and whispered, "Now we go silently. We're over the Assembly Hall now." Eishoxa crept as quietly as she could. She heard muffled voices and shouts as though there was an argument, but there was no sign of light or the end of the passage.

Suddenly it broadened out and they could walk normally again. A dim light appeared and Rush halted again. Slowly, step by step, they walked forward, finally crouching down. As they reached the light, Eishoxa saw that they were looking out over a hall about half the size of the Lily Hall. She and Rush were on a closed balcony, with rails in front of them but a roof and walls as well. Gresceva sat at the head of a large table in the centre of the floor. Down the sides sat the members of the Assembly. They were all men apart from Gresceva.

"Just like our Council," Eishoxa breathed.

"Yes, but they both have a female leader. These are the Faithful, those dedicated to keeping the peace," Rush murmured back, shifting slightly to sit more comfortably. Ember, Ash and Smoke were standing at the other end of the table facing Gresceva, directly below Rush and Eishoxa.

Ember was speaking. "It is the right time to attack! You ask for peace, and this I understand. But it is cowards who quake here, hiding away from the reality of our world. We are at war and you are as well, no matter what you think or decide."

Eishoxa raised her eyebrows. Ember's words were strong, but insulting as well – not the way to win people over to his side.

Gresceva spoke now. "We are a long way away from the war, Ember. If the Empty start to arrive, then perhaps we will consider your proposition, but until then I don't think there is a lot that you can do." Her tone was scathing and Eishoxa was not surprised to see Ember bristle. "My Lady, the war is coming here. As we speak, Empty are moving towards your lands. They come not from the Sorrowful Mountains but bend around to the east, to where you are." He gestured to Ash, who brought forward a map and laid it on the table. The members of the Assembly leaned forward to look at it.

Ember jabbed the map with one finger. "These are the Sorrowful Mountains. This is where you are and this is the Tree. We're fighting the Empty on the plains in front of the left-hand side of the Sorrowful Mountains and we're coming from both sides, straight through our holy ground and up through the desert. But we've been informed that they're now doubling back and attacking from the right, having found a way through the Cursed Marshes. They will move through your lands and approach the Tree that way. If they can cross the Cursed Marshes, then we have no hope."

"How do you know that?" called out one of the Faithful sitting near Gresceva. Ember looked up. "Spies, scouts, all kinds of things. The problem is not how I know, but that your lands are in danger. The

Empty will wipe this people out, once and for all, unless you act now. We are ahead of them, but we won't be for long if you keep up this stubborn attitude. You need warriors! And now!"

"Ember," Gresceva called out. He looked up. She rose and all the Faithful rose around her. "A word in private please." Ember nodded and those around the table, as well as Ash and Smoke, sat down. Gresceva and Ember walked towards one corner of the Assembly Hall.

Eishoxa looked to one side and saw that the passage they'd come through continued towards the corner where Gresceva and Ember had gone. "You wait here," she told Rush in an undertone. "I'm going to find out what they're saying."

"It's too dangerous!" he hissed. But she was already gone, scrambling quickly along the side. Rush stayed where he was.

Eishoxa went forward until she was quite close to where they stood below. That was fortunate, as they were whispering. The ground was gritty underfoot and Eishoxa had to move carefully so as not to make a sound.

"Ember, you're straying onto dangerous ground. You need to slow down," Gresceva was saying.

"Can't you just agree and finish this?" Ember demanded. Eishoxa stiffened in shock. What did he mean?

"No!" Gresceva exclaimed. "If I agree now, it looks strange. We need to give it time enough for some of the Assembly to agree as well, and then we will move."

"It's taking too long," Ember said. "If I go too slow, then Ash and Smoke will be suspicious." Suspicious of what, Eishoxa thought. What were they doing? Had they agreed something else? Was this why she was not allowed into the meetings?

"And what about Eishoxa?" Ember asked. Eishoxa jumped at hearing her name.

"What about her?"

"She'll get suspicious as well."

I'm suspicious already, Eishoxa thought. She shifted slightly, causing a little shower of grit to fall to the ground. Eishoxa froze and stopped breathing.

"What was that?" Ember asked. There was an excruciating pause as Gresceva presumably looked about. "Nothing," she said finally, and Eishoxa let out a slow sigh of relief. They started to return to the table where the others sat when Eishoxa heard another door open below her and she heard Leap speaking in his native tongue.

"Eishoxa isn't in her room," Gresceva told Ember.

Eishoxa scrambled back up the passage. "Rush, we have to go!" she hissed. "Now! They know I'm not in my room!

CHAPTER 14

IT TOOK HIM just a moment to react. Back down the passage, going as quickly as they dared, sliding sideways between the thin, narrow walls all the way to the bottom. Rush stepped in front of her and placed one hand on the door.

"There's no one there," he said. "Now, we must hurry." They stepped out into the corridor and Rush closed the passage behind them. To everyone but those who knew it was there, it looked simply part of the wall.

They ran through the Ice Lily until they got back to Eishoxa's room. "Good!" Rush said. "Now, inside – and I must go!"

Eishoxa nodded, threw open the door and closed it behind her. She seized a scroll, leapt onto her hammock and opened it. She barely made it in time. Just as her eyes focused on the words, the door opened again, this time showing Ember and Leap. Eishoxa looked around. "You know, you used to knock," she reflected. "I wonder what I did to lose that honour."

"We don't knock when we don't think someone is here," Ember replied, looking around the room suspiciously. "But you told me to stay in my room," Eishoxa pointed out. "Why would you think it was empty?"

Leap stepped forward. "Lady Eishoxa, I was here just now and you were not. Where were you, and who were you with?"

"You must have been mistaken," Eishoxa replied coldly. "I've been here all this time, since this morning."

"You're lying!" hissed Leap, taking a step towards her. Ember barred his way. "That's enough, Leap. You may go. I will deal with this."

"Sir, this is a matter that involves Gresceva and my people as well."

"I have Gresceva's favour," Ember said. "I can sort it. Thank you, Leap." Leap gave Eishoxa a look of severe dislike and left. Ember watched him go, then turned back to face her. "Eishoxa, he came here and you were not here. You're a good liar, but not good enough to fool me."

"I've been here all this time," she repeated, keeping her voice flat and even.

Ember shook his head. "As you know when I lie, I know when you lie."

"Maybe you don't know as well as you think," Eishoxa said.

"He came to your room, Eishoxa!"

"And between him and me, he's the one you trust more?" Eishoxa asked. "I've said that I've been here all this time and he said I haven't. You were nowhere nearby, so you have to trust one of us. Now you decide."

He didn't reply at first. "Eishoxa, do you remember an Ewdicani called Rush? Do you know him?"

"How can I answer if you don't trust me?" Eishoxa answered coolly.

Ember threw his hands in the air. "Leap was here! He came to your room! The evidence points against you!"

"His word against mine!" Eishoxa continued.

Ember put his hand up. "All right, say you were here and he's the one who's lying. Improbable, considering he is an Ewdicani and they don't usually lie."

"*Usually*," Eishoxa stressed.

"So, do you know an Ewdicani called Rush?"

Eishoxa looked at him, straight in the eye. "No," she said. "Never heard of him."

Ember turned on his heel. "Make sure it stays that way."

It wasn't many days after that incident that Eishoxa was summoned. A female Ewdicani, whom Eishoxa had never seen before, knocked on her door and told her that she was to come immediately to the Lily Hall. Eishoxa had a sense of foreboding as she followed the girl. She knew the way almost off by heart now, despite many twists and turns along the path. When they arrived, the girl bent her knees to Eishoxa and walked away. Two Ewdicani at the doors opened them for her. Every time she came in here she was struck by its beauty, but now she suspected that beauty of hiding something else – something that could only be hidden under beauty, like the statue in the Mother's Nest.

Gresceva stood in front of her chair, watching Eishoxa approach. Rush and other the guard, whose name Eishoxa had learnt was River, were stationed on either side of the chair. Ember stood beside Rush. "Eishoxa, welcome," Gresceva said. She was using her strange, floaty voice, the gentle one with which she'd greeted them on their arrival. "I trust that your coming here did not inconvenience you."

"I wasn't doing anything else," Eishoxa replied.

Gresceva nodded. "Good. Well, if you could come with me. Ember as well."

Gresceva beckoned to Eishoxa to follow. The three of them went to the room that Eishoxa had been in before, the room hidden just behind the screen. The minute they were there, Gresceva pointed to a chair. "Sit," she ordered. Her floaty voice had disappeared. Ember nodded to Eishoxa and she sat, although that was the last thing she wanted to do. She could feel waves of anger pouring off Gresceva, big, dangerous waves. Ember was watching Gresceva with a carefully guarded expression.

Gresceva folded her arms. Her foot was tapping agitatedly. "Eishoxa, do you remember what I told you when I brought you here before?"

"Yes," Eishoxa replied.

"Tell me."

"That I was to stay in my room no matter what."

"And did I give a reason?"

"No," Eishoxa said.

"No," she affirmed, "I did not. But does that diminish in any sense your obligation to obey?"

Eishoxa didn't answer straight away. She could feel Ember's eyes on her and Gresceva's penetrating stare. "Well?" Gresceva asked. Eishoxa looked at her. "It shouldn't."

"And did it?"

Eishoxa paused. "If you already think you have the answer, why are you asking again?"

"You have asked me a similar thing before. It doesn't matter what I think. If it did matter, I wouldn't have troubled to bring you here. If it mattered, then I'd have dealt with things differently. But here at Dulcacohefen we like to hear things from people's own mouths."

"I told Ember the same thing that I will tell you," Eishoxa replied defiantly. "Nothing in that respect has changed."

"I see," Gresceva said. She walked towards Eishoxa and stopped in front of her. Eishoxa could see Ember out of the corner of her eye and watched as he took a tiny step back. Suddenly Gresceva's hand shot out and grabbed Eishoxa's, the one she had set the swan on. The long red mark was clearly visible. "Do you know what I think?" Gresceva asked, turning Eishoxa's hand over. Eishoxa shook her head. "I think you're lying. Again." All Eishoxa saw, once more, was a flash, but her hand was stinging again. Gresceva released it with a disgusted look. "A guard will be posted at your door."

Eishoxa looked down at her hand. The wound had opened again. "That's a warning," Gresceva added. "You may have heard something at the Assembly Hall, but that's all. And I know who your companion is as well. Ember, take her to her room – and make sure she stays there."

Ember took Eishoxa's elbow and forcibly marched her out of the room. Gresceva stayed behind.

"You're a fool, Eishoxa," he hissed as they entered the Hall again. Eishoxa said nothing. Ember stopped and dragged her around to face him. "Did you hear me?"

"I heard you," Eishoxa said.

"Don't go crossing Gresceva! She's far more dangerous than you seem to realise! This" – he grabbed the hand that Gresceva had scratched – "is a warning. And a big warning at that. Is it so difficult to stay in your room?"

"While I know that you're doing something? Yes, Ember. I lied to you. I was in the Assembly Hall that day and I heard you speaking with Gresceva. You're not doing what everyone else thinks you're doing, are you?"

He didn't reply but started walking again, pulling her along with him.

"I'm cleverer than you give me credit for," Eishoxa said sharply.

"I know," he said. When they got to her room, he pushed her towards the door. "You will have a guard on your door," he said. "Around the clock." Eishoxa was about to reply but he continued. "And Rush will be locked up for one day."

"What?" Eishoxa gasped. Ember nodded. "That's the penalty for disobeying the leader here. Be happy for him; at the Tree it's far worse."

"That's your consolation?"

"I told you, didn't I? I told you to stay away from him. I warned you. And you lied to me."

"Now you know the truth."

Ember narrowed his eyes. "I know more of the truth than you do. Now, get in there."

Eishoxa passed through the door and slammed it behind her. Walking away from the door, she heard the lock turn. Running back, she tried the door and found that she had indeed been locked in.

"Perfect," she muttered. She leaned against the wall. Poor Rush. Locked away because of her.

Footsteps sounded outside and she put her ear to the door.

"Sir Ember," came an unfamiliar voice.

"Are you to guard the door?"

"Yes. Ripple will come at midnight."

"Good."

There was the sound of receding footsteps. Eishoxa shoved against the door again but it wouldn't budge. She sank down to the floor and leant her head back against the door. Her hand was stinging and she rubbed away the drop of blood that had rolled down her wrist. Gresceva was not to be trifled with. Ember had told her that; Gresceva herself had told her that. But what Eishoxa still couldn't work out was why. Why did they hate her so much here? And what exactly was Ember doing with Gresceva? That, above all, was what had sparked Eishoxa's curiosity.

Her thoughts drifted to Rush. Locked up for a day. Did prison here mean the same thing as the prison Eishoxa pictured in her head? She couldn't imagine a place like this having a dark cell with a barred door. She closed her eyes and let dreams take her.

CHAPTER 15

THE FOLLOWING DAY was the worst she'd spent there. The door to her room was locked and she was aware of the guard's constant presence. Someone had come in the night and locked the balcony doors so she had no way out at all. She spent the day lying in her hammock, wishing she was outside with Rush and wondering whether he'd even want to see her again.

She didn't expect Ember to come to see her that day. He'd been coming most days to remind her that she wasn't allowed out, but now he knew that she couldn't get out anyway so what would be the point of his coming? Even so, in the evening, when she was sure the Assembly meeting had finished, she heard the guard stand up. She swung herself out of the hammock and placed her ear to the door. She could hear Ember's brusque tones.

"Let me in," he demanded.

The guard hesitated. "We've been told to let no one in, Sir Ember, I'm afraid. My Lady Gresceva said total solitude."

"Yes, I know that," Ember snapped. "I was the one who suggested it. But I have her favour. Now, let me in." Eishoxa could imagine Ember seeming to grow taller, the way he did when he was angry. The guard paused but a moment before there was the sound of fumbling keys and a lock being hastily turned. Eishoxa backed away as the door opened. Ember stood in the doorway and, behind him, the guard, a tiny little Ewdicani with a frightened look on his face. Eishoxa felt sorry for him. Ember could be terrifying if one wasn't used to him.

"What do you want?" Eishoxa asked.

Ember nodded to the guard, who stepped further away but kept glancing back into the room. Eishoxa suspected he wasn't used to seeing Indocani, let alone two in the same room.

"I've come to tell you that the guard will be removed from the door tomorrow."

"Oh, so soon?"

"Would you like them here longer?" Ember asked sarcastically. He sighed when Eishoxa only glared at him. "If – and only if – you promise to stay in your room and actually stay. Gresceva has had enough."

"I make no promises."

Ember ran his hand through his hair with frustration. "Eishoxa, listen to me. We've never seen eye to eye, and I understand that. Be as angry as you want with me, but please take care with Gresceva. She's not the person you think she is, she's not who anyone thinks she is. I shouldn't tell you that, but you need to know. If you make her angry, she will hurt you because she can."

"Nor am I the person you think I am," Eishoxa retorted coldly. "I know you're lying to me. I know that Vera lied to me. I know there's something else going on."

Ember threw his hands into the air. "What would you have me do?" he shouted. "I've already done everything I can. I asked Gresceva to take the guard away. I told her you've learnt your lesson. But I will not see you get hurt, Eishoxa. Count on that. I will live with your hate, but not with your hurt. I lost you once – we lost you once – and I won't let it happen again. Promise me that you'll stay here."

"I make no promises," Eishoxa replied.

Ember nodded. "Then the guard stays," he replied. Eishoxa didn't reply. Ember turned to go. "I will not stand by idly again, Eishoxa, waiting for you to get hurt, so don't ask me to."

"I don't need your protection."

"You don't want it," Ember corrected. "But you don't know how much you need it."

Ember, she knew, would stick to his word and not remove the guard until he got the promise out of her. But she'd made her own promise to herself. She didn't know whether Rush had been let out yet, but she knew that she couldn't spend another day stuck in her room, no matter how beautiful. She needed the wind on her face and the sunlight, however weak, on her skin. Another day in here and she would go mad.

The balcony doors had remained locked, so Eishoxa had searched every inch of her room looking for another way out. After her third search yielded nothing, a plan formed in her head. The doors to her balcony were made for beauty, not security. If her idea was correct, the lock that held them together on the other side could easily be broken. Pushing against the doors to test her theory, she felt them yield slightly. Smiling, she shoved them with her shoulder and felt them give a bit more. Hurrying back into the room, she seized a blanket from her hammock and approached the balcony again. After wrapping the blanket around the handle to quieten to damage she was about to cause, she kicked it as hard as she could. Something yielded, with barely a sound. She paused to make sure the guard hadn't heard anything and then pushed on the doors. They opened. The latch had broken on the other side and the wood around it had splintered and cracked, but there was nothing wrong with the actual door frame.

Eishoxa closed the balcony doors behind her and fitted what was left of the latch into the wood, barely managing to piece it together. Looking down, she saw no one about. She swung herself over the rail and scrambled down the side of the petal, finding with relative ease the handholds and footholds that Rush used. Once on the ground, she looked around again. No one. She tilted her face to the sky and took a deep breath of the cool air. Immediately something brightened inside her, as if the sun had worked its way into her skin and body.

She walked towards the garden and vaulted the small bushes that edged it. Passing the statue of Wella, she looked up again at the Goddess of Peace. Wella's face, she noticed now, bore a resemblance to Gresceva. Was this deliberate, or was this how the Ewdicani saw Gresceva, as the personification of peace on Earth? As she crossed towards the river, the eyes seemed to watch her, suspicious and harsh like Gresceva's eyes. Eishoxa wondered whether there was a single thing that wasn't subtly polluted here with the distortion that people put upon beauty. She remembered Rush saying that beauty here had a symbolic meaning: everything considered beautiful was so for a reason, beauty didn't exist simply for its own sake, as Eishoxa had thought when she first arrived. She walked down to the riverside and looked around, disappointed. The boat was safely pulled out of the water, but of its owner there was no sign.

She was about to turn back when she heard a bird chirping in the distance, followed by a voice singing softly. She looked about, but there was no one to be seen. She pushed her way through the undergrowth, following the bend of the river. The voice was getting louder and louder as Eishoxa first walked, then broke into a run, tearing through the ever thickening undergrowth and she could feel the ground getting softer underfoot. Still she heard the singing but couldn't find its source. Suddenly the voice stopped, as did the bird. Eishoxa stopped walking, wondering where she should go. She was about to turn away when she heard it again, much closer this time.

"Rush?" she called.

"Little Flame?" came the answering question. Rush stepped out from behind one of the tree trunks. He looked more tired than Eishoxa had ever seen him. "You got out!" Rush smiled. He stepped towards her but stopped just before he reached her.

"Did they give you a hard time?" Eishoxa asked anxiously. "I heard they locked you away for a day."

Rush nodded gravely. "Yes. For betraying Gresceva and the task that she has charged me with. I told her that I must follow what I think is right according to my conscience and pay the consequences of my actions."

"Rush, you need to be careful. You're taking too great a risk."

"Eishoxa," Rush replied seriously, "I take the risk I want to take. You don't remember the things I do. This used to be a much better place. Now I feel as though something has gone wrong with it, with Gresceva. I will not follow a Protector like that."

"Rush," Eishoxa said, shaking her head.

"What about you, Little Flame?" Rush interrupted. "What did they do to you?"

"Shut me in my room for a day. Ember said the guard will be posted at my door until I promise to stay there."

"They put a guard there?" Eishoxa nodded. "How did you get out?"

"Broke down the door to the balcony."

Rush laughed. "That's the Eishoxa I know. Come, we shall take the boat and go to the other side of the river. They won't find us there."

When they reached the other side, Eishoxa sat on the bank and watched Rush pull the boat onto the shore.

"Why are you angry?" Rush asked. Eishoxa looked away. "It doesn't matter."

"It very clearly does," Rush said, sitting down beside her. "Is it someone you're angry at?"

Eishoxa sighed. "Ember," she replied finally. "He's angry that I lied to him and he's angry that I told the truth."

"What did you lie to him about?" Rush asked.

"About being in the Assembly Hall that day. Leap came to my room, and when I wasn't there he reported it to Ember. Ember then got angry with me and I was taken see Gresceva. That's why the two of us got into trouble."

Rush whistled quietly. "What was that like?"

Eishoxa traced the scratch on the back of her hand. "Awful."

Rush looked down. "She did that to you?"

"Yes," Eishoxa replied. Rush took her hand and looked at it.

"I think I'm allowed to hate her now," Eishoxa reflected.

"Yes," Rush admitted. "But no as well."

"Why not?" Eishoxa asked. "I think I hate her only a little less than I hate Ember."

"Oh, Ember as well now?"

"Yes, Ember as well."

Rush stood and walked several paces away from her. "You never have the right to hate someone, Eishoxa. That's what the Ewdicani teach. No matter what they do to you."

"Really?" Eishoxa retorted. "Well, that a stupid thing to teach."

"Is it?" Rush said. Eishoxa looked up. Rush's eyes were burning with a strong emotion. "Is it?" he repeated. "War. Suffering. Grief. They come when people forget that lesson. The war we have now. Every war that we've ever had. People, resentful and angry, leave their own kin every day and go and fight for evil, for evil things. Fuelled by hate. We never have the right to hate anyone."

"Easy for you to say," Eishoxa said, turning away.

Rush put his head on one side. "What's that supposed to mean?"

"What have you lost?" she asked viciously, staring out across the river. "Compared to what I've lost?"

Rush didn't answer for a long time. Eishoxa looked back up at him and saw that he'd turned away. The part of her that wasn't raging was suddenly shocked at what she'd said. Rush hadn't done anything to her. "I'm sorry," she said quietly. "I didn't mean it like that."

Rush turned around and Eishoxa could see his eyes bright with tears. He shook his head. "No, I understand. But you can't hate Ember, not for what he's done to you."

"You don't know what he's like," Eishoxa said.

Rush scoffed. "Oh yes I do. I've been here a lot longer than you have. I was here when you last were here and Ember came too. You had a different opinion of him then."

"Yes, I'm sure I did." Eishoxa rolled her eyes. "He's cruel and without compassion. That's my only opinion of him."

"Ember is a fine warrior, Eishoxa," Rush replied quietly, looking at the river again. "And a steadfast and fierce friend. He will never go back on his word, and that's a rare quality in a person these days when nothing is known for certain. And he has a heart of pure gold, hidden beneath everything that you see. I know that. I've seen it."

"Well, I haven't seen it – and I don't think I ever will," Eishoxa answered, but Rush's words held her back from saying anything more.

170

He spoke with something akin to jealously or loss, as though Ember had something he didn't. "I haven't seen it," she repeated, lowering her head, then added, "but I wish I had, now that you've told me."

Rush turned back to look at her. "You can see," he said suddenly. "Come with me."

He took her back to the Ice Lily and through the little twisting corridors until they reached the Mother's Nest. There, he took Eishoxa right to the back, past the plinth where the three Goddesses watched them from their staring eyes, to where there was a small shelf on which only a few books lay. They weren't in very good condition, with charring on some of the corners.

"These books were given to us by you from the limited selection in your library at the Tree. But," he took them all off the shelf and set them to one side. "I think this might interest you more." He reached to the end of the shelf and handed Eishoxa a folded piece of material tied with a red ribbon. "Last time, you left in a great hurry. These were found in your room, hidden in a corner. Gresceva read them and ordered that I keep them instead of returning them to you. I didn't know why and so I put them here. Of course I read them as well, but I think Gresceva and I are the only ones who know about these things."

Eishoxa looked up at him in confusion before tugging on the end of the ribbon and unfolding the material. They were letters, at least fifty of them, written in Düerasgörn. Eishoxa shuffled through them. The letters were written in a bold hand, a strong hand, a hand that knew glory and power.

"Are they …?"

"Letters from you to Ember and from Ember to you," Rush nodded.

Eishoxa looked down at them, shocked. Words were all very well but here was proof, physical proof, that there was more to Ember than what he seemed.

"You see?" Rush said. "You cannot judge him by what you see now. The war has done terrible things to him."

"It does terrible things to all," replied Eishoxa. She turned over the letters. "I didn't know about this."

"I for one don't know why we kept them, but they must have some purpose, otherwise Gresceva wouldn't have insisted." Eishoxa nodded. "And there's something else I must show you," Rush continued, "just to prove something." He turned and pulled another book from the shelf. This one was very large and thick. Rush carried it to one of the stands that stood around for this very purpose and opened it. Leafing through, he left it open on a page and stepped back. "This is war, Eishoxa. You would leave the Indocani, your people once upon a time, to such a fate?"

Eishoxa stepped forward and looked at the page he'd indicated. It showed a scene from a battle. The colours were smudged together, though, and the figures were distorted. "I can't see anything much," Eishoxa said.

Rush took her wrist and placed her hand on top of the picture. "Now look," he said. Eishoxa took her hand away. The picture was moving.

Dragons were flying over the field, dropping rocks down on the soldiers fighting below. All over the ground, people were dying: shot by arrows, stabbed by swords, crushed by a stampeding horde of warriors. Eishoxa could hear screaming and roaring and the clang of metal on metal and smell, seeping out of the page, the all-consuming stench of blood and fear and anger and revenge.

"When was this?" she asked.

"Thousands of years ago. This is the war that caused the Goddesses to curse the land and make the Cursed Marshes. It raged across the land, from the desert in the south almost all the way to Pellimeth in the north."

Eishoxa watched as a helmet was yanked off the head of one of the soldiers. She caught a glimpse of his face. He was young, a boy even. He was swallowed by a sea of blood that rose from the bottom of the page. Eishoxa averted her eyes.

"This is what war is. This is what you leave your people to."

"I don't think I could stop that even if I wanted to," Eishoxa said. But then she looked again and saw a little inscription at the bottom of the page: "I hope this is the war to end all wars."

"You can," Rush said. "Your warriors will fight with twice the strength and courage if you're with them."

"Don't try to convince me, Rush," Eishoxa said angrily. Then, in a quieter tone, "I've already made my choice."

"I'm not trying to do anything," Rush replied. "I'm just showing you the position." He shut the book with loud crack that sounded like a heart breaking in two.

CHAPTER 16

Eishoxa could sense that the days at Dulcacohefen were nearing their end. They didn't know that she'd found a way out of her room, and Ember no longer came to visit her. Eishoxa spent every waking moment with Rush. He too suspected that her time there was coming to a close, though neither could even begin to guess where it would end.

Rush took Eishoxa as far away from the Ice Lily as they dared to go. As the sun started to set, they knew she had to head back to her room. Rush had repaired the lock enough to fool anyone who didn't look closely. There was nothing to be done about the broken wood, he'd said. They just had to hope that no one would notice it.

Dulcacohefen, Rush had told her, referred not only to the Ice Lily but to all the rivers and land around it, from the edge of the Cursed Marshes all the way to the sea. No one knew what lay beyond that sea. In the same way, he had assumed, Sicharenhafan did not simply mean the Tree but the desert and holy ground.

"Holy ground?" Eishoxa had asked.

"Yes," Rush replied. "Fiera gave the Indocani a special piece of holy ground that protects them from that side of the Sorrowful Mountains. We had one too, apparently, but it turned into the Cursed Marshes. I suppose that's why the Empty are going to attack through Dulcacohefen, if they can find a way through the Cursed Marshes." Rush showed her a map, pointing out Dulcacohefen, Sicharenhafan and the holy ground. "And one day," he said. "I wish to show you the sea. I saw it once when I was very young, and there's no other sight to match it."

"I don't think I would be able," Eishoxa replied. "Can you see Ember letting me do that?"

"We can be optimistic, Little Flame," Rush countered. "You never know what will happen."

Eishoxa posed him the question she'd wanted to ask for a while. "Will you watch Gresceva for me when I go? I don't trust her."

"I'll try," Rush promised. "But I can't promise any more than my attempt."

"Will it be a strong attempt?" Eishoxa pestered.

Rush ran his hands through his hair. "I can't promise anything," he repeated. "She's guarded by more people than me. Leap is one of them. He suspects me anyway. I have to be careful. You understand this."

"She's dangerous," Eishoxa continued, but Rush cut her off sharply. "Eishoxa, I will not go back to prison." He paused and then said quietly, "Not even for you."

Eishoxa nodded. She knew she couldn't force him. "Can we go and see the Assembly again then? I want to prove to you that she's dangerous. I want something to show you. We can't discover anything out here."

Rush looked at her. "Eishoxa, we agreed that the safest way to stay out of trouble is to be here, far away from the Ice Lily."

"But I want to know what's going on. I want to find out things."

Rush smiled. "You sound like an Ewdicani. An Indocani wouldn't even ask."

"What are you suggesting then?" Eishoxa asked teasingly.

Rush gave her an exasperated look. "I've shown you the secret tunnel and I know you'll go whether I say it's dangerous or not. I've seen that look on your face before."

Eishoxa smiled. "Good. Can we go now?"

"No." Rush replied bluntly. "By the time we get back, today's session will have finished."

"Tomorrow?"

"I'll take you," Rush agreed with exasperation. "But may Wella forgive me if I'm doing the wrong thing."

Ember was angry. "Why are you taking so long?" he demanded. Gresceva was sitting in her chair in the Lily Hall. Rush and the other guard had been sent away and the door where Leap frequently emerged had been locked. Gresceva rested her cheek in her palm and looked up at him.

"Most of the Faithful agree with you now. It would be fine to agree now! No one would suspect you of anything." Gresceva gazed at him with heavily lidded eyes. "You think that, but you don't know. You're thinking with an Indocani's mind. Vera knew – and so do I – that that's not the mind I have to persuade. It is a mind like Eishoxa's, which is still suspicious."

"She's suspicious, but not because we've been taking too long," Ember reminded her painfully.

Gresceva nodded, as though just remembering. "Ah yes, it was because she sneaked into the Assembly Hall. Speaking of which, did you find out how she did that?"

Ember shook his head. He had examined every wall and ceiling, but there was no way in except through the door that he and everyone else entered. "Anyway, you were saying …?" he prompted.

"Yes," Gresceva continued. "We need more time to evaluate. My mind works much more quickly than many of the Ewdicani, and anyway I already know the answer."

"Every moment you delay, I lose more and more respect from Eishoxa," Ember protested.

Gresceva looked up at him, amusement dancing in her eyes. "An affair of the heart. How interesting. Does this mean that our secret is not safe with you?"

"It's perfectly safe," Ember replied angrily. "And it isn't a matter of the heart," he denied, and then realised he hadn't another answer to give. Finally he stuttered, "She is a fine warrior."

"Oh yes, I forgot," Gresceva nodded. "We are taking this road. Well," she sat back in her chair again. "I expect another week or so would do it. And then there's a banquet to be held. After that you're free to go and take your precious Eishoxa away from Rush."

"They are still meeting?" Ember questioned harshly.

Gresceva shrugged. "I get Leap to check on her, but she's there so I don't know. She hasn't been anywhere nearby with him, at any rate. I have people check the gardens and the rivers. Relax, Ember. You look ridiculous with your face like that."

Ember bristled. "A week?" he asked.

Gresceva nodded. "A week. I will inform the Assembly and I expect you to do the same with Smoke, Ash, and of course Eishoxa."

Ember nodded. "I shall. Right away." He turned to go, but she called him back for a moment.

"Another thing, Ember." She had sat forward on her chair, and the expression on her face was very intense. "In order for Vera's plan to work, Eishoxa needs deep ... immersion, shall we say, in water. Otherwise, nothing will happen."

Ember halted. "She almost died the last time. How ...?"

Gresceva sat back in her chair. "Aside from pushing her into a river, I had another idea – but it would involve your co-operation."

"Does it involve her death?" Ember asked bluntly.

Gresceva gave a tinkling laugh. "Ember, we haven't finished with her yet. Do you think I would kill her?"

"I don't put anything past anyone anymore," Ember replied stiffly. "What were you thinking?"

"I will tell you," Gresceva promised, "but not just yet. It is important not to say things until it's necessary. That way you don't have to put your trust in so many people." Ember refused to recoil from the awful precision in her voice. Gresceva laughed again. "I'll inform Vera that you'll be back with her within two weeks. You may go, Ember."

CHAPTER 17

EMBER VISITED EISHOXA that evening. She'd been back from her daily excursion with Rush for a long time and had been reading the scrolls that Rianox had given her. The knock on the door surprised her.

"Oh, you," Eishoxa said, looking away pointedly. He stood by the door, unwilling to move further into the room. "Have you come for anything specific, or have you been sent by Gresceva to check that I'm here?" she asked coldly. Standing up, she held her arms wide open. "Look. All of me. Still here."

"Your words are too harsh for one in your position," Ember accused.

"Oh yes. I'm sure." Eishoxa retorted. "What are you doing here?"

"I've come to tell you that we'll be leaving in just over a week."

Eishoxa froze. "A week?" she asked, her urge to argue and fight suddenly gone. Ember noted the abrupt extinction of the defiant light in her eyes, how her shoulders rolled forward and her head drooped slightly. She loved it here, that much was obvious. Ember hoped it was for the scenery.

"Yes," he repeated. "So I suggest, Princess, that you start to say your goodbyes to your room or whatever. We don't have very long."

She didn't move. "You're cruel, Ember."

"It's what you need, because niceness didn't work with you." He shrugged, forcing down the emotion that was building inside him.

She pointed to the door. "Get out."

"With pleasure, Princess."

Eishoxa was asleep when Rush came to take her to the Assembly Hall. She woke to the sound of him playing his flute. Sitting up in her hammock, she felt an overwhelming sadness fill her.

"Are you ready to go, Little Flame?"

"We're leaving, Rush," Eishoxa announced, sliding out of her hammock.

Rush stopped. "What? When?"

"In a week," she said, folding her arms. "Ember told me yesterday."

"A week?" he repeated. Eishoxa nodded. "And do you want to go?" he asked tentatively. Eishoxa shrugged. Rush sighed. "That's not an answer, Eishoxa."

"Why are you asking me that?" she objected. "Don't ask me to choose."

Rush regarded her for a moment, then looked away. "Fine," he said. "Well, do you still want to go to the Assembly Hall?"

"Don't be like that either," Eishoxa replied quietly. "You're asking me to make an impossible decision – and one that's already been made for me anyway."

"I didn't ask what you were going to do," Rush denied. "I asked what you wanted to do ... Shall we go?"

Eishoxa sighed. "No," she said. Rush looked surprised. "Why not?"

"We'll know the outcome in a week anyway. Let's go to one of the rivers instead. You're right, it's safer anyway."

Rush's face brightened. "Very clever."

There was a sudden knock on the door. "Lady Eishoxa?" It was one of the guards. Eishoxa looked around in panic at Rush.

"Yes?" she called.

"Are you all right?" he asked tentatively, knocking again gently at the door.

"Why wouldn't I be?" Eishoxa called back through the locked door.

"I can hear voices," came the apologetic response. Rush took Eishoxa's hand and began gesturing towards the broken balcony doors. She shook her head wildly. He nodded in response. "Come on!" he mouthed. There was a rattling of her bedroom door. Eishoxa kicked open the balcony doors and pushed Rush through.

"My Lady?" came a questioning call.

"I'm fine," Eishoxa shouted. "I'm fine!"

The guard didn't take the hint from her tone. Rush was still standing outside, and anyone who came in would easily see him. There was nowhere to hide now. Eishoxa made a split-second decision and rushed through the doors. They caught with a loud bang. She swung herself over the balcony rail and started to climb down, Rush ahead of her. Once safely on the ground, they looked up. The guard, peering down at them, obviously hadn't believed her when she'd said she was alone. Eishoxa burst out laughing.

Rush clapped his hand over her mouth. "What are you doing?" he demanded.

Eishoxa pulled him into the shadow of one of the petals. "We can't hide now, Rush. He's seen us."

"Then what are you laughing about?" he asked, perplexed. "This is not a good thing." The guard's face disappeared. Rush watched him go. "And now he'll go and find Ember and Gresceva and Leap, and all three of them will hunt us down mercilessly."

"Rush, I don't care anymore," Eishoxa said. He looked down at her, confused. "It doesn't matter to me whether I get into trouble or not. I'm afraid for you, it's true, but the more they do, the more they're proving that they have something to hide."

She started walking towards Gresceva's garden and Rush followed. He pushed his boat into the river and helped her inside. Eishoxa sat down facing him. He watched her silently as he pushed off from the bank. At last he spoke. "I don't understand you, Eishoxa. But maybe that's a good thing."

He took her to one of the rivers far away. The Ice Lily was a smudge on the horizon amid the lush green grass and tall forests and winding, silvery rivers. Birds were singing, and along the water glided a swan, her young cygnets, balls of squeaking feathers, bobbing behind. The sun was high in the sky, but its heat didn't reach the ground as it did in Sicharenhafan. Eishoxa sat by the river with Rush at her side and watched two birds fly together along the surface of the river. She could see their reflections in the water and from time to time they would dip down and one wing would skim a wave. They flew in patterns together, piping their diminutive songs all the while.

"It's so beautiful here," Eishoxa said, smiling a little to herself. Rush turned to look at her. "Would you go back to the Tree if you didn't have to?"

Eishoxa looked around, as though to justify the answer rising up in her throat. "No, I wouldn't. But I have to go back."

"Do you?" he asked. His blue eyes, always so bright and cheery, had darkened and there was a deadly serious sharpness to them now. "We could ask Ember. We could persuade him."

Eishoxa made a scoffing sound.

"What?" Rush asked. "You don't think that would work?"

"No, I don't think that would work," Eishoxa replied in frustration. "Why are you talking like this? In a week I leave and in a week we'll be separated forever. That is the truth."

"Eishoxa, please don't be like that. If we have to part, it should be as friends, shouldn't it?"

Eishoxa turned to look at him and sighed. "If we could persuade Ember, I would stay. Of course I would stay. I've never had a friend like you, and I never will."

He smiled, slightly embarrassed. "I showed you the rivers, Eishoxa. I haven't done that much."

"And you think I should stay just because of them?"

His face glowed with scholarly enthusiasm. "Well, of course. Who wouldn't?"

"Rush, be sensible."

He looked affronted. "I'm always sensible. You won't find nature anywhere else in the world like the nature here."

Eishoxa laughed. "Is this really nature though? It seems too peaceful."

"Why can't nature be peaceful? Look." He edged along the bank and lifted a water lily from the river. The great waxy leaves fell over the sides of his hands and he gently cradled the pale pink flower. "Look at how beautiful it is. Why search for beauty in proud victories or dominating battles? Why look for it in loud, wild ways that die? Why not look around you and just see it? Because it's always there."

Eishoxa had no answer for him. He lowered the flower back into the water and came back to sit beside her. "Before Gresceva, we had a leader called Ahumaia. She believed that the races would one day return to Pellimeth. You do know where that is, don't you?"

"Pellimeth? Rianox has mentioned it and so have you … but no, not really."

"It's where the Goddesses first touched the Earth. It's where they put us to live, before we divided ourselves. Pellimeth was razed to the ground, except for one tower that stands alone to this day in the middle of the devastated land." Rush was silent for a moment, his words ringing in the air between them.

Although Eishoxa had never been there, an image formed in her head of the lone tower in the midst of desolation. "And Ahumaia believed that you would return?" she prompted, as it didn't seem that he was going to continue. "Why?"

Rush turned to look at her. "She said that one day people would realise that, to achieve peace, there must be peace in oneself. Everyone has an aura, Eishoxa. You can sense it when you're around them. Even the Goddesses have an aura, and so do the Empty, although they have no minds or souls. And until you're at peace, you'll find peace nowhere else and the world will always be a terrible place." Eishoxa pondered his words, spoken lightly but with a meaning and truth about them. "This is what I believe anyway," Rush finished.

He shook himself gently, as though coming out of a trance, and looked around. "And now we have Gresceva as our leader, and I fear she has ruined our people."

"Oh good, so you don't like her then?" Eishoxa deduced.

Rush sighed. "It's not up to me to say whether I like her or not," he said carefully. "However," he continued as Eishoxa opened her mouth to say something, "however, I wasn't happy when she became leader. She has no real urge to preserve beauty and strives towards another future, outside of the good of the people she promised to protect."

Eishoxa nodded. It was clear that Rush was meticulously guarding something. She didn't want to pry; she didn't sense that he was holding anything important back from her, just something personal.

They sat in silence awhile, then Rush cleared his throat. "I have something for you. It belonged to my sister, who was called Lily. But as she's no longer with us, I'd be honoured if you had it instead." He walked to the river's edge and held his hand over the water. For a moment, nothing happened, and then the water began to bubble. A moment later something shot up out of the river and Rush caught it.

"She made it herself. She would be glad for me to give it to you." He held it out to Eishoxa, who took it a little nervously: a long white dress, somehow completely dry, made of a rich, heavy material. The sleeves were long and wide, and around the waist was a narrow beaded belt.

"Thank you," Eishoxa said, knowing she held something very precious in her hands.

"I don't expect you to wear it," Rush assured her. "But she told me to find someone special to give it to."

Eishoxa folded it and smiled up at him. "I'll look after it for her."

He stood rather suddenly and held out a hand to help her to her feet. "We were seen, remember? It's time to return. We have to go earlier than usual, I'm afraid."

Eishoxa helped him push the boat back into the water and they got in. She held the dress in her arms. "What will happen to you, Rush?" she asked, concerned, as he started to row back towards the Ice Lily.

"Nothing, I hope," Rush answered, with an attempt at cheerfulness. Eishoxa wasn't fooled. "Don't worry about me," he laughed. "I'm glad to be with you. You've done many things for me as well, and I'm grateful for them."

He left her at the foot of the ice petal. "I must return to my rooms. If they've found out you're not there, it will be best if at least we're not together when they find me." Eishoxa nodded. As she started to leave,

Rush stopped her. "Don't forget about what I said. If we could persuade Ember, you would stay, wouldn't you?"

"Of course I would."

Rush smiled and then gave her a little push towards the wall. "Climb," he said. "Go on, climb. And look after Lily's dress. It was made for someone special."

When Eishoxa reached her balcony, she looked over the rail for Rush. He was already gone.

CHAPTER 18

RUSH HAD RETURNED to his rooms when he was summoned to the Lily Hall. Gresceva was meeting again with Ember, and Leap wanted both guards at her side. As Leap came to tell him, Rush could tell that he was annoyed.

"Watch that Fire," he said nastily in their native tongue. "He's getting on my nerves. His obsession with meeting privately with Lady Gresceva is highly suspicious. In fact, we should all watch him, for our nation's sake."

Rush replied in the same language. "Gresceva trusts him, Leap. That should be enough for you." He was taller than Leap by about a head, and he used his height now to tower over him. "If she trusts someone, then it's not our place to tell her otherwise."

Leap stepped back but didn't flinch. "I have her favour," he replied. "I'm her loyal advisor."

"The Ewdicani do not have advisors. And neither do the Indocani. They have a divine right, Leap, remember that."

"You sympathise with the Warrior Race, don't you?" Leap sneered. "You like the Fire Princess, don't you?" Rush didn't reply immediately. He would not defend himself against this slimy character. Leap wanted to trip him up, to make him say something he'd regret later on.

"She is a noble Princess," Rush stated simply.

Leap's eyes flashed. "But have you forgotten your last encounter with her? Not this time, but the last life. I wonder, have you told her?"

Rush looked away. The shame of his past was building up inside him, as it had been ever since Eishoxa had first smiled at him – in this life – looking at him with trust in her beautiful eyes, instead of disgust and spite and hate. It had been a long time since that smile had been directed at Rush, and now he didn't want to lose it.

"Gresceva would like to see you," Leap finished, turning away in his dismissive fashion, as if to say Rush was no longer important.

Rush let it pass and followed Leap back to the Lily Hall. Ember was yet to arrive, but Gresceva was there already, along with River, the other guard. Rush took his place on the other side, his hands behind his back, his face rearranged as a featureless mask, just as Gresceva liked him to look. He could sense she was watching him now. Eishoxa was right not to trust her, Rush thought. One look into those icy blue eyes and you knew she was everything she told people she wasn't. He knew this more than anyone.

"You like our guests, do you not?" Gresceva asked. Rush remained silent. Gresceva laughed. "I see you refuse to talk to me. Well, that's understandable. But I would like to remind you that you're my guard, and I command you in everything you do. If I say you cannot be with Eishoxa, then you cannot, no matter how innocent your meetings may be. Do you understand me?" Her voice had risen until it was almost a shout. Rush realised that she was not just angry but frustrated, and that gave her a weakness – a weakness she was well aware of, which pushed her to anger. She didn't have the evidence she needed to condemn him, no eyewitness who'd seen them together. Unable to prove anything, she was building to a fury.

Ember was announced before she could say anything else, and Gresceva immediately turned to face him. Rush noticed out of the corner of his eye that Leap entered through the side door and stood just inside the Hall, watching the pair. Rush suppressed a smile. Leap couldn't have been more obvious if he tried.

"My Lady," Ember said. Rush's gaze turned to him.

"Ember, we shall have a banquet in honour of the Indocani who have come. You, Ash, Eishoxa of course – and who was the last one? Charcoal?"

"No, my Lady. Smoke. Charcoal ..." and Ember trailed off. Rush stood more stiffly, knowing that Gresceva would finish the sentence.

"Oh yes, Charcoal came with you the last time you were here. He died, didn't he? What a pity. I did like him."

"Yes, my Lady," Ember said awkwardly.

Rush wanted to shout at him: "She's doing this because of me, not you!" Rush knew what had happened to Charcoal, and why. This was Gresceva's way of once again reminding Rush of the shame of his past.

"Soon would be good," she was saying. "I expect you want to return to your people very soon."

"Yes, my Lady."

Gresceva sighed. "Will you tell Eishoxa, or shall I? I'm sure she'll pleased. Cooped up in her room for so long, she must be desperate to get out."

Rush saw Ember stiffen. "Yes, my Lady," he said finally.

"That is decided, then. You may go, Ember."

"Thank you, my Lady." Ember bowed and left the hall.

"You see, Rush?" Gresceva asked, so quietly that only he could hear. "Cruelty is the only thing he understands, and I expect the same is true for you."

Eishoxa was on her balcony when Ember arrived to see her. She was sitting on the floor, her knees pulled up to her face, and her loose red hair hung over one shoulder. Ember paused at the sight of her. Her cheek was resting on one knee as she stared over the forest with a look of serene happiness. He stood in the doorway, unsure of what to do. He was spared a decision because she heard him and turned. She rose slowly to her feet. Ember noticed that around her waist she was wearing a slim beaded belt, but he made no reference to it.

"Yes?" she said. Ember said nothing, although the words were in his mouth. Her eyes were hard and cold and he couldn't bear to have her look at him like that. The old Eishoxa would have understood what he was doing. She wouldn't have liked it, but she would have understood. This Eishoxa didn't, and Ember found that he couldn't bear it anymore.

"Will you hate me forever?" he asked quietly. Eishoxa looked shocked for a moment but didn't answer his question, instead saying, "Is that what you've come to say?"

"Eishoxa, I've made mistakes and I know that, but ..." His voice trailed away. His mouth could form the words, but no sound came out. Eishoxa's face softened slightly. "What?" she asked.

He shook his head. "I wanted to say ... that ..." But the words stuck in his throat. He watched as Eishoxa took one step towards him and then another. He didn't know what she was going to do, but the quizzical look she'd fixed on him suddenly brought him to his senses.

"I'm sorry," he said, and left the room.

The small brook was so shallow that the bottom of the boat occasionally scraped along the riverbed. "There's a banquet planned for you and the rest of the Indocani," Rush was explaining to Eishoxa.

"When?"

"Tomorrow. Maybe the next day."

She had told Rush how Ember had reacted the day before, but he couldn't make sense of it any more than Eishoxa could.

"But why would he have behaved like that just to tell me that?" Eishoxa asked.

"He must have had his reasons," Rush said. "I heard about the banquet yesterday when Ember received the news from Gresceva." Eishoxa shuddered slightly at the sound of her name. Rush laughed. "Still don't like her?"

"I don't understand how anyone can," Eishoxa retorted.

"Leap can," Rush said. He pulled something out of the bottom of the boat and handed it to her.

"I didn't give you these yesterday. They go with the dress Lily made." It was a little collection of white, blue and green ribbons of different lengths. "I thought if you didn't want to wear the dress, then at least you could wear one of these, to remind you of Dulcacohefen."

"I won't need a ribbon to remember it," Eishoxa smiled. "But thank you." She stowed them away in the pocket of her gown. "The days are slipping away from us," she reflected.

Rush nodded. "They are indeed. But we've had a month or more, and that's a lot."

"Just not enough," Eishoxa replied.

Rush shook his head. "But you find that. If we'd had a year, we would have wanted more. If we'd had a lifetime, it still wouldn't have been enough." Eishoxa agreed.

Rush put his hand over the side of the boat and pushed them slightly in the other direction. "And that's probably the saddest thing," he said slowly. "No matter how much time you have with someone, it's never enough."

CHAPTER 19

Ember himself, with Ash and Smoke, came to escort Eishoxa to the banquet. Ember acted as though his earlier encounter with her hadn't happened at all. The three of them had replaced their belts and were carrying their sheathed knives. Eishoxa had donned the clothes she'd worn for the banquet at the Tree but had added the beaded white belt around her waist and had woven blue and green ribbons into her hair. She saw the shock on Ember's face when she opened the door.

"Why are you wearing those?" he asked, pointing to the ribbons. He made no comment on the beaded belt.

She shrugged. "It seemed appropriate."

"Where did you get them?"

"Would you like to guess, or shall I tell you?" Eishoxa asked sweetly.

Ember took her arm. "Let's go," he growled. They walked to the Lily Hall and the doors were opened for them. Crowds of Ewdicani were already there, dressed in their customary colours of blue, green and white. They spoke very quietly together and so, even though there were many, the sound of gentle music being played in the corner was quite audible. Tables edged the room, leaving a large, clear space in the centre. Ember held her elbow firmly and steered her towards the table furthest back in the room, where Gresceva sat with a guard standing behind her on either side. All along the table sat the members of the Assembly. There were four empty chairs, two on either side of Gresceva and two at each end of the table. Ember nodded to Ash and Smoke, who dutifully went to either end. Ember took Eishoxa up to sit on Gresceva's left side, while he sat on her right.

Gresceva looked beautiful. She had abandoned her usual shawls and was instead wearing a floor-length gown. It was strapless, which was unusual for Ewdicani garments. Around the hem it was a midnight blue, but the colour lightened until, at the top, it was of the palest blue. Her hair fell over her bare white shoulders. Around her wrist she wore a leather brace, which sparked Eishoxa's curiosity. Normally one wore such a thing when carrying a dagger. But Gresceva wouldn't carry a dagger, not at such a public event.

Gresceva turned immediately to Ember and completely ignored Eishoxa. The latter was fine with this and instead examined everything on the table. At the feast with the Indocani, the dishes and goblets had been crudely made out of wood, but here they were all of glass and rimmed with pure silver. There was a hush as Gresceva stood and tapped her fingernail against the edge of her glass. It rang out eerily in the almost silent room. The Ewdicani arranged themselves around the edge of room, sitting down on the chairs provided. Eishoxa noticed that there were many empty chairs and wondered who would sit on them. At the Tree, they had had benches to sit on communally.

"Welcome!" Gresceva called out into the silent room. "Welcome to this banquet of ours to celebrate our foreign guests and to say good-bye to them. Our business is almost done, and they will leave soon to return to their country. But for now, let us eat and celebrate!"

She clapped her hands and the screen at the back of the room was pulled back to reveal a line of Ewdicani, each bearing a different platter. They divided uniformly and set their platters on the table. Eishoxa recognised some of the food, but there were a great many dishes she didn't recognise. Those bearing the platters, once they had performed their task, took the empty chairs. No one touched the food yet though. Eishoxa looked around, wondering what would happen, and noticed that everyone was looking expectantly at Gresceva. She poured something into her cup, stood up again and then drank from it deeply. She then sat down again.

Now there was a great ripple of movement as everyone around the room started to eat. Huge fish lay on their sides on beds of seaweed, and little pink creatures that Eishoxa recognised as shrimp and large prawns, looking grotesque with all their legs and eyes, and all around the room large jugs held liquids of a variety of colours. Big-bellied bowls held soups of all kinds, from clear broth to stew-like creations.

Eishoxa spooned a small helping of whatever was in front of her onto her plate and started to eat it very slowly. She still couldn't get used to the taste of the Ewdicani's food, no matter how often she ate it. Looking down the table, she noticed that Ember was not eating and had not served himself anything but was simply drinking from his goblet and talking to Gresceva. Ash and Smoke were doing their best, but Eishoxa caught a glimpse of the pucker of Ash's mouth, which meant he was not enjoying whatever he was eating. Eishoxa picked up the jug in front of her, a tall narrow one, and poured herself a measure of whatever was in it. Then she focused on that instead.

"It's strange that my Lady should wear that," came a voice from her other side. Eishoxa turned and saw that she was seated next to Leap, whom she hadn't noticed before. He was looking at the band of white around her waist.

"Yes, I know. But I thought it would be appropriate," Eishoxa explained.

Leap raised his eyebrows. "Did you? And why is that? Do you feel loyalty to here now?"

"I feel as though the people here have been very kind to have treated us so well," Eishoxa replied carefully, wondering where Leap was going with this.

He put his hand out and pulled out one of the ribbons from her hair. He twisted it around one of his fingers and examined it. "Someone must have given this to you. They were not left in your room. May I ask who?"

"A friend," Eishoxa answered hotly, touching her hair unconsciously.

He raised his eyebrows again. "Does that friend have a name?"

"Why would you care?"

Leap sighed. "Lady Eishoxa, I remember from the last time you were here that you had a particular liking for not doing as you were told. I had hoped that you would have grown out of that fault, but perhaps I was wrong. You were told to stay in your room. Now," he reflected

185

as he twisted the ribbon around his finger again, "I can only imagine what would happen to the person who convinced you to disobey those in charge here."

Eishoxa said nothing for a moment and then asked, "What is your evidence that I've been out?"

He took hold of her wrist and began tying the ribbon around it. His hand was very cold and reminded Eishoxa of a dead thing, but he held it so tightly that she couldn't pull away. He finished tying the knot and the ribbon too was cold on Eishoxa's skin. He picked up his goblet but didn't drink from it. "I wonder whether it is the same person you were so interested in last time."

Leap turned away to talk to his neighbour on the other side. As he did so, Eishoxa felt a searing pain shoot through the underside of her wrist. Gasping, she flipped her hand over and did not miss the name written in ice-blue letters along the white ribbon. To hide her shaking hands, Eishoxa grabbed her own goblet and drank deeply from the blue liquid. She dared not remove the white ribbon from her wrist – that would prove he was right. But keeping it there meant something as well. What else did they know about? Did they know that she'd made Rush promise to watch Gresceva? And what did Leap mean? If she'd met Rush the last time, then why hadn't he said so?

She glanced to her left. Rush and the other guard stood behind Gresceva as usual, statue-still and staring straight ahead. If he felt her eyes on him, he did nothing. Eishoxa lowered her head. No, it must be a misunderstanding. Her drink was cold as it flowed down her throat and sat in her stomach like a block of ice.

"Eishoxa, are you all right?" Gresceva had turned back to her. Her eyes had flitted to the white ribbon around her wrist, and she was looking at Eishoxa in a peculiar manner.

"Yes, quite all right," she replied, her voice higher than usual.

"You're looking very pale," Gresceva reflected. "Is something wrong?" Her voice was concerned, but Eishoxa could see the sarcasm defining her face like an ugly drawing.

"No, nothing's wrong."

Gresceva picked up her goblet and ran a finger along the rim of it. A clear high tone rang out. "Good. Then you're ready to dance," she said. At the sound of the glass, everyone in the hall had stopped. Gresceva rose to her feet. "I hope you have all eaten enough, for we are now going to dance."

A few Ewdicani stood up and walked to the corner of the room. There they picked up their instruments – the flutes and pipes that Rush played as well as others that Eishoxa didn't recognise. Gresceva smiled. Sweeping her arms around, she invited everyone to stand. They did. And with another wave of her hand, she moved the tables back against the walls. When she clapped her hands, blue drapes fell down from the ceiling to encircle the standing Ewdicani and hide the tables from sight. Gresceva smiled again. To Eishoxa, it looked like a cage. There was one opening in it and the table blocked the view.

"Now, let our guest of honour begin the first dance," Gresceva called.

"Eishoxa?"

Eishoxa froze. Dance? Her? In front of all these people? Maya could dance. She couldn't. Panicking slightly, she turned to Gresceva who was looking at her in a particularly nasty way. Eishoxa realised something then: this was a punishment. A punishment for not doing as she was told … or perhaps she was paying for what she had done to these people all those years ago.

"Eishoxa?" Gresceva asked again. Putting her hands on the table, Eishoxa stood. Gresceva took her hand and, holding it tightly, took her onto the floor. The Ewdicani waited silently. Gresceva let go of her hand and looked around.

"Eishoxa requires someone to dance with," she said loudly, looking around. No one moved. Gresceva tutted. "Come, come, someone must dance." Eishoxa stood there and felt as though she were standing in a bright light. She could feel herself blushing but she refused to lower her head. If Gresceva wished to humiliate her, then humiliation was the last thing she was going to show.

"I'll do it," came a voice. Eishoxa looked around and saw the ranks near the table opening as Rush walked towards her. Gresceva did not pause for a moment. "Rush, as one of my guards you are not allowed. You must stay where I put you."

Rush now stood beside Eishoxa and he took her arm. "My Lady, with the greatest respect," he said quietly so that only Gresceva and Eishoxa could hear, "it is not Eishoxa on whom this will reflect badly, but on you yourself, as you suggested it." Gresceva glared at him. "You forget your place, Rush. You will be put back in prison unless you do as I say."

Rush remained where he was. Gresceva was floundering. She rounded on Eishoxa. "Dance with him then." She turned to face the table. Ember had a look of disbelief on his face and his hand was on his sword. Eishoxa looked up at him for a moment before turning back to Rush. Gresceva snapped her fingers at the musicians. "Play!" she demanded. "Play!"

They broke into a tune and Eishoxa recognised it immediately. "It's the one we play together," she said. Rush took her elbow. "And the one we'll dance to together, for your humiliation and mine."

He set both his hands on her waist and, with that, she had to walk out into the centre of the circle. The Ewdicani were murmuring amongst themselves, and Eishoxa could hear it as loudly as though they were shouting in her ears.

"I don't know how to dance," she admitted to him. He smiled at her. "And you didn't know how to play either. Follow the music in your head and it will tell you how."

The tune increased in dynamic and tempo. Eishoxa recalled the two birds she'd seen, twisting and swooping around each other by the river. She thought about the little cygnet that had swum close by to her, and about how smoothly the water rushed over the bow of the boat. And as she did, she realised that nothing she was thinking about had anything to do with the Indocani. It was as if she wasn't one of them at all, but Ewdicani. It was as if she was part of the race that she loved more, not the one that everyone told her she belonged to. And as she thought, she realised that there was nothing difficult about dancing at all. The dancing of the Indocani was wild and uncontrolled, but with the Ewdicani, each step was precise and important and made a tapestry of music and notes.

As the last chords died away, Eishoxa smiled to herself. If only Maya were there to see her. There was a quiet, polite round of applause and then the musicians started again, on a tune that Eishoxa had never heard before. The Ewdicani broke into pairs and made their way around the dance floor, turning and twisting and stepping. Eishoxa had never seen dancing like the dancing of the Ewdicani. They moved together as one, like a shoal of fish, barely making a sound as they moved across the floor. Each couple seemed to do something different, yet it all made sense.

Rush tugged on Eishoxa's elbow and tilted his head towards the break in the curtains. Eishoxa looked over at Gresceva. She was talking to Ember again, who kept shooting glances in their direction. Neither of them would be able to reach her, they were too far away. And in that knowledge, safe but under observation, Eishoxa felt a reckless urge to break for freedom, if only one last time. Leap was staring in their direction, but he too was prevented from reaching them by the many couples dancing around them.

"Leap is looking at us," Eishoxa whispered.

Rush shrugged. "He can't get to us, can he?" Eishoxa saw his grin and shook her head. They kept to the edge of the curtain, and when the music stopped for a moment, Rush pulled Eishoxa through the gap and they left the Hall.

CHAPTER 20

For a long while, they could still hear the music being played from the Hall. "It's the way the Ice Lily is designed," Rush explained. "Music can be heard along most of these corridors when it's being played in the Lily Hall."

Eishoxa smiled at him quickly but then fell silent again. Rush stopped. "What is it?"

"Why was dancing with me to be your humiliation as well as mine?" she asked. Rush absentmindedly took her hand as they started to walk along.

"There was a reason Gresceva asked you to dance first. You've been shut away in your room, supposedly, for your whole stay. No one has met you. No one knows you like I do and so, in everyone else's mind, you're still the same person you were before. And so no one was going to dance with you. As I'm sure you suspected, it was Gresceva's way of humiliating you."

"She really hates me, doesn't she?" Eishoxa mused.

Rush laughed dryly. "She doesn't really like anyone. But yes, you she particularly doesn't like. And so it will be considered a humiliation for me that I danced with you."

"Then why did you do it?" Eishoxa asked, halting in her tracks. Rush looked down at her. "Must you ask? I knew I couldn't leave you standing there all by yourself."

"But you'll be in trouble now. They've already locked you up. What will they do next time? I'm worried," she added.

"Eishoxa, don't worry about me," Rush urged sincerely. "I'm Gresceva's guard. Very few people want to do it and she needs us. Our leader has always had two guards. She can't do anything to me that she hasn't already done. I'm safe." Eishoxa narrowed her eyes at him disbelievingly. Rush laughed. "You don't believe me?"

"In my shoes, would you?"

"We try not to lie, Eishoxa," Rush reminded her. "And it's not in my repertoire to do so either."

Eishoxa considered this for a moment. "But Ewdicani try not to dance with me either," she pointed out.

Rush took her hand again. "You've spent too much time with me, Eishoxa. And I cannot work out whether that's a good thing or a bad thing."

"A good thing," Eishoxa decided. "A very good thing."

Rush decided that it would be better if they left the Ice Lily and went outside, as he couldn't be sure that all Ewdicani were at the banquet.

"Also, Leap had his eyes on us," Eishoxa reminded him.

Rush scoffed. "Leap cannot do anything. He values his position too much to openly break any rules. He won't leave the banquet." They avoided Gresceva's private garden, but in his boat Rush took Eishoxa further downriver to another secluded garden. As he said, it was too risky to go to places they'd been to before.

Eishoxa stepped off the boat and Rush lifted it onto the bank. It was dark and cold– even more so under the tall trees – but the moon shone brightly and the night sky was peppered with stars. "Go that way," Rush said, pointing up a small stone path that moved uphill, away from the river. Eishoxa found herself in a small glade surrounded by poplars that grew tall and strong. She couldn't see through the thick trunks, but the moonlight shed a dazzling, ethereal light on the centre of the glade. Eishoxa gave a little laugh of excitement as she looked around.

"The Grove of the Poplars," Rush said, pulling her further into the centre. "It's said to be the most magical place in Dulcacohefen."

"It's beautiful," Eishoxa said.

Rush smiled. "I knew you would like it. I didn't want to show you before, but now I know that you deserve it."

The place was indeed magical. Eishoxa felt its power rising from the ground at her feet and smelt it in the earthy scent that filled the grove whenever the wind blew. With each breeze that whistled around her and whispered things in her ear, she could sense that this place did know magic – deep, ancient magic. She knew why Rush hadn't wanted to bring her here earlier. This place was for water, and no matter how much she loved the Ice Lily, she loved the sun and the desert and the stifling heat even more. That didn't belong here. She looked up at Rush. "Thank you for showing me this," she whispered.

"This is the first place of Dulcacohefen that was built," Rush added. "Deep under the ground runs the last seawater spring. The others dried up a long time ago, but not this one. That's why this place is so special to us."

Eishoxa smiled again. "It is amazing," she said.

"What's that?" Rush asked, pointing at her wrist. Eishoxa looked down at the white ribbon. In the silver moonlight, it was glowing vividly against her dark skin.

"Nothing," she said, moving her hand behind her. "Just something Leap did."

"Show me," Rush replied. It sounded like an order. Eishoxa brought her hand out from behind her back and showed him. Rush turned her wrist over and unpicked the knot. Immediately, her skin seared again and the icy letters showed up again. Rush stared at them in disbelief and then looked down at the ribbon.

"I'm sorry, Eishoxa," he said, taking her hand and laying the ribbon across her palm.

"Sorry for what?" she asked. Rush shook his head and muttered something to himself. "Rush, what is it?" She touched his shoulder and he turned to face her. In the strange light, his face looked different, older and more dangerous.

"I can't tell you," he said with feeling. "I mustn't tell you." She let go of him and he sighed. "Not because I don't want to, Eishoxa," he said. He looked at the white ribbon that still lay on Eishoxa's palm and swung slightly as she curled her fingers around it. "But it's too dangerous for you to know," he finished. His words were so final that

Eishoxa didn't argue with him.

"I'm not a little girl," she said finally, so quietly that she didn't think he would hear. "I know there are things that everyone is keeping from me because they don't think I'll be able to bear the truth, but I value honestly above stubbornness or determination."

"Eishoxa, this is not a matter of determination or stubbornness. Listen to me. I have been bound by oaths that I cannot undo. And as long as the fire burns inside you as brightly as it does, I cannot reveal secrets to you. Believe me – Ember and your people may be kept silent by stubbornness, but for me that's not the reason. Do you believe me?" Eishoxa nodded.

"Now," Rush grinned. "There's something else we must do. You cannot leave until we do." He took her hand and led her back to the boat. "Climb in," he invited, raising it into the air. Eishoxa sat down in the front of the boat. Rush leaned over her and pulled on something that protruded from the bottom of the boat. "I put this in recently," he said. A large screen rose from around the prow of the boat, shimmered slightly as though made of water, and disappeared. "Now, stay where you are," he said, scrambling back over to stand at the back.

"What was that?" Eishoxa asked, reaching forward. She couldn't feel anything.

"A shield."

"Why haven't I needed it before?" Eishoxa asked.

"Because we've never done this before," Rush replied. "Now, hold on tight." He pushed them off the bank and started propelling them down the river. Almost immediately, they were picked up by a fast current rushing under the surface of the water. Eishoxa looked down. The water was creaming beneath them much faster than before. The shore was flying past, and the boat slipped in and out of the moonlight so fast that her eyes could hardly take in what she was seeing. Rush pushed them around a bend.

"Eishoxa," he called. She looked back. He'd seated himself on the other end of the boat and was stowing the large pole beneath the seats. "Hold on," he advised, and she gripped the edges of the boat. Rush reached over to the other side of the boat and took out a much shorter, stouter pole. "Do you trust me?" he asked. Eishoxa looked back around at him, wondering what he was planning. "Do you?" he asked again.

Eishoxa felt the wind get stronger as the boat speeded up. She held on more tightly. "Yes," she shouted. "What are you doing?"

He didn't reply but started to push them down the river ever more quickly. Presently Eishoxa heard a roar in the distance. It was the thunder of falling water. As she leaned forward to try to glimpse what lay ahead, Rush shouted, "Hold on!" She sat back immediately. Rush had now put away his single oar and held his hand over the water. The current was pulling them faster and faster. And then Eishoxa saw the foaming water drop out of sight.

"We're going to go over!" she shouted, spinning around to face Rush.

He laughed and yelled something back that was lost in the sound of the crashing water and the pounding in her head. The current dragged them towards the edge, where they slowed for a moment. The river was plummeting down, with a thunderous crash at the bottom. A scream built in her throat and then they were falling, down, down, down. Rush was laughing loudly and whooping with glee as, still upright, they were thrown from side to side, yet not a drop of water touched them. Deafened by the roaring water, Eishoxa could see sharp black rocks lurking beneath the surface, but her blood was on fire with adrenaline and Rush's delight was contagious. When they hit the water, a great wave rose up all around them. Eishoxa gasped, waiting to be drenched, but again it didn't touch her. Rush was still laughing as he took out the shorter oar and guided the boat away from the rocks.

"What was that?" Eishoxa asked, turning around to look at it.

"A waterfall," Rush answered. "I've only ever fallen down a waterfall once before, but that time was much better. Tell me you didn't enjoy that!"

"I could have died!" Eishoxa said, turning back to face him.

Rush shook his head, grinning from ear to ear. "I put a barrier all around you – the water couldn't touch you. Even if you'd fallen in, you would have been expelled from the water onto the bank. You were perfectly safe. Plus, my boat is the sturdiest vessel ever built – I made sure of that."

Eishoxa could still hear the waterfall. She tapped the side of the boat. It seemed so light and fragile.

Rush rose to his feet, took out the longer pole and moved them down the river along many twists and bends. Everywhere was deserted. "I thought Ewdicani came out at night," Eishoxa said, looking around. Apart from the hoot of an owl, there was not a sound.

"They do," Rush replied. "But everyone is at the banquet and no one has time to do this."

"It did seem a rather daring thing for an Ewdicani to do," Eishoxa teased.

Rush chuckled. "Well, I've learnt things from you – as you have from me."

They travelled in silence for a while. At the Tree, there were always sounds of some sort, but here, with the night sky stretched lovingly over them, Eishoxa could hear nothing but the gentle lapping of water beneath the boat. The river was inky black, looking cold and uninvitingly, but where touched by moonlight it shone like liquid silver, so beautiful that Eishoxa wanted to touch it. But even nature's beauty couldn't drive the night's events completely from her head.

"Do you see what I mean now? I don't trust Gresceva," she said abruptly.

Rush nodded. "I know. You've said before. Neither do I now."

"Really?" said Eishoxa.

"Really," Rush replied. "She speaks with the Assembly everyday but has secret meetings with Ember nearly every day as well. She carries a dagger on her wrist and she wears inappropriate clothes to formal events."

"Like the dress she was wearing today?" Eishoxa enquired.

Rush nodded. "And in public view. No, I don't trust her. And now she'll be more careful. We guards are meant to do exactly what Gresceva tells us. We can't take part in banquets unless she allows us, and when she needs us we must be at her side. By dancing with you tonight, I've shown her that she doesn't have my complete loyalty. And that means she'll be even more careful."

"And I don't trust Vera either," Eishoxa said. She didn't know what Rush could say about that, but she had to tell someone.

"I've only met your leader once," Rush admitted. "And to me, she seemed like everything an Indocani should be: loyal, brave, fierce—"

"Arrogant, cruel," Eishoxa finished.

"You shouldn't be so harsh."

"I thought Ewdicani told the truth."

"We also strive to be kind, Eishoxa," Rush reminded her. "Ember may have polluted your image of an Indocani, but he is only one and there are many."

"He will be a Lord," Eishoxa said. "And the Lords have control and influence. And he is great friends with both Vera and Gresceva. I don't like it."

"We know nothing for certain. It's all speculation," Rush told her firmly. "We must let events unfold in order to see the truth behind them."

"And when will we take action?" she asked. "When all our friends lie dead at our feet?"

"Eishoxa, you think I'm being patronising but I'm being realistic. You cannot fight this battle by yourself, and you cannot convince people to join your side so easily. You must be patient. If you're right, the truth will show itself. Just keep your eyes open."

"An optimist's answer," Eishoxa concluded.

"Like a leaping fish," Rush replied.

The boat scraped to a halt beside the bank and Eishoxa realised they had pulled up next to Gresceva's garden again.

"We should go back now," Rush pointed out. Eishoxa hesitated before standing. "I know ... but I don't want to," she said. Rush tied the boat to a tree, then raised it back onto the ground and secured it.

"Come," he said, taking her hand. They walked towards the garden, but as it came into sight Rush wrenched her back into the shadows. He put a finger to his lips and peered around.

"Leap," he mouthed. Footsteps approached and Rush drew her deeper into the undergrowth, where they crouched side by side. Through a gap in the leaves they saw Leap stop and look around. He walked on, then paused again. He must have seen the boat on the shore. Then he turned back, walking the way he had come. He stopped where they could see him again but then continued on, back through the garden. Eishoxa made to stand up but Rush held onto her, shaking his head. "Stay here," he mouthed. He stood and, cautiously looking around, pushed his way through the leaves. Eishoxa heard his footsteps retreat, then stop, then come back.

"He's gone," he whispered. "But we need to get out of here in case he comes back. My boat is still wet so he probably guessed we were in it."

Eishoxa came out and stood up. They were walking back through the garden towards the door when suddenly she heard a rustle sound. She looked over her shoulder to see Leap coming down the path towards them. He must have doubled back.

"Run!" she cried, seizing Rush's wrist to pull him towards the door. Rush spun around, saw Leap and took Eishoxa the opposite way. They dodged through the undergrowth and leapt over the little garden wall. Rush pulled her back into the shadow of the Ice Lily, under the petal beneath her balcony. They heard Leap running past them.

Rush looked around and above, then pulled Eishoxa forward. "Climb!" he hissed. "Climb up!"

Eishoxa set her hands against the cold wall and felt for a handhold. Tiny little notches had been cut into the ice. She climbed as quickly as she could towards the room above, and heard Rush behind her.

"Come on – faster!" he whispered urgently. When she reached the top, she pulled herself over the balcony and moved to one side to let Rush over.

"He's coming!" she warned him. Leap was climbing swiftly after them. Rush kicked open the door. "Inside, quickly," he urged. He slammed the door behind them and, taking a book, wedged it over the lock to prevent it opening. As they ran from the room into the corridor, they saw Leap hauling himself onto the balcony. The two of them burst into Eishoxa's room, laughing. But their laughter was cut short when they saw Ember sitting in there.

"Ember! What are you doing here? Why aren't you at the banquet?" Eishoxa demanded.

"I might ask him the same question," Ember replied, standing up and pointing at Rush. The tension in the room was palpable and growing. Eishoxa looked between the two of them: something unsaid was passing between them.

"We were at the river," Eishoxa said quickly, placing herself between them. "And it wasn't Rush's fault. I was the one who decided to leave."

"You're defending him?" Ember asked disbelievingly. Eishoxa shoved him away from herself and Rush.

"He has done things for me that are worth defending," she hissed.

"Really? And you think that, because of that, you'll have the chance to be friends, do you? You're from different races! Only fools try to convince themselves that an Indocani and an Ewdicani can live happily side by side," Ember sneered.

Eishoxa felt a hot blush flood her cheeks. "We are friends! More than I can say about you and me!"

"He is an enemy of yours," Ember said, stepping very close to her. "An enemy in more ways than one!"

Eishoxa looked back at Rush. He had said nothing, gave away nothing.

"Leave us, Rush," she said. Rush nodded and left the room, all too eagerly it seemed.

Ember stood back and watched him go before turning on Eishoxa again. "I don't even want to hear your lies! Throughout this time, I've told you to stay in your room! Gresceva has told you to stay in your room! And now you leave the banquet that was prepared in your honour!"

"For my humiliation, you mean!" Eishoxa retorted. "In Bareth, I didn't even do what my father told me to do – and I loved him! I don't listen to you and I don't listen to Gresceva." The back of her hand tingled where the swan had slashed her. The scratch would scar. "She doesn't scare me!"

"You don't have a father!" Ember reminded her viciously.

"No thanks to you," Eishoxa spat.

"Gresceva is the leader here!" Ember shouted. "You have to do what she says! And you should be scared of her! She has power that you cannot imagine. Water will still hurt you, it can kill you – and she controls it!"

"You try it then!" Eishoxa shouted back. "You try sitting here day after day with nothing to do, after being told you were coming here to do something, and then tell me to do what I'm told!"

"And so you turn to Rush for help? He is dangerous!"

"How?" Eishoxa demanded. "Tell me how!"

"I can't tell you!" Ember yelled, throwing his hands up into the air. "But he is, you just have to trust me!"

"I trust those who've given me reason to trust them!" Eishoxa said, taking another step towards him. "You haven't."

"I know you've asked him! I know you've asked him to tell you everything you want to know. And he hasn't. So what makes him so different?"

"I trust him! He's told me why he can't tell me and I believe him!"

"Oh really? And what great reasons has Rush given you to trust him?" Ember asked, resisting the urge to slap her.

"He is my friend and has no reason to lie to me!" Eishoxa said.

"You've known him for a month!" exclaimed Ember. "Maybe a month and a half, and you call him a friend?"

"In that month I've known more friendship from him than I have in the three months I've known you!"

That stopped him for a moment, but then he came back. "It sounds like you're desperate!"

"Yes, maybe I am!" Eishoxa yelled. "But you would be too!"

I am, Ember thought to himself. But he couldn't say it. Instead, he gave Eishoxa another long look, then bowed deeply and threw out his arms as sarcastically as he could. "I must return to the banquet, so must take your leave," he said.

"Your spying duties are over," Eishoxa said bitterly.

Ember drew his sword and put the point of it under her chin. She looked back at him without fear, knowing that he wouldn't do anything.

"I have been a patient man, Eishoxa," he said very quietly. "But I swear by this sword that if I see the two of you together again, I will do something you will regret. And it won't be to you. So, for his safety, stay away from Rush." He jerked his sword back from her chin, knocking her teeth together painfully. "Goodnight, Eishoxa," he said, slamming the door behind him.

CHAPTER 21

Eishoxa did not see Rush the next day. He had the good sense to stay away, and Eishoxa stayed in her room. To even try to go out again would be asking for trouble. It was the first time that she'd done so for a while.

She took out the scrolls that Rianox had given her and unrolled them, looking at the scratchy writing on the page. There was a story she particularly liked in one of them. It told of a young Indocani who, after losing all his family, travelled far from his homeland in search of something worth living for. On the way, he had many great adventures, fighting demons and saving cities from great monsters, but none of the events were told in particular detail until the one where he saved a little human girl from drowning. He had always had a great disdain for humans, that point was strongly emphasised. But he had seen her playing beside the river, and she had said hello to him with such friendliness, and an assumption that he would reply, that he was instantly curious about her. But he hadn't replied, just left her sitting by herself. Next thing, he heard a splash. Turning around, he saw that the girl that fallen into the river. Without hesitation he dived in, knowing that he would die. And when he pushed the girl back onto the bank, she helped him out as well. He realised then that it was things like this that made life worth living.

Eishoxa reread the story several times. It was a strange story to have found its way into an Indocani book – normally stories concentrated on fighting and battles to show the strength and glory of war. And the little girl was human, not even Ewdicani, but the lowest of the low. She hadn't missed the look of disgust that briefly revealed itself in the Indocani's eyes when they spoke of the Ignorant. Like me, Eishoxa thought.

She went to the corner of the room and picked up the big flute. It seemed so long ago that she had played this with Rush. She still had his little flute but hadn't touched it yet. It was too precious to her. She remembered the night before, when they'd danced together, knowing that with every step they brought upon themselves more and more trouble. But it hadn't mattered. They'd been there for one another. As they always would be. It didn't matter that she would leave and he would stay. Their friendship was different from the one that she'd had with Maya. It would be cemented with the secrets that they kept and the distance they had to spend apart, and not weakened. She didn't know why she trusted him, that much she had made clear to Ember the night before. But for some reason she did. And an instinct that strong, similar to the one that had told her that Ember and Gresceva were untrustworthy, was good enough for her.

The door opened suddenly and Eishoxa looked up to see Ash standing there. "Eishoxa, you're to come to the Lily Hall. The Assembly has finished debating and a final decision is about to be made."

All the Ewdicani were grouped in the Lily Hall, perhaps even more of them than had been there the night before. Gresceva was sitting in her chair, the white stone glowing in the centre of her forehead. Eishoxa sat next to Ash at the back of the crowd on a raised bench. Smoke sat on her other side. Ember was standing next to Rush, on the platform, near Gresceva. A low hum spread through the waiting ranks of Ewdicani, like ripples on a pool of water, the sound of many conversations happening at the same time. Gresceva was sitting up very straight in her chair, but she was brooding. Eishoxa could sense it like a massive storm cloud over her head.

All of a sudden, Gresceva stood and clapped her hands. The room became silent as though under a spell. She moved into the centre of the hall. Ember stood up straighter, seeming to prepare himself for something. What had been decided? What was Gresceva going to say? Surely they had agreed to join the war – after everything that had happened, everything that she had seen?

"You know that we have been playing host for a while now to some guests from the Tree. To a party of Indocani who have travelled to us in the interests of securing an alliance between our race and theirs. For a long time, I have thought this matter over with our Assembly, the group of distinguished Ewdicani who have been chosen to keep the peace across the whole of Dulcacohefen. After long discussions, and with the approval of the Indocani, we have come to a decision."

All the Ewdicani were looking at her expectantly. Eishoxa remembered how Rush had told her that Gresceva had risen in power because she had a truly exceptional way of speaking and of convincing people that she was right. What did she want to convince people to do this time?

"We have been asked to join this war. This war does not look to be in the interest of peace, and we Ewdicani have been told to keep the peace, no matter what the consequences. However, these are difficult and dangerous times. We have been given this land by Wella herself and we must protect it. But is fighting the way to do this?" It sounded as though she were debating with herself, as though she hadn't yet made up her mind, or as though she were buying time, wondering whether her answer was the right one.

"Will fighting bring the peace that has been promised to us? The water that we strive to be like is the water that is peaceful and calm. When it is not, destruction of the most terrible sort will follow. This is not what we look for. This is not our goal. In the past there have been many wars. Think about those. We have not seen peace, and despite the wars our world is in a worse place today. But the Empty are coming. The Cursed. The ones who have abandoned their identities and joined the Goddess Nezrax, the Goddess of Evil. Evil of the worst kind. The Assembly and I have come to a decision, but as you know, that means very little. With all I have said in mind, I ask you to discuss and, by popular vote, come to a unanimous verdict." Gresceva strode back to her chair and sat down.

"What are they doing now?" Eishoxa asked. Gresceva didn't look as if she would stand up and speak again.

"It's the way political decisions are made here," Ash whispered to her. "Unlike us, they must keep the peace. They'll discuss and then vote on what will happen. Those opposed to the plan are then expected to see why their opinion wasn't considered the right one."

"And what do we do – the Indocani?"

"The Council advises Vera and Vera makes the final decision. She listens to the Council but doesn't have to agree with them. The rest of the Indocani are not consulted at all."

"So a dictatorship?" Eishoxa asked.

"That's one way of looking at it, yes," Ash replied. "But she speaks with the tongue of Fiera, remember. Nothing comes to us before passing through Fiera first. We must trust our leader."

"Famous last words," Eishoxa muttered under her breath. The hall had been silent at first but now discussions broke out across the hall. Small groups soon opened up, like a flower blooming, into bigger groups. Hundreds of Ewdicani were standing there, all talking to each other, yet Eishoxa could barely hear a sound.

"How are they so quiet?"

"Listen not to the voices," Ash advised "but to the energy. Listen with your mind. They discuss in their heads so that they may be truthful with each other."

Eishoxa closed her eyes and stretched out her consciousness into the Hall. For a moment she felt nothing, then suddenly it rushed upon her: hundreds of minds, joined together as one, pulsing with intelligence, like the different parts of a plant linking together to form the flower. It felt like a beautiful thing. Eishoxa opened her eyes to see that the Ewdicani had split into two huge circles, one on either side of the Hall. She opened her mind again, and when she could feel it, she looked for it in the Hall. It was high above them, in the centre of the ceiling: a mass of countless little lights, joining together to form a masterpiece. Then, all of a sudden, it was gone. The Ewdicani broke apart and returned to their seats. The Hall was silent again.

Someone was walking. It was Leap. He went over to Gresceva, bent down and spoke very quietly to her. Eishoxa couldn't hear a word of what he was saying.

"Be patient," Ash said. "We'll hear the verdict in a minute."

"What if it's no?"

"Then we will lose our war," Ash replied simply. He sounded so calm and sincere that Eishoxa knew he had thought about this many times and had finally come to terms with the possibility. Without any allies, they would die. Gresceva nodded to Leap, rose to her feet and straightened her dress.

"The decision has been made," she called out. "We will not join the war with the Indocani." The silence that greeted her words soon disappeared. There was a quiet round of applause and the Ewdicani started to disperse.

"Well," Ash said. "We tried."

Eishoxa shook her head. She couldn't believe what she'd just heard. Cautiously she rose to her feet and felt the eyes of all turn towards her.

"Eishoxa," Ash hissed. "What are you doing?"

Ignoring him, she addressed Gresceva. She felt her mouth open and a single word fell out, like a stone into water. "Why?"

A great silence greeted her words, but it was full of fired anticipation instead of tranquillity.

"Why what, Eishoxa?" Gresceva asked.

"Why won't you join the war?"

"We have stated our reasons, Eishoxa."

"I didn't understand. Could you repeat them?" She wondered what Gresceva would think of the sarcasm in her voice.

"We are people of peace, Eishoxa," Gresceva pointed out. "And this war will not be peaceful."

"You mean you're cowards," Eishoxa shot back. A ripple of furious whispering broke out across the Hall. Ember gave her a threatening look. Ash and Smoke were staring at her, horrified. Eishoxa swallowed but stood her ground.

"Cowards?" Gresceva repeated. "We are not cowards. We are Peacemakers. We value peace as much as you value war."

Eishoxa ignored her and instead looked around at the Ewdicani. She realised that calling them cowards probably hadn't convinced many of them to side with her, but she had to try. "I was shown the library while I've been here. And in one of the manuscripts I saw a picture. A picture that was drawn long ago. It said that it had been drawn during the time of the war that caused the Goddesses to make the Cursed Marshes. It showed the horror that happened and begged that this war would be the last, that finally people would learn that, by war, the only thing that's achieved is the opportunity for more war. I don't pretend to know a lot about this war. I don't pretend to know a lot about your people or heritage or what you believe in. But I do say that I'm a different person from the one you know from before. That Eishoxa is no more. And whatever happened in that life will exist only in the minds of those who remember it. I cannot remember and so, to me, this is my life and here I am.

"I did not come here of my own accord. I do not even come here on behalf of the Indocani, to plead for the race that has claimed me. I come as myself, to ask each and every one of you to remember the unspoken code of human decency and of humanity. You do not know this human code as well as I do, but there are morals that you will stand by as well. Now I speak to those morals and to the individual conscience of every person in this room.

"You distinguish between their race and yours. You point out differences between their race and yours, between Empty and Ewdicani, between Empty and Indocani, between Ewdicani and Indocani. As do the Indocani. You live for these differences and take pride in them. But you forget one important thing: the Empty will not. And when they come – as they will come – they will not distinguish between races, they will not spare anyone. They will kill all; they will destroy all. And so think of that. This is not a grudge that must be held onto from the past. This is a war rising in the present, and the whole world will fight it. You were born with peace written on your hearts, and the Indocani were born with wildness and fervour on theirs. The Empty have no hearts – and therefore they will let no one go. So do not fight for our sake. Fight for yourselves, and help us too."

Silence. Eishoxa sat down, willing her words to have an effect, any effect. Then, slowly at first, as though they couldn't believe they were doing it, the Ewdicani started to move again. They broke into circles; they joined minds; their energy hummed through the air.

"Good work," Ash whispered.

Eishoxa smiled tightly. "Thanks. I just hope it will work." This time the discussion was louder and more prominent. Eishoxa could see the Ewdicani talking, gesticulating. Gresceva didn't move and neither did Ember. They just watched as the proceedings took place.

This session was over much more quickly. Leap rose to his feet and walked towards Gresceva. She listened to what he had to say and shrugged.

"We have changed our mind," she called. "We will join the war. This discussion has finished."

Eishoxa allowed herself a small smile before forcing it away. She had convinced them; she had done it. But was it for the good of everyone, or for her own selfish gain?

Eishoxa walked through the corridor, swinging her arms. She had hoped that she would see Rush, but so far there was no sign of him. She walked through the Peace Corridor, looking at the mural on the wall and running her fingers over it. It was such exquisite workmanship. While there, she had come to never take beauty of this kind for granted. She recalled the crudely made huts hacked out of the trunk of the Tree and shuddered slightly. She didn't want to go back. It seemed too much. And leaving here meant leaving Rush as well. Eishoxa smiled sadly at the thought of saying farewell to him.

"You still like it here, don't you?"

Eishoxa turned around and grinned. "I was just thinking about you," she confessed. "It's as if you were conjured here by my thoughts."

He grinned back at her. "Maybe I was, Little Flame."

Eishoxa laughed and took his arm. "Do you really have to keep calling me that?"

"That is your name from now on."

"Are we going to the garden?"

"We can't, I'm afraid. Gresceva is there today. But we can go to the other side of the river, to the swing. When are you meant to be back? Or are you still closeted?"

"Not closeted anymore. I think they realised they can't do anything. But Ember will definitely come to my room, so I don't have long. He still doesn't like the idea of us together."

"Then we'd better go," Rush smiled. They took a different path this time, bending around the Ice Lily until they emerged facing a very similar door. Rush led the way through it and they arrived at the edge of the river. Eishoxa went straight away to the swing and climbed on. Rush smiled and went to stand by the river.

"What are you thinking about?" Eishoxa asked, stopping the swing and looking at him. He turned and smiled at her. "Just something that Ember said the other day when he caught us." Eishoxa dug her feet into the soft ground and leaned forward. "You shouldn't think about it. He shouldn't have been there."

Rush walked towards her. "No. He said that it was fools who tried to convince themselves that an Indocani and an Ewdicani could be together."

"What? Why were you thinking about that?"

"And yesterday as well, something you said to Gresceva. You said that we distinguish between races, when really we aren't that different. We think in different ways, we look different, but are we different?"

"Rush, I don't understand what you're talking about."

"Ember saw me as someone different, someone maybe not worth you spending time with. He was jealous, " Rush concluded simply.

Eishoxa looked down at the ground. "Well, he is very loyal to his people."

"I know," Rush nodded, but his tone seemed dissatisfied. Eishoxa sat back on the swing and kicked off again, swinging back and forth.

"Do you have to go back?"

Eishoxa stopped again and looked at him. "Do I have a choice?"

He shrugged. "I guess not."

She got off the swing. "I'm not going of my own free will. You know that more than anyone. If I had my way, I'd stay here … with you."

He looked up at her. "Then why are you going? Why don't you stay?"

She looked back at him hopelessly. "How can I stay? It's too dangerous for you; it's too dangerous for me; it's too dangerous for your people."

He raised his eyebrows at her. "How so?"

"The Indocani won't let me go. If I stay here, they'll come and pick me up themselves. I've seen how they do it. Your people wouldn't be able to withstand them."

"Are you calling us weak?"

"You are a weak people," she replied, deciding to be truthful. He sat down on the side of the river and looked out across the water.

"Only in some ways," he contradicted.

She shrugged. "When it comes to fighting, you wouldn't stand a chance against them."

"You call them them instead of us," he pointed out, turning his piercing blue eyes on her.

Eishoxa shrugged again. "I don't really feel like I belong to them."
And then she added, "Yet."

"Will you belong to them?"

"I want to go back to Bareth," she said quietly.

He looked at her for a few seconds and then turned his gaze back to
the river. "Why?"

Eishoxa was startled by the question. "What do you mean, why? I
want to go back because I belong there."

He raised his eyebrows and muttered something to himself. "Once
again, I have to say, sometimes I don't understand you, Eishoxa."
He said this as if it should have insulted her, but it did nothing more
than increase her confusion. He stood up. Stepping away from the
river he came towards her saying, "If I asked you to jump into the
river, would you do it?"

Even by human standards he was tall, and he towered above her.
Eishoxa looked up at him, perplexed. "Rush, what has this got to
do—"

"Just answer the question," he said, cutting across her. She shook
her head deliberately. He nodded, as if he'd expected her to say
that. "But if I asked you to jump into fire, would you do that?" She
nodded.

"But why?" he pressed.

"Because I know it won't hurt me."

His smile was without humour. "There you have it. If you belonged
to Bareth, you would have said the opposite. If you belonged here,
you would have said the opposite. So the obvious conclusion is that
you belong with the Indocani."

"What are you saying, Rush? What is the point of this?" she asked.

"The point is, the only place where you really belong – if that's how
you want to look at it – is the place that you don't want to return to.
You haven't changed yet. You're still not wholly Indocani. And you
could stay here … if you wanted to."

"But I can't. It's too dangerous for your people. It's too dangerous
for you."

"Why? What do you mean?"

Eishoxa sighed. "Ember has said that if we meet again, as we've
been doing, then he'll do something that we'll both regret. I can't let
that happen to you. I can't take that kind of risk with someone who's
done nothing to deserve it."

Rush considered this for a moment, then shook his head decisively.
"He wouldn't do anything. He's almost a Lord. To attack one of the
race that you're trying to form an alliance with would lose him the
favour he has. I'm safe, and I'm more worried about you anyway."

Eishoxa shook her head with exasperation. "Rush, there's no point
talking about it. It isn't going to happen. Can you really see Gresceva
letting me stay here?"

"You wouldn't have to stay at the Ice Lily. We could hide you
elsewhere. Just convince Ember, that's all."

"You're dreaming, Rush. That's never going to happen."

He leant back against the tree. "It won't happen because you won't let it."

Eishoxa got off the swing, ignoring his last remark. "We should go back," she said.

"Of course," Rush agreed. "Definitely." Neither of them commented on the blatant sarcasm in his voice.

CHAPTER 22

Eishoxa lay in her hammock, regarding the ceiling. They would be leaving the next day. The dragons were coming to pick them up at dawn. Eishoxa could picture Zeexa flying through the air towards the Ice Lily, flying right in the middle of the pack. Would Ferac be in charge as Ember had been? Would Zeexa be arguing with him all the time, or were the two of them friends again?

This could be her only chance to say goodbye to Rush. Sliding out of her hammock, she pulled on the boots that Rush had given her to protect her feet from the water and tied them up tightly. Pulling on her light red clothes and taking one of the blankets off her hammock, she padded towards the door. She wasn't sure that she would find Rush at all, but she had an idea where he might be. And if she couldn't find him, then at least she knew that she'd tried. Opening the door slowly, she looked up and down the dim corridor. It was deserted, as she'd hoped it would be. Everyone else was sleeping. Ember, Ash and Smoke would be either in their room or with Gresceva.

She met no one as she moved silently through the corridors, although usually the Ewdicani were very active at night. It was very cold in the corridors, and Eishoxa shivered violently. The journey took a lot longer than usual. Eishoxa felt every one of her steps drag. She didn't want to say goodbye, but she didn't want to leave without saying it. She passed by the mural she loved. Rush had shown this to her on her first day there. So much had happened between then and now. She ran her fingers over it. So much for beauty. The very heart of the world despised beauty. She had learnt that now.

Eishoxa placed her hand on the door to the garden. It felt colder than it ever had before. But before she could move, someone spoke behind her.

"Eishoxa. Where are you going?" She jumped and turned around slowly, her hand still on the door. Ember stepped out of the shadows, arms folded. He seemed to have been waiting there for her.

"Nowhere," she said, stepping away from the door. He looked from the door to her and back again.

"You were going to see Rush again?"

"Why does that matter to you?"

Ember stepped forward and took hold of her shoulders. "I've told you already, he's dangerous. Does that mean nothing to you?"

"And why should I believe you," she retorted, "when you've spent almost our whole stay here lying to me?"

He dropped his hands. "Will you continue to accuse me regarding everything I do? But leave this place as the hero?"

"You didn't secure the peace," she hissed, "I did."

"He is dangerous," Ember repeated.

"But you've not told me why," Eishoxa countered.

"Must you have everything set out in black and white?" said Ember, exasperated.

"I'm just as capable of handling the truth as you are."

"You're a child compared to him, Eishoxa. If I could tell you, I would."

"Is this about preserving your precious honour?"

"Be careful what you say."

Eishoxa stepped back and leant against the door, holding onto it as if it would keep everything from falling apart. Ember shook his head. "You're not allowed to say goodbye."

"I'm going," Eishoxa said, turning around blindly and pushing on the door. She dropped her blanket. The cold air greeted her with an icy embrace and beckoned her into the garden.

"Eishoxa, come back!" Ember seized her arm.

"Leave me be!" she cried, trying to free herself.

"No! You will not go!" he shouted.

"Why not? Do you think I love him?"

Ember reeled back from her words and his grip on her arm became painfully tight. Eishoxa could feel a manic carelessness rising from inside her. The words were bubbling up in her throat, the things that she wanted to yell at him.

"I've seen the things that we said to each other and I know – I know that you loved me before. Hear me now! I will never love you in the same way again! You will be alone. Alone forever, because my heart belongs to someone else. Now let me go!"

He released her arm suddenly and she stumbled. And then she ran. At the river she looked left and right for Rush, but there was no sign of him. She heard Ember running behind her. He was much swifter and she could hear him gaining.

"Eishoxa, come back!"

She took off along the riverbank. The ground beneath her feet was soft and yielding and too late she remembered Rush's first warning about the ground that could break. Ahead of her she could see a gap where the river split. If she could make it there, she could jump and get to the other side. Ember wouldn't follow her there. He couldn't cross it there. She tried to run faster, but Ember was still gaining.

"Eishoxa, wait!" She threw herself towards the other side. After a terrifying moment in mid-air, she crashed onto the other side and grabbed a branch that hung over the river. Her feet couldn't get a grip and she slipped down the muddy side.

"Rush!" she shouted. "Rush!" There was no sign of him anywhere. Ember skidded to a halt on the other side. She could feel his terror like her own. The water churned beneath her, splashing up in little waves. Taking little steps, she tried to climb back up the bank, but she couldn't. The branch was slipping through her hands. She noticed a stronger branch further down and reached out for it. Just as her fingertips were about to touch it, she heard a crack as the first branch snapped and she fell into the black waters below.

If Eishoxa could have had one wish as she fell, it would be to not feel. Not feel the water attack every inch of her body with knives of ice. Not feel the current dragging her down, down, down into the water where there was no escape and no place to hide. Not feel the unnatural, excruciating coldness that froze her body and stopped her brain from thinking rationally. Not feel the ceaseless battering as she was pulled down the river and thrown against the rocks. Not feel the band of fire around her ribs as she struggled for air. And to not feel a thing as she fell was a wish that never came true.

Something was brushing her hair back from her face. Her eyes were so swollen and bruised that she couldn't open them, and her face felt distended and torn. Every fibre of her being felt damaged. Water was still lapping over her feet and her cheek was pressing against wet mud. Her left shoulder ached as if it had been hit with an iron fist. She spun in and out of consciousness as she was lifted up into someone's arms, someone whose tread on the ground was soft and gentle and did not jar her. And it was only when she was in this person's arms that she felt safe.

CHAPTER 23

*E*ISHOXA WAS SWIMMING. *She was swimming through deep water, so deep that she couldn't see the bottom and she couldn't see the top. She was diving deeper and deeper. The water was cool as it ran by her skin and bubbles burst from her mouth. She could hear the sounds of many creatures swimming around her, although she couldn't see them. The pressure was like a comforting weight around her. When she saw a light approaching, she went towards it. As it got closer, she saw that it was a little green light hanging in the centre of a cave, a cave deep under the sea. She swam towards it, sure that she was meant to go there, that she was being called there. The mouth of the cave was decorated with many carvings. Inside she saw that the cave was lit by a strange green light, the same colour as the lamp hanging from the centre of the cave. It was deserted, but she was sure that someone should be here. She swam around the edge of the cave. When she turned back to face the entrance, she was not surprised to see that someone was there, hovering in the water.*

"Wella," Eishoxa said, and the woman smiled and entered the cave. She looked like she did in many pictures and carvings, but as she got closer Eishoxa could see lines around her mouth, and these made her look very old and very sad. She carried herself with pride, and Eishoxa could sense a deep peace rolling off her, radiating through the water and enveloping Eishoxa in its tranquillity.

"Yes. I thought I would see you again, Eishoxa, but I didn't expect it to be so soon."

"Why am I here?" Eishoxa asked. "Did I bring myself here?"

"No one can control you, Eishoxa," Wella reminded her gently. "If you are anywhere, it is because you choose to be there."

"Or I have been made to stay," Eishoxa added.

Wella shook her head, smiling. "I don't think so. You're talking about the Tree, aren't you?"

"The Tree?" Eishoxa's mind was hazy and she couldn't remember why she should know this name.

"Yes. Where the Warriors live, remember? The Indocani?"

Eishoxa nodded, suddenly remembering. "I didn't want to go there."

"No, I know. But you stayed, and now you're with my people at Dulcacohefen." The name flowed so beautifully off her tongue it was like two oceans merging seamlessly together.

"Is that where we are now?"

"No. This is where the Ewdicani come before their final rest. You have brought yourself here. I cannot summon you here because you're not an Ewdicani."

"I'm not?" Eishoxa asked.

"No."

"But look at me. I look like one and I feel like one," Eishoxa protested. There was a mottled mirror hanging on the wall and she swam over to it. Her eyes were round and green. Her skin was white, and she had no legs but a long tail below her waist. Her long hair, the palest shade of blue, was plaited across her head and the braid fell down over her right shoulder. She had gills on the side of her neck that opened and closed as she breathed. She smiled in satisfaction

at herself. She was beautiful just the way she was. Wella swam up behind her, gliding effortlessly through the water. She tilted her head to one side. "Do you look like that?" she asked. "Or do you look like this?"

She lightly brushed something on Eishoxa's left shoulder with one gentle finger. A burning pain spread through her, starting at the shoulder and spreading outwards until her whole body was consumed by it. And in the mirror she saw herself change. Her skin darkened, turning instead into a dark brown. Her eyes narrowed and changed colour until they were a golden brown, and her tail morphed into two strong, slim legs, built for running on land, not swimming through the water. The gills closed and disappeared and her lungs filled with cold seawater. Her hair hung loose around her shoulders and it was a deep, vibrant red.

"You fell in the river, remember?" Wella asked. "You were so close to dying that you brought yourself here. You will have characteristics of the Peacemakers for your whole life. The water has marked you and made you one of its own." She turned Eishoxa gently so that she could see her left shoulder in the mirror. Embedded there, about the size of Eishoxa's fist, was a mark, a brand in the shape of a swan. "This is my sign," explained Wella. "I have given you some of the Peacemakers' powers. You will need them for the times ahead, I think. You need to go now. This is not your place yet."

Eishoxa nodded. Her shoulder was still burning, but less intensely. "Where do I go?" she asked.

Wella smiled. "Wherever you want to," she said. "You're free, remember?"

The Goddess was disappearing, her form getting fainter and fainter until it was gone. The lights on the walls of the cave went out and Eishoxa stood in pitch darkness. She made her way to the front of the cave. She could walk quite easily through the water, and breathing was no problem despite having no gills. She stepped out of the cave, but instead of swimming out into water, she felt herself falling forward until she landed on her feet in a very different place.

Looking around her, Eishoxa knew there was only one place she could be: Fiera's palace. The ground was made of glowing coals, as were the walls. Heat radiated through the air from the many fires that were burning.

"You've finally arrived. You took your time, I have to say."

Eishoxa turned to see another woman descending a flight of stairs that led up out of sight. She was by far the most beautiful of the three Goddesses that Eishoxa had seen, but she also looked the cruellest, crueller even than Nezrax. Eishoxa instantly recognised her as the Warrior Goddess. She carried no weapons but had the poise and grace of a fighter, of one who is not accustomed to losing, one who refuses to lose. They stared at each other, Fiera with appraisal and Eishoxa with dislike. This woman was her mother, and her mother had given her away.

Fiera swept across the room and sat gracefully in a chair. Eishoxa stood watching her. She could see the similarities between them; the same red hair arranged around the face; the same eyes, keen and sharp; and the same brown skin. Fiera's skin was not mottled like the Indocani's, but brown like Eishoxa's had been in Bareth, only much darker.

"I don't blame you for looking at me like that, but I wouldn't advise it. It does absolutely nothing for you."

"What do you mean?" Eishoxa enquired.

"To dislike something is one thing, but to show you dislike it is another. It shows a weakness." She sighed in exasperation. "Your time with the Ignorant has ruined you. You had some potential when you were younger."

"To be what?" Eishoxa asked.

"To be a great warrior."

"Like you, you mean."

"Mind what you say, Eishoxa. I am your mother, after all."

"One that didn't want me," Eishoxa replied angrily. Fiera stopped, confused. "Didn't want you? Who told you that?"

"Well, it's true, isn't it?" Eishoxa said resentfully. "I wouldn't have gone to the Ignorant if it weren't for you and all the wars you were starting."

Fiera stared at her for a moment before bursting out into laughter. "That's what they told you? Oh, my people! So determined not to take the blame for anything. Just as I remember them. They've gone rotten, Eishoxa, you know that?"

Eishoxa nodded curtly. "Yes, Rianox told me."

"Oh, the half-breed? I wondered what you would make of him this time. Poor Ember seems quite abandoned. But then, he always was a little too arrogant for my liking."

"The half-breed?" Eishoxa asked, confused.

"His loyalty is divided," Fiera sighed, resting her forehead on the tips of her fingers. "Very difficult. But I think he has chosen the right path."

"Why am I here?" Eishoxa enquired.

"How many times must people tell you that no one controls you in this world?" Fiera replied heatedly. "You control yourself. Many people have said that to you and you refuse to pay them any attention."

"But I don't understand," Eishoxa cried. "I have no control over what I do. I cannot even control fire yet. How can I be your daughter?"

"You cannot control fire yet because you're frightened! Frightened of accepting who you are, attached as you are to that pathetic country."

"Don't you dare speak that way about Bareth! They took care of me there, which you have failed to do! The fire wouldn't accept me; it said I wasn't ready."

"No, of course you weren't," Fiera said vehemently. She violently threw her hand out to one side and a great eagle made of fire erupted from her palm. It screeched its way around the room before colliding with the wall and exploding in sparks. "Would you be ready to make and control something like that?" Fiera asked.

Eishoxa threw her hair over one shoulder out of her way. "You wouldn't know, would you? You've never given me the chance."

That seemed to strike something in Fiera. "And you would like the chance? Even though it reduces your chances of returning Bareth? You would be burnt as a witch — but then, you could never be burnt. So you would be drowned — and you can't be drowned either. So you would be buried alive, or stoned, or hacked to pieces and it would be such a waste. I can sense the water in you now. It is strange that you still want fire although you have already been claimed. But maybe you will use it to your advantage."

"I want fire," Eishoxa said slowly.

210

Fiera sighed. "Very well. You may have it. And may it serve you well." She waved her hand through the air and Eishoxa felt herself falling backwards, blown into a tide of memories that picked her up with them and swept her into a pool of nothingness.

Eishoxa opened her eyes again to the sound of children laughing. She raised her head and looked around. The sun was a bright, white circle in a cloudless blue sky. As she sat up, her head spun and she put her hand on the grass to steady herself. It crumbled under her fingers. She turned her head to one side and saw the Tree, except it looked much younger. It wasn't as knarled and it was shorter and slimmer, as though it didn't have so many branches. Sitting in the shade were three giggling children.

Eishoxa stood up and walked towards them, sitting down nearby. She could already tell that they couldn't see her. One of them was Ember, another was Amber. She stood and circled them, looking down at the child version of herself. She was almost identical to how she had looked in Bareth. Indocani's skin darkened as they grew up, so the olive-skinned girl sitting here was a near perfect image. There were slight differences. The child Eishoxa's skin was patterned with the lines and shapes customary for the Indocani. She carried herself with an imperial air, strange in one so young but becoming to her nonetheless, and she seemed to have an inborn way with fire.

Eishoxa sat down next to the child Ember. There was no reaction; he simply clapped his hands and shouted, "Do it again! Do it again!" The child Eishoxa smiled regally and opened her hand slowly. A small flame blossomed in the centre of her palm. She blew on it gently and it took the shape of a flower, glowing and twisting. Eishoxa watched in surprise as her child self took the flower off her hand with gentle fingers and gave it to Amber. "For you," she smiled.

"Can you make one for me as well?" Ember asked hopefully. The two girls laughed at him.

"Boys don't have flowers. That would be very silly," Eishoxa laughed. "I'll make you something else." She closed her hand tightly again, then uncurled each finger one by one. A miniature eagle flapped off her palm, and Ember caught it with a look of delight.

"Thank you, Eishoxa."

"How do you do that?" Amber asked.

Eishoxa shrugged, and opened and shut her hand several times. A shower of sparks shot up into the air. She shrugged. "I've always been able to do it."

"But only the adults can do that," Amber persisted.

Her friend shrugged again. "I don't know."

Eishoxa had the sensation of being picked up and thrown against something. Immediately everything changed. She was standing behind the children again, but they were in the forest now and hiding behind a large log. An Indocani was calling their names irritably. "Amber! Ember! Eishoxa! Where are you? Where have you gone?" He stood with his hands on his hips, looking around. The children were giggling quietly, but could no longer restrain themselves when he started calling again. Ember burst out laughing and Eishoxa joined in. The children stood up, revealing their hiding place. The Indocani smiled *tiredly when he saw them.*

"Please, Eishoxa. Vera would like to speak to you in her room."

Ember and Amber turned in surprise to Eishoxa, their eyes wide. "What did you do?" Ember said in an awed voice. Eishoxa shrugged nonchalantly and followed the Indocani. Ember and Amber were left in the forest. The older Eishoxa followed her younger self and the Indocani. They seemed to move impossibly quickly, and Eishoxa kept pace with them.

Eishoxa sat on a chest in the corner of Vera's room. Vera had her back to her and was facing the child standing in front of her. Her voice seemed distorted, but became clearer as Eishoxa listened. She was speaking in a much gentler tone than Eishoxa had ever heard her use.

"What can you do?"

"I can control fire and it speaks to me," the child said in a worried tone. Vera nodded encouragingly. "I can make animals and plants out of fire and I can shoot sparks and flames out of my hands."

"Show me," she invited. The child opened one hand slowly, and a shower of sparks bloomed from her hand and rained down from the ceiling. She did the same with the other and the same thing happened, except with flames. With a flick of her wrist, an eagle burst from her hand, followed by a cawing phoenix. From the corner of the room Eishoxa watched in wonder. The child standing before her handled the flames with such grace and ease. And it was herself.

"This means you're special," Vera explained. "You've been given these things because you have a very special mother. You know who that is?"

"Fiera," breathed the child.

Vera nodded. "Yes. How did you know?"

"She speaks to me when I sleep," the child said. "She tells me that she has some very important things planned for me to do."

"Because you're special," Vera continued in a more serious tone. "We have decided that we will train you now. You will learn how to ride a dragon and learn how to be one of the army."

"Why?" Eishoxa asked.

"Because you're very special." Vera smiled, and the child nodded.

Eishoxa, Ember and Amber, with a boy Eishoxa recognised as Coal, along with several others, were standing at the front of a silent group of Indocani. The other Indocani crowded behind, looking at someone just behind Vera. Eishoxa moved slightly and saw it to be Rianox. He was very young, just a toddler. He was held in the arms of someone who could only have been his sister. She too was very young but she looked up with defiance at Vera. They both had very pale skin, so pale they could almost have been Ewdicani.

"You will be taken to the forest. You will be left there and you will stay there," Vera was saying.

Eishoxa watched herself stay expressionless, but Amber tugged on her arm. "Why are they going there?"

"Because they're different," Eishoxa replied in a bitter voice. The older Eishoxa suddenly realised why she spoke so bitterly: it could have been her. She was different but could do nothing about it, just like Rianox and the other girl. But she was being praised for it while they were being sent far away. And it could have been her.

212

The scene changed again and Eishoxa could hear the sound of clashing swords. She was in the forest again, close to the dragons' pit and watching as she and another Indocani were duelling furiously with one another. Although her opponent was much taller and stronger, Eishoxa was using her speed and agility to her advantage.

She saw very little of this scene before it changed again. The younger Eishoxa was by herself, shooting arrow after arrow at a tree in the middle of the forest. Eishoxa came up directly behind herself and watched. She was aiming her arrows at a vertical row of tiny red dots drawn on the tree all the way up. The bow melded with her fingers as though it was part of her. She took aim before hitting her target every time. She was a natural.

Again the scene changed. Eishoxa was back in Vera's room. She was older now. Her skin was darker and she had belted around her waist a thick leather strip.
"You are getting stronger," Vera pointed out, "but you're not strong enough yet."
"I want to train with my friends. Ember and Amber are starting to learn; why can't I be with them?"
"They're not as good as you. It would set you back to be trained with them. No, we will continue as we have started. I'm sorry, Eishoxa, but that's my final word."
The scene began to blur, but before it disappeared Eishoxa saw herself bow her head, looking at the floor.

Next she was standing beside the Tree. In the shadow of one of the branches, she could see herself and Ember sitting there. Eishoxa crept forward, even though she knew that she couldn't be seen or heard. They were older but still looked younger than Eishoxa was, maybe fourteen or fifteen in human years. She knew that age worked differently for the Indocani.
"How are you finding the training?" she heard herself ask.
Ember grinned. "I love it. I don't understand why you complained so much. I'm better than Amber already."
"Do you know how to do this?" Eishoxa teased, opening her hand and watching an eagle fly from her palm. Ember moved to catch it, but Eishoxa snapped her fingers and the bird disappeared in an explosion of sparks.
"If you want one, you have to give me something," Eishoxa challenged.
Ember sat up. "What do you want?"
"A kiss. From you," Eishoxa giggled, tapping her cheek. Ember sighed and leaned forward, kissing her awkwardly. She smiled and opened her palm obligingly. An eagle flew towards Ember. He caught it. "You're welcome," Eishoxa said. They were silent for a few minutes and Eishoxa felt herself dragged back slightly. The picture became a little blurry and then focused again. She scrambled forward towards the pair to hear what they were saying.
"What do you think we'll be doing a few years from now?" Eishoxa was

asking. Ember shrugged. He lay back on the branch and put his hands behind his head. "Whatever we're supposed to be doing, I guess."

"Do you believe in the Goddess?" Eishoxa enquired, looking down at her hands. Ember sat up, confused. "Of course I do. You're her daughter. If you exist, then she exists."

"But do you believe that because you've been told or because you actually think that?"

"I've been told," Ember admitted, but then hurried on to say, "but it makes sense. You were able to control fire from a young age, you were able to do all those things, remember?"

"Who do you think we will be, years from now?"

"You asked that question already?"

"No, I didn't," she denied. "I asked what we would be doing. But who do you think we will be? Do you want to be leader, like Vera?"

"I can't," Ember laughed, settling himself back down. "Only a woman can do that. Maybe I'll be a Lord and lead our people to many victories."

"And I'll be leader and we can lead them into war together!" Eishoxa exclaimed, lying down beside him. He smiled and closed his eyes. "So we will be together, years from now."

Eishoxa sat up slightly. "Of course. That's the only thing I'm sure about."

She was standing on the edge of the Tree, watching as two figures ran and jumped off a branch quite high up, rolling perfectly in unison as they landed on the ground. The young Ember and Eishoxa had grown up a lot since last she saw them. They ran swiftly together towards the forest where the dragons were. Eishoxa followed. Her feet didn't touch the ground; she glided over it, making no noise whatsoever.

"Come on! Come on!" she heard Ember shout to his companion.

Eishoxa had crouched on the ground to look at something, but as Ember called she jumped up. "Coming!"

"I want to show you Ferac before anyone else sees him." Ember smiled. It was one of the smiles that Eishoxa had seen in the Forest of No Flame, one of the smiles that transformed his face, and it seemed to be reserved for her.

"I'm coming," Eishoxa answered, and took off running into the forest, so that Ember had to sprint to catch up. Reaching the top of the dragons' pit, they saw that only a few dragons were there, definitely not as many as there had been when her older self was there. The girl made a flying leap into the centre of the pit, but Ember scrambled down the side.

"Eishoxa, wait for me!" he called, hurrying after her. Eishoxa watched herself approach a golden dragon. In Eishoxa's opinion, it was the most beautiful dragon she had ever seen, even more beautiful than Zeexa. Every scale on its body was gold, and its wings were small but strong. Ferac was there too, easily recognisable by the way he carried himself and the jet black of his scales. He was still very small, much smaller than Eishoxa's dragon, but he would grow. The two dragons were lying close together, but when the girl approached, the golden dragon lifted its head and rose to its feet. Ember hurried to his dragon's side.

"Is he not the most beautiful dragon you've ever seen?"

"Not as good as my Fiera, but beautiful nonetheless," Eishoxa teased, rubbing the golden dragon's nose. The watching Eishoxa remembered Rianox's words about how her dragon, called Fiera, had left and had not returned. Looking at this dragon, Eishoxa knew that this was her dragon, her dragon that she should have been riding, the dragon whose place in her heart had been poorly filled with Zeexa. The scene suddenly blurred and Eishoxa couldn't see what was happening.

She had the sensation of being thrown backwards again, and then she was standing in a room looking down on herself. She had the strangest feeling of déjà vu: she had seen this scene already, in the tunnel back at the Tree. She watched herself rise and start pacing back and forth and back and forth. The door opened and Eishoxa started. A young Indocani, whom Eishoxa did not know, entered and bowed low.

"Princess Eishoxa," the Indocani said.

"How is he, Charcoal?" Eishoxa asked, walking towards him in distress.

"He will survive, Princess, he will survive. But many of our people have been killed. It was an ambush. We were not prepared."

"All right, thank you, Charcoal. You may go." Eishoxa resumed her pacing. She started talking to herself, mumbling words that the watching Eishoxa had difficulty catching. Then she turned and looked directly towards Eishoxa. "Fiera!" she called. "You are the Great Warrior and now I promise that I will avenge this day. I will avenge the loss of our people."

The scene changed again. Ember and Eishoxa were standing before a younger version of Vera. They both looked tired and battered; Ember had multiple wounds over his neck and chest, and Eishoxa was bleeding from one arm.

"It was a great victory," Ember was saying. "A few losses on our part. They will not think of attacking us again."

"Thank you, the both of you. You have done well. Hopefully this will teach our enemy that we are not to be underestimated."

And again the scene changed. Eishoxa was sitting next to Ember and the two of them were laughing about something. They were sitting very close together, holding hands. As Eishoxa watched, Ember took her chin and turned her face towards him gently. He kissed her on the mouth very slowly and she responded passionately, wrapping her arms around his neck. Eishoxa saw herself rest her head against Ember's shoulder and he laid his cheek on top of her head. This scene was over very quickly.

The next scene happened on the plain in front of the Tree. Eishoxa was shouting at someone and brandishing a sword. Ember was standing off slightly, watching her with a calculating look on his face.

"Why did you come back?" Eishoxa was screaming. The watching Eishoxa hurried around to see who it was. A cold shiver of horrified dread ran through her as she saw it was Rianox. He had wounds in his side and shoulder, and the scar that would later trace his body from shoulder to hip was not there. He was doing nothing to defend himself, and this seemed to infuriate her even more. She was jabbing at him with her sword and Eishoxa could only stand by as Rianox sank to the ground, exhausted, his skin split open like an overripe

215

berry. Ember did nothing but watch.

"Half-breed! Outcast!" Eishoxa mocked. "I told you never to come back! I told you to stay in the forest, where you belong!"

Rianox was shivering on the ground, but at her words he looked up. With intense hatred written all over his face, he whispered in a voice that Eishoxa could hear as clear as day: "I belong where I choose to belong, and nothing you can say will change that."

The scene dissolved, but not before Eishoxa saw herself raise her sword high above her head and bring it down, a silver blur through the air, right across Rianox's heart.

She hung in limbo for a while, no new scene appearing. But then she heard the sound of arguing, and a picture took form before her eyes.

"Why are you going? Why do you want to? You can stay here! You can! We will protect you!" Ember's voice sounded more desperate than Eishoxa had ever heard it. He was pacing up and down in a room that Eishoxa recognised as the glass room back at the Tree. Eishoxa herself was sitting on the bed, which looked exactly the same.

"I have to go," she said. "I cannot stay here anymore. This place is not for me."

"You're going to leave because of the words of a few Ewdicani?" Ember asked in disbelief. Eishoxa remembered. Rianox had told her that the Ewdicani had wanted her to leave because she was becoming too influential.

"No. Never," Eishoxa said. "Because I have no choice. I want a new life, Ember. A new life away from this."

"But ..." and his voice sounded hopeless. "But what about me?"

Eishoxa's face, which had been set hard as flint, softened as she looked up at him. "I will come back," she said. "I'm not going away forever. I will prove to the Peacemakers that they cannot control me. But I must leave, Ember. I must leave everyone behind. Even you."

"But you will come back?"

"Yes, I promise. I will come back and we will fight together once again." The watching Eishoxa saw the two of them embrace. The raw emotion on Ember's face scorched through her as if that was actually her, in the present, standing there and saying goodbye.

"What if you forget me? And when will you come back?"

"You will know when to come and get me. I won't forget you, of all people. I could never forget you."

The rest of her dreaming was in snatches of scenes and words and war. Lots of war. Eishoxa felt every death of an Indocani as if it were her own. This went on and on and on until she heard two voices vibrating through her head. One she had never heard. The other was Fiera: "This is what I feel like. If I give you fire, you must join the Indocani. When one dies and joins me, they all feel it. Every death. In every war. And this is what I'm giving you."

Then Fiera's voice disappeared and the other voice spoke alone. "When you return home you will see me, and I too will give you power. Fire and water together obey your voice, and your voice alone. Hold onto it, Eishoxa, and never give it up."

Something streaked across her vision, a bright, white light. Followed by another, and another, in quick succession. Then she saw herself back at the Tree, but this time it was her. She identified the night of the banquet when the fire had not accepted her, when Fiera had not accepted her. She could feel the fire in her mind, vibrating through her being until it reached the place where her whole existence was. There it stopped. And it spread. And the burning light reached the corners of her mind and grew and grew and grew. She was on fire. Flames were spreading over her body, filling her head with warmth and light and heat. So much heat. Then it stopped and she was left to float in wherever she was.

Fiera spoke one more time. "You're one of us now, Eishoxa. Remember that."

CHAPTER 24

Eishoxa opened her eyes slowly. She was looking at an unfamiliar ceiling and she felt awful. Every bone in her body ached, and her skin, although infinitely better than it had been before, still felt swollen and sore. She tried to turn her head, but her neck hurt so much it brought tears to her eyes.

Tears. So Wella had given her power over water. Indocani couldn't cry. Her left shoulder hurt the most and felt oddly detached from the rest of her. She heard someone moving somewhere out of sight and tried to turn her head to see who it was. This movement caused a sharp intake of breath, and instantly there was someone at her side.

"Eishoxa! You're awake! At last!"

"Ember?" Eishoxa croaked. Her voice sounded as though her throat were filled with grit.

"Yes. Do you want to sit up?"

"I can try, but it might not work very well," she forced out, gritting her teeth. He slid his hands under her shoulders and one of his fingers brushed the mark left by Wella. She reacted immediately to the burning heat and pain. He smiled sadly down at her. "That's where the water left its mark."

She nodded. "Come on, help me up," she said, and then clenched her teeth even tighter as her body was forced into a painful position.

"You're so stupid," he said softly. "I warned you, didn't I? Let it be known that I warned you."

Eishoxa didn't really take in his words. "I saw us, you know. When I was asleep. Fiera showed me some of my memories from when I was here. You were in almost every one."

He nodded. "I wasn't so bad back then, was I?"

"We really loved each other, didn't we?" she mused, thinking over what she'd seen. He nodded again slightly. "I loved you more than you loved me," he ruminated.

"I made you kiss me," she remembered.

Ember chuckled. "For an eagle? I still can't make those."

"I didn't know … I wish I had now. It was beautiful," she realised.

"Yes … but I don't blame you anymore. In fact, I have something for you." He reached down to pick up something from the floor and handed it to her. It was her coin. The coin that Rosemarie had given her, which she'd lost that day by the river when she'd drunk water for the first time.

"How … how did you get this?"

"When you drank water and I was trying to wake you up, I took it away from you. I didn't know what it was, but I decided that it was unfair to keep it from you." The surface was so dirty that Eishoxa could barely make out the letters. She smudged her thumb across it but the metal refused to shine.

"You can make it shiny again," Ember explained quickly. "If you use a little fire."

Eishoxa set it down for a moment. "I saw Fiera," she said quietly.

"And she gave me fire. She gave me control over it and made it mine. Wella too, with water."

Ember nodded. "I know about the water," he said. "That mark on your shoulder won't go away, but it might heal slightly."

"Fiera told me," Eishoxa said, as though puzzling something out in her head, "Fiera told me that I was once a great warrior and that you and I went into every battle together."

He smiled at her. "She was right. Side by side, we went into battle, and you were the better warrior. Particularly on dragon-back. We were friends from a very young age and it just grew, I guess. I don't think I was ever anything more than a friend to you," he sighed, "but to me … I was head over heels in love with you and could never forgive myself for letting you go. Even now, all I want to do is make you happy."

"I think," she said, "I think we should start again. From the beginning."

"As friends?" he asked, holding out his hand.

She smiled. "As friends," she agreed, and put her hand in his. It fit there so perfectly, almost as if it had been made to stay there forever.

As it happened, she did get to say goodbye to Rush. She had been unconscious for eight days, eight days of just lying there. When the dragons arrived, Ember had sent them back home and asked for only three to return. Zeexa would be staying at the Tree. Eishoxa was too weak to fly a dragon by herself, and everyone understood that she would ride back with Ember on Ferac. Ember had not left her side for those eight days. She finally ordered him to go away and talk to Gresceva about the treaty because his constant worrying was starting to annoy her. But now she could talk to fire and play with it to her heart's content. Fire had its own language, she learned. The Indocani had Düerasgörn, but she learnt there was something else about fire. It wanted to play and dance, it wanted to leap and twist and twirl. It didn't want to be used to fight constantly, to do nothing but destroy. It wanted to create as well.

Late in the afternoon of her third day after awakening - the day the dragons were due to come back – Eishoxa heard a faint tap at the door. It opened to reveal Rush. His white skin looked even paler than usual and his face was drawn with worry. He let out a sigh of relief when he saw her. "Eishoxa! You're all right!"

"Yes," Eishoxa smiled. He closed the door carefully behind him and took the chair that Ember usually sat in.

"I'm so sorry—" he started.

"I know what you're going to say," Eishoxa said, waving his apology away. "But it wasn't your fault. I shouldn't have gone out."

"But I was there," Rush explained. "I was there, but I saw Ember and thought that if he saw me you would get into even more trouble. You know that we're not meant to meet anymore."

"You were there?"

Rush nodded desperately. "I thought you'd be able to pull yourself up. Seeing you fall was the worst moment of my life. I jumped in immediately and tried to get you, but I couldn't see you anywhere." He gave a rueful laugh. "And I'm meant to control water."

Eishoxa stroked his hand consolingly. "You couldn't have done anything about it. And I'm fine now – see?"

"I heard that you saw Wella." Rush looked at her with awe. "What was she like?"

"Much nicer than Fiera, that much I can tell you. And she gave me powers over the water. Look." Eishoxa put out her hand and released a small stream of water from her palm.

Rush smiled. "Yes, I heard about that as well. There are many rumours circulating now. But what did Wella look like? What happened?" he asked again eagerly.

"She looked like the carving in the garden. Almost identical. She was the first person I saw. I swam down to her cave, the cave that she said the Ewdicani go to when they die. And I had a tail, a tail like Wella's."

"You went down the cave?" Rush asked in wonder. "Why did she let you down?"

"I looked like one of them. I looked like one of you." Eishoxa looked at her hand and tried to imagine it pale and white like Rush's was.

"But with a tail," Rush finished for her.

Eishoxa nodded. "Yes, with a tail. But it felt right, Rush. It felt like I should have been one of them. And when I went to Fiera and saw her, all I could think about was how I wanted to be back under the sea."

Rush nodded in understanding. "You've been given power over both water and fire now and they'll compete for dominance. Have you changed your mind about Fiera now?"

Eishoxa shook her head. "She is disgusting. I can't understand why anyone would look up to her."

"Have you told anyone that? Ember, for instance?"

Eishoxa looked at Rush to see whether he was joking or not. When Rush looked back at her with deadly seriousness, Eishoxa laughed. "No, of course not." She looked down at her hands again.

"There's something else, isn't there?" Rush asked.

Eishoxa put her head on one side in thought. "I recalled some memories of Ember and me together. We were really in love. At least he was. And I saw the time when I promised to come back, to return to him. And …" she trailed away, shrugging.

Rush gave her a small, sad smile. "Listen to me, Eishoxa, and hear me when I say you owe me nothing. You must understand that. We may have walked the same path for a while, but if you think we walk different paths, then that's fine."

She gave him a bittersweet smile. Rush put one hand up to her face and brushed something off her cheek. "Tears," he said. "You really are one of us now."

"That's what Fiera said," Eishoxa replied quietly.

"And which one would you rather belong to?"

"Right now? I don't know. I just don't know."

CHAPTER 25

Rush had long gone by the time Ember returned to take her to the dragons.

"Are you ready to go now?" he asked, tapping on the half-open door. He had her pack in his hand. "Check that everything is in it and then we can leave."

Eishoxa leant forward, wincing slightly, and picked up the pack. She opened it and looked inside. The scrolls were in there, as well as Rush's flute and the ribbons. She could just see Lily's dress underneath it all. Everything seemed to be there except her bow.

"But where is my bow?"

"Already by the dragons," Ember said. "Ash took it with him."

Eishoxa nodded briskly. "All right, let's go then. No," she said as Ember made to pick her up. "No. I'm going to walk." She swung her legs over the side of the couch and set her feet on the floor. Slinging her pack over her shoulder, she gripped the side of her couch and pushed herself to her feet. She staggered; it felt as if all her weight had slid down into her feet.

Ember grabbed her arm to keep her steady. "All right?" he asked.

Eishoxa nodded. "All right." After the first tentative steps she was fine. But even though they moved slowly, every step drained Eishoxa in a way she wouldn't have expected. Ember took them up to the petal where they had arrived. From far off, Eishoxa could see three dragons waiting there, along with a small group of people.

"All right, that's enough," Ember said. He took her pack off her shoulders and picked her up in his arms. "I don't want you tiring yourself out." He carried her the rest of the way to the dragons and set her on her feet once there. Ash and Smoke were there, already mounted and ready. Gresceva and Leap were there, as well as Rush. Eishoxa tactfully avoided looking at him as she thanked Gresceva.

"You did well, Eishoxa," she said with surprising warmth. "How is your shoulder?"

"Better," Eishoxa replied.

"Wella blessed you with powers over the water as well, I understand."

Eishoxa nodded and Gresceva looked at her shrewdly. "I'm not here to question my Goddess. If she believes you're worthy of those powers, then I must trust her. Goodbye, Eishoxa. I hope that we shall meet again another time." Eishoxa nodded. She bowed to Leap and Rush. "Goodbye," she said. Ember was in brief but deep discussion with Gresceva, so Eishoxa approached Ferac alone who was looking down at her from his great height.

"I am to ride you, Ferac," she said. The black dragon's mind was very different from Zeexa's. It felt much older and wiser. Eishoxa's voice, as she spoke, seemed to echo, as though the dragon's mind was filled with deep chasms. He bent down low enough for Eishoxa to scramble up onto his back. Ember bowed to the three Ewdicani and then strode over to his dragon. His pack was already up on Ferac's back.

He swung himself in front of Eishoxa and tied her pack to his, hanging them over Ferac's neck where they swung gently.

"My bow?" Eishoxa asked.

"I have it," Ash called. "It's in my pack."

Eishoxa nodded. Ember wheeled Ferac around to face the open sky. Ferac readied himself, his great black wings unfurling. They were so big that the Ewdicani had to take a few steps back.

Ferac was gathering himself to take off into the sky. His mouth opened wide and a great twisting snake of flame poured out of his mouth. Eishoxa turned to look at Rush. He smiled at her and she smiled back. His words echoed in her head: "You owe me nothing." She wondered whether that was true, or whether she owed him more than either of them could express.

Ferac took off. As they rose higher and higher into the sky, Eishoxa looked back at the beautiful white lily, deserted and empty, growing smaller and smaller. As they neared the ridge that took them over the Cursed Marshes, Eishoxa thought the lily looked almost like a face, with the rivers that surrounded it looking like tear tracks running down its icy cheeks.

CHAPTER 26

THE CURSED MARSHES were just as vile as Eishoxa remembered them. She looked around nervously as they flew over them, wondering whether the creatures that had attacked them before would come back.

"Do you think they'll come back? The creatures from before?"

"No," Ember said with enough conviction that Eishoxa believed him. "They hadn't seen dragons for a long time and they'd forgotten our strength. We won't be bothered by them again. They'll remember."

"*And we have made sure that they will not forget our strength again*," Ferac snarled, lashing out violently with one of his feet. Ember smiled and patted the dragon's neck. "Yes. Exactly."

Ferac growled his approval. As there were only three dragons, they flew quite closely in a line. Smoke flew ahead, Ember and Eishoxa flew in the middle, and Ash brought up the rear. The day was much clearer, without a cloud in the sky. Eishoxa looked over the side and watched as the marshes bubbled and roiled beneath the surface. The stench of rot hung in the atmosphere.

"Is it because of one battle that it is called the Cursed Marshes?" she asked Ember.

"A battle was fought here long ago, it is true," Ember explained, looking down as well. "But it was the nature of the battle that gave this place its name. Soon after their separation, the Indocani and Ewdicani met here in an attempt to wipe out the other race, so intense was their hatred for each other. Nezrax joined the fight, hoping that they would destroy each other. There were three armies, each fighting against another two. Finally, the Indocani and Ewdicani realised that they would be destroyed if they did not join forces. So they drove Nezrax back. Fiera and Wella were so disgusted that they cursed the marshes."

"Was I there?" Eishoxa asked, half to herself.

"No. And neither was I. It happened long before either of us was born. Nowadays you may only cross it on a dragon's back. No one may take a step on that ground."

"Why? What would happen?"

"You would die," Ash called out bluntly, spurring Jerath closer. "And you may not join your Goddess either. It is a terrible price."

Eishoxa stared down at it. "Because of the war?"

Ash nodded. "But I thought Fiera liked battle."

"That was not battle," Ember said solemnly. "It was a suicide mission."

"Isn't that what battle is?" Eishoxa wondered, more to herself than to Ash or Ember. She could feel the latter's eyes on her but kept her gaze trained downwards. When she eventually looked up again, she could make out a little smudge of something on the horizon. "Is that the Forest of No Flame?" Eishoxa asked.

Ember replied, "Yes. We need to get there by nightfall. We can't camp anywhere near these marshes. It's just too dangerous." He whistled loudly and Ferac roared, soaring up into the sky with renewed strength and increased speed.

The sky was dark by the time they reached the Forest of No Flame and descended into the green glow below the forest canopy. Ember conjured a ball of flame and, a moment later, Ash and Smoke did as well. Eishoxa remembered the last time they'd been there, but Ember, as though sensing what she was going to say, turned to her and shook his head.

"Not this time, Eishoxa. We're going to light a fire whether you like it or not. So don't argue."

"But—" Eishoxa protested, trying desperately not to lose her temper again. He was almost slipping back into the way he was before, patronising and refusing to see reason. "Ember, I don't know how I know, but I know that lighting a fire here, after doing it before, is wrong."

"We did it before and nothing happened," he pointed out.

"Yes, but we can't be sure of that this time," Eishoxa objected.

Ember sighed. "Eishoxa, you're one of us now. The fire has claimed you. No matter what the water has done, you know how much we need it. And I won't allow you to go even one night in this place without a fire."

"Fine," Eishoxa conceded. "But let me take no responsibility for the consequences."

A twig snapped very loudly somewhere and Eishoxa started awake. The fire was burning still, and the smell of smoke suffused the air. Everyone was asleep, even Smoke, who was meant to be keeping guard. She looked quickly around and grabbed her bow, which lay beside her. Crack – another twig. She jumped to her feet and scanned the forest, slinging her quiver onto her back. She put an arrow in her bow and brought the string up to her shoulder, training the arrow tip into the trees where she'd heard the twig snap. The green light in the forest still glowed brightly, enabling her to see all around, but the leaves had stilled. Now she could hear footsteps approaching.

"Who's there?" she called into the forest, pulling her bowstring tighter. The voice that responded did not speak aloud but seemed to reverberate around the trees, murmur in the boughs, whisper in the bark, communicate through every blade of grass and trembling leaf.

"Are you going to shoot, Eishoxa? Please do. I'd like to see what would happen."

"Who are you?" she called again, turning on the spot and trying to pinpoint something to shoot out. But the forest looked normal, with no wind, no breeze.

The voice taunted her again. "Shoot. I dare you. Shoot." A wind suddenly sped through the branches and Eishoxa's loose hair whipped around her face. She let go of the arrow and it sped through the branches. She couldn't hear it hit anything.

The voice came again. "Very good. And now … I reveal myself."

Eishoxa turned and turned, trying to see where the voice was coming from. Suddenly the trees around her started to move and the bark started to open. Smoke stirred slightly in his sleep as someone, stepping out of the tree his back was leaning against, crept around him. Eishoxa plucked another arrow from her bow and rotated slowly on the spot.

From all the trees around them figures were emerging, stepping across the forest floor, approaching her and her companions deep in sleep. When these people moved, with their tall lithe bodies and long green frizzy hair tied back with moss and leaves, it looked like the forest itself was moving. Their faces were marked with berry juice, and around their waists were belts of bark from which hung pouches made from leaves. Old and young were there, watching her, waiting, and all the while the voice kept whispering,

"And here's another … and another … and another." When all the trees had emptied themselves, the voice paused for a minute and then started again. "These people whom you see are all part of me. These are the Dwellers. Your companions are not welcome here. They have lit a fire in the middle of their homes, a fire that is burning through the ground and damaging the roots in the earth. This fire is forbidden here."

"I told them not to light it," Eishoxa whispered. She didn't understand what was going on.

"Obviously you didn't convince them. But you are not one of them, are you?"

"I am different," Eishoxa said, so quietly that she was sure the voice wouldn't hear – but it did. None of the people around her were moving or speaking. They simply stood there, watching the fire, watching the sleeping bodies. The voice spoke again to Eishoxa.

"Of course you are. And that is why we have tolerated your presence here. Now, the others must go. They must not be here when the sun rises."

"Who are you?" Eishoxa asked again. The voice laughed and Eishoxa felt another wind against her cheek. "I am the Forest, of course. Who else would I be?"

"Do I know you?" Eishoxa enquired. She felt she had heard this voice before, but couldn't pinpoint where and when.

"Of course you know me. I have spoken to you many times, but perhaps you did not have the ears to listen."

The people started to move. Each of them reached into the leaf pouch hanging at their belt and approached the fire, then threw a handful of soil on the fire, causing the flames to sputter and flicker. Eishoxa felt no regret as she watched the fire die. She knew that this was not the place for fire, of any kind.

"Remember," said the voice, "*you* are welcome here."

When she awoke again, she was not in the forest. A strong, cold wind was blowing, buffeting her from side to side. She was standing on the very top of a mountain. There was space for her two feet to stand side by side, but around her was a sheer drop on all sides. If she overbalanced she would fall, and it was a long way down. She could see other mountains, a whole ridge of them, made of black granite. They rose out of the ground like spines on a dragon's back. She turned carefully in a circle, wondering why she was here.

There could be no doubt where she was. She knew she was by the Sorrowful Mountains. But as to why she was here, she had no idea.

Something swept by her ear and she started, almost falling. Turning, she watched as something formed in the air beside her, floating without any support. It formed the shape of a woman, a woman clothed entirely in black, with skin as white as ice. She had a keen face, with waves of jet-black hair blowing out from behind her. Around her feet, a dark cloud was brewing, crackling with miniature lightning forks and rumbling with thunder. It was the third girl from the statue at Dulcacohefen.

"Nezrax," Eishoxa said. The figure smiled.

"Of course." Eishoxa's voice seemed not her own. It came out in a monotone.

"And my sisters – you know them too, do you not?"

Eishoxa nodded. Nezrax smiled again. She looked so young and carefree. She couldn't have been very much older than Eishoxa herself, even though she knew the Goddess had been here since the beginning of time.

"Why have you brought me here?"

Nezrax's eyes widened with surprise. "I brought you here? No, you brought yourself here. I was about to ask you the same question. I have no control in your dreams."

"You're lying," Eishoxa said bluntly. "I would never have brought myself here. This place is evil." Nezrax's face didn't change and neither did her uncaring demeanour. She spun in the air and her hair, black as a crow's wing, swept over her shoulders. "Evil? That's a matter of perspective. It depends on who you talk to."

"I don't think so," Eishoxa retorted immediately, shaking her head.

"Everyone has a seed of something bad inside them. All it depends on what you choose to tend to."

"What do you mean?" Nezrax turned in the air once more and slowly morphed until Eishoxa could see Rosemarie standing there, smiling down at her.

"You see?" Nezrax said. Rosemarie's lips were moving whenever the Goddess spoke. "I can take many forms, but I cannot take the form of something that does not have that seed."

Eishoxa turned away. "Stop it. Let me go back to the forest."

"Oh, to the people who don't think you can do anything. I have heard what my sister has said to you and I feel sorry for you. She has said similar things to me many times. Noble Fiera, thinking that she can save the world with a few sword strokes and clever words. And now I'm here to help you, if you want it."

"There's nothing that you could possibly help me with," Eishoxa spat. Nezrax slowly turned back to her former self and then changed again, taking the shape of Maya. Eishoxa froze. "Stop it," she whispered. "Stop it."

"If you wanted to stop me and you were able to, then you would. But you're weak and you cannot do what you should be able to do. Fiera is right in some things, but she offers no alternative. I, on the other hand, am willing to help you. I will teach you magic beyond anything anyone is capable of."

"I don't need your help and I don't want it," Eishoxa answered, refusing to look at Maya's shape. Nezrax shrugged and flipped over in a perfect somersault. Her form rippled once again and she changed back to her old self.

"You have brought yourself here and now you may go back," she said. "But *you know how to get here."*

"Leave me alone. Don't walk in my dreams again," Eishoxa said darkly, clenching her fists.

Nezrax smiled. "You will come back. I know you will. And I have all the time I need to wait."

CHAPTER 27

Eishoxa woke suddenly as if she had been drenched in cold water. Remembering her encounter with the Guardian, she rolled over and looked towards the fire. It had gone out and the ashes were cold. Smiling contentedly, she lay on her back looking up into the sky. But as she lay there, she remembered the other dream and the smile was wiped off her face. Nezrax wasn't what she'd expected. It was unnerving how normal the Goddess looked, how normal she seemed, but Eishoxa knew she was far from normal.

A bird chirped somewhere. Eishoxa turned and looked into the trees from where she'd heard the voice of the Forest talking to her. Picking up her bow and quiver, she crept out into the forest. The trees were silent and there was no sound or sign of any other life. Eishoxa rested one hand against a trunk. The Dwellers had come out from the trees as though they lived in them. The moss was soft and damp against Eishoxa's bare feet and the air was cold and still heavy with morning dew. Eishoxa ran her hand over the mark on her left shoulder, a scar she would carry forever, a memory of her baptism in the river. The water would not harm her now.

Walking through the forest, she caught the glimpse of something familiar ahead: her arrow, embedded deeply in the trunk of a huge oak. Ivy had grown over it, although it had only been shot there the night before. She hurried up to it and took hold of the end. Immediately another wind blew through the forest and the ivy retracted, curling off in slow spirals away from the arrow. Eishoxa pulled it easily out of the wood. Green leaves fell from the trees and brushed gently against her face.

"Remember, you're welcome here." She could hear the words in her head and feel them in the air around her. This Forest of No Flame was alive – alive in every branch and leaf. In every bird that sang and every creature that moved, she could see the forest living and breathing through them.

She headed back to her companions. When she heard the crackle of the fire, she knew already that it was too late. The ground rumbled as she tore back through the trees.

"Ember!" she shouted. "Don't light a fire! Don't light it!" As she burst back through the trees, she arrived in time to see a vine wrap itself around Ember's ankle and hoist him into the air. Ash and Smoke were similarly trapped. The dragons too had been forced to the ground by vines; however much Ferac roared and fought against the entanglements, he could do nothing to free himself. His fire went out the minute it left his mouth. He was truly trapped. The fire in the centre was still burning brightly though. Eishoxa rushed beside it and heaped earth upon it.

"Eishoxa, what's happening?"

"We must go!" she said. "We must leave now!"

Ember was thrashing around on the end of his vine, trying to reach the knife he kept in his belt. The ground rumbled again, louder and longer this time, and Eishoxa watched as the trees opened and the Dwellers emerged. Ash and Smoke looked shocked, but not as if they were wondering what they were.

"I told you not to light a fire," Eishoxa said quietly, but she became silent when one of the Dwellers gave her a piercing look. They came in their multitudes, as many as the Ewdicani or Indocani. There was a whole race here.

She looked at Ember, who was staring at the Dwellers incredulously.

"We told you not to let them light a fire," the Dweller said to Eishoxa. His voice was low and accented, a strange mixture of all the tongues that Eishoxa had heard.

"I tried, but they lit it when I'd left." He nodded. "We watched you return to get your arrow. The fault is not yours."

"We must light fires to survive," Ember shouted from his vine, still dangling by his ankle. There was a roar from deep within the forest and Eishoxa felt the trees shake.

"Have you no respect for the world that you live in? Fire can only destroy! You want to destroy in the place that is meant to create. A curse on you, Fire!"

They all heard the fury in the Forest's voice. "I've put it out," Eishoxa offered, but she met with no response.

The Dweller who had spoken continued. "We will not decide your fate here but with the Forest. Come, bring them." He motioned to three Dwellers, who cut the vines holding Ash, Smoke and Ember. The three fell to the ground and were pulled to their feet. The dragons were left where they were, even though Ferac roared even louder. Eishoxa was glad her companions had the good sense to keep quiet for once, although their eyes asked many questions.

The Dweller who was in charge spoke to Eishoxa. "You're coming, are you not?" Eishoxa nodded. He gestured between the trees. "Lead on, then." Eishoxa walked forward. She knew where to go. The Dwellers holding Ash, Smoke and Ember followed close behind and the rest brought up the rear. When they reached the oak from which Eishoxa had taken her arrow, they stopped. The Dweller took from his pouch a handful of dirt and sprinkled it over the roots that protruded from the ground. They stirred in the ground and Eishoxa heard the voice again.

"Ah, the Fires and Eishoxa." The Dwellers were silent in awe. Ember said nothing but seemed to understand what was going on. Ash and Smoke were looking around in puzzlement, as though wondering where the voice was coming from.

"Come forward, Fire, and tell me your name." The Dweller pushed Ember forward. He looked up at the tree and said, "My name is Ember."

"Ember. A fitting one for a Fire."

He enquired in turn, "What is your name?"

"I have many names, but I am the Forest. The forest in which you stand and the forest that you wanted to destroy."

"Never to destroy," Ember said. "We lit a single fire."

"Eishoxa warned you not to."

"She does not understand our ways as one would like. She is ... different from us."

Eishoxa frowned. She felt Ash's and Smoke's eyes on her and her hand drifted unconsciously to the mark on her left shoulder.

"Yes, I see what you mean," the Forest said, rumbling through the trees.

"Where are you?" Ember asked boldly. "What do you look like?"

"I am all around you, but you do not have the eyes to see," replied the Forest. Eishoxa turned, hearing the voice come from somewhere behind her. The Dwellers dropped to the ground as a woman stepped out from behind a tree. Eishoxa smiled at her and received a smile back. She felt that she knew this woman already. The woman had long brown hair and was dressed simply in a green tunic. She had a pale green face, traced with ink tattoos of ivy leaves. As her long tunic brushed along the ground, the forest floor bloomed with the most beautiful flowers.

"I am the Guardian of this Forest," she said in a slightly singsong voice. "Whenever you harm the Forest, you harm me too." She showed them two small burns just below her elbow. "You see? You have wounded me."

Ember was staring at the woman as if he couldn't believe his eyes. She smiled coolly back at him and then turned to Eishoxa. "I walked among the Fires once, but they sent me away. They sent me to the forest, to this forest, and I have become it. The Dwellers are those rejected by their people, rejected by those who should have loved them the most."

"What do you mean?" Eishoxa asked, turning back to look at Ember. He nodded grudgingly.

"If a child shows signs of being like the other race, it is abandoned in the forest. It is not expected to survive."

Eishoxa turned to look the Guardian, her eyes wide as she remembered something. The Guardian smiled again and then held out her hand to Eishoxa. "Walk with me, Eishoxa. I can see that you have a lot to say."

Ember started forward. "Where are you taking her?"

"I wish to walk," the Guardian said firmly. "And I wish to walk with her. This is my forest, Ember. Remember that."

"Guardian," replied Ember stiffly, "we must get home. We carry important news to the rest of our people."

The Guardian inclined her head. "I will not be long, but I must insist that I talk to Eishoxa. It is of a matter of great importance." Eishoxa put out her hand as Ember opened his mouth again. "It's fine. I will speak with her and then we shall go."

Eishoxa looked at the Guardian for confirmation and she nodded. "Yes. And in the meantime, you may pack up your things and prepare yourself to leave. Dinor, accompany them back to their camp." She lingered slightly on the last word. The Dweller who was in charge, Dinor, stood up and started to walk back with the rest. Ember gave Eishoxa one more look before following. Eishoxa turned back to the Guardian, who said, "Now we can walk and I can say things to you

230

that I have wanted to say for a while."

Eishoxa nodded assent. The Guardian led her deeper into the forest, where the light was green and dark and the trees grew close together. She said nothing for a while and they simply walked. Eishoxa bit her lip and said suddenly, "I didn't know about the abandoning of people in the forest."

The Guardian turned to her. "That is strange. One of your close friends should be one of my people."

Eishoxa stopped. "So it's true then? Rianox is one of you?"

The Guardian smiled. "His blood is a mixture of both Ewdicani and Indocani."

"I saw him in a memory. He was being held in the arms of a girl. He was being sent away."

"And what did you think about that?"

Eishoxa thought back. "I felt very bitter," she remembered. "Because he was different and so was I, but I was praised and he was condemned."

"You were very young. Had you tried to do anything, they would not have listened to you." The Guardian smiled sadly. "Unfortunately, it is the way to keep pure blood running through the races."

"But how does that happen?" Eishoxa asked. "The two races are forbidden to mix."

"It is a strange pattern that appears throughout races of all different species. In the forest the strongest survive, and with the Ignorant as well. However, with water and fire, sometimes it is the one who can hide and be silent for the longest who survives. Rianox has that. Only the Goddesses decide what blood you will have."

"He didn't tell me," Eishoxa said quietly.

The Guardian sighed. "Well, they do not like to be known for that, although it is common knowledge about Rianox's bloodline. It is strange."

"But why did he stay? How was he allowed to stay? I saw," she swallowed, "I saw him return and I … I attacked him for who he was. I called him a half-breed. And you, who were you?" asked Eishoxa.

The Guardian raised her eyebrows. "It is hard to say. I do not know enough to stay truthful to the real story. I suggest you ask him when you return. As for who I am and was, that is none of your concern. I promise that you will find out soon enough. But that is not what I wanted to talk to you about." She stopped suddenly and rested one hand on a tree. The leaves, which had been looking wilted, became fresh, and flowers opened on the end of each little branch.

"You are part of each race now, woven into their history by your actions or by who you are. You're Indocani because of your mother. You're Ignorant because of your choice to go there when you had to leave this world. You're Ewdicani because they have marked you. And you're one of us as well, because you have not chosen a race but are a combination of them all. That is a lot of power, and as you grow, your powers will increase until perhaps you're as powerful as the Goddesses themselves. There are dangerous times ahead, and you will be called upon by many races to fight and defend them. You will have to make many choices about what is right and what you want to do."

Eishoxa wondered whether the Guardian knew of her dream of Nezrax the previous night. She wondered whether she had indeed taken herself there out of her own free will.

"It is hard to choose, I know. I had to choose to leave a race that I loved and make my own race here." The Guardian opened her hand slowly and a flower grew gradually out of her palm. "I had to choose to put away the sword and bow, and grow flowers instead." She looked up at Eishoxa through her eyelashes and smiled. "It doesn't sound very interesting, does it?"

"I don't know," and Eishoxa shrugged. "I don't know what sounds interesting."

The Guardian closed her hand and dropped the flower on the ground. "Listen to me, Eishoxa. You have a friend, do you not? A friend whom you seek, who you believe may still be alive."

Eishoxa's eyes widened. "How do you know about Maya?"

"I can see out of every forest, forests all around the world. You're not alone in your search to find her."

"Other people are looking for her? Where is she?"

"This I cannot tell you. If I knew, I would, but she is hidden from me. All I know is that she is alive."

Eishoxa's heart began to pump very fast. "Really?"

The Guardian shook her head. "But she must not be the person you sacrifice a nation for. She must come second or third. Listen to me, Eishoxa" – because she had started to shake her head and back away – "The world is corrupt now, and the only way to mend it may be to start again. I hope this is not the case. The world needs you. The life of one Ignorant must not stop you from saving it."

"But Maya needs me too. It's my fault that she is wherever she is, and I am going to put things right. I owe nothing to these people, nothing at all." Eishoxa argued.

The Guardian bowed her head and her hair blew across her face. She raised her eyes again and Eishoxa saw that they had changed colour. They were a dark gold now, like the dappled sunlight on a forest floor, like the richest colour of a flame, like the dawn light that glows on the sea in the morning.

"Is that true, Eishoxa? Do you not owe anyone anything at all? Not even the Ewdicani you left behind, who risked everything to show you some hope in the world?"

"How do you know about Rush?"

"I know about many people. I operate outside the usual rules of nature and I can create them. Look at the world, Eishoxa. Look, and see its fate."

Eishoxa felt herself thrown into something and then pulled out. She was looking down on herself from far above and she could see that her body was frozen. The Guardian moved forward and placed one hand on her forehead. Suddenly Eishoxa was dragged forward again and she was looking through a huge eye, an eye that encompassed the world.

Waves crashed down, one after the other, in great acts of destruction. Fire burned through the forest and a great pit was swallowing up the ground. Continents toppled in like stacks of cards. Eishoxa saw a total obliteration of everything.

"This is the pit that our world is falling into," said the Guardian. "All elements will destroy each other, and there will be no salvation for anyone who looks for it. This is our world – your world and my world. You cannot let that happen."

Eishoxa felt her head spin with intense vertigo, then suddenly she was back in her body. "What if I can't stop it?" she asked. The forest erupted with sound. The wind howled through the trees and the ground rumbled and shook. Eishoxa could feel with every iota of her body that the Forest was raging.

"I would not have told you if I did not think you could do it. I am outside of time, Eishoxa, and so I see the future and the past and the present. You're the only one in this world or in any other world who can stop it if you would put obstacles aside." Then the sound stopped and the forest was silent again. Eishoxa shook with fear. The Guardian smiled. "When you're ready, you may come back to the forest. It will help you to be here, I think. But there is a fight that must be won first." Eishoxa nodded, but wondered what she was talking about.

"And now," said the Guardian, "let us go back to your friends. I think Ember wants to leave as soon as possible."

When they arrived back in the clearing, the others were ready to go. The Dwellers formed a silent crowd on one side, and the Guardian stood, leaning against a tree, on the other. Ash handed Eishoxa her pack and she slung it over her shoulder. Ember was already astride Ferac, who was snapping his jaws and growling warningly at the Dwellers, who kept their distance from him. Eishoxa took the hand offered to her and swung herself up onto Ferac's back.

"Shall we go home, then?" Ember asked. Eishoxa, still reeling from what she'd learned, heard only one word. "Home," she whispered. "Yes, I'm going home."

As they landed on the wide grassy plain in front of the Tree, Eishoxa breathed deeply of the air that felt so strange now to be back in her lungs. She slid down off Ferac and took her pack from Ember.

"Look!" Smoke called. Eishoxa turned to see two figures running towards them from the base of the Tree. Even from here, she could distinguish Amber's voice floating towards them on the breeze.

"You're back!"

Eishoxa put her pack on the ground and took the bow off her shoulder. As Amber collided into her, Eishoxa laughed. "I've missed you, Amber."

"And me as well?" Rianox asked in mock hopefulness. Over his shoulder, Eishoxa could see Ember turn away, as if he knew that Eishoxa was back among those she preferred. She paused for a moment, remembering what she had found out about Rianox in the Forest. Then she put it to one side. If he wanted to tell her, he would.

"Yes, you as well," Eishoxa said. For better or for worse, she was back. And she had succeeded.

PART 3

CHAPTER 1

Rianox and Amber accompanied them to Vera's room. Ferac, along with the other two dragons, had left immediately for the dragons' pit. Eishoxa had asked Ferac to say hello to Zeexa for her, but she didn't know whether he would. He'd been treating her in an aloof manner on their journey back from the Forest of No Flame and across the desert, as if she should be honoured to be riding him. Or maybe he was just angry with her because of the incident with the Dwellers. Ember had said that Ferac was shy. Eishoxa strongly doubted it.

As the six of them started to climb the Tree, Eishoxa was surprised to see that everything looked normal. She didn't know what she'd been expecting, but then she realised: most of the Indocani probably didn't know they were at war. They didn't know that the Empty were advancing, at this very moment. It was now her task to say that the rival nations of the Indocani and the Ewdicani, enemies for thousands of years, had united against their old enemy and were going to war. But right now, the Tree looked just as she had left it. Although Sicharenhafan had no seasons, pale green leaves were sprouting from the bark of the trunk, like springtime in the gardens at Bareth. She wondered how the Tree grew so well with no water, and pondered how the Indocani had tricked it into thriving in a drought-ridden land.

Ash and Smoke stood behind them as they knocked on Vera's door. Rianox and Amber stayed outside while the four travellers entered. Vera had her back to them, looking at something on the wall. Eishoxa could see that it was a map, similar to the one she'd seen at Dulcacohefen but with different-coloured lines all crossing over each other. The map was new; at least, it hadn't been there when they'd left. As they walked forward Vera turned around and her face lit up with a look of surprised delight. "Eishoxa! Ember! You've returned!" Ash and Smoke, stepping forward, were then greeted in the same way. Giving the map a final glance, Vera took a seat behind her table and smiled up at them.

"I didn't expect you back so soon. You must have set a punishing speed, Ember," Vera smiled. Ash and Smoke looked uncomfortable. Although Eishoxa had been given the task of securing the peace with the Ewdicani, it was Ember Vera was praising and treating like leader.

"We tried to get back as soon as we could," Ember replied, agreeing with his leader.

"Well, it is a very good thing that you have done, a very good thing indeed." She looked at each of them in turn and noticed that Eishoxa's eyes had been caught by something else. She followed Eishoxa's gaze to the map. Standing, she turned and looked at it. "I see you have noticed our map. I had it brought up from our library as soon as Gresceva sent news of the successful alliance. I'm charting our progress in the war against the Empty. As soon as you secured the treaty, Gresceva sent a waiting battalion to the Sorrowful Mountains." She pointed to a line, tracing it from one point to a place where all the lines converged. "This definitely helped us, so I thank you for that, Ember."

"Actually, Vera, Eishoxa secured the treaty," Ember replied. Ash and Smoke turned in surprise towards him. It was not like Ember to give up a compliment. Eishoxa could feel her cheeks burning: Ember couldn't have forgotten the last time she'd reminded him that it was in fact she who'd secured the peace. Vera looked from Eishoxa to Ember, who avoided looking at each other.

"Really? When Gresceva wrote to me to say that you were returning, she told me that it was you, Ember. But I suppose it doesn't matter who it was. The point is that you've done it between you, and we have been saved."

Eishoxa moved closer to the map on the wall. It was shaded lightly in three colours, black, red and blue.

"What do these colours mean?" she asked. Vera stepped up behind her. "Those colours signify which land belongs to whom."

"This is the Forest of No Flame, isn't it?" Eishoxa asked, resting one finger on the map. Vera squinted slightly at it and nodded. "Yes it is." Across it was written in small letters occupied territory.

"Doesn't that belong to the Dwellers?" Eishoxa asked, turning around to look at Vera, who blinked in confusion.

"I don't think I know what you're talking about, Eishoxa."

"The Dwellers," she repeated, looking at Ember for confirmation. He cleared his throat and stepped forward. "The Outcast, she means," he said. Vera made a sound of understanding.

"The Outcast do not have land," she said in a voice that brooked no argument. "They betrayed their people and therefore they do not merit the right to land." Eishoxa opened her mouth to speak but Ember cut in, giving her a warning glare.

"Quite right," he said. "I suggest that we speak in private, Vera, and let the others go."

"Why?" Eishoxa asked, turning around to look at him. "What can't the rest of us hear?"

"Eishoxa," answered Vera, before Ember could speak. "Ember is a Lord. There are going to be things that he cannot share with you and are for my ears only."

Eishoxa glared at Ember, but he wasn't looking in her direction. She turned back to the map and examined again, taking her time.

"Vera," she began, puzzling over something in her head.

Vera turned again. "What now, Eishoxa?" There was an almost imperceptible sigh from Ember, but Eishoxa ignored him. "You said that the only problem with the Ewdicani joining us was that their land would be destroyed. But on this map, the war doesn't come anywhere close to their land."

"What's the matter with that, Eishoxa? Do you want their land to be destroyed? True, that was a potential problem: if the Empty found out that the Ewdicani were helping us, then they might destroy their land, and with Dulcacohefen being much less practical to defend, they would be wiped out."

Eishoxa shook her head. "That's not what you said."

"What are you trying to say, Eishoxa?" Vera's voice was calm, but it contained a hint of menace as she dared Eishoxa to voice her thoughts.

"You said the only way for the Empty to reach us here was through the Ewdicani's land. But the war is coming the other way." She traced one line on the map with her finger. "There's something else, isn't there, something you don't want anyone to know about." Silence in the room, so tense that Eishoxa felt just able to breathe. Ash and Smoke were looking at her, horrified.

"Ember, Ash, Smoke – leave us for a moment please?" Vera asked, sitting behind her table once again.

"Is that necessary?" Ember asked.

Vera pointed to the door and it swung open. "Out, Ember!" she commanded. Once they had left, she looked up at Eishoxa. "Tell me, Eishoxa, what are you trying to do?"

"What do you mean?" Eishoxa asked.

"Are you trying to prove something to Ember about me? Or to Ash? Or Smoke? Or yourself? Are you trying to prove something to me? Why does it bother you if their land is not destroyed?"

"I could ask you a similar question: wasn't that what you wanted to happen? Better their land be destroyed than risk Indocani lives?"

"I do not wish any land to be destroyed. I do not wish there to be a war. But there is. There is a war, Eishoxa. And sometimes that happens."

"I know that. But I think there's something else. I heard things while I was there at Dulcacohefen, Vera."

"Oh? What kind of things, Eishoxa?" Vera asked. Her voice sounded dangerous, but Eishoxa carried on. "Something that you're doing with Gresceva."

"I am doing many things with Gresceva, Eishoxa. We are leaders and there is a war."

"I don't think it's that, Vera. I think you are lying."

"You cannot prove that, Eishoxa," Vera answered. Her eyes narrowed. "Remember that you are only one of my subjects here. I am leader, and as leader I am owed your respect."

"I'll give you my respect when you earn it," Eishoxa retorted. "And so far I haven't seen anything that does deserve it. And I am not your subject. I was never your subject. You are not my leader."

Vera gave a little intake of breath. "Watch what you say, Eishoxa. You are not seated in your castle at Bareth. You are not seated with your mother in her heavenly palace. You are here. On Earth. This is my land and these are my people, and you will do as I say."

They glared at each other. Eishoxa spoke first. "I wasn't allowed in the Assembly, did you know that?"

"Gresceva mentioned it."

"But you said that I would be actively involved. You said that I needed to go."

"You did," Vera replied.

"I don't think you keep the promises you make, Vera. But even so, there is one promise that I won't forget."

"And which one was that?" Vera rejoined. "I seem to make a lot of promises to you, Eishoxa."

"I've done what you wanted. I've secured an alliance for you, and now you must let me go back to Bareth. That was your promise." Vera didn't even blink. "Of course you may go back to Bareth, if that is what you want to happen. However, I have one condition. Ember is the only one who would and could take you back, but I need him to perform a small task for me. When he returns, then he may take you back."

"Why can't he take me home before?"

"This task is of the utmost importance."

"Why can't someone else take me?"

"The decision has been made!" Vera shouted. "I will not have you arguing anymore with me. If you are not satisfied with this, then please go off into the Black Forest and you will die, alone. I am the leader here and I have made the final decision! Either you go back when Ember returns or you do not go back at all. Take your pick. And now leave me. I cannot bear to listen to you anymore!" Eishoxa turned on her heel and stormed out, slamming the door behind her. The silent group of waiting Indocani watched as she raged away out of sight. Amber took off after her. After a moment, and a quick glance at Ember, Rianox followed.

Ember nodded to Ash and Smoke. "You may go. There are matters that I need to discuss with Vera. Thank you for what you've done." The two of them bowed and Ember gave a quick bow back. Then they left. Ember pushed on the door and entered. Vera was lounging in her chair, absentmindedly playing with the papers in front of her.

"She knows," Vera said, looking up and staring thoughtfully at him. "She knows there's something not right. We have underestimated her. We must continue to perform the task with utmost speed." She looked up at Ember as if he had an idea of what to do. He shrugged.

"I told Gresceva this, but she didn't understand. She thought that if we left her in her room, she would lose interest. But it made her all the more dangerous."

Vera nodded. "Gresceva's mind is brilliant, but she's not used to dealing with someone like Eishoxa, who has been given a great power." Ember made an affirmative sound. "She fell in the river, didn't she?" Vera asked, and when Ember nodded, she continued, "She is marked by the water, and Wella has given her powers of her own. You can sense them in her, can you not?"

"Very much so," Ember agreed. "But she doesn't know about all of them, only the ones on the surface. The fire recently claimed her. If she focuses on that, then it will destroy the other powers that she's been given. The Guardian also has blessed her. She has control over all elements now but rock and air."

"Nezrax," Vera mused.

Ember nodded. "We'll need to watch her. I'm sure that Nezrax will do everything in her power to convince her to join them."

"And with her on their side—" Vera began.

"They will be unstoppable. She is still essential to our plan."

"My plan," Vera corrected. "Of course she's essential. She's the only one who can do it."

"When will you take her to the Mountains?"

"I don't know. It won't be easy now, Ember. We must tread carefully from now on. I understand that she heard things she wasn't meant to in Dulcacohefen."

"She was more suspicious than I thought. She was put in the most beautiful room, as instructed, but it wasn't enough this time."

Vera raised her eyebrows. "Rush," Ember replied by way of explanation.

Vera nodded. "Gresceva told me that he'd be a problem. It doesn't matter, though; he can be dealt with. And besides, he's not important to the plan. Has she been to the Sorrowful Mountains yet?"

"Of course not," Ember stated. "How could I have taken her there?"

Vera slammed her hand on the table. "In her dreams, you fool! Of course I'm not asking if you took her there in person. Has she been there in her dreams?"

"I don't know," Ember admitted.

"We'll need to find out."

"I know someone who can help with that," Ember replied.

"But she wants to go back to Bareth," Vera pointed out.

Ember lifted his gaze to the ceiling. "Do you remember what we discussed?" he enquired. Vera started to smile. Ember looked back down at her. He could feel a deep sadness welling up inside him, like tears. But he couldn't cry.

"I don't agree with what I have to do, but …"

"For the good of the Indocani," Vera prompted.

Ember took a deep breath. "I will do whatever it takes to keep her here."

CHAPTER 2

Eishoxa sat in the shade of one of the boughs in the Tree, opposite Amber. The two of them had been spending more and more time together since Eishoxa had returned from Dulcacohefen, and she had found that, if there was a substitute for Maya, it was Amber. She was everything Eishoxa wanted a friend to be. She showed the caring nature and attentiveness of Maya, but she also had the energy and vitality that Maya lacked. Ember had disappeared immediately after they'd returned to the Tree. When Eishoxa had commented on this, Amber had shrugged. Clearly, it was nothing unusual, and Eishoxa did not pursue the topic.

"So what were the Ewdicani actually like?" Amber asked, throwing a pinecone into the air and catching it again. "You haven't told me that yet. We've just spoken about your journey and what I did while you were gone."

Eishoxa shrugged and adjusted her position on the bough. "Different from what I expected."

"Was that a good thing or a bad thing then?"

Eishoxa thought for a moment. "Good thing, I think. Definitely a good thing."

"But how was Gresceva?"

Eishoxa rolled her eyes. "Worse than Vera, I'll tell you that." Amber laughed and winced in sympathy. "Yes, she is very hard to get along with, from what I've heard."

Eishoxa thought back. "She was worse than that. There was something not right about her.

"She's an Ewdicani," Amber shrugged. "There's something not right about all of them."

Eishoxa nodded. "Maybe. A lot of them were like that. But not all."

"Was Ember unbearable?" Amber grinned.

Eishoxa put her hand into her pocket and brought out the coin. The bronze was still shiny and warm from her pocket. "Sometimes, yes. And sometimes worse than unbearable. But he gave me back my coin."

"Yes, he told me about that." Amber leaned forward. "What is it?"

Eishoxa handed it to her. "It's the currency of Bareth."

Amber looked up, bemused. "What's a currency?"

Eishoxa leaned back against the tree. "It's what they use to buy things from each other and pay for things. Money. Rosemarie, my adopted sister, made that for me specially."

"What does it say?" Amber found the Base Tongue hard to read.

"Along the bottom it says *Princess of Bareth*, and then beneath it *My Sister.*" Amber handed it back and Eishoxa put it away. They stayed in silence for a moment and then Amber spoke again. Now, I want to know the truth. What happened to your shoulder?"

Eishoxa put her hand up unconsciously to touch the little mark. "What do you mean?"

"I saw the Ewdicani mark on it." Eishoxa pulled her sleeve higher up her shoulder. She'd been trying to hide it. Amber laughed. "Did you really think I wouldn't notice?"

Eishoxa shrugged. "Maybe."

Amber stopped smiling and asked again, "What happened? Ember never said."

Eishoxa sighed. "I fell in the river."

"What?" Amber's eyes widened. "How?"

"It was an accident," Eishoxa supplied, unwilling to say anymore.

"But … how did you survive?" Amber questioned.

Eishoxa shifted slightly on the branch, deliberating whether or not to tell Amber what had really happened. "I saw Wella," she finally replied. "And she gave me powers over water.

Amber blinked, looking confused. "So you have control over two elements now, not one?" Eishoxa could hear a trace of fear in Amber's voice. Control over more than one element was only associated with the Empty. "Yes," Eishoxa answered truthfully.

"Will that mark ever go? Will you ever lose that power?" Amber enquired.

Eishoxa shrugged. "It doesn't hurt anymore."

"But it won't go?"

"I don't think so, but I don't mind. I can't use much water here anyway."

Amber didn't look convinced. Eishoxa sighed. "I know what it can do and I promise I will never use it against the Indocani. But please, don't tell anyone. Ember wants it to remain as secret as possible."

Amber nodded slowly. "Well, I can see why."

Eishoxa smiled. "And I saw memories, from when we were younger."

Amber looked shocked. "Really?"

"Yes. The three of us were inseparable, weren't we?"

"We were called the Trio of Trouble," Amber laughed. "But with you at our head, no one could correct us."

"And I saw how much I could do, even when I was so young."

"Yes, you were so talented. Both Ember and I were so surprised when you chose to be our friend. We never asked. You just approached us one day and said, 'Let's be friends.' Wouldn't it be amazing if you learnt how to do all that again?" Eishoxa concentrated for a moment and her hand burst into flames. "Well, I can do simple things: start fires, put out fires, make the fire move a little bit."

"But you are learning, that's good."

Eishoxa suddenly thought of the Forest as Amber finished speaking. "We saw the Dwellers."

Amber looked puzzled. "Who are they?"

"They live in the Forest of No Flame. Ember called them the Outcast. They've been banished but they've made their own race."

"Who has been banished?" came a curious voice. Eishoxa turned to see Rianox approaching. He sat down on the branch next to Amber and looked at each of them.

"Who was banished?" he asked again.

"The people in the Forest of No Flame," Eishoxa replied. She found it impossible to look away from the scar on his chest. She knew how that had happened now, and seeing his warm smile made her feel even worse. He didn't know that she knew. So she cleared her throat and tried to speak casually. "We saw the Dwellers and I spoke to the Guardian." She kept her head lowered, but out of the corner of her eye she saw Rianox stiffen. So the Guardian had been right: he was indeed one of them – or at least he knew them.

"She mentioned you," Eishoxa said slowly and carefully, lest Rianox should not want to speak of it. To her surprise, he raised his head and gave her a tight smile. "I know. She would have done. She told you that I was one of them, didn't she?"

"Yes." To Eishoxa, Amber's lack of reaction seemed to mean she already knew about it. So maybe it was common knowledge, as the Guardian had said. "How did people find out that …?" She didn't know how to voice it.

Rianox understood. "Well, I was always much cleverer than everyone else. Languages came easily to me, and I preferred reading books to sparring with the others. That's usually a sign, especially when you're young – you don't know what to hide then. And my skin, of course, was always so much lighter than the others. It's funny – the one thing I couldn't change gave me away the most."

Eishoxa said nothing. It was hard to know what to say when there are no words to comfort someone. Rianox sighed. "Well, I chose to come back. There was no reason why I should have left. I'm proud to be Indocani."

Amber patted his hand comfortingly. "Well, I'm happy to have you here." He gave her a forced smile, but his voice sounded genuinely amused when he spoke. "That's good, Amber. At least someone thinks that."

"Is that why you have that scar? Because you didn't leave?" Eishoxa asked, pointing to it. The words spilled out before she could stop them, and she cursed her stupidity. The last thing she wanted to do was talk about it.

Rianox looked down. "No. Someone else gave me that." He didn't elaborate, and Eishoxa stayed silent. Amber took a deep breath and cut through the silence that hung awkwardly between them. "Why did you come back on Ferac?"

Eishoxa turned to her gratefully. "Because I fell in the river, I wasn't trusted to fly a dragon by myself."

"Yes, I heard Zeexa was very annoyed that she wasn't allowed to fly with the others."

Eishoxa grinned. "I can imagine."

"She is a good dragon, isn't she?" Rianox asked, rejoining the conversation. Eishoxa nodded vigorously. "Oh yes, very good. But very competitive. She was always trying to beat the others, even though she's the smallest."

Rianox laughed. "Yes, that sounds like her. She'll grow, though, and then maybe she'll have a chance."

"I need to go and see her," Eishoxa thought aloud.

"Yes, that would be a good idea. I don't think she likes being abandoned." Amber laughed. Rianox smiled and eased his posture on his branch.

"What are you going to do now, Eishoxa?" he questioned in his quiet voice.

"Try to find Maya," Eishoxa answered with conviction. "I've done what I had to do for the Indocani, and now they must honour their promise and let me go back to find her. I know she's alive. The Guardian told me that. And now I must find her."

Eishoxa caught a look that passed between Rianox and Amber. "What?"

"Will Ember let you go?" Amber asked apprehensively.

"Vera said I may go when he gets back."

"But he would be the one taking you," Amber pointed out. "And he isn't going to let you leave without a struggle."

"Do you want to leave that much? " Rianox enquired. "What if your friend is dead and it's a suicide mission?"

Eishoxa heaved a sigh. "I want to leave a lot less now than I did when I got here, it's true. And I have all these powers now, which mean that I'm more Indocani than I was before. But if I went missing, would you look for me? Even if you thought I was dead?"

"I would keep looking for you until the day I found you or knew you were dead," Rianox said, and Amber agreed with a nod. Her face, usually so keen and cheerful, had taken on a sad look. It made her look so much older.

"That's why I need to leave, to find Maya. She would do the same for me, and I owe her no less. I have done what I have to do here."

Rianox and Amber said nothing. Eishoxa couldn't think of anything else to say.

"So we have until Ember returns then?" Amber asked finally. Rianox raised his head to check.

"Until Ember returns," Eishoxa said.

After their conversation in the Tree, the three of them spent more and more time together. Mostly, Amber did the speaking and shouting, Rianox did the answering and bickering, and Eishoxa did the listening and laughing, but none of them minded the part the others played. Yet Eishoxa couldn't quite drive from her head another trio, a trio that fate had reshuffled with new people – with Ember exchanged for Rianox. Eishoxa could tell that this was sometimes on Amber's mind as well.

Rianox and Amber coached Eishoxa. They spent a long time in the Dragon Forest together, refining Eishoxa's archery. Amber taught her to run through the crunchy dry leaves and twigs making barely a sound, and to track prey by reading the claw marks left on tree bark. Eishoxa was enjoying these days. Her time with Rush had taught her that, no matter what she wanted, she had to enjoy herself sometimes because that was how she could be free, and when she was with Rianox and Amber, listening with a smile on her face to the two of them arguing about something, it was very hard not to be happy.

CHAPTER 3

*E*ISHOXA WAS BACK *in the Forest of No Flame. She was running, and the ground felt cool against her bare feet, whose rhythmic thud was the only sound she could hear. The trees were swaying from side to side and the tendrils of ivy that hung down in green curtains moved aside as she past. With every step, leaves sprung from the ground, burgeoning around her feet. She ran and ran, with no purpose or destination, and her mind felt blissfully clear for the first time in a long time. No worries clouded it, no problems weighed it down. The density of trees varied as she ran, from very thick to very sparse. But then she sensed something change beneath her, and her feet started to slow of their own accord. She stopped and looked down, pushing her toes into the soft earth. The leaves that had sprung up wherever her feet touched the ground began to grow again. A damp, sweet aroma rose up around her. Holding out one hand, she focused on the earth that still peeped between the huge, dark, waxy leaves. Within moments, flowers were springing up all around her, filling the gaps with bright colours. Beautiful flowers in shades of red and orange, pink and deepest blue. She twirled around in delight, and the flowers grew higher and higher as she commanded them.*

She heard the sound of laughter behind her and turned to see the Guardian walking towards her. "Eishoxa! How wonderful to see you again."

"I think I'm dreaming," admitted Eishoxa. "But it's good to see you as well."

"Of course you're dreaming, Eishoxa, but why should that affect your happiness at seeing me?"

The Guardian waved her hand through her air, and the flowers that Eishoxa had made shrank and turned green again, then disappeared into the ground. She smiled and said, "We can't have too much colour here, though it is fun to make it. You've found out, I see, that you have control over the Earth, as you do with water and fire." She held her hand out to Eishoxa. "Walk with me. Run with me. Talk with me. Laugh with me. We have little time, I'm afraid, and as always there is much that needs to be said. It's always the best times that must be cut short, and the worst that drag on."

Eishoxa took her hand and the Guardian started to run with the swiftness of a deer. Eishoxa could somehow keep up. They ran on and on through the forest, and still the Guardian kept running.

"Where are we going?" Eishoxa called.

"Come and see," the Guardian said mysteriously. After a while the Guardian slowed and stopped. Here the trees grew even more densely, and brambles and ivy wound around them, making it impossible to see past them.

The Guardian let go of Eishoxa's hand. "Behind this wall," she said, walking towards it, "lives the Forest's secret. Can you guess?"

Eishoxa shook her head. The Guardian smiled again. "The elements," she whispered.

"The elements?"

"Yes – the wild and wonderful parts of them that weren't allowed out when the Goddesses recreated the world." She rested her hand against the green wall for a moment, as though she wanted to push through. Then she spun around gracefully and took Eishoxa's hands again. "Unfortunately, I cannot

enter, although I've tried many times. Only those decreed worthy of meeting the elements may enter. And now I feel as though, sometime soon, you're going to need to be somewhere, somewhere where you can hide – safely. And I also feel that a time is coming soon when you will need to speak to the elements, to ask them for advice and consult with them. This is where you may succeed where others before you have failed. Failed terribly."

"What are you talking about?" Eishoxa asked. The Guardian looked very gravely at her. "There is danger ahead of you, Eishoxa. Much danger and much sorrow. Sorrow that will drive you to your knees, and death all around you. You will have many battles soon, both externally and internally."

"Can I stop it?" Eishoxa asked before she could stop herself. The Guardian shook her head. "I'm afraid it is already happening. But remember as I said, you are welcome here."

CHAPTER 4

EISHOXA LEFT THE TREE and walked off towards the Dragon Forest. Her dream from the previous night was at the forefront of her mind, and although it worried her, she hadn't spoken to anyone about it. The Forest of No Flame was alien and dangerous to those who didn't respect its rules. And, by extension, that meant that the Guardian was also dangerous, because she was the Forest personified. In everything she did, her two different natures collided: the maternal side, nurtured during her time leading the Dwellers, and the predator side, which she retained from her time with the Indocani.

She didn't want to share with the Indocani what the Guardian had told her in her dream because they wouldn't understand how important it was for her to know what the Guardian had meant. When she put her hand on the ground, the soil shifted weakly under her fingers. She could control three elements now. Rush had said that it was dangerous to have control over more than one, that it changed a person. Even now, she could feel all three elements fighting each other for dominance inside her, a constant battle. Even now, they scared her.

She entered the Dragon Forest and adjusted the strap of her quiver and bowstring on her back. She had got so used to not wearing it during her time at Dulcacohefen that it seemed almost wrong to put it back on now, as if she were violating some deeply held principle. She only had to look around once to remember where she was now. But it took a little longer to convince herself that she was meant to be there.

Walking slowly through the forest, Eishoxa concentrated on the crunch that every footstep made. She was getting so good at walking quietly that sometimes she had to remember that she was able to make noise.

As she approached the dragons' pit, she could hear the familiar sounds that many dragons made when snoozing in the late afternoon: rumbling, growling, with the occasional puff of smoke or muted roar from one trying to prove he was stronger than the rest. She reached the top of the hollow and clambered down into the pit. The dragons were accustomed to her now, and with her braided hair and her bow on her back, she didn't look all that different from the Indocani. Zeexa had said that dragons get a sense of someone by connecting to a person's heart, emotions and intentions rather than judging by what they see. Eishoxa wondered what her heart gave away. Through the mounds of sleeping and stretching dragons, Eishoxa scanned the groups for the little black dragon that she was looking for. When she caught sight of her, Eishoxa smiled. Zeexa was one of the better reasons for coming back. Eishoxa had missed that little dragon.

"*Zeexa!*" she called, and she felt the little flower open again. That was the only way Eishoxa could describe Zeexa's mind. She felt it open slowly in the corner of her consciousness and then flood her all at once.

"*Eishoxa! I was hoping you would come and see me soon!*" The dragon scurried over, shoving her way through the other dragons to reach Eishoxa. Zeexa purred with a deep cat-like sound as Eishoxa put her arms around her neck and leant her face against Zeexa's shoulder.

"You've grown!" Eishoxa exclaimed, stepping back to take a better look at her. Zeexa nodded proudly. *"Not very much – I'm still one of the smallest here. But I am much faster since last you rode me."*

Eishoxa grinned. *"That's very good."*

"Why wasn't I allowed to come and take you back home? They never told me."

"I wasn't able to fly a dragon because I was too weak," Eishoxa explained.

"So who did you ride then?"

"Ferac, with Ember."

Zeexa made a disgusted sound. *"Did you have to ride him?"*

Eishoxa laughed. *"You were the better dragon, Zeexa. I promise. We can ride now, if you want."* The dragon made a deep sound in the bottom of her throat as Eishoxa climbed up onto her back.

"It's been too long since we've ridden together," she said.

Zeexa growled in agreement. *"But you're back now and now we can ride whenever we want because you're not going anywhere."* Eishoxa's happiness at being back with Zeexa disappeared momentarily when she heard the dragon's words. She'd done what she said she would do, and now she wanted the Indocani to honour their promise and let her go back to Bareth. Rianox had said that time worked differently here: days and weeks here could mean hours back there. She had to find Maya and she had to put things right. She could feel the weight of Rosemarie's coin in her pocket. The coin weighed not only in her pocket but also in her heart.

Zeexa, who hadn't noticed anything wrong, took off into the air, through trees and branches and swift as an arrow into the sky. The dragon was right – she had got a lot faster. They coursed through the air, the wind whistling in Eishoxa's ears, the icy air making her eyes stream. However thrilling her rides with Rush on the rivers, Eishoxa felt a unique rush of adrenaline whenever she rode a dragon.

Zeexa spun around and shot up into the sky, towards the sun. Eishoxa imagined seeing them from below, streaking across the blue sky like a comet. Suddenly the dragon nosed up and then, in one smooth motion, turned around to dive headfirst back towards the ground. Eishoxa was screaming, gripping Zeexa with all her might. Zeexa leveled off and went forward again even faster, her wings beating strongly. Eishoxa felt electrified. The dragon paused in mid-air for a moment, and Eishoxa adjusted her position to balance better. *"Will you go to war with the rest?"* Zeexa asked.

The question was so unexpected that Eishoxa couldn't think for a moment. She looked down towards the ground. From here, she could see a world that had never known a life with water: the grass was burnt and brown, the Tree's green leaves wilted and pale. This was not the land Eishoxa wanted to fight for. It was ironic that she wasn't allowed to go to the land she did want to fight for, while the land she cared nothing for was the one she was meant to defend to the death.

"I don't know. Maya's alive, Zeexa. I have to find her, learn what happened to her. If the Guardian is wrong and Maya's dead, then it's my fault. If she's

not wrong and Maya's alive, then I owe it to her to go and find her. We were more than just friends, Zeexa. We relied on each other. We were like soul mates."

"But what if you die in the process?" The dragon's tone was non-accusing but she sounded tired and maybe a little exasperated. "When we were travelling to the Peacemakers, you said that you didn't pick fights. That it wasn't your fault. But what if, by leaving, you make the war last longer so that even more of us die? We need you just as much as your unfortunate friend. And there are more of us. What would you do then?" Eishoxa had no answer to Zeexa's question. Zeexa sighed in her mind. "Do you really hate it here so much?"

"No!" Eishoxa protested. "No, but I cannot abandon those who've given me no reason to abandon them. And she is in more danger than you. Please don't try to convince me, Zeexa. I've made up my mind." The dragon gave a sad little whine. "If you say so," she said.

When she opened her eyes, she was back on top of the mountain.

"Nezrax," she shouted. "Why am I here?"

"Because you want to be," came the mocking voice from all around her. Eishoxa pushed her hair out of her eyes and looked around. Nezrax slowly materialised in front of her, spinning around in the air.

"You see? I knew you would come back," she smiled triumphantly. "It's easy to tell when someone will."

"What do you mean by that?" Eishoxa snapped, shaking her hair out of her face again.

Nezrax tutted. "They haven't told you yet?"

"Who hasn't told me what?" Eishoxa asked, curious despite herself. Nezrax sighed in seeming sympathy, shaking her head. "Well, let's just say that the people you're with are not what they seem. Ember – what is he up to these days?"

Eishoxa stiffened as she caught on to what Nezrax was saying. "He went away, but he didn't tell me where. Why? Where has he gone?"

Nezrax laughed. "You see? The man who says he loves you so much won't even tell you where he's going. Does that seem fair?"

Eishoxa could think of nothing to say and turned her head away. Nezrax's smile slipped off her face and was replaced by a sinister look. She flew around so that she could look into Eishoxa's eyes.

"Fire, water, earth," she whispered. "All these under your spell – but look! You cannot control everything. And you want to, don't you?" Eishoxa felt tentacles of consciousness twisting into her mind, taking hold of her thoughts gently but ominously. She shook her head. "You have nothing that I want!"

Nezrax smiled knowingly. "Really? I have the Pentelement. Look around you. Wouldn't you want to control the air, the rock? Everyone desires power, and you're lying if you deny it. Good or bad, it's natural to want it."

"Get away from me," Eishoxa said very clearly. "Get away and stay away." A crow, cawing loudly, landed on Nezrax's shoulder. "The more power you could have, the more you want it. And you could have a lot of power, Eishoxa."

"Go away," Eishoxa said, feeling a raging pressure build in her head.

Nezrax continued. *"Haven't you always wondered what it would be like? To have the power to move mountains, to dry up seas, to do anything you wanted?"*

"Go away," she repeated more loudly, trying to block out the voice and wake herself up. Nezrax continued, in a strange chanting tone. *"Wouldn't you want the power to go back to Bareth? To go back home?"*

"Go away!" Eishoxa screamed with a violent gesture. There was a loud cracking and rumbling, and the ground gaped beneath her feet. An avalanche of black granite began spilling down the mountains towards them. Nezrax simply flicked her hand and the rocks dissipated into thin air. She smiled at Eishoxa, a proud smile, a satisfied smile. Then she spun in the air and disappeared in a cloud of black feathers, with a final shriek from the monstrous bird.

CHAPTER 5

Eishoxa gasped and sat up. Her blanket was twisted around her, as though she'd been thrashing about in her sleep. She was drenched in cold sweat and covered in goose bumps. She closed her eyes for a moment and saw Nezrax again, had a sense of being in a black pit that wanted to suck her in, never to escape. Throwing her blanket off, she went to her mirror. She looked as she had always done, except for her eyes. They had a wild, haunted look, like a trapped animal desperate to get away. How had she done that? She stared at her hands, willing them to provide an answer. Nothing. The rock had crumbled like sand. She had done that. She could control four elements now. Did that mean that she was becoming like an Empty? Part of the Pentelement? Did that mean that she was becoming like Nezrax? She couldn't drive Rush's words out of her head. They had been haunting her more and more recently. Madness followed those who controlled more than one element. Eishoxa went outside. The cool air relieved her clammy skin. She walked to the edge of her branch and looked down. It hadn't always been this big, the Tree. She knew there had been a time when it was a sapling, a mere shoot, until the Indocani had come and decided to make it their home. She wondered whether they'd grown the forest as well, before the dragons burnt it down. The sky was clear, as it always was here, but it looked different from how she remembered it. Maybe it was because of her time with the Ewdicani: she'd got used to the majestic, noble night there, and the night here couldn't begin to compete. She remembered how, in Bareth, night and day were equally beautiful. But in a desert, night was always beautiful. It brought a coolness not possible during the day. She took another step towards the edge of the branch and looked down, leaning out over the side.

"Bad dreams?" Rianox asked, coming forward out of the shadows. He smiled at her.

Eishoxa sighed. "Yes."

"I couldn't sleep either."

"So you decided to just come and see if I couldn't either?" Eishoxa asked teasingly.

"I was right, wasn't I?" They stood side by side for a minute before Rianox spoke again.

"I know you know, Eishoxa. I knew from the minute you returned."

She turned to look at him, surprised. "Know what?"

"How I got this scar," he said softly.

Eishoxa froze. "Oh that," she murmured. "Yes … I know."

There was a silence again, a silence that anticipated tension but could find none.

"I was a monster," Eishoxa realised.

"No," Rianox contradicted immediately. She turned to look at him. "How can you say that? I almost killed you."

"But you didn't. And it was no fault of yours anyway. Everyone hated me. You were no different, but you decided to show your feelings, that was all. You were loyal to your people but you were Indocani through

251

and through, and their thoughts were your thoughts. You saw me as a threat and you acted like that because that was who you were."

"How did you know I knew?"

"I have my connections," Rianox replied, shifting a bit on the branch. Something clicked in Eishoxa's head. "The Guardian?" she asked.

"She's known as that, but her name was Flame. She changed it to Morika, which means Child of the Forest. She spoke to you when you fell into the river."

Eishoxa thought back. "So hers was the voice I couldn't distinguish. Was she the girl carrying you?" Rianox gave a tiny nod. Eishoxa took a little sharp breath. "Then the Guardian is … your sister?" Eishoxa asked. A long silence followed. Then Rianox took a deep breath and said, "Yes, she's my sister. But very few people here remember that, or are even old enough to know."

"Why did she stay in the forest and you come back?"

"She never thought she belonged here. When we went to the Forest of No Flame, she kept telling me that we should be happy to be there, that we could thrive there. That we didn't need the Indocani. But I always knew where I belonged, and it was right here."

"So you left and she stayed." He nodded heavily. "Yes, I left. But she stayed. She renounced all claims on fire and took both water and earth to grow and nurture the Forest."

"I thought she was the Forest. That's what she called herself." Rianox put his head to one side, considering what she'd said. "Yes, she is the Forest in some ways. At least, it belongs to her, and the Dwellers consider her their saviour. But she was born Indocani, and she has removed a part of herself that she should never have done."

"She seems happy," Eishoxa protested quietly.

Rianox shrugged. "We no longer speak face to face so I can't contradict you. But to get rid of something like that hurts you, for your whole life. You know, it's said that the Forest of No Flame is considered sadder than the Sorrowful Mountains themselves. That's because it thrives on something that should never have happened."

Eishoxa felt very strange standing there. He was reminiscing about the past, and she was a part of it, but she had no idea what he was talking about. She smiled tightly and said quietly, "I've seen the Sorrowful Mountains in a dream."

Rianox looked up sharply. "When?"

"Twice," Eishoxa admitted. "Once in the Forest of No Flame, and the other in my dream just before I woke up this morning."

"Did you see Nezrax?"

"Yes. She's trying to convince me to join her," she said softly. She didn't know why she was telling Rianox, but she had to tell someone.

"And what did you say?" Rianox asked gently.

"I told her I wouldn't, but she didn't give up." Eishoxa looked up desperately, all her previous fears flooding back. "She told me I could have power over all the elements, and then I destroyed the rock. She'd made me angry and I just wanted her to leave me be, and I threw out my hands and the rock broke. It shattered, just like that."

Rianox thought in silence.

Eishoxa spoke again. "What if she has given me power over rock? What if I'm becoming like her?"

"No, Eishoxa, you're nothing like her, no matter what you did. She is evil. That's what her essence is. That's what she's there to be – to be the contradiction of everything that's good, so that people can see and distinguish one from the other. It's natural that she wants you on her side – everyone wants you on their side."

"But ..." Eishoxa trailed off. There was nothing to say.

"Listen, Eishoxa. Fiera and Nezrax both have the power to meddle with people's perceptions and their minds. Fiera rarely uses it, but for Nezrax it's one of her greatest weapons. After all, if you created a picture of something in someone's mind and they can't understand it or explain where it came from, they think it's the truth. The twisted truth is even more dangerous than an outright lie, Eishoxa. You don't know that you shattered the rock – she might just have put that idea in your head. It's not your fault. All you have to remember is that she is evil and you've won half the battle. One of her greatest powers is changing people's minds – but if you have control over yours, then she's at a disadvantage and she can't hurt you."

Eishoxa gave him a small smile and nodded.

"Just remember that," he repeated. "Be brave, Eishoxa. Just be brave." Eishoxa put her arms around him and he paused for only a fraction of a second before returning the hug. As they broke apart he added, "For the worst fight is still to come."

"You shouldn't talk to him, you know," Fiera said, looking bored. Eishoxa had opened her eyes to find herself in the fiery palace. Fiera was wearing a magnificent robe of red and yellow that complimented her dark brown skin. She had abandoned her sword and bow and instead, strapped around her waist, carried a small knife in a bejewelled sheath.

"Why do you keep entering my dreams?" Eishoxa enquired.

"Why do you keep returning to my palace? I don't want you here, you know. It's not part of my leisure time to converse with a silly little girl like you."

"Your daughter," Eishoxa reminded her hotly. "If you think I'm silly, then you have only yourself to blame."

"Spoken like a true Indocani. Taking no blame for what you do. I said, you shouldn't talk to him."

"Why not?" Eishoxa asked.

"He's a half-breed. He has divided loyalties."

"Don't call him that," she snapped. "I'm a half-breed too, if you're looking at it that way."

"You are not!" Fiera denied. Then she made a small sound – pfft – and flicked her had dismissively. "You're too troublesome to argue with."

"You mean I'm not worth the effort," Eishoxa said.

Fiera looked hard at her. "Yes, I suppose that too."

"Where is Ember?" Eishoxa asked.

"I wouldn't know."

"Rianox said—"

"The half-breed," Fiera muttered.

"Rianox," repeated Eishoxa angrily. "He said that you could see the whole country. Can you tell me where he is?"

Fiera turned away. "I cannot see him. He is outside my realm."

"What does that mean?" Eishoxa asked urgently.

"You don't trust Vera." Fiera remarked, avoiding her question.

"If someone doesn't trust me," Eishoxa retorted, "then I make a point of not trusting them. Vera keeps things back from me, which means she has something to hide."

"Something to hide," Fiera mused. "Is that what you think? Interesting."

"Why did you choose her as leader?" Eishoxa asked curiously. "What was so special about her?"

"She was strong and clever. She was an excellent warrior and her mind was absolutely brilliant. As keen and sharp as an eagle's claw. I looked into her mind and I could see her loyalty, her loyalty to me, to her people."

"She isn't like that now," Eishoxa said quietly.

"Everyone starts life with good qualities," Fiera reflected.

"And then what happens?" Eishoxa asked.

"They choose whether or not they want to keep them."

CHAPTER 6

EMBER PUT HIS HAND on Ferac's neck to soothe him. The great black dragon was frightened of the Black Forest around them and the portal to the other world that he could sense in front of them.

"One last step, Ferac," Ember urged gently. Ferac looked back at him resentfully. *"Can we not rest? You've been driving me for five days and we haven't stopped once."* Ember sighed. It was true. Ferac didn't have endless reserves of energy. And neither did he. He would need determination and strength once they reached the other side of the portal, and it simply wasn't possible if both of them were exhausted. *"All right,"* he agreed, sliding from Ferac's back onto the ground. *"For a little while."* The dragon slumped to the ground and Ember laid his hand on Ferac's head. *"You did well,"* Ember praised him. *"I forget that we aren't as young as we once were."* The dragon grumbled, his eyes half-closed. *"I can go as far, but maybe not as fast. And besides, once upon a time, I had Fiera to race against, as you had Eishoxa. I could never let that dragon win."* Ember smiled fondly at the memories. *"I seem to remember you lost on several occasions."*

Ferac sniffed. *"Because I let her."* Ember laughed and leant back against Ferac's warm flank. He looked around. "This is where I brought Eishoxa from Bareth. I was so sure that the portal would make her into an Indocani her, that she'd remember everything once we were here. But when we arrived and the only thing in her head was Bareth, I was at such a loss. I didn't know what to do." The dragon gave a low growl and lifted his head to look around. Ember was lost to the world at this moment, wallowing in his own despairing thoughts.

"I don't want to do it, Ferac," he whispered. He could hear the fear in his voice. He was disgusted with himself, but carried on. *"I'm going to lose her again. I can see it. I know it. And I don't want to."*

"We have no choice. We swore fealty to Vera, promised to obey all her commands. We can't pick and choose now. And anyway," Ferac concluded, *"we'll never be good. It's too late to redeem ourselves."*

"We used to be the favoured ones," Ember recalled. *"Everyone was jealous of us. We commanded awe wherever we went. And now I'm lucky if she looks at me."* Ember was pulled out of his dreaming by the sound of beating wings. He nudged Ferac and stood up, preparing to meet whatever came at him. Then he heard his name.

"Lord Ember! Lord Ember, where are you?"

"Here!" Ember shouted. "Who are you? What do you want?" He sheathed his sword as an Indocani came into view, leading a dragon that looked as tired as Ferac. They were both young and, by the looks of them, must have flown as if an army of Empty were breathing down their necks.

"Vera sent me with news," the Indocani panted quietly. His dragon had collapsed gratefully on the ground and closed its eyes. Ember took the proffered letter. What would Vera want to tell him? To return home? That she had another plan? Had something happened to Eishoxa? With all eyes upon him he tore open the letter. It was only a few lines, written in Vera's bold strong hand – very much like Eishoxa's used to be, he reflected. Focusing on the characters and forcing Eishoxa out of his mind he read:

We are in luck. She has been visited by Nezrax in her dreams multiple times. You were right. Your spy proved most useful. Return immediately, after your task is complete. We have more work to do. Vera.

"I've betrayed her," Ember whispered to himself, crumpling the letter. Ferac was looking at him questioningly. "*Time to go,*" Ember told Ferac as he mounted him. He turned back to the Indocani. "Well done," he said. "You did well. Rest here for a while, make a fire to keep yourself warm, and then get back to the Tree as soon as you can. Tell Vera that I shall be with her as soon as I can." His eyes scanned the boy. He was unarmed. "And next time, bring a weapon," he remarked. "The Black Forest can be a dangerous place." He tossed the boy a knife from his belt. Then he wheeled Ferac around to face the portal. To everyone's eyes it looked like part of the forest, a little more densely grown perhaps, nothing exceptional. But Ember knew otherwise. Closing his eyes, he murmured something under his breath, so quietly that even his dragon couldn't hear. When he opened them he saw the telltale shimmering to show him where the portal was.

"*Fly where I guide you,*" he told Ferac. "*And don't be afraid. Nothing is going to happen.*" He urged Ferac forward, guiding the dragon straight through the portal. They felt a tugging sensation, and then saw ahead, instead of trees, a castle built on a hill, at whose foot a sluggish river flowed.

Eishoxa resumed her lessons with Rianox while they waited for Ember to return. She usually didn't want to study, so the two of them just talked. Rianox was clever and funny and, even more than Rush, he had the energy that Eishoxa loved about the Indocani. Nevertheless, whenever Rianox made Eishoxa laugh or smile, she felt a sting of guilt as she remembered Rush. She'd told him that she would never forget him and she meant it, yet whenever she was with Rianox, Rush left her mind. Eishoxa saw very little of Vera because the latter was so caught up in preparing for battle. Ever since Eishoxa had returned from Dulcacohefen, the Tree had been all astir. Everyone knew now that war was inevitable. Ewdicani ambassadors travelled to the Tree more and more often, although Eishoxa never got to speak to them: the moment they arrived, they were whisked away by Vera and her Council. The Tree itself had been fortified and branches that got in the way had been cut off and burnt. Eishoxa thought it made the place look very bare and ugly. She saw more Indocani than ever, practicing sword fighting, shooting at trees in the forest, and taking their dragons out for regular flights. Rianox had taken Eishoxa deep down under ground, far beneath the Great Hall, to the magnificent armoury and forges. She'd not seen them before leaving for Dulcacohefen, so it was with great excitement that she learnt she was finally going to visit them. She'd found it odd that she'd seen so few weapons and signs of fortification in the Tree; after all, this was a warrior nation. But underneath the ground was where the Indocani took the most pride, just like the Ewdicani with their library. It was here that they all went, night and day, so that usually the Tree seemed almost deserted. It was as big as the Great Hall but lined with stone, and in front of the walls were racks for newly made weapons. Dotted around the hall were forges where Indocani struck huge hunks of metal into shape. After her return the Indocani had flocked there, making swords and shields, bows and arrows, with great love and care. Eishoxa had never seen such exquisite workmanship.

"It is what we live for," Rianox had reminded her. An Indocani ran past, carrying an armful of blunt swords. As he passed them he bowed quickly to Eishoxa. "Princess Eishoxa," he said before hurrying about his work.

"Your return has made it clear that war is coming. The Empty have spies everywhere. They will know of our movements as we know of theirs. That is to say, they'll know that we've made an alliance. I'm surprised that they haven't made another move yet, that they haven't yet tried to attack the Tree."

"Yes, but they have sent their Goddess to try to convince me to join them," Eishoxa pointed out, and Rianox nodded thoughtfully.

"True, true. But I'd expected something more." They left the armoury together and walked back up through the tunnels to the Great Hall. Then Rianox took Eishoxa along another passage and towards an old-looking door.

"This is our library. You may be surprised to learn that I spend the majority of my time here, trying to salvage what I can."

Eishoxa smiled. "I'm not surprised." Rianox pushed open the door and they were met with the reek of neglect. "Unfortunately, our race puts little time aside for learning things," Rianox reflected. The library was illuminated by many candles hovering in the air. The room was circular and they stood on one edge, facing a narrow pathway that curved out of sight in a spiral fashion. The shelves nearest to them were quite short and Eishoxa could see over the tops of them. Closer to the centre of the room, the shelves rose in height, almost touching the ceiling. As they walked through the room, the smell of rotting parchment and dust became ever more noticeable.

"Vera doesn't care for them at all," Rianox said as he led her to the centre of the room, where the shelves were tall enough to touch the ceiling.

Eishoxa shrugged. "You can't expect her to, though, can you?"

"I suppose not," Rianox said. "But then again, I *would* expect her to. We're not meant to be imbeciles, you know."

Eishoxa turned and ran her fingers over the spines of the books and the ends of the scrolls packed into the shelves. "What's this?" she continued, holding up the book.

He took it and thumbed through it. "A book of spells. Speaking of which, how is your magic coming along?" He turned another page over, paused slightly, then snapped the book shut.

"Very well," Eishoxa replied. "Fire is my strongest, followed by earth. With water, I still have difficulty."

"Well, that's understandable here," Rianox replied, rearranging some of the books on the shelves. "Ideally, you would have an Ewdicani teacher to show you how to master that, but in the circumstances that's not possible.

"I wish it were," Eishoxa said quietly. Rianox tucked a few books under his arm and started walking towards the entrance. As he did, one of the books in his arms shifted and a piece of very old paper fell out of it. It fell open as it landed. Eishoxa picked it up.

"What is this?" Rianox saw what she was holding and took it from her, almost warily. "It's a spell," he said.

Eishoxa looked back down at the paper. "Yes, but what does it do?" Rianox put his head on one side and looked down at the paper.

"Well, it causes the destruction of a pair of countries. From one country, all the water is taken and the other is flooded with it. It used to be quite a common way to flush out enemies."

"That's barbaric," Eishoxa said.

"I agree," said Rianox. "But it used to be quite effective."

Eishoxa saw that his thumb was covering something that looked familiar. "What's that?" she asked, pointing.

"A map," Rianox said, without elaboration. He tucked the paper back under his arm.

"A map of what? I thought it looked familiar," Eishoxa persisted, taking his arm as they walked out.

He looked down at her. "Never you mind."

Eishoxa was left to her own devices again as Rianox was called by Vera and Amber was nowhere to be found. But as soon as she sat down in her room, she had a sudden urge to go back to the Great Hall and to the tunnel where she'd seen her life carved out. She left her room and, as she jumped from bough to bough, felt quite apprehensive. The tunnel showed the truth of a person's life, the good and the bad, and sometimes it wasn't at all pleasant. When she got to the Great Hall, she walked beside the wall, brushing her fingers over the roots. When she got to the entrance of the tunnel, she placed her whole hand on the wall and it retracted into itself, revealing the stone passage, dimly lit with flaming torches. Eishoxa entered and took one of the torches from its bracket. Touching her hand to the stone, she raised the torch to see the carvings appear. There she was – in the time she'd been here before. She walked back towards the door, looking at the past she couldn't remember.

Eishoxa found herself as a young child with Amber and Ember. Again she placed her hand on the wall and the carvings started to move, just as they had the last time. The three of them were running through the woods … discovering the dragons' pit … sparring with branches in the forest. Then the others disappeared; that must have been when she was told that she was different, special. That she had to train separately from her friends. That their path couldn't be her path. A seriousness hung over Eishoxa now as, walking down the tunnel, she watched herself grow by leaps and bounds. And then Ember re-entered the carvings. Eishoxa traced them with her finger. Just as it showed the bad, it showed the good as well. They were out on their dragons together, Fiera and Ferac – one golden, one black, although the carvings didn't show that. They were sparring in the woods, but with swords this time. They were leading an army into battle, side by side.

Eishoxa walked on and on, reaching the event she was dreading: the moment when she attacked Rianox, giving him the scar. When she reached the point before she went to Bareth, there was a stretch of empty wall separating the carved sections. And then came Bareth. That beautiful, beautiful time. She held the torch closer to the wall to see better. There she was with Maya. There was Rosemarie, growing much faster than she did. Eishoxa watched as Rosemarie got married and left, and saw how, from then on, she matured and grew up, distancing herself from Eishoxa. She continued walking, transfixed by this account of her life depicted on the wall. Suddenly the carvings looked new. She wondered who had created them – or did they simply make themselves, as events occurred? Here, she was being taken out of Bareth. She saw that Ember now looked very different from before. What had happened in his life during the years she was in Bareth? Had he missed her all that time? Time moved much more quickly here.

Then she was at Dulcacohefen. Eishoxa watched as the scenes brightened up again, were happy again. A certain quality of light seemed to shine out from the stone itself now. The only other time she'd seen herself like that was before, with Ember. But whereas her image had previously had a harsh glare, here she glowed with a soft golden hue.

Eishoxa walked further down but then the carvings stopped. They took her to present day but not into the future. Eishoxa looked back the way she had come. She'd had a long life and it was all recorded here, deep underground. This tunnel told her life, it was true, but without reasons or explanations. And that was sometimes the hardest thing: not to understand why things happened, not to be given a reason. One just saw them, relived the mistakes, but had to work out the reasons oneself. She returned the way she had come, replacing the torch in the bracket and leaving the tunnel. But she didn't walk away. Instead, she watched as the door closed in on itself and became part of the wall again. Perhaps one day she would understand why she had done those things, would remember what she'd been thinking when she'd done those things ... when she'd thought that attacking a helpless person, simply because he was different, was right. Eishoxa walked away slowly, wondering whether the right thing to do was ever simple for anyone to know.

CHAPTER 7

Eishoxa was sitting with Zeexa in the forest. They'd walked away from the dragons' pit together because Zeexa wanted to have a proper conversation with her. Now Zeexa was crouched comfortably on the ground and Eishoxa was sitting on a pile of dry leaves, leaning next to her and shooting little sparks out of her finger tips.

"*It's great that you can do that now,*" Zeexa said, moving her head forward slightly. Eishoxa rested her hand on Zeexa's head. She'd been debating with herself whether to tell Zeexa about Nezrax. But dragons had proved to be wiser than Eishoxa had thought, so she decided to risk it.

"*I saw Nezrax, Zeexa.*"

The dragon hissed. "*Dragon murderer! That woman has the blood of thousands of dragons and Warriors on her hands. Where did you see her?*"

"*She came to me in a dream. She claimed that I took myself there, but I don't think I did. If I did, I have no idea how I did it.*"

"*Where did she take you?*" Zeexa demanded.

"*The Sorrowful Mountains.*"

"*And what did she say?*"

"*She was offering me a place with her ... she was asking me to join her.*" Eishoxa ignored Zeexa's menacing growl. "*I didn't accept, but she said that I could have power over all the elements. I could join the Pentelement.*"

The dragon shuddered beside her. "*To leave fire? To replace it with water and earth and rock and air? She's a monster. Don't listen, Eishoxa. Block her out.*"

Eishoxa was shaking her head. "*You don't understand, Zeexa. I got angry with her and wanted her away – and that's all I thought – and I caused an avalanche! All the rock crumbled around me, just like that! I just wanted Nezrax gone and I destroyed a mountain.*"

"*She can invade your dreams, Eishoxa,*" soothed the dragon. "*She can make you see things that aren't there.*"

"*I know she can do that,*" Eishoxa said. "*But it looked real. It felt real. What if it was? What if I have that power? What if she has already given it to me?*" The dragon had pressed her warm snout against Eishoxa's hand. Eishoxa looked down and the dragon was blinking huge eyes up at her. "*Eishoxa, dragons can read people's hearts. They can read their intentions. You are not a bad person. Bad things have happened to you, and they are happening and will continue to happen until the day you die. For you more than anyone else. But you know you've done wrong, and that will work in your favour. Those you surround yourself with have done wrong and are doing wrong, but they can't see it and so they're doomed to repeat it. But you are not bad. I can read your heart and it is good. Confused, but good.*"

"*Why confused?*"

"*It just seems confused. As though you can't make up your mind,*" said the dragon perceptively.

"I can't," whispered Eishoxa out loud.

"*And there's someone who won't leave your mind,*" Zeexa said suddenly, narrowing her eyes in concentration.

Eishoxa was surprised. *"Who?"*

"They are pressing down upon you." Zeexa concentrated again, shutting her eyes. *"They are holding you back and trying to bring you forward, all at the same time."*

"Rush?" Eishoxa asked.

Zeexa opened one eye but then shut it again and shook her head. *"No, someone far more powerful."*

"More powerful? In my mind?"

Zeexa nodded, then opened both eyes. *"That is all I can see."* Eishoxa frowned and picked at the ground. Then the dragon surprised her by speaking again. *"Be careful who you give your heart to, Eishoxa. No matter what they say, there are few in this world who are what they seem."*

When Eishoxa returned from the Dragon Forest, she learnt from a passing Indocani that Amber had been looking for her.

"Do you know where she went?"

"She is waiting for you in your room, Princess Eishoxa."

"Thank you," she said, and bowed to him. She swung herself up through the branches and went to her room. Amber was indeed there, as was Rianox. They were speaking in worried tones to each other but stopped as Eishoxa opened the door. As she entered, Amber rose to her feet.

"Eishoxa," Amber said. Her voice was rather forced and breathless.

"What's happening? What are you two doing here?" Eishoxa asked, straightening her bow where it rested against the wall. Amber glanced at Rianox, and the two of them seemed to be communicating with their eyes. Finally, Amber cried, "I don't care, Rianox. I'm going to tell her."

"Tell me what?" Eishoxa asked.

Amber hesitated, a look of fear on her face. She walked forward and took Eishoxa's hands. "Eishoxa ..." she began. Rianox was looking at her intently, willing her to continue or to stop, but saying nothing himself. "Eishoxa," she repeated. "We've always been good friends. This time, we haven't spent much time together, but believe me when I say we were great friends and I hope one day that you remember how much."

Eishoxa smiled. "I know that we were. I saw that in the memories I was shown. Is that all you wanted to tell me?"

Amber shook her head. "Not quite."

Rianox stood up and interrupted. "Amber, that's quite enough. There's no need for any more." He put his hands on Amber's shoulders but she shrugged him off.

"I'm going to tell her," she snapped. She turned back to Eishoxa. "But however much we are friends, it's the law to honour and obey our leader before anyone else in our race. And for us, that's Vera, not you."

Eishoxa replied. "I know, don't worry. I know what it's like to have divided loyalties."

"But you must worry!" cried Amber. "You don't know what is going on!"

"Why? What's happened?" Eishoxa asked.

Rianox jumped between them. "Amber, that's enough."

"No – tell me!" Eishoxa demanded.

Rianox pushed her aside. "No. It's not for you to know."

"Does everyone get treated like that here?" Eishoxa enquired. "Rianox, if it's about me, then it's my right to know."

"No!" Rianox rounded on her. His face looked fierce, and she took a step back. "Vera has forbidden us to tell and so we cannot tell."

"Vera has always struck me as a liar," Eishoxa retorted, folding her arms.

"We must follow our leader," Rianox insisted. "She's the one who guides us. She speaks with Fiera."

"And? Amber stepped forward again and pushed Rianox to one side. "Rianox, that's enough from you as well!" she snapped. "Eishoxa, I am bound by loyalty to my leader, but I have loyalty to you as well, which Rianox seems to have forgotten!" Rianox grabbed her arm and said something so fast in Düerasgörn that Eishoxa couldn't catch the words. Amber stood very still but then shook her head and turned back to Eishoxa. "You must go to Vera's rooms, Eishoxa. You must speak with her there." Rianox let go of Amber's arm and looked at Eishoxa so seriously that Eishoxa took a step back. "Why? Is something wrong?"

Amber hung her head. "Go, Eishoxa, and … I'm sorry."

When Eishoxa left, Amber rounded on Rianox. "What were you playing at? Why didn't you let me tell her?"

Rianox shoved her away from him. "My loyalty lies with my people. And my people have a law. And the law is that we obey Vera. And Vera said that we mustn't tell her. What do you think is going to happen to us now? No, Amber, in fact what is going to happen to me? Not you. You have the security of not being a half-breed. And now I'll be a disloyal half-breed. I'll be sent away again!"

Amber shook her head. "That's ridiculous. We have loyalty to Eishoxa too. She's the daughter of our Goddess. In my opinion, we owe more loyalty to her than we do to Vera. More to the point, we're her friends. We are," she insisted as Rianox snorted with derision. "We are. And you know there's something wrong with how Ember's been acting. And I know that one of your guesses is the same as mine. We know where Ember has gone. And if Eishoxa finds out we knew and that we didn't tell her, she won't forgive us, and I couldn't live with that. Enemies lie to each other, and I refuse to be her enemy."

"Vera knows what she's doing. We have to believe it's for the good of the people."

"The good of the people?" Amber laughed incredulously. "You can't be serious. This is for the good of Vera and Ember."

"Eishoxa approved of Vera's election as leader," Rianox began. "Furthermore," he continued as Amber opened her mouth, "Eishoxa agreed that there wasn't anyone better. Therefore, Eishoxa pledged her own loyalty. And even if she doesn't remember it, we stand by a law." He took a deep breath as though steadying himself. "And that law is what keeps us alive."

"You and your laws," Amber said, giving him a push. "What about decency? And friendship? What have your precious laws got to say about that?" Rianox looked down at her, glowering. Then he said very quietly, as though forcing himself to say each word, "Eishoxa is a strong, proud and noble warrior. But she drove me away, with no fault on my part. She gave me this scar, and as I bear scars from her, she too will bear scars. The scars from what she has done. Scars from the consequences of her actions."

Amber took a step back. "Rianox, you can't be serious. She's changed. You know that more than anyone."

"She hasn't changed enough," Rianox said firmly.

"But you love her. You told me that you did," Amber entreated quietly, unable to believe that Rianox was saying these malicious words.

Rianox stiffened. "Obviously not enough, Amber." Then he turned and walked out the door.

Eishoxa knocked on Vera's door and entered.

"Vera?" she called, closing the door behind her. For the first time she could remember, the room was empty. Vera was not seated behind her table as she usually was; instead there was simply a pile of papers on the table, along with a strange object. Eishoxa, despite herself, walked to the table and looked down at the object. It was a small almond-shaped vessel, made of glass and filled with a clear liquid. Eishoxa touched the liquid very briefly. It was water; she could feel its bizarre coolness, even though it no longer affected her. But what was Vera doing with something like this? Water – in the heart of the Tree, in the heart of Sicharenhafan. Eishoxa picked it up carefully; the bottom of it was icy cold. Vera wouldn't even be able to touch this thing, let alone use it. As she set it down again, a little water splashed onto one of the papers on the table. Eishoxa hurried to the other side and, as she mopped at it with her sleeve, she caught sight of her name. She picked up the piece of paper. It was all in Düerasgörn, which she could read quite well now. However, this writing was so hastily scrawled that much of it was illegible. Random words jumped out at her, but she could make no sense of them. *Destruction … traitors … Ewdicani … Eishoxa.* She held the paper closer and tried to distinguish more. Her name was written there: Eishoxa. As clear as day. Eishoxa … She traced her finger over the letter. *Eishoxa has taken charge … The place has been destroyed.* And then, underneath, the single word *Dulcacohefen.* A terrible shock hit her as she remembered what Rush had said: *"I lost them in an unprovoked ambush to one whom I started to hate with all my strength."* Had she led that ambush? Had that been her doing? She was scrabbling frantically through the papers when the door opened with a bang and Vera entered. Eishoxa stuffed the papers into her pocket and spun around, hiding her action behind the table that stood between them. Vera looked shocked but not angry. Her eyes fell on the papers, but she made no move. "Eishoxa? What on earth are you doing here?"

"I must go back to Bareth. I must return. Now," Eishoxa stuttered.

Vera nodded. "I'm afraid I have something to tell you, Eishoxa. It's about Bareth. Rianox told me that he sent you here. Although you're not allowed in my rooms when I'm not here, in the circumstances I will overlook it." She smiled sweetly, a smile as fake as the honeyed sympathy on her face.

"What is it? What's happened to Bareth?"

"I think I can only show you," said Vera regretfully, shaking her head. Eishoxa suppressed a shudder as she felt a chill slither down her back. Vera walked around behind her table and past Eishoxa to stand in front of the water-filled vessel. She held her hand over it, almost touching the surface of the water. As she took her hand away, a picture formed in the liquid. Vera pushed the vessel towards her. Eishoxa looked down at the image and saw Bareth Castle atop its hill. Behind it, the sky looked dark and bruised, and smoke filled the air. The castle started to shake violently and there was a loud rumbling. Then the image zoomed out to show the whole hill and the villages that surrounded it, all shaking and rumbling. Fire was raging through the houses, and the turrets of the castle were tumbling. She could hear the faint sounds of people screaming and then the castle fell. Eishoxa stepped back in horror. Vera was looking at her in concern. "I'm afraid that many fires and earthquakes struck the castle while you were in Dulcacohefen. This was the last of them and, as you see, it caused the castle to fall." Eishoxa was shaking her head. "No, the castle isn't like that. It was built to withstand earthquakes. We had them when I was there … It's strong and the fires couldn't have burnt it down." She was stammering, groping for words. Her brain hadn't caught up with what she'd seen. She couldn't understand; she refused to understand. She stumbled backwards and the glass vessel fell from her hand, splashing a drop of water on her hand. Vera lunged forward to catch it but it shattered on the floor. The drop of water on Eishoxa's hand quivered. The pieces of broken glass came together perfectly again, and the drop of water on her hand rose to join the rest of the water that had reappeared in the little vessel. Eishoxa picked it up again and looked into it.   Vera was frozen, unable to decide whether or not to take it from her. Another image was forming in the water, but this time it was distorted. This time Bareth Castle appeared slightly further away, and in the distance was someone riding a dragon. As Eishoxa watched, the figure soared towards the castle, sending bolts of fire at it. As they hit, the castle shook and trembled. The figure then flew over the village and the dragon opened its fiery mouth to torch the ground. Eishoxa could hear the screaming clearly now. She looked again for the dragon and its rider but couldn't see them. Suddenly they appeared again. Eishoxa could no longer deny what her mind had been telling her. She had recognised that rider on the dragon. It was Ember.

As if the water had conjured him, Ember walked through the door. He stopped short at the sight of Eishoxa standing there, tears in her eyes, the glass vessel clutched in her hand.

"You were at Bareth?" Eishoxa asked hesitantly. Ember froze as well now, just like Vera. Eishoxa asked again, "Were you at Bareth?" Slowly, Ember shook his head. Eishoxa threw the glass down upon the floor again. It hovered there for a split second before breaking again. Eishoxa could see her heart in the fragments on the floor.

"I saw you," she hissed. "I saw you destroy my city." She could feel Vera's hand on her arm, but all she could see was her castle disintegrating in smoke and dust, all she could hear were the cries of her innocent people burning to death. And Ember's words reverberated through her head again and again: *"Even now, all I want to do is make you happy."*

"It was done for your own good," Vera said gently.

Something snapped inside Eishoxa. She spun around and slapped Vera right across the face, with such strength that her hand stung with the pain. She gave Vera a look of deepest disgust before turning back to Ember. "I trusted you! I thought you trusted me!" She could see him trying to reason with her but his words weren't getting through to her. "Why didn't you tell me? Why did you do it?"

"I thought it would make you stay here!" shouted Ember desperately. Eishoxa, near the door now, backed away from him, and her feet stumbled on the threshold.

"You thought that I could be persuaded to stay in the place where the people who destroyed my city lived?" she asked with an acidic iciness in her voice. "You thought that I would even consider it? How many innocent people have you killed, Ember? They did nothing! They didn't deserve to die like that! Did that even cross your mind?"

"You should care about this place more! This is your home!"

"I care more about Bareth than I could ever care about this place! You know that!" At this, Ember's whole demeanour changed. Vera laid a restraining hand on his shoulder, but he threw it off. "Do you? Do you want to know why that place was so fertile and green? Because it belonged to the Ewdicani. Why did the people of Bareth suffer for a hundred years with droughts and fires? Because you made it so! You destroyed that land to punish the Ewdicani! That land and Cara!"

Eishoxa's ears were ringing. She was walking away from Ember, from the words she had heard, from the words that had struck true in her. Ember's shoulders dropped and he started towards her. "I'm sorry, Eishoxa. I'm sorry." She heard words come from her mouth, cold, hard words in a voice that didn't belong to her. "You are a liar and a murderer! I don't want to ever see you again!"

She ran out of the room, and Ember followed. Leaping into the branches above, she swung her way higher and higher, as though by running she could escape what she'd learnt.

"Eishoxa, wait! Stop!" She ran to the edge of the branch. He'd caught her up easily. "Eishoxa, you must hear me out! You must listen to what I have to say!"

"You want *me* to listen now! Why didn't *you* listen? Listen when I said that I wanted to go home? Listen when Vera said that I could, after doing what you wanted? Listen to when I said that I never wanted to see you again?"

"Eishoxa, please!" The wind was blowing and the branch shook violently. If he came towards her, she thought, she would have nowhere to go but backwards and she would fall, fall from the Tree, down, down, down, until she hit the ground. Her foot slipped fractionally and she tilted, feeling her balance threatened.

"I wasn't the only one!" he shouted, his words desperate and disjointed, as though he was trying to think of what to say, to explain away what he'd done. "Other people were involved with it as well! It wasn't just my fault!"

Eishoxa shook her head. "Lies won't get you out of this one, Ember." She stepped backwards and fell.

"Eishoxa?" came a singsong voice, one that she knew well. "Eishoxa. What do you think now? Does what I said make sense to you now?" The wind skimmed her face as Eishoxa struggled to sit up. She couldn't. She wasn't on the mountain but lying on the ground. Her arms were stretched out on the grass and her legs were bent. Above her she could see the huge boughs of the Tree, shadowing her. Nezrax hovered closely over her. "Am I dead? I wanted to die."

Nezrax threw her head back, laughing. "No, not dead, just unconscious. You fell, remember? You tried to die, but I'm afraid it didn't work."

"Bareth," Eishoxa remembered, looking back up. "Ember destroyed it."

Nezrax said nothing. Eishoxa realised something. "You knew that, didn't you?"

"I told you they were always going to lie to you about something, but you didn't believe me. Ember, the great warrior." She spat on the ground. "Ember, the great liar. Oh, his words are pretty enough, but they lack that rare quality of frankness. Truth."

"Have you come to gloat then?" Eishoxa asked. Her head throbbed painfully and every bone in her body ached. She couldn't sit up because Nezrax was right above her. Nezrax looked surprised. "You think so poorly of me, Eishoxa. You think so poorly of everything I do. But am I really any worse than those you surround yourself with? If you join me, you have nothing left to lose, have you? You must use all your power. If you do not, you are useless to everyone, including yourself."

"You're evil."

"Only to those who think I am. I am powerful. Evil, maybe. Powerful, definitely."

"You don't deny it. You don't deny that you are evil." Nezrax said nothing. "So you are?"

"You can call me what you like, but I didn't destroy a country for no reason," Nezrax said, rising slightly higher. Eishoxa had turned her head onto one side and felt a tear roll down her face. "What more do you want to do to me?"

"Say that you'll join me, Eishoxa, and I'll show you. I'll put a seed of power in you and it will grow and you will know what strength and courage are, beyond that of any Indocani."

Eishoxa said nothing. Nezrax played with a strand of her black hair, wind-

ing it around her finger. "Tell me now: if you say yes, what have you lost?"

"What have I gained though? I am still here, with the Indocani." The word sounded so heavy on her tongue.

Nezrax swooped down towards her. "Maybe here is where you can do the most. Where you can prove to the most people that they have underestimated you. That's what you want to do, isn't it? To prove to Ember that he made a mistake by destroying Bareth ... poor, poor Bareth?" Eishoxa felt herself crying again. Nezrax's words were flowing over her, slimy and false and sickening, but Ember's lies had felt worse.

Nezrax smiled. "So what do you say, Eishoxa? I won't wait forever. Do you accept?"

Eishoxa looked at her, the tears on her face drying. "I accept."

CHAPTER 8

Eishoxa returned to her room, her head bleeding slightly. The smell of smoke from the burning fire pervaded the space. Smoke. Fire. Ember. His lying to her hurt more than anything. She had given him another chance; she had tried to trust him; she had trusted him. And he knew that. Why had he done it? All she could think of was what she'd seen in the tunnel deep underground – what she'd seen of before, when they were friends, when they were more than friends, when they relied on each other. When they almost existed for each other. One question refused to leave her. But why had she destroyed Bareth? She could see in her head the seared land, the farmers hacking at the dry soil, exhausted by their efforts, the misery and starvation that resulted. She could see the village children, bones painfully visible, their little legs stick-thin. She could see the fields that would yield no crops, the plants that would not grow strong and green – these were her fault? That was all because of her? Eishoxa sat heavily the edge of her bed and one of the legs broke with a low, mournful creak. The bed sloped at one corner and she fell to the floor. Looking down at her hand, she tried to imagine being the one to conjure fires and earthquakes, to suck the water out of the land, to destroy an innocent country, an innocent place. Bareth: the name hadn't made sense before, but *bareth* meant *the cursed one*. And she had cursed it.

They were never going to let her go home. It had never been their intention. Another lie. How many could she count? How many people would she look at from now on and never know whether they what they said was true or not? Eishoxa rose to her feet and went to the dresser in a trance. She felt no connection with the person who looked back at her. This skin was the colour of skin from Bareth. These eyes belonged to Bareth. She belonged to Bareth, she was part of Bareth, part of the cursed country. She herself was cursed. She thought about what Nezrax had said, how she had nothing left to lose. And she didn't. She had lost her country and her people and her home. Rush was far away, where he couldn't help her and where he couldn't be hurt. When she cared, she got hurt. And she was tired of being hurt. Remembering the encounter with Vera, she retrieved the papers from her pocket, surprised they'd stayed there. Letting the others fall to the ground, she looked at the one that had her name on it. It was a letter, she realised, written by her to the Indocani.

"*The traitor has got ahead of me again. But it doesn't matter. I'll catch up with him in Rerath.*'"

"Rerath," Eishoxa whispered to herself. The Blessed One. Was that what it had been called before? "*He cannot run forever, and my feet fly much faster than his. He is the one leading ambushes, and I have promised myself that those Indocani who died will be avenged. The Ewdicani have gone too far.*" A black line had been drawn under the last sentence. The letter continued. "*The traitor has hidden himself deep in the Ignorant's land. I cannot get to him through force. He has conjured a great shield around the whole land. But do not worry. I have a plan. By this time tomorrow, the water in that land will have gone and he will be able to hide no longer."* The words were vicious and cruel, written in a strong, arrogant hand. This was her? The young girl she had seen making toys for her friends had become this grotesque thing, relentlessly tracking down a traitor. What had the traitor done? And who was the traitor? Monster they had called her, and monster she was. She collapsed to the ground, her head in her hands. A world built on false hope and lies started to crumble around her. As she lay there despairing, something crept into the ruins of her broken heart, something dark and full of evil intent. It sat there, growing, confident that it would not be turned away.

When Amber saw Eishoxa, she knew immediately what had happened. She'd seen Ember return, and from the despair on his face had known instantly what he'd left in ruins. Amber sat in the shadows of the boughs above Eishoxa's room, watching her friend through the glass. She saw as Eishoxa slowly crumpled to the floor and felt her heart shudder under the weight of forbidden secrets. When Eishoxa emerged, Amber stood up. Eishoxa's eyes were expressionless. Amber approached her.

"I'm sorry," Amber said, knowing that the two words would simply add to the burden her friend carried now.

"Tell me something," Eishoxa replied. "How much did you know, and for how long did you know?" Amber said nothing and Eishoxa slumped to her knees. Amber crouched down beside her immediately, a wave of panic and guilt making her feel ill, and put her hand on Eishoxa's trembling arm. "I wanted to tell you, I swear, only Vera made me vow that I wouldn't." Eishoxa was silent. Her eyes had focused on something behind Amber.

"You knew as well, didn't you?" she asked. Rianox stepped out of the shadows.

"Ziach," he said by way of answer. "That is what the spell is called. Everything is nothing." Eishoxa recoiled from him, a single tear spilling down her cheek. The sight of that hurt Amber as much as if the tear had been her own.

"Why didn't you tell me?" Eishoxa asked them. And then, turning to Rianox, "Why did you hate me so much?"

"I didn't," Rianox said, cutting through Amber's attempt to answer. "I never hated you. I only resented you for having another chance. You had another chance at innocence, although after what you have done, you didn't deserve it. Another chance at redemption, to prove that you have changed. I've been an Outcast once, Eishoxa, for doing nothing! For being born a colour that was out of my control. And for being different I was cast away, into the Forest. And you – who killed so many of the Indocani by leading us into battle after battle, simply because you wanted to, because Fiera had told you that you would never die in war, and because you thought your troops were endless – you were welcomed back with open arms! Vera praised you while she threatened me! You had it all, and you deserved none of it!"

Amber leapt to her feet and pushed Rianox away from Eishoxa. "Rianox, that's enough! Stop it now!"

"Well now, I suppose I have my justice," Rianox shouted at Eishoxa, "now that Bareth has been destroyed and you have no chance of seeing Rush again. I suppose I have it!" He shoved Amber aside and leapt down the tree. Amber watched him go and then turned back to Eishoxa, who was still cowering at the edge of the branch, as if to hide from his words. She'd buried her face in her knees and her shoulders were shaking.

"Can I help you …?" Amber asked, her voice trailing away. Amber dropped beside her. "Eishoxa, I'm sorry. I didn't think he would do it. I didn't think he'd go through with it."

Eishoxa lifted a tear-streaked face to Amber. "Go through with what? Of course you knew! You're all the same!" She slapped Amber's hand away from her and stood. "You lied to me and pretended to be something you weren't. If you ever come near me again, I'll treat you like I promised to treat your brother. I'll kill you!" And she leapt back up into her room.

For the second time that day, Eishoxa entered Vera's room. The leader looked up in surprise as Eishoxa burst in, and then stood. Eishoxa didn't wait for her to speak.

"Take me to Bareth," she demanded. Vera stared at her. "Take me back now."

"There's nothing left for you there," Vera stuttered, looking behind Eishoxa for support. Eishoxa turned and saw Ember sitting there. He'd had his head in his hands but was now looking up. "Everything was destroyed. We made sure of that," he finished for Vera hoarsely.

Eishoxa shook her head. "There's nothing left for me here either. I want to go back."

"You would die," Vera said.

"I don't care – take me back!" Eishoxa shouted. "I have to find Maya, I have to find my family!"

"Your family is here!" Vera insisted.

"You will never be my family," Eishoxa stated flatly. "There are monsters here – monsters, murderers and liars. I don't want to spend a single moment longer here. Take me back!" Vera said nothing, looking towards Ember for support once again. He had risen but he said nothing. Eishoxa stood in the centre of the room, her fists clenched, looking between the two of them.

"Take me back to Bareth," she said again, although uncertainty was clouding her mind. What were they saying, the two of them? What meaning had been exchanged in those looks they gave each other? After another glance at Ember, Vera turned to Eishoxa. "You *cannot* go back. In order to prevent your return ever happening, Ember destroyed the portal."

"What? Destroyed what portal?"

Vera looked to Ember, but again he said nothing. "The portal to get to Bareth. To the other world. I ordered him to close it and now it cannot be opened again."

"Why?" Vera sighed, then pressed her lips together tightly. In a much harsher tone, she continued, "Eishoxa, I will not explain things twice to you. You cannot go back. You would die there. Your powers now trap you here and make you one of us. There is no way you can live there safely anymore. You need to forget that world. You belong here now and, since you do, I am your leader and my actions are not to be questioned, regardless of whether you understand them or not. Do I make myself clear?" Her voice then softened. "You don't understand, I know—"

"I am the daughter of your Goddess," Eishoxa said quietly. "My words are her words. Her words are your law. You cannot hold me here against my will. I demand that you take me back to where I belong."

"The daughter of my Goddess?" Vera scoffed, looking as though she wanted to laugh. "You don't even want to accept her existence, let alone claim your heritage! There's nothing more to be done. Unless you want to wander the Black Forest for a few days – and I assure you, I will send soldiers to fetch you back – there is nothing more to be done. Bareth is finished."

"How dare you speak that way!" Eishoxa shouted.

"Silence!" Vera screamed. Pain shot through Eishoxa from the head to foot, and she found herself instantly frozen in position against her will. "I should have you punished for speaking this way. You are an Indocani, and you will follow our rules or I will treat you like any other one of my soldiers! You accepted my leadership and you said that you would follow me. And now I hold you to that." She threw her hand in her air and Eishoxa could move again. "Now leave me," Vera ordered. Eishoxa turned to go, but before she stepped outside she looked at Ember. Although he didn't return her look, she could see he'd averted his gaze from Vera. Disgust covered his face.

Her dreams were nightmares from then on. She never realised when she was in the middle of them and never remembered them the next morning. But they came to her every night, stealing into her subconscious and whispering maliciously to her. They were full of shadows pursuing each other, and when she awoke the next morning, she felt just as exhausted as when she'd lain down the night before. And the blackness in her heart had grown a little bigger and become a little stronger. She told no one. She didn't even admit it to herself: that would be too terrifying. She told herself that to be afraid was to be weak, but could never understand where she'd got that idea from. It was as if the little germ of darkness in her heart had made a place for itself in her mind as well, and there it sat, like a malevolent spider, spinning a web in which it would be safe from harm and in which it could trap and devour any thoughts of goodness.

CHAPTER 9

Eishoxa went to the dragons' pit. It was the only place where she could be herself, the only place she knew that the truth would be spoken to her. She reached the forest and started to run, faster than she ever had before, dodging around trees and leaping over boulders. As she ran, she called out to Zeexa and heard the sound of dragon wings ahead of her. Zeexa landed inelegantly on the forest floor and was shaking some dead leaves from her wings, but stopped at the sight of Eishoxa's face.

"Eishoxa! What's wrong?"

Eishoxa put her arms around Zeexa's neck and breathed in the warm, earthy scent. She let her memories convey what words could not and felt Zeexa's initial shock, and then sorrow, even deeper than her own. *"I knew there was something strange about Vera. I knew she was up to something ... I was a monster, Zeexa. I destroyed a country, a country of innocent people – people who'd done nothing to me – simply to get to someone who I thought was a traitor."*

Tears were pouring copiously down her face and she shut her eyes and rubbed them, trying to stop them. *"And there's more. Ember destroyed the portal that would take me back to Bareth. I'm a prisoner here, Zeexa."*

Once more she put her arms around the dragon's neck and Zeexa growled in sympathy, a low long growl that vibrated through her neck and into Eishoxa. The dragon's warm waves of consolation washed over Eishoxa's tormented mind and soothed it, but only a little. She was hiding so much from the dragon, and it was hurting too much.

How could Eishoxa tell her about the seed of evil that she had let Nezrax plant inside her, that she was growing and nurturing in her heart? How could she show the dragon the depth of her black despair, now that she had nothing left to fight for, now that everything had been taken away?

Suddenly, Zeexa stiffened in Eishoxa's arms and pricked up her ears, staring deeper into the forest.

"What's wrong? What's happened?"

"Someone's there," Zeexa whispered and growled warningly. Eishoxa turned around, scouring the landscape. Zeexa snuffled, sniffed the air and strained forward. Her eyesight was also much sharper than Eishoxa's. Suddenly she shot forward and disappeared into the trees.

"Zeexa! Come back!" Eishoxa called, but there was no reply. *"Zeexa,"* she called aloud cautiously, looking through the burnt trees. She jumped as a crash sounded above her and something dropped at her feet. Zeexa landed a moment later and stalked, growling, towards the thing she had dropped.

"I found this walking through our forest as if he owned it. Traitor! I should kill him now," Zeexa snarled, hissing and spitting.

Eishoxa looked to see who it was, confirming her guess. Jumping between the two of them, she put her hand on Zeexa's muzzle. *"It's all right. He's a friend."*

The dragon stopped in surprise. *"He's one of the Water Dwellers. How could he be a friend?"*

Eishoxa nodded. *"I know. But he is."* She turned to him. "Are you all right, Rush?"

He nodded. "Dragons are more vicious than you said they were."

Eishoxa shook her head, smiling, and looked back at Zeexa. "No, that's just because she doesn't know you. Isn't that right, Zeexa?" Zeexa growled and raked her feet through the leaves.

Eishoxa smiled but then turned back to Rush and said urgently, "What are you doing here? Do you want to be killed?"

Rush shook his head. "I had to come. I discovered something after you left and I knew that I had to tell you."

"What? What is it?"

Rush looked anxiously at Zeexa, who narrowed her eyes at him and flapped her wings threateningly. *"I don't trust him,"* the dragon snarled. *"What is he doing here? What does he want?"*

"Zeexa, be quiet," Eishoxa ordered irritably. And then to Rush, "Tell me."

"Someone else is coming!" Zeexa hissed suddenly.

"Come on." Eishoxa took Rush's hand and pulled him through the forest, away from the dragons' pit. Zeexa followed, on the alert. When they reached a secluded spot, Eishoxa turned to Zeexa. *"Will you go back a bit and keep guard, in case someone comes?"*

Zeexa growled and bared her long teeth. *"I don't like him. He smells weird."*

Eishoxa smiled despite herself. *"He's a friend, I promise. I wouldn't lie to you. Don't go far. If I need you, I'll call."*

Zeexa glared once more at Rush before walking a distance away and settling herself on the ground, ears pricked, head shifting from side to side. Eishoxa faced Rush.

"Come on," she whispered again and took him further into the trees. Once they were out of sight of Zeexa, she stopped and pulled him behind a trunk. Rush looked down at her, taking in her tear-dampened cheeks and her reddened eyes "Are you all right?"

Eishoxa took a jagged breath and immediately tears flooded from her eyes. Rush pulled her into his arms, resting his chin on top of her head. "What is it? What's wrong?"

"I was wrong about them all, Rush. I turned Rereth, which meant the Blessed One, into Bareth because I hated the Ewdicani. I was tracking down an Ewdicani traitor who took shelter in Rereth and I destroyed it trying to get to them. All the fires and droughts were my doing."

Rush was silent, knowing that words wouldn't help. Anything he said would be lost in the pool of sorrow Eishoxa was drowning in. He could only hold her up and not let go, not let her sink and be lost forever.

Eishoxa squeezed her eyes tight shut, but when she opened them a fresh wave of tears poured down her cheeks. "And there's something more. Ember destroyed the portal to get back to Bareth, so I can never return. I have nowhere to go and nowhere to hide from them. I hate them so much it scares me, Rush. I hate them so much."

"The world can be a cruel place," Rush mourned quietly.

Eishoxa lifted her head. "No, not the world," she denied, "just the people in it. Vera and Ember."

"Vera?" Rush asked, stepping back a bit.

"Yes," Eishoxa spat vehemently. "Vera was the one in charge of it all … What is it?" Rush was suddenly looking very uncomfortable. "What is it?" she repeated. "Do you know something more about Vera? Is that why you've come?"

He paused for a moment and then took her hands and said, very quickly and urgently, "Eishoxa, why did you have to come to Dulcacohefen? Did they tell you?"

"To form an alliance with the Ewdicani. Then, after I'd done that, I could go home." He was shaking his head. "What?" she asked.

"You were right," he replied tonelessly. "They were lying to you."

Eishoxa froze. "What do you mean?"

"It wasn't to form an alliance. I listened to what you said about Gresceva and I watched her, and it's true, she did behave strangely after you left. So I broke into her rooms and took what I could find."

"Rush! What if you'd been caught? You were in enough trouble when I left!"

"But I wasn't," he grinned. He took something out of his pocket and showed it to her. "Letters from Vera to Gresceva and from Gresceva to Vera. Not only is that not allowed, look at this." He moved his finger over the paper. "The Pentelement … How much to you know about it?"

"Not a lot," Eishoxa admitted.

Rush jabbed the paper with his finger. "The God Pentelemence was defeated by his three daughters, but he didn't die – being immortal, he can't. He was only banished. And I think they're trying to bring him back, trying to restore the world to how it was."

Eishoxa looked at him in horror. "Are you sure?"

"Yes – at least, that's what I've understood from these letters."

"So why was I taken to Dulcacohefen?"

Rush shoved the letters back into his pouch. "That's the worst part of all. You're the daughter of a Goddess, one of the two most powerful Goddesses. In order for anyone to raise Pentelemence, it must be you or one of the Goddesses who re-awaken the elements. They must use the power of those who put them to sleep in the first place. In other words, the power of the Goddesses."

Eishoxa shook her head. "I don't understand you, Rush. What does all that mean?"

He sighed. "The elements – Fire, Water, Rock, Earth and Air – are things. They exist in us, but they're alive as well. When Fiera, Wella and Nezrax defeated their father and banished him into the far corners of the universe, they put to sleep the wild part of the elements, the parts that are dangerous in each, and left them in a secret sanctuary hidden in the Forest of No Flame. No matter how powerful anyone becomes, that's only a fraction of how powerful Pentelemence used to be. The elements we have now are tamer versions, not constantly trying to destroy each other. Do you understand so far?" Eishoxa nodded.

Rush continued, "And in order to reawaken them, you must visit the home of each of the five elements: Sicharenhafan, Dulcacohefen, the Sorrowful Mountains, the Forest of No Flame and the Great Mountains of the Air. You've visited three of those five places, you've been claimed by three of the five elements. And now you're trapped here in the Tree, it would be very easy for Vera to take you to take you to the Great Mountains of the Air. And tell me, have you ever seen the Sorrowful Mountains in your dreams? Ever spoken to Nezrax?"

Eishoxa looked away. Rush took her face gently between his hands and turned it so that she was looking into his eyes. "Tell me. Have you?"

The look on her face gave him the answer. His mouth twisted anxiously. "So you've visited four of the five places. Now the only place you need to go is the Great Mountains of the Air and you'll raise Pentelemence. Because Nezrax is so good at twisting minds, she can trick your soul into inhabiting your dream body." Eishoxa backed away slowly, her hands held over her mouth in horror. Rush nodded grimly. "Exactly. Would Vera or Ember know about your visiting the Sorrowful Mountains?"

Eishoxa started to shake her head, and then stopped. "I told Rianox," she confessed. "He must have told them."

Rush nodded. "And would Vera have told Ember of the plan to raise Pentelemence?"

"She would have," Eishoxa said without hesitation.

Rush nodded. "Maybe. But we can't be sure. Vera wouldn't have given her secret up to anyone. Then again, Ember has destroyed the portal and that means you're trapped.

"Would Gresceva have told anyone?"

"No," said Rush with certainty. "She trusts no one. She's betrayed our people as Vera has betrayed yours."

"So did anyone else know about it? Anyone in the Assembly, or our Council even?"

"No. They would've discussed an alliance and argued it out, but it was already planned. That was all a show. And Vera, knowing that you didn't trust her, needed you there in Dulcacohefen but away from the Assembly. She suspected you as you suspected her."

"So why have you come? To tell me that?"

"To take you away. We shall go to the Forest. We must learn how to Change you."

"Change me?"

"Yes. You're neither wholly Indocani nor wholly Ewdicani. You're a mix of many things, as I'm sure you've been told: parts of you are human, parts of you are Indocani or Ewdicani, and you've been blessed with powers from the Guardian of Earth. When you Change – change into a true Indocani – the power you will been given by your mother, which will turn you into a fully fledged Indocani, will cancel out your going to those four places, simply by erasing your human existence. Unfortunately, I don't know how a Changing may take place, but the Guardian of the Forest of No Flame would know."

"You know the Guardian?" Eishoxa asked, raising an eyebrow.

"I do," he said. "It's taken me a long time to get here. I couldn't cross the Dead Marshes, of course, so I had to go around them. As soon as I found out about Gresceva, I left. I've left the Ewdicani."

"But I don't want to Change. I don't want to be an Indocani," Eishoxa said, turning her face away. "They only remind me of what they've done to me."

"What about an Ewdicani? Would you be one of those?"

Eishoxa spun around to look at him. "I could be?"

"Theoretically, yes," Rush said. "You've been blessed by the Water Goddess and she put water inside you. You're as much Ewdicani as Indocani. You have a choice now."

"And do you think that we could do it?" Eishoxa asked. Things were happening too fast. It seemed too risky to think about.

Rush took her hands and looked earnestly into her eyes. "Eishoxa, we can. Together we can get away from this place. It's too dangerous for you here. Do you understand? If anything happened to you and I knew that I'd not even tried to get you out, I would never forgive myself."

Her mouth opened to utter one word. "Bareth?" It was a question, not asked of Rush but of herself. Could she abandon all possibility of getting back, leave everything behind her, to go with the person she loved away from the place she hated? She would have to give up not only Bareth, but Maya as well.

Rush lifted her face to meet his gaze. "Eishoxa, Bareth is lost. I know you don't want to hear that, but it is. The portal has been destroyed and the only other portal in this world is in the Sorrowful Mountains. Only Nezrax knows how to use it, and you're not going to the Sorrowful Mountains. We can do it. We can get away from here. Will you come?"

Eishoxa nodded, just once. "I will come. But how are we going to get there? How are we going to cross the desert unseen?"

She noticed that Rush was looking tired and worn. Nevertheless, he smiled. "I got across it before."

"Why don't we take Zeexa?" Eishoxa suggested, feeling her heart warm just thinking about the sprightly little dragon. "I don't want to leave her here and she can fly fast, even with two of us. The Guardian, I'm sure, won't mind her staying in the forest – but if she does, we can send her back."

"The dragon?" Rush asked dubiously.

"Yes, the dragon," Eishoxa urged. "It's safer. No one will question a dragon flying away, even with two riders on its back. It's a marvel you haven't been caught yet. I'm not risking it again."

"All right," Rush agreed with a little laugh. "If it makes you happy."

"Very happy," Eishoxa smiled. She called for the dragon, "*Zeexa, come here!*" She waited for a while, but there was no reply.

"*Zeexa!*" Eishoxa called again. She took Rush's hand and they went back through the forest. "*Zeexa?*" she repeated, but trailed into silence when she saw the place where they'd left her. All that was left was a smoking depression in the leaves where Zeexa had been sitting.

"*Zeexa?*" She looked around. The dragon would never have left them, not without telling Eishoxa. "*Zeexa!*" she shouted.

Suddenly a dragon's roar sounded ahead of them and an almighty crash reverberated through the trees. "*Zeexa!*" she yelled, and tore off into the trees, leaving Rush to follow. She came to a halt when she saw the dragon lying on the ground. "*Zeexa!*" she cried, and ran to her side. Rush joined her then. The dragon wasn't moving.

An almighty yell came from above and someone dropped from a tree to the ground between Rush and Eishoxa. It was Ember. His sword was out and he bore a look of deadly fury. Before Eishoxa could react, he had slashed at Rush and caught him across one arm. Rush staggered backwards, holding his wound. Dark blood – not red but blue – seeped between his fingers.

Eishoxa struggled to her feet and leapt at Ember, shouting in his ear: "Ember! Stop it! He's not doing anything wrong! You're not thinking clearly!" Without even looking at her he struck her in the face with his free hand, with such force that she spun and fell. Ears ringing and head throbbing, she turned onto her back just in time to see Ember strike Rush in the face with the butt of his sword. Rush fell to the ground.

"Ember, he's innocent! What are you doing?" She stood up only to fly at him again, trying to stop Ember's blade finding its way into Rush's heart.

"Innocent?" Ember sneered. "Innocent?" He threw her off him again.

"Oh, pretty he may be, but innocent he is not. That traitor you tracked through the forest and into your precious Bareth – who was it? Who led ambush after ambush on innocent Indocani, some of them children, to prove a point? Who killed many of your friends and wounded you yourself in an unprovoked attack on the Tree? Who was it, Eishoxa? It was Rush!"

The words pounded through Eishoxa's head. Some of them lingered but most of them passed straight through. But she understood the tone. Rush? Really? Could it be?

"Is it true?" she whispered. Then Ember slashed again. Rush fell, blood pouring from his side. But as she leapt to help him, she was seized from behind.

"Eishoxa! There's nothing you can do!" Rianox was holding her in a vice-like grip, having appeared out of nowhere. Her arms were twisted tightly behind her, and his hold was so strong that soon her hands went numb. No matter how hard she fought, she couldn't break free.

"Ember! Stop it! Stop it!" She was screaming now and her throat burned with the strain. Rush had stopped trying to get away and now lay on the ground, curled up in a ball. Ember was looking down at him dispassionately. Suddenly he became aware of Eishoxa's screams and turned to look at her. She was still resisting Rianox, who was holding her in his unyielding grip.

"Keep fighting, Princess," Ember said. "You'll never get free. You think me cruel, don't you? I learnt from the best, Eishoxa. I learnt from you." His free hand burst into flames. Eishoxa screamed again, fighting even more violently, but Ember no longer paid her any attention. He spun around and shot the flames at Rush. At that moment, Eishoxa could not say whose scream was louder, hers or Rush's. All she could see was him thrashing around, flames coiling around his arm and setting the ground alight as well. While his skin burned and blackened, all she could hear was Ember's manic, unending laugh.

Then it was over. Rush lay still, making no sound. Eishoxa was gasping for breath and choking on tears and fury.

Ember's unsheathed sword was back in his hands. "The real world is cruel, Eishoxa. I know that you know that. But don't judge me for this because you have done the same to many others. And I learnt from the best – I learnt from you."

Eishoxa barely heard what he said. She was focusing instead on something inside her, something that was crawling out from her heart and filled her with strength beyond any she'd had before. The force exploded from her, throwing off Rianox, then sped her across to Ember, her only intent being to hurt him as much as he had hurt her. Her short knife was now in her hand. She collided with Ember and both fell to the ground. She wrenched his sword out of his hand and threw it away. Then she stabbed down, over and over. Ember tried to roll away but couldn't move fast enough.

When it was over, she stepped off him. From the corner of her eye she saw Rianox lying crumpled at the foot of a tree. She ran to Rush's side, took hold of his shoulder and rolled him onto his back. She recoiled at the sight of his mangled face and blue unseeing eyes.

"Rush! Rush! Don't be dead! Please don't be dead!" But Rush did not stir. She conjured water to trickle it over his wounds, but he made no sound. "Rush," she whispered. A single, lonely sound.

Straightening his legs and crossing his arms over his chest, she conjured green shoots to grow around him, cover him, hold him to the ground; shoots that wound over his chest, that hid the wounds and burns on his face and blossomed with flowers. She rested her forehead against his until the shoots completely covered him. Gathering bark and brambles, she strengthened his forest tomb and on the top wrote *Rush*. A single word.

They were going to run away. They were going to do it. It was going to be the two of them together, forever. And now there was only Eishoxa.

She stood, refusing to look at Rianox and Ember, and walked away.

CHAPTER 10

Eishoxa went back to the Tree. As she reached it, she raised one hand into the air and a rope of bramble snaked down from one of the boughs. She clung to it, ignoring the thorns stabbing her palm as it pulled her up onto the branch. In her hand she clenched a ball of dark magic. It had simply appeared there – and with it in her hand she was unstoppable. She strode to Vera's door and kicked it open, releasing the black magic as she did so. The energy exploded the door in a cloud of dust and wood fragments. Eishoxa didn't pause but walking straight in. Vera sat very still at her table, her hands on the arms of her chair.

"Eishoxa? What's going on? What are you doing?"

Eishoxa kindled another ball of magic and immediately Vera was silent. Eishoxa spoke in a monotone but each word was enunciated clearly: "Rianox and Ember are in the dragon forest. They attacked me and they lost. Rianox is not dead. I do not know about Ember." She put her hands on Vera's table and leaned over.

"I know what you are trying to do. I know all about Pentelemence and your lies. I know why you sent me to Dulcacohefen and I know what you were going to try to do. You must be frightened now. I know you are afraid of what I can do and what I am going to do. Well, be afraid. By lying to me for this long, you have made yourself my enemy. And not just my enemy but Fiera's as well. I am going to ask her to abandon you, you and all your people, to abandon everyone here, until you suffer as much as you have made me suffer." She lifted herself up from the table with purpose. Vera's face, usually so composed, had drained of all colour. The brilliant gold bangles and necklaces she wore made her skin looked even more washed out. Eishoxa left her without another word.

She walked towards the Black Forest, the forest that Coal and Ember had brought her through when they'd taken her from Bareth. She looked back towards the Tree and, beyond it, to the smudge that was the Dragon Forest. There Rush lay, on soil not his own, unhonoured and scorned.

A huge wave of anger engulfed her, and the power of rage stirred something deep within her. A tug, like a deep ocean current, yanked at her insides and everything she knew was heaved upside down. She seemed to be standing at the edge of a black hole in which the swirling depths frothed and bubbled. And she let herself fall in.

Magic seized her and rippled powerfully through her, knocking her off her feet and into the air. Nezrax's voice reverberated through her, in her head and in her ears: "You must use all your power. Otherwise you are useless to everyone. Take this. I am giving it to you now. And use it. Do what you want. And then come to the Sorrowful Mountains where I will be waiting."

When she came to, she was lying in the middle of a glade in the Black

Forest, and the trees around her were full of singing birds. The word *'useless'* echoed in her accusingly. Turning her head she saw a stream. She crawled on all fours to the water's edge and put her hand in it. It didn't harm her. Calling on her magic, she parted the stream and then joined it back. She need only think something and it happened. The birds' songs rang louder and louder in her ears. Eishoxa looked down at her reflection in the water. Her hair had come loose and her eyes were narrower and darker. Her mouth had taken on a cruel sharpness. She looked like an Indocani. She looked like her mother. She looked like her old self. She was her old self. What had Ember said? That he'd learnt cruelty from the best – from her. Well, she would teach him now that he was not cruel, just cowardly. And cruelty meant so much more than what he thought. While the birds still twittered in the trees, oblivious of the magic that thrummed through Eishoxa's body, a large crow landed on the water's edge opposite. The crow, symbol of Nezrax, just as the eagle was Fiera's and the swan was Wella's. The crow *was* Nezrax; it carried her spirit wherever it went. With its head cocked to one side, the bird fixed her with a beady eye. Eishoxa looked back and felt the anger rise again. She turned away and saw the Tree, silhouetted in the approaching dusk. She could make out the figures of people dancing on the branches, unaware of the danger they were in, unaware of her power. As the voices of the birds rose to a crescendo, so did her fury. The crow hopped along the ground and cawed at her. This was the limit. She couldn't take anymore. With an unearthly scream, she flung her arms out.

The clearing was silenced. Every one of the birds dropped down to the ground, muted by death. Eishoxa rose to her feet. She pushed her hair back from her eyes and turned towards the Tree. Raising her arms, she called on the magic again. The crow, still there, hopped and strutted; its hideous voice cawed and cawed, a harsh fanfare of triumph. She stretched out her hands. A dark cloud started to brew over the Tree, ugly and purple like a bruise. Eishoxa expanded it, grew it, adding smaller clouds all around, gorging them with water. Trees wilted around her as she took the water from the ground. The air around her shimmered as heat radiated from her body, setting the trees and the ground on fire. She could see the Indocani at the Tree taking cover, trying to shelter themselves, heard orders being given loudly on all sides. She thought of Rush lying on the burning ground, as dead as the birds around her, and her heart hardened. She clapped her hands. A massive mushroom of steam drenched the Tree below as the cloud split in two. She watched as people dropped from the branches, flailing desperately as they fell. Then she turned and faced the clearing. The trees were only smoldering but great fires were starting in the dead leaves beneath the trees. She stood there, treacherous but beautiful in her great, black, twisted snake of sinfulness. She stamped her foot and the ground shuddered as it prepared for her next attack. She slammed her hand against the air and trees toppled like dominoes. She picked one up, pivoted and threw it at the Tree.

She couldn't be stopped. This was her time now. Calling to the earth and the rock, she pulled more trees out of the ground. Lightning forked down from the sky at her command and the trees combusted in a blaze of fire and light. Ash rained from the sky like water. It fell on her face, her hands, her body, and it felt like freedom.

PART 4

CHAPTER 1

THE JOURNEY TO the Sorrowful Mountains was uneventful. A towering black castle, hewn from the rock and built with misery for mortar, loomed up from the centre of the mountains. This place was rightly named, Eishoxa thought, looking around. Crows, the only birds to be seen, sat in the skeletal trees and cawed at her. Weeds had pushed their way through the cracks but then given up and wilted at the surface. Old stems of horned bramble arched over the black boulders that hunched their shoulders against the ground, and bindweed licked its way up between them. There were no other plants. The ground beneath her feet was unyielding and peppered with sharp stones that she had to pick her way across. The sky was overcast, the air humid, as if the weather couldn't make up its mind what to be. And of course, hemming her in on every side were the Sorrowful Mountains. She met no Empty on her way up to the castle. Eventually she crossed a small bridge to reach the metal drawbridge, which was closed and overlooked by four guard towers, each one bristling with the Empty and their weapons. There was a sentinel standing at the end of the bridge, who barred the way as Eishoxa walked forward.

"Who are you?" he demanded. "What is your business here?" The Empty had black faces, not the warm chocolate brown of the Indocani, or the delicate light blue of the Ewdicani. No, this was black: the black of the deadest, darkest night, the black that filled a despairing heart, that ate away at anything good in you. The black that nightmares were made of. They wore tight, black clothes that looked like snake skin, studded on the shoulders, and running along the outside of the arms and legs were long, sharp metal spikes. The guard carried a spiked mace and looked as if he wouldn't let her pass.

"My name is Eishoxa," she said.

"And what business do you have here?"

"I've come to speak to Nezrax. She told me to come here."

"Is that so?" he sneered.

"Yes."

"I think you're lying."

"Do you?" Eishoxa responded. "Well, will you let me pass anyway?" Another Empty came up behind him and struck him on the head with the butt of his sword. "You idiot. This is the daughter of the Warrior Goddess. Can you not tell?"

The first Empty looked Eishoxa up and down. "She doesn't look like much."

"Neither do you. I could probably get past both of you but, because I am being polite, I have decided to ask you. So, will you let me go?" Eishoxa asked. The Empty stopped arguing and turned to looked at her.

"Is that a threat?" the first one asked. Eishoxa felt her fist clench of its own accord and did nothing to stop it. "I don't know," she replied calmly. "That all depends on what you call a threat." She snapped her fingers and the Empty who had refused her entry flew against the rock. He hung there, suspended by a skewer of wood that pierced him through the chest.

"Now," Eishoxa said, smiling at the other one who regarded her with fear in his eyes. "Are you going to let me pass?" The great drawbridge groaned as it was let down, the thick rusted chains unused to movement. Eishoxa wondered how many times it had been let down, how many times prisoners had been brought back here, how many times people had been let out. She reckoned it was very few, on all counts. The Empty who had come to the bridge had stayed with her but was keeping his distance. On the other side of the drawbridge was a large plain. It was full of activity.

"This is where we prepare for battle," the Empty told her hurriedly as she looked at him questioningly. Eishoxa nodded. In the corner, about fifty Empty were testing catapults made from wood, throwing large granite rocks at the castle walls. Fires were being stoked and all kinds of weapons being made. Dented armour was being repaired and new armour was being made. No grass grew on the hard ground. Eishoxa was led by the Empty towards the castle gates. These were made of thick wood strengthened by strong iron bars and were defended by even more guard towers. Large cauldrons made for boiling pitch or oil were suspended on either side of the great doors. The Empty approached the guard standing there and spoke a few words. The guard shook his head. Apologetically, the Empty turned back to Eishoxa.

"You are not allowed in," he said. "Nezrax has not allowed visitors." Eishoxa raised her eyebrows at him. "She will see me," she told him and walked forward towards the guard on duty. The other Empty stayed where he was. "Let me in," she said.

"I cannot do that," the Empty replied, standing up straighter. Eishoxa looked up and loosened the chain that held one of the cauldrons in place.

"I would advise you not to disagree with me," she said.

"Oh? And why is that?" he asked, with a bored look.

She turned slightly and could see the other Empty shooting him warning glances which he ignored. "Because …" she started, and released the chain that held the cauldron. It crashed onto his head and he fell to the ground. She stepped over his body. The Empty who had accompanied her hurried to her side and pushed open the gates to the castle.

"Nezrax is in the Star Hall," the Empty said. The walls of the castle were made from the blackest quartz and towered high. Eishoxa knew at once why Nezrax had fashioned her lair like this. The high walls and towers were sinister and forbidding, forming the perfect prison for any unfortunate victim who passed through her doors. The Empty led her on through the castle to a large hall. As Eishoxa entered it and looked about, she saw that the place was Nezrax's ironic counterpart to the Star Hall at the Tree. Where twisted roots had formed the walls, here they were made from rock and metal. Where the Tree hummed with controlled energy and fervour, this hall felt dank and dark and black. She could feel all through its walls its parasitical power, absorbing life from any who entered it.

On the floor of the hall, etched deep into the stone, was a strange symbol, a huge five-pointed star, and in each corner was a further different symbol. It was the same symbol Eishoxa had seen tattooed on Nezrax's arm in the Mother's Nest at Dulcacohefen: the Pentelement. So Nezrax did have control over all elements. A throne, resembling Gresceva's chair in the Lily Hall, stood at far end. Perched on its back was a large crow, like the one in Eishoxa's dream. Nezrax reclined with all the rapacious grace of a predator observing its unsuspecting prey. Her white skin glowed beneath her black hair, which was draped over one shoulder. Seeing Eishoxa enter, the Goddess straightened, then stood. Eishoxa saw that her legs were enveloped by a black cloud – the roof of Hell – with only her bare feet visible underneath. Eishoxa shuddered when she saw the empty throne: it was made from bones. Nezrax was slight and very small, with a young childlike face. But her eyes were windows revealing the darkness inside. She smiled, a smile that touched nothing but her mouth. She waved the other Empty away. "Eishoxa. You've come."

"I had no choice. I could no longer stay with the Indocani," Eishoxa said.

Nezrax's face contorted in a look of sympathy. "Oh yes. I heard about what happened. Poor you." Eishoxa looked away from her ghastly expression, and her eyes, Nezrax noted, fell on the star in the middle of the room.

"That's the Pentelement," she explained. She walked towards it and lightly traced each point with a foot. "It shows control and mastery over the five elements. My sisters think that one element is enough, but I," she smiled again. "I can control all five. That is what I teach my followers."

"I don't want to learn that," Eishoxa interrupted. "I left the Indocani because they were trying to make me into a mindless, thoughtless follower, someone who follows and says nothing." Nezrax looked up, a calculating look on her face. "Then why are you here?" The crow sitting on the chair cawed accusingly. Eishoxa glanced towards the gruesome bird and then looked back at Nezrax. "Revenge. I'm here for revenge against those who hurt me."

CHAPTER 2

Eishoxa was taken straight from the Star Hall to the armoury. There she was given the same clothes that all the Empty wore: a tight pair of black trousers and a tight black jacket. Silver spikes projected along the outer edge of each arm and leg. Eishoxa looked down at the strange snakeskin garments she held in her arms, and then at her flowing red clothes. She couldn't stay here dressed in the clothing typical of the Empty's enemy.

"You can put those on," said the Empty who'd fitted her out. "The things you're wearing now won't help you at all here." She was led to a large room and left there. At the Tree, her room had been bold and made a statement, with strong angles and bright colours. At Dulcacohefen, her room had been delicate and beautiful, full of exotic things and interesting artefacts. Here in the Sorrowful Mountains her room was completely different. It was made from the same rock as the castle, and its walls were covered in strange scratches and gashes, as though they'd been savagely attacked with a knife. The bed was a simple one, similar to the one at the Tree but supported on poles that had been carved like bones.

Laid out on the bed were a variety of weapons. Eishoxa walked towards them slowly. There was an unsheathed sword, with its scabbard beside it. There were throwing knives and knives for keeping at hand. There was a bow with a quiver of arrows. Eishoxa was drawn to it immediately, but the arrows smelt odd and she realised that they'd been dipped in poison.

She left them on the bed and walked over to the window, the only one in the room. There were no shutters and nothing to close it with. It looked directly over the courtyard where the Empty were constantly preparing for war. For a war that might come. For a war that might never come. She realised, for the first time, that her mind was silent. These people had no conscience, no principles, nothing that might want to join with her mind. And here, her own mind would be silent. Even the faintest presence of Zeexa had disappeared, and there was no life here to speak of.

Life. Rush. She put her hand over her mouth to stop the grieving, rasping noises escaping her throat. The image of him lying there motionless, his eyes staring up at her, shocked at what one person could do to another, refusing to believe it in his good, naïve head. She remembered what Rush had said about the good of the world, that the instinct to be good was in all of us, if we would just follow it. He was wrong, but she found she couldn't contemplate hating him for it. If he'd been right, she wouldn't be here, but she couldn't blame him. He'd paid the ultimate price. She clenched her teeth and forced the noise back down her throat. No one would know. No one would hear. She looked down at her unfamiliar clothing. This was a different girl entirely. This was not the Princess of Bareth, holding tightly onto the few months of freedom and innocence she had left. This wasn't even Fiera's daughter, revelling in the strength and awe of her people. Was this the Eishoxa at Dulcacohefen, confused and refusing to believe what she was seeing and hearing, or the Eishoxa in the Dragon Forest, powerless and held back while an innocent man was killed? No, Eishoxa didn't know who this person was, this girl with awesome power within her, power that enabled her to summon winds and fell trees with mere thoughts. It was as though Nezrax had lent the power to her and now had taken it back, until the next time she deserved it. Tight, black and scaly, her clothes made the perfect place to hide in. Hide from the world. And anything good in it.

After a sleepless night, Eishoxa was summoned to the Hall and was led there by Sorperstat, the Empty who had taken her there the day before. He seemed to have got over his fear of her and was almost indifferent to her as they walked through the castle.

The Star Hall was darker than Eishoxa remembered it, and Nezrax was not sitting in her chair but hovering high above the centre of the symbol of the Pentelement engraved in the floor. Two of the star's points had been ignited, and Nezrax was speaking softly to herself, twisting and swaying on the black cloud that enveloped her feet. The moment they entered, Sorperstat put out his arm to stop her from going any further. Nezrax, however, seemed to sense their presence and turned around. The star was still alight below her. On seeing Eishoxa, she smiled and descended. When she touched the floor, the light of the star went out.

"Thank you, Sorperstat," she said and he left. Nezrax turned to Eishoxa. "Now we may begin your training."

"Training?"

"To become one of the Pentelement," Nezrax reminded her. Eishoxa looked at the star cut into the floor. She remembered how she had controlled the lightning and the thunder, how for one glorious moment she had felt invincible, how she had felt incredible, as if nothing could hurt her. How she had turned huge trees to dust with a single thought. How she had so easily thrown off Rianox and attacked Ember. Was that what she wanted? That type of power? The power that Nezrax had, and had promised her?

Eishoxa felt her head shake. "No. I don't want that." Nezrax took a step back, giving her a calculating look. Eishoxa spoke again, keeping her gaze trained on the star on the floor. "I just want to go home. They said that you knew how to get me home. Rush said that there was a portal here, a portal that would take me home."

"And where is home for you?" Nezrax asked tauntingly.

"Bareth," Eishoxa whispered in reply.

Nezrax made a sound of contempt. "I thought Bareth had been destroyed. What are you going to do, cry on the ruins?" Eishoxa looked up at her with intense dislike. The reason she had come was to get what she wanted and nothing else.

"I am going to find my friend. This world doesn't deserve me, and the way to take my revenge is to do what they tried so hard to stop me doing. I'm going back."

"And what if your friend is dead?" Nezrax asked dangerously.

"Then I will find her," Eishoxa insisted, clenching her fists. "For too long I've done what I was told. Now I'll make my own choices." Nezrax turned away from her. "I have something to show you, Eishoxa. I know that you won't like it, but I'm sure that in time it will serve you well to have seen it." She clapped her hands before Eishoxa had time to respond. Sorperstat entered the Star Hall.

"Take Eishoxa to the dungeons," and Nezrax gestured with her chin. Sorperstat glanced at her before walking towards the door. Eishoxa followed, still not quite sure of what was going on. Nezrax floated in the air just behind them.

"I must tell you that you may be quite shocked," Nezrax warned as they left the Star Hall. The passage they followed, cut into the rock, twisted and turned as it led steadily down into the ever colder bowels of the castle. Quite suddenly, the passage opened out into a large room where several cells, divided by thick walls, were secured with rusty iron locks. The uneven floor held puddles of stagnant water and there was a strong smell of rot. Sorperstat held out his hand and Nezrax handed him a large set of keys. He flicked through them and picked out the smallest key, then walked towards the last cell. Eishoxa followed slowly. Sorperstat peered inside, unlocked it and opened the door for her. Eishoxa looked back at Nezrax, who nodded at her, and then took a few tentative steps. Sorperstat still held the door and did not meet Eishoxa's eye. She stopped at the threshold and looked inside.

It was a tiny space, just tall enough for Eishoxa to stand, and just three paces in length. Lying on a raised stone platform opposite was someone dressed completely in white. She was small and shrunken, and her head was turned away. Her hands lay crossed on her chest, in the way the dead were laid out. She looked back at Sorperstat, who still did not meet her eye. Nezrax had come to the door of the cell and was watching her. She said nothing, but Eishoxa could hear a small voice in her head whispering, "Are you afraid? Afraid of someone who can do nothing to you? Afraid of the dead?" Eishoxa turned away from her and crept towards the body. As she approached, she became aware of a very sweet smell, sweet and clean, like the smell of hoarfrost in the morning. Eishoxa froze, almost staggering as she realised who it was. It was Maya.

"No." The single word came forth, as if it would somehow reverse time and bring her friend back. Eishoxa touched Maya's hand and an unearthly cold crept through her. Maya's face was composed. There was nothing horrifying about her, no mark on her white, white skin, no sign of force or abuse on her face or hands. It was that apparent pathetic acceptance – willingness even – to be gone, to be dead, that cracked Eishoxa's heart right down the middle. She could feel it shatter. Something welled up in her. Not anger; no, this was something different. Something much stronger, much darker. When Eishoxa lifted Maya's shoulders to embrace her, she was lighter than a feather.

Her skin was so cold that the life in Eishoxa retreated in fear. This was not death. This was not how death was supposed to be.

"What happened? The Guardian said she was alive." Eishoxa said.

"It happened when Ember destroyed Bareth," Nezrax said. She came to Eishoxa's side and put her hand on her shoulder. "I saw it happen," she added solemnly. Eishoxa closed her eyes. She felt nothing but a burning, furious loathing towards Ember. That was it: she would shut herself away in her head and live off whatever was left inside her, good or bad. That would be her world now. She shrugged off Nezrax's hand and felt the Goddess crouch beside her. Eishoxa looked down. The cloud around Nezrax's feet was dark grey and stormy. Through it she could just make out Nezrax's feet, bare and white. It was on those that Eishoxa focused so that she didn't have to look at anything around her.

"Eishoxa, listen to me. Do you want revenge?" Eishoxa raised her head only a little but still caught the Goddess's gaze. Nezrax was looking up at her with big, innocent-looking eyes, and in them Eishoxa could only interpret sympathy. Eishoxa turned away again and rested her head against Maya's hair. She could still smell the freshness that Maya carried around her, the smell of water and ice. It was like the smell that Rush had, the smell that hung over the Ice Lily, but lighter, more delicate. Eishoxa, with her head still bowed, nodded. Nezrax took her arm. "Now do you know what you want to do?"

"Leave this place," Eishoxa said hollowly. "Leave this world." Nezrax shook her head. "No, that will only work for a little while."

"Then what do you suggest?"

"Learn what I have to teach you. Become their enemy, as we are. And avenge your poor dead friend." Eishoxa heard barely a word of this, but the words *become their enemy, as we are* hit her. The Empty and the Indocani were enemies, and she too was the Indocani's enemy. This was where she belonged then. Nezrax was right. Here in this dark castle, with its strange walls and carvings. Here in the lap of evil was where she would be safe. She felt Nezrax pulling her upright, unwinding her arms from Maya and guiding her out.

"Maya will be safe in the earth there," Nezrax promised. Her voice was low and comforting now, and Eishoxa let it wash over her like waves on the beach. "I will teach you all that I know, Eishoxa. And then we shall go to war, and you may take revenge however you wish." Eishoxa stopped and steadied herself. "Yes," she agreed softly. "Then we shall go to war."

CHAPTER 3

Eishoxa stood in the centre of the star. She had removed all her weapons and held her hands out in front of her, preparing herself. Nezrax circled the outside. "My sisters decided that they would co-operate with the elements that they chose," Nezrax said with a sneer on her face. "Fire and water 'dance' for them, as they say. That way of thinking is for cowards. But you and I, we are not cowards. The elements need to be controlled, mastered – then they must do what you want. The Indocani are weak. If the fire doesn't do what they want, they try to convince it. I know better. It doesn't argue with me because I don't let it. That is what I will teach you." Nezrax snapped her fingers and a fire blazed up where the fire symbol was. Nezrax circled it, moving her hand through the dancing flame.

"When my sisters and I conquered our father and sent him to the out-ermost edges of the universe, we divided the elements of this world, the wild from the tame. The tame is what my sisters listen to. I control the wild. This requires superior skill and strength." Eishoxa nodded and closed her eyes as Nezrax instructed. "Now, listen to the fire in your mind. Find it and hold onto it … Can you feel it?"

Eishoxa nodded silently. It was a bright, dancing light in the corner of her consciousness. She could find such lights all over her mind, ban-ishing the shadows and inviting in the bright rays of day. She chased the lights into one corner, and suddenly, cowering together, they didn't seem so big.

"Open your eyes," Nezrax said. Eishoxa did, and gasped in surprise. Over the flickering flames she could see a translucent oval, strangely hued, as if all the colours in the world were mixed together, but un-happily – blues and purples, green and yellows, reds and pinks, swirl-ing about in that oval. And on one side was a small cluster of circular lights floating together.

"This is your mind," Nezrax explained, moving slowly over to it. "These lights here, this is fire. You must put out the lights to gain con-trol."

"Put them out?" Eishoxa asked. Nezrax simply looked at her. "How?"

Nezrax smiled. "This you must work out. When you have conquered fire, then we can move on." She drifted out of sight.

Eishoxa examined the oval image of her mind. She reached out to touch it and her hand went straight through, as if through thin air. But she felt something brush against her subconscious. So this really was her mind. She put her hand out again and touched one of the little balls of light. A burning sensation streaked across her mind. She stepped back, putting her hand to her head. She looked towards Nez-rax, who was watching her.

"Work it out," Nezrax repeated. "Otherwise you are useless to ev-eryone." Eishoxa put her hand once again towards the balls of light, this time locating the light in her mind as well. She stretched out black snakes of shadow towards it and watched as they grew and elongat-ed. Her head was burning and aching. As the shadows touched the light, a blinding flash crossed her vision. She staggered backwards and watched as the shadows devoured the lights, one by one. With each one that disappeared, another flash streaked across Eishoxa's eyes. She backed further away and tried to rein in the shadows, but she no longer had any control over them. They had their own life now. As she tried to back away even more, something stopped her. Nezrax held her there.

"You must not leave the circle," Nezrax said. Eishoxa looked down and saw that she was nearly outside the point of the star that held the fire. As she watched, the flames flickered and died back, then flared up again. This time, however, the flames were black. When the last little ball of light flickered and died, the shadows slowly disappeared.

Nezrax pushed Eishoxa back towards the oval that showed her mind.

"Now look," Nezrax commanded, floating around to the other side. The balls of light had disappeared, but the shadows Eishoxa had just seen vanish were forming again. And something ignited again in her mind, feeling like fire but stronger and less inclined to bow and bend and obey. The shadows circled her mind like ravenous wolves. They listened to no one, belonged only to themselves. That was what she had unleashed inside herself.

"This is Fire," Nezrax whispered. The black flames lit up the Goddess's face with an eerie glow and Eishoxa was unable to look at her. "The shadow of fire. We are all shadows, shadows of what we could be, and shadows of what we should be. Now, get on with water."

"Another one?" Eishoxa asked, shuddering inside.

"There are five to master," Nezrax reminded her.

"I didn't think it would be so hard," Eishoxa admitted.

Nezrax laughed. "That's just a fraction of it. It's a shadow, remember?"

"And will each be as hard as that?" she asked.

Nezrax looked at her. "Are you afraid or weak?"

Eishoxa clenched her fists. "I'm not either," she stated. "It's just not what I expected."

"The elements are wild, Eishoxa. Have you ever seen a forest fire, or a fire in land ravaged by drought? Is there any force in heaven or on earth that can stop it?" Eishoxa shook her head. Nezrax smiled. "Exactly. It is that which you are mastering. Now, get on." Eishoxa crossed to the water section. Nezrax followed her. Eishoxa put her hand over the symbol, and from the ground there came a jet of clear, cold water.

"But how do I summon the oval? My mind? How do you take your mind out of your body?" Eishoxa asked.

"Will it," Nezrax replied. "You are in charge. You may stop when you have conquered water." She drifted away. Eishoxa heard a door shut and turned to see that Nezrax had exited the Star Hall. She turned back to the water. The cool, clean jet was bubbling up through the stone floor. Eishoxa watched it, remembering the happy times in Dulcacohefen. Those few times when the Assembly didn't even cross her mind and she could freely enjoy the beauty around her. The times she was with Rush. A cold knife pierced her heart as she thought of him. No more could she recall that smile that came so easily, or his thoughtful comments, or his gentle chiding, the kind of comment that only wanted to help. No more could she remember his gentle, loving face with his sweet blue eyes. Now all she could see was the coffin of living plants that she had buried him in. The water now drained away and stopped. Eishoxa looked over to the fire section. The flames had gone, but she could feel them in her head, urging her on. Something at once snapped and mended itself inside her. She suddenly felt stronger. Closing her eyes again, she projected her mind out into the world. All at once, she felt a terrible iciness and, opening her eyes, saw the oval suspended in front of her eyes. She held her hand out again over the carved symbol of water and the clear spring bubbled up again. She searched her mind again for water. She knew it would be there. Yes! There it was, like a little trill, flute-like, hiding away in the corner of her head. Now it appeared in the oval, a small silver wave bumbling along, unaware of the danger that surrounded it. Then the shadows overcame it, gulping and devouring it in the most sickening way. Eishoxa felt a slimy explosion in her head that trickled down the insides of her skull. The spring gurgled and shrank away, leaving mud oozing across the floor. Eishoxa, shaking, stepped out of the star. The moment her feet touched normal ground, her legs crumpled and she staggered. Soon she felt a burning pain up the side of her left leg. She drew up the leg of her trousers and saw etched into her skin, one above the other, the symbol of water and the symbol of fire.

"The mark that all my followers bear," said a voice above her. Nezrax hovered above her, regarding the marks with satisfaction. "And which I wear too. When you have all five, then you wear the symbol of the Pentelement. Eishoxa nodded her acceptance.

Two Empty, garbed in full armour, hurried down the Sorrowful Mountains, away from the castle. They looked neither left nor right but kept moving onwards. When they reached the scrubby undergrowth, the taller one looked around furtively and ducked behind one of the large bushes. Then he straightened, pulled off the black helmet and shook out his long red hair.

"I think we're safe now," he said. "I don't think we've been followed." The other did the same. He was much younger than his companion, but his face bore a battle scar and his eyes were old and weary.

"I'm glad to be out of there, Flame," he said, turning to look back at the castle that loomed above them.

"There's no chance of kidnapping her," Flame remarked. "The only answer is war. She will come and then there may be a way."

"War?" the younger one asked. Flame bowed his head.

"I wished never to live through it," he answered. "But there's no choice. If she has gone against her will, as Ember said, then we must get her out."

"And the Pentelement? You know as well as I do that she's been trained in their footsteps now." Flame whistled. It wasn't long before his dragon emerged from the surrounding undergrowth. He mounted and pulled his companion up behind him. Only then did he answer his question. "Then we need to take immediate action." He urged his dragon into the sky and pointed him home.

From then on, all Eishoxa did was learn the way of the Pentelement. Nezrax wouldn't let her do anything else until she had defeated all five elements. Water and Fire were the easy ones, Nezrax had said. The others would be much harder. Rock would be the last one, and the worst.

It was the day after she'd conquered water, and her leg still ached from the mark branded into her skin by the Pentelement. Eishoxa was standing in the Earth section. Nezrax herself had conjured the earth: little shoots that grew sturdy, supple and strong. Eishoxa drew her mind out, shuddering as she did so, for it was the worst of feelings to draw something out that was meant to stay in the privacy of one's being. And like a surgeon cutting away something that was corrupted in the body, she severed the little green shoots. They died almost immediately. And when the shadows destroyed them, and they crumbled and turned to dust, Eishoxa felt a trembling inside her, as though her own body had succumbed to the force. She understood then that whatever she felt was the other side of the elements, the dangerous side, which only those greedy enough or reckless enough dealt with. She wondered which she was. She watched as the plants now grew back crooked and black and weak. With the earth's defeat came the burning sensation that had preceded the branding on her leg, right above the symbol of water.

Air took a few days. As Eishoxa tried to harness it, it resisted and threw her out of the circle. And her head ached with a strange, new pain as her mind was forced back inside her head against her will. Nezrax explained that the mind could only be drawn out inside the Pentelement star. Otherwise, the mind had no use outside the head and therefore was forced back in. When Eishoxa finally conquered Air, she felt herself falling forwards, tumbling through space with nothing to hold her. The power of the wind swept through the Hall as she unleashed it and Nezrax stood there with a satisfied, triumphant look on her face. Lightning, thunder and wind, they all came under Air. And Eishoxa felt the mark burn into her skin as the shadows found a way into her heart.

Rock was indeed the worst and took the longest to conquer. Rock belonged to Nezrax and she did not give up its ownership easily. Eishoxa spent hours searching for it in her mind. When she did find it and the shadows enveloped it, she felt a rumbling at her feet and, through squinted eyes, saw the mountains outside the Hall shaking from their roots. Eishoxa took control of Rock and, before the shadows devoured it completely, a crushing pain pressed down on top of her. She could barely breathe as she struggled to stay standing. She envisaged herself lying under a huge pile of boulders, and the more she struggled, the more the pile grew until the weight of the world pressed down on her and there was no way out.

When all five symbols were burnt onto Eishoxa's leg, Nezrax stood her in the middle of the star. The edges of the star ignited and she felt the five-pointed star tattoo itself on the top of her left arm. She felt claimed by it, as though it had taken a part of herself, a part she couldn't get back. She was part of the Pentelement now. Nezrax told her that she only need will something and it would come about.

"Now that we have made you a sorceress," Nezrax said, "we must make you a warrior."

CHAPTER 4

NEZRAX FLOATED AT Eishoxa's side as she took her out of the Star Hall and directed her down a corridor that gradually descended. Eishoxa felt that they were heading back to the dungeons. The walls were tall and strong and made from blackest rock. There were torches set brackets but their light was dim and only cast vague shadows along the walls. Now came the sounds of metal upon metal, growing louder with every step. Suddenly the corridor opened up into a colossal room. The ceiling, arching high above them, turned every clash and shout into an echoing cacophony. Eishoxa couldn't focus on anything with the sounds pounding into her. This was the training place of the Empty – those who had once been Ewdicani and Indocani. Every Empty was dressed in full body armour, so Eishoxa couldn't see any faces. They were without identity, simply one body learning how to fight. No, not how to fight: how to kill in a thousand different ways. Eishoxa saw swords and arrows and spiked maces and bludgeons and spears and javelins, and they were used with even less mercy here than on the battlefield. On one side of the hall, several Empty were charging about and jumping against the walls, wielding ignited whips and chains. Eishoxa noticed, with a heavy heart, that the dummies they were attacking each had a feather stuck in its head, red to signify the Indocani and blue for the Ewdicani.

Eishoxa turned towards Nezrax, but the Goddess's attention was focused on a nearby platform where a duel was taking place. One Empty was vastly superior in strength and skill. Every blow he landed weakened his opponent until the smaller one dropped to his knees. Nezrax walked towards them. The defeated Empty struggled to his feet and held his sword out to continue. The other attacked again, and before long his opponent was on his knees again. The smaller one held up one hand. "I'm done," he said, and Eishoxa could tell from his voice that he was young, no older than she was. He stood again as the other Empty had caught sight of Nezrax. She was looking at the two of them, her face expressionless, and Eishoxa knew that this was not a good thing. The Goddess walked towards the pair. The winner lowered his sword but the loser had shuffled back. The duels around them had stopped. Nezrax had everyone's attention.

"Tell me," the Goddess said, taking the younger one's sword from him, "what was the first lesson you were taught when you came here?" The Empty swallowed and said fearfully, "That the Indocani are the enemy?"

Nezrax smiled. "Sorry, my mistake. The second lesson you were taught then." The Empty said nothing. His eyes were fixed on the sword Nezrax was now pointing at him.

"The second lesson, soldier," Nezrax demanded. The Empty mumbled something.

"I didn't hear that," Nezrax replied. "Speak up, or it is into the Pit with you." The Empty looked up and said, "Never give up."

"Never give up. And what have you just done?"

"Given up," the Empty replied. His voice was shaking.

"So, correct me if I'm wrong, but you have disobeyed an order given, almost directly, by me to you?" The Empty nodded.

"Speak!" ordered Nezrax. The Empty cleared his throat and said very quietly, "Yes. But I'll try harder next time, I promise." He barely got to finish his sentence. Nezrax had nodded at his opponent and there was a flash of metal. The Empty barely made a sound as he slumped to the ground. Nezrax threw his sword next to him. It landed beside his hand.

"Good," Nezrax smiled. "I'm sure you will." The bloodlust had died from her eyes. Nezrax nodded to the victorious Empty. "Get rid of this," she said, nudging the dead body with her foot. Eishoxa glanced down and saw that his helmet had fallen off. His hair was changing colour, and she saw with a shudder that it was turning red. He was an Indocani. The other Empty hauled him over his shoulder and walked away. Eishoxa jumped as Nezrax's pale, cold hand landed on her arm.

Come, Eishoxa. There is something I want to show you."

Eishoxa followed blindly. The Empty around the walls were watching her as she walked away and Eishoxa wondered if it was with disgust or awe that they were looking at her. Everyone knew that she had arrived, Nezrax had made sure of that, but no one had seen much of her. Her days so far had all been spent with Nezrax, mastering the Pentelement.

"We train warriors, not cowards," Nezrax said coldly as she took Eishoxa out of the dungeons. "Those who cannot kill have no place here. Mercy is another form of surrender, and we do not surrender. Ever." Eishoxa knew that in some twisted way Nezrax had quoted something the Indocani believed. There was a reason that Ember hadn't let Rush go. There was a reason why he hadn't stopped until Rush was dead. He had challenged him, and a challenge ended in a death. The strongest survived, while the weakest were picked off one by one. That was the law of nature and the Indocani were bound to it. Nezrax led her through the castle to a staircase. As they climbed higher and higher, Eishoxa was sure they were going to emerge on the roof. Suddenly the stairs stopped at a metal door. Nezrax unlocked it with a key that hung around her neck. "Come in," she said. The room reminded Eishoxa of something, but she couldn't decide what. It was inviting in some way, not beautiful but desirable. It both fascinated and terrified her. She turned around and saw that Nezrax still stood at the entrance, watching Eishoxa taking it in.

"Like it?" the Goddess asked. Eishoxa shrugged. "It's strange," she answered honestly. Nezrax laughed, stepping forward. "Yes. Strange. It could be described like that." The room was circular and Eishoxa assumed that they must be in the tallest tower of the castle. The only window overlooked the courtyard, where the Empty were swarming all over the ground like a horde of fire ants. Outside the castle grounds the Sorrowful Mountains sloped down to the vast plains below. Nezrax cast a glance over the room before turning back to Eishoxa.

"It's strange. My sisters do so much to hold onto you, but in the end you walk freely into my arms." Eishoxa said nothing. In this place, silence was her greatest weapon, just as it had been her greatest weakness with the Indocani. How different the two places were! Nezrax turned around. Eishoxa's eyes were drawn to the cloud at Nezrax's feet. It looked different now, changing from its usual dark, stormy grey to a milky white, and certainly more transparent.

Nezrax followed her gaze downwards. "There are many spirits in the walls, Eishoxa. Tormented souls who never found peace when they died. These walls hold them – the walls of this room in particular. The more concentrated the spirits, the whiter and more transparent my cloud."

"That cloud is the roof of Hell, isn't it?" Eishoxa asked.

Nezrax took the key off her neck and shrugged nonchalantly, glancing at the cloud she was standing on. "Depends on what you call Hell. This is the roof of that place where the souls of my enemies can never find peace. They are doomed." Nezrax moved her hand in a circle, and on the ground around her feet, under the cloud, there appeared the Pentelement star. Nezrax said something under her breath and the cloud darkened again, losing its milky whiteness. Eishoxa took a step back. The cloud was growing, obscuring more and more of Nezrax's body. As it reached her shoulders, Nezrax turned the key in the air itself, and a deathly cold swept across the room.

"Come," she said. The last thing Eishoxa wanted was to walk any closer, but she obeyed. As she stepped into the circle, the iciness intensified: it felt like thousands of knives stabbing at her. She shuddered, then jumped. Nezrax's hand closed over her wrist and pulled her closer, so that the cloud covered her body as well. In Nezrax's black eyes, Eishoxa saw a picture forming: in the centre of swirling black smoke, a massive door was opening. Wails and shrieks filled the air. Behind the door nothing could be seen, but Eishoxa could feel a penetrating cold, one that spoke of all the anguish and despair in the world. Strange, cold hands pulled at her clothing and suddenly she was falling forwards, tumbling into that terrible, desolate place. Then Nezrax blinked, and she saw nothing more. Eishoxa now realised: Nezrax was Hell. Hell existed inside of her, was part of her. Nezrax raised her eyebrows and made a satisfied sound. Eishoxa stepped back out of the star, and the sudden warmth that surrounded her again felt scalding by comparison.

"Hell," Nezrax said softly. "Yes, maybe it is."

CHAPTER 5

EMBER HAD CALLED a War Council after his recent findings. His wound still pained him. His fight with Eishoxa had cost him more than the use of two limbs; it had cost him his pride as well. Rianox, who'd been invited to the Council meeting, strongly suspected that Ember was there simply to make an appearance because his face was still twisted in pain. Rianox himself had come out of curiosity. His feelings towards Vera's plan were neutral now; he neither agreed nor disagreed. He had done his part, had shown his loyalty, and now there was forgiveness to be sought and consequences to be paid. That was the way of the Indocani. Act first, accept the consequences later. Vera sat at the top end of the table, looking grim. Rianox could imagine the thoughts rushing through her head. She knew what danger they were in and what danger she was in. It was a crime against the Goddesses to try to bring back Pentelemence, as she had done, and now Eishoxa had found out, Vera knew that there was nowhere to hide. When everyone in the Council had settled, she rose to her feet.

"Lords of the Council, we cannot deny what we see before us. We are in mortal danger since Eishoxa abandoned us: our only advantage is gone. Not only this, but scouts along the Sorrowful Mountains have told us that Eishoxa is being trained in the cult of the Pentelement. We must decide what to do." Rianox had to commend her for her acting. Of course she would not reveal to the War Council her own plans to raise Pentelemence. The way she presented their situation, Eishoxa was entirely to blame and Vera looked like the victim once again. And once again, Rianox had to congratulate Fiera for choosing her as leader. Vera was ruthless but her mind was brilliant. She always had a plan. Nothing slipped past her – and it was precisely that which made her so dangerous.

One of the Lords spoke up. "What are our options?" Vera looked around at them all. "We have three that we can consider. First, to try through the power of words to get Eishoxa back. The danger of this is great, but if we succeed, the reward will be greater. We know she is very powerful now, much more powerful than she was before. Our second option is to hide and wait for them to come to us. We've done this before, but now there is a difference: it would mean the loss of many Ewdicani lives. Given our present circumstances, I cannot advise that we lose any of the allies that we still have. Battles have cost us dearly and our numbers are starting to wane. Our third option is, of course, to go to war and fight to the death as we've always done. We can hope this will convince Eishoxa to return to us – but we cannot be certain it will." The Lord who had spoken called out again. "Is Eishoxa essential to our plan?" Vera looked at him. "I have not heard Fiera speak to me or felt her presence since she has left." Everyone sitting around the table looked up. Even Rianox was surprised to hear this. Vera continued, looking grim.

"I know that Eishoxa called to Fiera and, as a last wish from daughter to mother, asked her to abandon us, but I did not believe that Fiera would do such as thing. A great warrior puts the greater good before matters of the heart." Vera looked slightly disgusted. Rianox stood up. "Vera, if I may." Vera looked at him. Rianox sighed. He knew they weren't going to like what he had to say.

"We cannot fight her. And that means we cannot fight them. There are wars going on as we speak, and they are powerful – we have a powerful enemy. To provoke their anger even more would just be too dangerous." Vera nodded, but she was the only one who did so. One of the other Lords spoke up.

"We knew that our enemy was powerful, and now we must prove that we are as well."

"Vera," appealed Rianox, "they will destroy us." Ember slammed his fist down on the table. "We must go to war! We have no other choice!" Rianox shook his head. "Against Eishoxa? We stand no chance. In our present situation the power of words is far greater. We have seen and shown what violence can do!"

"You are a warrior and you want to fight with words? What's the matter with you?" sneered Ember. Rianox blushed but kept a civil tongue, "I would rather fight with words than risk the death of thousands of Ewdicani and Indocani. Our people are not limitless."

"Maybe you're just being a coward," said Ember. Rianox fought his rising anger. "Maybe I'm looking beyond instinct and thinking rationally! We can't win against her – there's no point denying it. You thought you were stronger than Eishoxa and you're not. You were wrong. We were both wrong. Quenching the power of a Goddess only makes it stronger, and that's what we tried to do ever since she got here. We must face the truth, something that we very rarely do: Fiera has abandoned us and we are by ourselves. We must call a halt to our arrogance and try to make amends."

"Amends?" scoffed Ember. "Thousands of us are dying and you want to make amends?"

"Not to our enemy. But to Eishoxa!" shouted Rianox. "It's you and I who have wronged her, not anyone else. We failed; we lost her. Now forgiveness must be sought – for the safety of everyone."

"With a war, we can get her out quickly," Ember countered, looking around the War Council and appealing for support. Rianox stood up. "Your concern for Eishoxa is clouding your better judgement."

Ember stood up also. "I cannot bear to think of her in that place!"

"She is safe where she is. They won't harm her there, not any more than we have. She is their advantage. But we must think about what to do now – what the best plan is, not the quickest. She has powers that neither of us understands, powers she's received from all manner of people and elements. No ordinary Indocani can make it rain, can control the earth and rock and sky as she can. No ordinary Indocani has power like that running through their veins. To attack would be a terrible mistake."

"You don't know that she's safe! Yes, I would risk lives to get her out of there. I care for her, no matter what I've done. It seems that you, a half breed, do not," Ember retorted.

"Don't you dare call me that!" spat Rianox furiously. "I've proved my loyalty a thousand times over, and a thousand times again. I've proved it at the cost of everything I hold dear!" Vera raised her hand. "Sit," she said. When neither moved, still glaring wrathfully at each other, she repeated more firmly, "Sit, or I shall be forced to ask you both to leave." The two of them lowered themselves into their chairs, Rianox poised on the edge as if to jump up again. Vera looked wearily at the two of them.

"It's true that Eishoxa is powerful now and that she thinks we've wronged her, and this makes her angry and dangerous. But we must uphold our beliefs: to fight for what we think is right, no matter the consequences. That is what it means to be one of the Warrior Race." All around the table, the Lords were nodding their approval. Only Ember and Rianox stayed still. They knew the web Vera's words could spin to entrap someone in their own convictions and removing them from her path. Encouraged by the general reaction, Vera continued, her voice getting stronger.

"This could be the biggest war of our time, and if the world is destroyed in the undertaking of it, then so be it. It is what we were made to do." She stood abruptly and turned to face the wall. All eyes were trained on her, and yet she did not turn around as she spoke. "We are warriors above all else. I was told once, long ago, that the Indocani's overwhelming need to fight until we die would be our undoing. Perhaps we have now arrived at that point. We have been betrayed – betrayed by one of our own!" She hit the wall and the ground shook with the force. The room was still. Vera didn't turn around but kept speaking, as if to herself.

"And our Goddess – the one who said she would stay with us for all eternity – has abandoned us. Well, then, we will abandon ourselves. We shall go to war and we will fight. If we win, we bring Eishoxa back and treat her like the traitor she is. And if we lose … then we all die." Her words hung in the air, reverberating in the silence as it dawned on them what she meant. Rianox stood. "You mean, kill Eishoxa?"

"How do we deal with traitors, Rianox?" Vera reminded him, without turning around. "You're a clever man; you know the law. Why don't you tell us?" Her cold, hard voice brooked no disobedience. But Rianox could say nothing. Every fibre of his being screamed against this injustice towards a girl who had done nothing, who he knew was not the girl who'd taunted and tortured him, who'd turned him away, refused his vow of service and loyalty. Since the day he'd arrived and been forced to swear that he would help Vera in any way he could, he knew that his promise to her was wrong. But his pride, that terrible pride of the Indocani – which set them apart from the Ewdicani, who were humble and penitent – his pride had refused to give in. But now he'd had enough.

"She is not a traitor!"

Vera spun around. "She is!" she spat. "She has betrayed our people, she has betrayed her own. How could she have done that if she is not a traitor?"

"We did worse to her!" Rianox protested. "You know we did!"

"Silence! You will not speak to me in that way!" Vera shouted. "Or I will treat you as a traitor as well. I will not be surrounded by disloyal subjects. I am the leader. I am the Commander. I need warriors, not cowards." Rianox flinched and turned to Ember. He had said nothing, hadn't looked at anyone. Vera looked to him as well. "Prepare our people for battle. We will attack from the front of their army, right into the Sorrowful Mountains. It is time." Ember nodded. Rianox looked aghast at him. "Ember, you don't think Eishoxa is a traitor, do you?" But Ember said nothing.

Rianox left the War Council in a fury. He stalked back up through the Tree. Eishoxa's attack on it had left noticeable scars that would not heal quickly. Just like Eishoxa. Amber sat in Eishoxa's room. She very rarely left it now. It had become her haven. For her sake, Rianox and Ember had agreed not to tell her what had happened in the Dragon Forest between them, Eishoxa and the Ewdicani. Rianox didn't speak to Amber about Eishoxa at all. He knocked as he opened the door and entered. Amber looked up. The spark had gone from her eyes and on her face new lines had been etched by sorrow at losing Eishoxa again for no reason. Rianox sighed internally. So many scars, so many mistakes, for so many people.

"Still no sign of her?" Amber asked. Rianox shook his head. "I've just come from the War Council," he said.

Amber stood up from Eishoxa's bed. "What have they decided?"

"We're going to war," Rianox replied, hanging his head.

Amber sat down again heavily. "We're doomed," she whispered. Rianox nodded. "Yes. Your brother was the one in charge of the proceedings on that front, I'm afraid."

"Yes, I know he was," Amber said. She ran a hand distractedly through her hair. Rianox looked at her again. Beneath the many colourful tattoos on the warm brown skin of her face and neck, a sickly pallour showed through. She'd known about Vera's plan almost from the beginning. She'd been smart enough to realise that Ember had been acting differently and had immediately started to badger Rianox. Once Rianox had told her, she was sworn to secrecy. But without knowing the whole story now, she was suffering more than any of them. Poor Amber. She believed it was her fault that Eishoxa had left, when in fact Eishoxa's departure was because of him and Ember and what they'd done to Rush. Amber only knew that once again she had lost her best friend and had stood by while Eishoxa was repeatedly lied to. The events of the past few weeks had taken their toll on her, who had been once so full of life. Rianox sighed, sitting down beside her. "Amber, I have something to tell you."

She forced a smile. "What is it, Rianox?"

"I know why Eishoxa left, and it isn't because of what you think. But if I tell you, you cannot let anyone know that you know. This information is supposed to be strictly between me, Ember and Vera."

"I wouldn't tell anyone. You know that." Rianox shook his head. "No matter how shocking you think it is, you can't tell anyone. Your word, Amber?" She narrowed her eyes at him. "Your word," he repeated. "Otherwise I cannot tell you. I promised Vera."

Amber nodded. "My word."

Rianox revealed what had happened in the forest, how Ember had killed Rush, and that Eishoxa had left because she couldn't bear to be with them anymore. As he spoke, Amber's eyes never left his face.

"You didn't tell me," she said when he had finished. Rianox shook his head. She stood up, moving away from him. "I thought it was my fault. I blamed myself. I thought you and Ember hated each other. I thought …" She trailed off. Rianox again shook his head, standing to.

"We don't hate each other. It's more …" He also couldn't find the words. Amber suddenly slapped him across the face with all her strength. Rianox did nothing. "I'm sorry," he said.

"Ember I can imagine doing that," Amber began. "Ember has it in him. But you? You who know what it's like to be punished for something that you can't help, to be hurt for it." Her eyes moved down to look at his scar, and he nodded. His face was burning from her hand.

"She was your friend. She trusted you! You know she did! You know you were someone she loved, that from her you had everything you wanted! And you turned on her! Like an animal! Like a half-breed!" He sat there, numb. Angrily she shoved him away from her.

"I trusted you! I thought we told each other everything! I thought you trusted me! How could you let me suffer like that?"

"Vera made me promise." Even as he said it, he knew his excuse was inadequate.

"Vera is a traitor against her people and her Goddess. Why would you trust her? Why would you follow her?" Amber made to leave the room, but Rianox grabbed her arm.

"You promised you wouldn't tell anyone else." She gave him a look of contempt but he held onto her arm. "You gave your word, Amber. You promised."

"A promise like that shouldn't be kept," she spat. "Unlike yours, my honour is not surface-deep. Yes, I'll keep your dirty secret, but I shall go to war. I shall go – and if I die, then you'll die too. After what we've done to her, we all deserve to die."

CHAPTER 6

FROM THEN ON, Eishoxa saw very little of Nezrax. All day, every day, she would spend training. And the more time she spent there, the more she came to both fear and to make her mark in this place. Mercy was unknown here. Murder, like that of the young Indocani, was not infrequent. She focused her energy on archery, unwilling to engage in a duel until she was stronger. She suspected that Nezrax had told the soldiers to leave her for a while, but she knew her day was coming. Even without duelling, Eishoxa went to bed every night with new cuts and bruises. They did not train warriors here, they trained murderers, who pushed their bodies to breaking point every day; if they couldn't do it, they were killed. No exceptions. The overseer of the training was a general in the Empty's army called Grimlock. He had clearly been an Indocani before: huge, broad-shouldered and with combat skills that only come from battle training from birth. He ran the training sessions with an iron hand and was even more ruthless than Nezrax. When Eishoxa's day to duel arrived, she was put in the ring with an Empty even smaller than she was. Within a few strong blows, the other Empty had fallen. Eishoxa stepped back and willed her to get up. Sometimes the fights didn't end in a death, although that was rare. If Grimlock thought they had gone on too long, he let both warriors out. The Empty on the ground stood up again and readjusted her helmet. The point of her sharp blade was trembling.

Again Eishoxa took the offensive, and again the other Empty fell. From the corner of her eye she could see Grimlock watching. She noticed her opponent glance towards him as well before looking back at Eishoxa. Eishoxa closed her eyes for a moment and silently begged the other Empty to stay standing. Another fall and she would lose. The fight had barely lasted five minutes. That usually meant death. The third time, the Empty seemed to have more fight in her. But, for the third time, after Eishoxa hit her with the butt of her sword, the Empty fell again. Grimlock stepped into the ring. He looked down at the Empty on the floor as at an insect. Eishoxa moved back, meaning to step out of the ring, but Grimlock stopped her.

"What happened, soldier?" he asked the fallen Empty. She stood and shakily resheathed her sword but didn't answer. Grimlock repeated the question, but again the soldier didn't answer. Grimlock reached out and pulled her sheathed sword out of its scabbard. The Empty froze. Grimlock held the sword out to Eishoxa.

"Death," he said.

Eishoxa did not take the sword. "No," she replied. All activity around them stopped. Grimlock, who'd been looking at the condemned Empty, now turned to stare at Eishoxa. "No?" he asked. "She lost."

"I won't kill her," Eishoxa replied. She had no idea what was prompting her to say such a thing. She cared less about these people than she did about the Indocani. Maybe it was because of the way the Empty's shoulders hunched dejectedly, the way her small body curled in on itself in a pathetic way. Maybe it was because she reminded her of

Maya.

"You won't?" Grimlock asked.

Eishoxa felt a rush of anger. "Yes, are you deaf? I won't!"

A shocked silence fell on the hall. An archer released an arrow, and the thunk as it hit the target was so loud that several Empty jumped. Grimlock looked around. "Respath!" he shouted. "Where is Respath?" The crowd parted and an Empty walked through. He was much taller than Eishoxa and much stronger. Grimlock struck the defeated, fearful Empty in the chest and she flew out of the ring to land crumpled on the floor.

"Respath, you will fight Eishoxa, and whoever falls first will lose. And die." Eishoxa drew her sword again. Maybe this was it then. Respath held his sword at the ready. Eishoxa waited. She never made the first move. She held her weapon with both hands. The blade gleamed. There was not a sound in the training room.

"Go!" shouted Grimlock. Respath stepped forward hurriedly, aiming a sloppy hit which Eishoxa sidestepped. But that was the extent of Respath's misjudgements. He pivoted on one foot and aimed again, this time at her head. She narrowly avoided his blade. Again he struck, and whenever their swords met, Eishoxa knew that she couldn't win. His every blow sent violent shudders down her arms, whereas he barely moved. She had neither the strength nor the will to beat him. She found herself kneeling on the ground.   Grimlock, who'd been leaning on his sword, straightened.

"Kill her," he ordered. Respath paused before raising his sword. Then he hesitated again.

"Are you a coward like her?" Grimlock jeered. He pointed his own sword at Respath. "Kill her or I will kill you."

Eishoxa looked up at Respath. He seemed to harden his resolve. But before he could move, another voice said, "Stop."

Everyone turned to see Nezrax leaning against the wall near the door of the training room. Eishoxa wondered how long she'd been there. The crowd parted again to let her through and she climbed up into the ring.

"What happened?" she asked, looking down at the kneeling Eishoxa. Grimlock stepped forward. "This one fought," he growled, kicking Eishoxa in the side, "and she won, but—"

"But she wouldn't kill," Nezrax interrupted him. Grimlock nodded.

"Get up," she said to Eishoxa. Respath stepped back and lowered his sword.

"Why not?" Nezrax asked. Eishoxa sheathed her sword and replied very clearly. "I didn't come here to learn how to kill. I came for a different purpose." Nezrax raised her eyebrows. "And what about in the battle you so deeply desire? Would you kill then?"

"In battle, I do not kill those who are my allies," Eishoxa replied. She knew that she was taking a risk, that behind Nezrax's smiles and small, graceful movements there hid an ancient being who was incapable of either mercy or remorse. But still, if Eishoxa was going to die, she was determined to die as herself, whoever that might be.

"Your allies?" Nezrax repeated. Eishoxa nodded once. Nezrax rubbed her hands together thoughtfully. "Good." She pointed to the fallen Empty, who was now stirring feebly.

"Grimlock, take her to the Pit." Grimlock jumped down off the platform, slung the Empty over one shoulder and departed. "The rest of you, carry on. Eishoxa, come with me."

Eishoxa followed the Goddess back to the Star Hall. Nezrax sat on her chair and kicked a stool towards Eishoxa. "Sit." When she had, Nezrax leaned forward on her chair. "Are you happy being here? And I want the truth."

Eishoxa had started to say yes but then changed her mind. "No."

"I thought so. But that's all right. For the same reason you came here, you will not leave."

"What do you mean?" Eishoxa asked.

Nezrax looked down at her in surprise. "It's obvious, isn't it? You had nowhere else to go." Eishoxa bowed her head. It was true. She'd only come here because she wanted to return to Bareth. Returning to any other place was unthinkable. Nezrax continued, "But you don't like our rules, and Grimlock won't stand for anymore disobedience. Neither will I." Eishoxa lifted her head. Nezrax's eyes were smouldering, as they had when she'd shown Eishoxa how to open Hell.

"I've brought you into my castle and I expect respect from you. You will not disobey anymore, is that clear? Or I will treat you like any other soldier." Eishoxa nodded, her nails digging into her palm. Nezrax sighed. "I'm going to take responsibility for your combat training. You've been in the hands of the Indocani too long and they've all but ruined you."

"I would be honoured," Eishoxa replied.

"And when you're strong enough to beat me, then we can go to war. Do you understand?" Eishoxa looked up. The shadows were reawakening in her mind and her head stung with the absence of good. She had invited darkness into herself and now she had to use it – otherwise it would destroy her.

"I understand," she replied.

If training under Grimlock had been hard, training under Nezrax was worse. Grimlock had hundreds of Empty to train, Nezrax only one. The Goddess never seemed to have anything better to do either. Any semblance of sympathy and toleration had disappeared. Nezrax was all taunts and jeers and mockery whenever Eishoxa couldn't meet her demands. In the Star Hall, from dawn till dusk, she had no break, until Eishoxa was convinced that Nezrax would kill her, given the chance. This must be some sort of punishment, or at least a test. The first day was the worst, but each day thereafter never seemed to get any better. Nezrax was malicious and cunning in her duelling, leading Eishoxa on one pattern before completely changing in one smooth move.

After a week of training, having knocked Eishoxa over again with a sweep kick under her feet, Nezrax said, "Tell me, Eishoxa, are you in fact even trying? Because in all my many years, I've not seen such a poor warrior."

Eishoxa stood up again. The last fall had winded her, and she was bleeding from a cut over one eye.

"I am trying," she answered, holding her sword up again.

"Then why aren't you getting any better?" Nezrax enquired, moving her sword so fast it was almost a blur. "You're almost as weak as the Peacemakers." Eishoxa gripped her sword harder and focused on Nezrax's blade, not her words. Crash, crash, crash. Blade met blade, not skin. Then Nezrax spun on one foot and her sword sliced down Eishoxa's arm. Blood seeped down her leather arm protector.

"Almost as weak as him," Nezrax taunted. Nezrax's blade swept past her legs, nicking her knees and sending her down. "What was his name – Rush, was it?" Eishoxa froze. The Star Hall disappeared around her and she was once more in the Dragon Forest, watching powerless as Rush died. Ember was laughing manically, but then it was Nezrax chuckling. Eishoxa scrambled to her feet again. In her head, Ember's jeering continued but his voice drove her on. When Nezrax's blade met hers, they locked together.

"Don't you dare say a word against him!" Eishoxa yelled. "He was braver than you'll ever be!" Nezrax threw Eishoxa's blade off hers and feigned to the left before bringing her sword around to the right.

"Was he?" she replied with a laugh. Eishoxa's arm stung where Nezrax's blade had pierced her skin, and the wound above her eye started to trickle again.

"Yes!" She wouldn't hear a word against Rush, not one. If he'd been alive, she would never have come here. If he'd been alive, they would have run away together, to the Guardian, to safety. Nezrax pulled Eishoxa past her and she struggled to keep her footing. Nezrax advanced on her, speaking very quietly, "But tell me, did he teach you anything? Anything worth keeping?"

"He taught me a lot," Eishoxa retorted. "More than all your lessons ever could."

Nezrax's eyes narrowed dangerously. "How to be weak, you mean?" At this, a huge tug pulled at Eishoxa's insides. Lightning forked down from the ceiling, catching Nezrax by surprise and knocking her back.

"No," Eishoxa whispered to herself. "He tried to teach me how to forgive. And I failed him." She raised her hand to the ceiling and blasted Nezrax again with a bolt of lightning. The Goddess flew backwards and landed on the floor. A scorch mark ran down the centre of her dress. Eishoxa gripped her sword tightly and strode towards her.

The Goddess was already on her feet. Then she started to laugh. "That's what we're looking for. Good, Eishoxa." Nezrax set her sword on her chair. "I think that's enough for today. Walk with me now. There's something I want to speak to you about." Eishoxa sheathed her sword and followed Nezrax out of the hall.

"You are talented now, in mind, magic and strength. I have been training you to the standard of a Goddess like myself, and you'll find other opponents to be easy. But you cannot achieve your full strength in the state you're currently in."

Eishoxa frowned in puzzlement. "What do you mean?"

"There is a weakness in you that, no matter how hard you try, will not disappear. It is what the Indocani and Ewdicani call goodness. You have strength about your heart and mind now, but it is not strong enough. And so I'll make you an offer. You may Change and truly become one of us."

"Why is that necessary?"

Nezrax nodded. "I see that you've heard others speak of it. You know then that until you remove your human state completely, you cannot achieve your full powers. I assure you, once you achieve your full powers, no force on earth will be able to stop you."

"But what if I am not meant to be one of you?"

Nezrax continued smoothly, "You have to agree that it makes sense. You've already agreed that you're not any of the other races. I heard you say that to the Ewdicani."

"Did you hear everything I said to Rush?" Eishoxa asked.

"I don't listen in, but my spirit exists in every crow you see, and what a crow hears, I hear. I live in every creature that can feel power."

"Evil, you mean," Eishoxa replied bluntly. Nezrax shrugged. "If you think the little mice that scurry around your Dragon Forest are evil ..."

"No," Eishoxa replied. "But there's a hierarchy, even among mice. And every mouse wants to be at the top of it. They want to feel power and strength. And if a creature has that desire, I may exist through them."

"So you can listen to everything." Nezrax smiled but didn't answer the question. "What do you think about my offer?"

"I need to think about it," Eishoxa decided. To Change meant to give up everything she was, everything she had, to an evil that would not let her rest until she had destroyed all good in the world. But she didn't want to do that. She just wanted to destroy the Indocani.

"Can I think about it?" Eishoxa asked. "I didn't come here with that in mind."

"You still think us evil, do you not?" Nezrax asked knowingly.

"That is what you are."

"It's true, then, as I suspected. You are only using us for what you want," Nezrax concluded. They approached a window and looked down over the other side of the castle. On this side, there were only mountains, stretching as far as the eye could see, and a sunset that was hidden by the black peaks.

"You are using me," Eishoxa replied.

"Oh, of course we are," Nezrax admitted. "But that is war. And every person is a piece in the game, a game that only the masters may play."

"And you are a master?" Eishoxa asked, staring over the black peaks.

"You are as well," Nezrax replied. "You choose where to go, you change your ideas, and whenever someone thinks that they have finally understood you, you evolve again and become a new person. Only the strongest can be masters, the cleverest, the most cunning, the bravest, the best. It doesn't matter how you define those words. They all mean something different for each person ... think about my offer,

Eishoxa." There was a rush of wind, and when Eishoxa looked to her right, Nezrax was gone.

CHAPTER 7

S HE WALKED BACK to her room, deep in thought about Nezrax's
Swords. She remembered what Rianox had said: that once upon a
time, Nezrax had been good and was doted upon by her sisters and
father. Her sisters had given her power over the Rock, even though
they hadn't wanted to, simply because she'd asked for it. She'd been
the little favoured one, the sweetheart sister. Nezrax moved with
assurance, with a confidence that Eishoxa recognised on her own face
in the mirrors at Bareth. The confidence that comes from being loved,
no matter what you've done; from knowing that someone holds
you in great affection. And the evil that drove Nezrax now came not
from her own heart, but from an evil that had grown throughout the
world, feeding on greedy thoughts and taking over the hearts of so
many people, even a Goddess.

Eishoxa opened her door and sensed, rather than heard, something
behind her. She raised her hand and caught the candlestick that was
about to crash onto her head. She wrenched it from the attacker's
hands and threw it across the room. Then she turned and faced a
young Empty, whose face was twisted and snarling.

"What are you doing here?" Eishoxa demanded. The Empty lunged
forward and seized Eishoxa's knife from her belt. In the same moment
Eishoxa drew her sword and held the Empty at bay.

"To hear you justify your actions." Eishoxa lowered her sword slightly. She suddenly recognised the voice of this girl. It was the Empty
she'd defeated, whom Grimlock had ordered her to kill.

"Justify them?" Eishoxa asked. "I let you live!"

"I wanted you to kill me!" the Empty snarled. "You should have
killed me! I wanted to die!" Eishoxa looked closer at the girl. The black
skin had started to peel away, revealing the white skin of the Ewdicani
underneath.

"You were one of the Peacemakers," Eishoxa said quietly. The girl
shuddered and suddenly leapt forward again, not towards Eishoxa
but towards the window. "You were, weren't you?"

"Yes," the girl said.

"Why did you come to this place?" Eishoxa asked.

The girl backed away against the window. "Why didn't you kill me?
I wanted to die."

"I will not kill those in my army," Eishoxa replied. "I will not kill my
allies. I came here with another purpose."

"Then you're a fool," the girl hissed. She stepped up onto the windowsill. Eishoxa took another step towards her.

"What are you doing?"

"What does it look like? I'm defying Nezrax in the only way I can."
She was gabbling now, the words pouring from her mouth. Eishoxa
could barely make sense of them.

"I came here only because of her. She came to me in dreams and
spoke in my head. Gresceva is a witch. Everyone knows it. She acts
like a great leader but she isn't. And Nezrax told me that I could fol-

low her and that everything would be better. But I didn't know who she was. I didn't know what it would mean. I gave up everything and I've gained nothing." Eishoxa could only listen. She had no words of comfort; the story was too similar to her own. "And I agreed and I've ended up here. I've given up everything, Eishoxa. And I tried to lose. I wanted to die. Because dying is the only way out of here."

"She put you in the Pit, didn't she?" The girl wailed and Eishoxa jumped. Her screech sounded as though it should come from the throat of an animal, not a person. "She put me in Hell! That's what the Pit is – Hell!" The girl leaned back further out of the window, holding onto the side with one hand and pointing the knife at Eishoxa.

"You won't harm her by doing this," Eishoxa said. "Nezrax has thousands of soldiers. All you'll achieve is your own death. You don't matter to her enough."

"But you do, don't you?" the girl answered. She stepped forward again. In the other hand appeared a ball of black magic.

"Do you know what they call this?" the girl asked. "Sweet death. Because death is the only way out. My death won't mean anything to her, but yours will." She raised her hand.

"Throw," Eishoxa replied. "Throw and take me with you."

"You didn't kill me," the girl said desperately again. "You let me live."

"It wasn't your time to die," Eishoxa replied. She didn't dare go closer to the girl in case she let go of the window. But at the same time, she was desperately thinking of a way to save her. The girl was speaking again.

"But if I leave you here, you'll suffer as much as I did. And that seems fair, doesn't it, Eishoxa." She looked out over the edge of the window. "Wella won't take me back, but at least I won't be with Nezrax."

"Don't—" Eishoxa began, but the girl had thrown the knife at her and Eishoxa had to dodge to avoid it. But in the moment that she dodged, the girl had jumped. Eishoxa ran to the window and looked down. The girl was falling, falling, falling. And as she did, as she fell, Eishoxa saw another girl fall away from her, carried away by wind or magic. Another girl, with white skin the colour of snow and pale hair that draped around her face. Eishoxa looked away as the girl landed, but when she looked again it wasn't an Empty who lay there, nor an Ewdicani. It was everyone she had left, everyone she had failed, lying there broken. She picked up the candlestick the girl had held. She recognised it as an Ewdicani one. Eishoxa wondered how she'd managed to bring it, why it hadn't been taken from her. Eishoxa hid it under her bed and wondered what was going to happen to her.

The following day, two Indocani scouts were captured on the Sorrowful Mountains. They'd been part of an ambush that had attacked a group of Empty returning to the castle. Eishoxa suspected that they had come for her. She was called to the Star Hall.

"Did you know about this?" Nezrax demanded. The cloud around her feet was roiling furiously, to match the temper of the Goddess.

Eishoxa shook her head. "Not at all. I knew nothing about it."

The Goddess reflected a moment. "I believe you … But the ones we've captured will taste my fury. They will indeed," she added darkly. "And you will watch and learn what happens when I'm angry. My sisters think they can get past me – but no, I refuse to let them this time."

Nezrax clapped her hands three times and the doors to the Star Hall opened. In came two pairs of Empty, each dragging an unconscious Indocani. Nezrax waved two of the four Empty away. The other two lifted the Indocani onto their knees over the symbol of the Pentelement. Nezrax crouched beside them and placed a hand on their foreheads. "Watch, Eishoxa."

A little oval appeared above each of the Indocani's heads, showing their minds. They were stirring now; Nezrax had awakened them. Eishoxa was fascinated at the sight of the ovals, which were completely full of the little balls of light. They were pure Indocani – they'd given their whole existence to Fire. Nezrax looked from one to the other.

"Are there other scouts on my mountains?" Nezrax asked them. "What else have your people sent me, apart from the two of you?" Neither answered. "Speak!" she shouted. She turned the face of one of them towards her. "I will have my answers, whether I take them from you or find them out myself." She let his chin go and he lowered his head again. "They have opted for silence," Nezrax said slowly. "I've always admired this." The other Indocani's eyes lifted and landed on Eishoxa. "What have you done to her? She's mindless!" he demanded. Nezrax followed his gaze. "To Eishoxa? Nothing. She has chosen her own path." Both Indocani now stared at Eishoxa. She held their gaze for a moment and then looked away. The accusation in their eyes was too much to bear. Nezrax stamped her foot and the two Indocani were forced to look at her again.

"I now give you a choice. You may join my army or suffer the punishment that befits your crime." Eishoxa wondered what Nezrax wanted to do. One Indocani looked at her as if appealing for help, but Eishoxa was silent. They must have known that she would make no sound, that she could not help them. Then, at Nezrax's unspoken command, the two heads of the Indocani hung. Their backs stiffened and they were pulled up straight. The little balls of light drifting in their minds moved faster and faster, then a humming sound began and the edges of the ovals started to blur. Nezrax made a slicing motion through the air and the Indocani nearest to her slumped over and lay still. Eishoxa saw that Nezrax held the tiniest of daggers. The oval above that one was cut in two. The Indocani appeared dead, but then he twitched. Nezrax held the dagger out to Eishoxa. "The other one," she said. "Do not disobey me again. Do it." Eishoxa took the dagger and stepped in front of the other one. She raised her arm but found that she had to close her eyes. She brought her arm down through the air and heard the Indocani fall. Nezrax took the dagger back. She nodded to the two Empty. "You know where to put them." The two guards dragged their charges out of the Hall. Nezrax turned to Eishoxa. "I didn't think you would do it."

"Neither did I ... he called me mindless," Eishoxa said slowly. "What did he mean?" Nezrax stepped towards her and placed a hand on her forehead. When her skin made contact, Eishoxa could feel all the shadows writhing around in her mind. She shuddered.

"Look," Nezrax said. Eishoxa looked up and saw her mind's oval with its writhing shadows. "Touch it," Nezrax said. Eishoxa drew her hand through the oval over her head. "What do you not feel?" Nezrax asked.

"I can't feel it in my head," Eishoxa realised, repeating the action over and over. Nezrax stopped her hand in mid-air. "Exactly. You've put barriers around it, shut it down."

"Shut it down?" Eishoxa asked.

Nezrax nodded. "Have you felt fear recently? Remorse? Have you felt anything?" Eishoxa slowly shook her head. Nezrax smiled. "Exactly. And what causes weakness – of any sort?" Eishoxa looked at her blankly.

"Emotion," Nezrax explained. "We who know this separate ourselves from emotion so that we're not affected by it. That is what you've done."

"So I'll never feel anything again – ever?" Eishoxa asked.

"Is there a problem with that?" Nezrax countered. "Is that not what you want?" Eishoxa wanted to shake her head but took another look at Nezrax's face and thought better of it. "Yes," she said quietly. "There's no problem."

Nezrax smiled again. "I think we're ready to go to war."

CHAPTER 8

AMBER WAS RUNNING through the Dragon Forest. She hadn't run like this in a long time. She kept her gaze forward, weaving her way through the trees and along the uneven ground. She had memorised this forest as a child, running through it with her brother and best friend. At the thought of the Eishoxa, a pain pulsed in her stomach. She was sick to the core at what Ember and Rianox had done. She couldn't believe that Rianox was capable of something so foul. Ember, maybe. She'd seen him in many different states and had watched him through the years when Eishoxa hadn't been with them; had watched as sorrow and loss turned his natural pride to arrogance, his strength to cruelty; and she, against her better judgement, had praised him for it, unwilling to tell him that if Eishoxa returned, he would be unrecognisable. There was nothing to be done about that. Once he started slipping, nothing would have held him back. But Rianox, sweet, careful Rianox, the one who found delight in boring her with something he had found, in sitting peacefully and calmly, who spoke passionately about the most mundane things – him? She could not believe it. He had changed. They had both changed. She had lost a brother and two friends. The brother who had advised her and comforted her, the friend she had laughed at and argued with, and the friend that she had been in awe of, had cherished like an irreplaceable treasure. She had lost everything.

Amber stopped running and looked around. There wasn't a place in this forest she didn't know. Ahead, the forest continued. She moved forward and quickened her pace, lengthening her stride, stretching her legs. The ground cleared a bit here; there were fewer burnt stumps and broken trees. On and on she ran. Suddenly she realised that something about the forest she had passed was different. The land here was supposed to be relatively flat, so what had that bulge in the ground been, noticeably green against the blackened leaves? She doubled back. Taking her bow, which she always carried with her, from her shoulder, she slid an arrow carefully into it before creeping towards the bulge. The trees grew here, tall and strong. It was probably the only place the dragons hadn't destroyed yet. The forest felt normal, filled with the usual sounds of life, not silent. But as she moved towards the mound, she felt the atmosphere change. Despite an inward shudder she carried on, her curiosity urging her forward. When she reached it she saw a mound of brambles and bark, perfectly formed. Green stems poked through gaps, its shoots searching for light, and although there was no source of water here or anywhere else in Sicharenhafan, the flowers were healthy and beautifully coloured. Amber crouched down beside the mound and laid her hand on top. Immediately, she withdrew it. It was damp and the water had seared her skin. She backed away, but not before she'd seen the word carved into the top of the mound. Rush. Amber said the word to herself, listening to the unfamiliar sound of it on her tongue. Then she realised where she'd heard that word, what this mound was. It was a coffin. A coffin for the Ewdicani Ember had killed. Rianox himself had told her that. Amber stumbled backwards in horror at the realisation. Then she noticed something else. The bark was cracked neatly along one edge. This was not the mark of an animal tearing into it for food. Nor was it the mark of someone trying to break out from the inside. This was a calculated cut, the mark of someone who knew what was in there and had opened the coffin and removed the body. Amber stepped closer but immediately hopped back with a sound of pain. The ground was soaked through. She took an arrow from her quiver and lodged it in the crack in the bark, levering open the mound. There was nothing. It was simply an empty coffin. She made a quick decision, left the coffin open, and tore off back to the Tree. She found the person she was looking for almost immediately. "Come with me," she said breathlessly to Rianox. "There's something you have to see." Amber led Rianox back to the coffin. "He's gone," she said. She put her hand on his arm as he took a step towards the damp ground, but immediately withdrew it. He paused and then looked around.

"He won't have gone far. We need to find him," he decided.

"You mean he's alive?" Amber asked uncertainly.

"He's no longer in this coffin," Rianox pointed out. "And the ground is wet. I expect we'll find him. We need to look around."

"Shouldn't we tell someone?" she asked. "I mean, this can't be a good sign."

"Who do you suggest we ask?" Rianox enquired. "Ember? Do you want to see this Ewdicani die again? And, I assure you, Ember will not put him back in his coffin."

Amber accepted this. "Where would he be?" she asked, looking around, but Rianox didn't answer. She turned to look at him and saw what had caught his attention. A figure had appeared as if from nowhere and was looking blankly about. With white skin and blue eyes, he could not have looked more out of place in this forest of dragons. He was dressed in long white robes and had a celestial look about him. His feet were bare.

"Who am I?" he asked and his voice was low and musical.

Rianox stepped forward and held his hands out, as if to show he was unarmed.

"Your name is Rush," he said. "I can't believe you're alive."

CHAPTER 9

NEZRAX WALKED OUT onto the battlement of the castle with Eishoxa at her side. The Empty had all gathered in the massive courtyard below and, looking down at them, Eishoxa knew that even with the Indocani and Ewdicani joined together, there wasn't a fighting force on earth as large as this one. Every warrior in the Indocani's army would be outnumbered ten to one, even twenty to one. The Warrior race, no matter how strong and brave, didn't stand a chance.

The Empty had cheered and shouted as Eishoxa and Nezrax made their appearance but fell silent the moment the Goddess lifted her arms. She took Eishoxa by the wrist and raised her arm into the air.

"This is Eishoxa, daughter of my sister and enemy Fiera, Goddess of Fire!" Nezrax's voice was carried on the wind, and Eishoxa knew that every last Empty in the courtyard could hear her. "She has proved to be stronger than her weak-minded kin. She has joined us with the same purpose in her heart that every last one of you joined us for. She believes what we believe: that the Warriors and the Peacemakers are our enemy!" Another cheer greeted her words. When the noise subsided she spoke again. "We have learnt that there are enemy scouts hiding in our mountains, spying on us. One of those very scouts revealed our plans to the Indocani, who ambushed a group of our soldiers. They all fought bravely and we captured two of the ambushers. They have been dealt with according to the severity of their crime. And now, Eishoxa will lead our army into war alongside our generals! So prepare yourselves, my people, and we will not lose!" A deafening roar rose from the ranks, vibrating through the mountains, echoing along the black rocks until hundreds of roars resounded. Nezrax took Eishoxa back inside the castle.

"Are they strong enough?" Nezrax asked her.

Eishoxa nodded. "Definitely. As soon as the Indocani approach, we attack. And then I will have my revenge."

The Empty were prepared for battle within a couple of days. Their spies had been watching the Tree for a long time, and when they saw the first signs of movement towards the Sorrowful Mountains, it took them very little time to ready their troops. When the order came, Eishoxa prepared herself. She slung her bow over her back and placed several long, sharp knives into her belt. She strapped her scabbard around her waist and slid the sword inside. She was ready to take whatever came her way. She stood by her window and looked out. There was always a gray light here. Gray days and black nights. The huge drawbridge was being let down. In all her time there, she had not seen it open. The great chains were creaking and groaning, loud enough to be heard over the noise in the courtyard. It landed with a crash on the other side.

Orders were being shouted on both sides of the courtyard. Giant catapults were being pulled towards the open drawbridge by monstrous creatures made from rock and metal – Nezrax's creations. Other machines were pulled out, made from wood and metal and rope. Diabolical inventions that shot arrows and hurled burning balls of straw and rocks. They all came.

On the plain in front of the black stone castle, the Empty were preparing for battle. They carried knives and swords and bows. They wielded sharp scythes and spiked maces and clubs – every type of weapon imaginable. And the helmet of each soldier, man or woman, bore one image: the face of Nezrax. The Empty rode on their own drakons, creatures made from black magic. They dragged catapults and carried mountains of rocks. Eishoxa looked out of the window and tried to feel something. Revenge, satisfaction, the tiniest inkling of remorse. Nothing. Not one emotion graced her. She tightened her belt and fastened her jacket around her. She wasn't wearing the same armour as the Empty. She wore what she wore every day, the tight black snakeskin clothes, spiked on the shoulders, arms and legs. She had fastened thick material around her shins and forearms.

Descending the steps, she walked out of the castle and stood next to the generals who were watching the troops get ready for battle. Her own drakon was ready. It had no name. It didn't need a name. As soon as she swung herself onto the saddle, the other generals mounted as well. There was a loud boom from inside the castle and people momentarily stopped what they were doing. Everyone but Eishoxa turned to see Nezrax soar out of her castle. She was dressed normally and carried no weapons, but Eishoxa could see the magic around her, the spirits of darkness that followed her and the key around her neck that could unlock the gates of Hell.

The troops had assembled themselves into battalions. Those flying on drakons were at the back, ready to soar into the sky at the first command. The catapults and other machines were ahead of them, pulled by Nezrax's creations of rock, huge animals with pointed horns and vicious teeth. Then came those on foot, armed with every kind of weapon. Eishoxa readied her mount and looked at Nezrax.

One of the generals asked her, "Are you going to say anything?" Eishoxa paused for a moment. "No," she said. "There's nothing to say."

"We're not taking prisoners?" another asked. She turned around to look at the general who had spoken. "No," she said. She kicked her drakon hard in the ribs and it roared. Answering howls shook the ancient stones around them. They were unstoppable. They were unconquerable. The Indocani didn't stand a chance. Eishoxa soared into the sky and felt her generals surround her. She was leading an army into battle, just as she had before. And this time, she wouldn't lose.

They left the Sorrowful Mountains and arrived at the place which the Indocani called the Plain of Despair. This was what their enemy would have to cross to get to them. Eishoxa ordered her soldiers to set up the field and await her commands. She flew high above her army, accompanied by her generals, watching and waiting for Indocani to come.

They did not have to wait long. Eishoxa saw the dragons first, flying up over the top of a hill, closely followed by the ranks of Indocani. Even from here she could sense their fear. It tainted the air like a foul cloud, and she felt her mount shift as it smelt it too. Let them be afraid. They should be afraid. There were many of them, far more than she'd seen at the Tree.

"Look," sneered one of the generals from behind her. "They've brought the Ewdicani with them." He was right. Eishoxa could pick out the pale white faces amongst them. But they must have brought all their people to have so many there. She wrenched her drakon's head around and faced the generals.

"We will have one more meeting with Nezrax before we attack."

"We do not attack straight away?"

"We're outnumbered," Eishoxa snapped. "By a lot."

"You underestimated them?" one asked. Eishoxa looked at the who had spoken – Respath.

"No. I've not underestimated them. They've underestimated me! Be prepared – I'm not planning to let them win." That seemed to be enough for them, and they flew back towards the ground. At the rear of the troops a tent had been set up for them. Eishoxa slid off her drakon and entered the tent, followed by her generals. Nezrax was already inside.

"They are here," Eishoxa said to Nezrax, sitting down beside her.

A thin smile curled her lips. "How many?"

"More than we are," Eishoxa admitted.

"Too many?" Nezrax asked.

"No," Eishoxa said with conviction.

"How will you attack?" Nezrax asked. Eishoxa nodded to her generals to speak. Grimlock, whom she'd chosen as second-in-command only on Nezrax's order, answered.

"We will attack from the air using the drakons. The catapults will follow immediately. We won't risk our foot soldiers until the enemy have been reduced in number and strength. They've brought the Ewdicani with them."

"So they are desperate," Nezrax mused. "This should be easy." She fingered the key around her neck. "Eishoxa, what are you planning to do?"

Eishoxa lifted her head. "You will see."

"Are you not planning to fight?" a general asked Nezrax.

"You have Eishoxa. I will be there, but I have other business to attend to." Nezrax smiled, then nodded at Eishoxa. "You've come a long way from the weak little girl standing on a mountaintop," she remarked.

"I'm not that girl anymore," Eishoxa replied. "I won't let any of them get away. They'll be taught their own lesson."

"And what is that?" Nezrax asked. Eishoxa drew her sword. It ignited with black flames that moved up and down the blade. "That there is no good in this world and no mercy, even for those who beg for it."

Eishoxa jumped onto her drakon and took off into the sky. The army that stretched below her was under her command; they would do whatever she said. She turned towards the other army. She could imagine Vera standing there in front of the army, or maybe it was Ember, talking to them, encouraging them. She would do none of that. She wanted this over.

"Drakons!" she shouted. "Attack!" A flock of them rose up into the sky, each one carrying in its claws a massive boulder. One of the generals flew at the front. Eishoxa watched as, over the other army, a cloud of mounted dragons rose into the sky and flew out to meet them. Fire blazed from their mouths and their claws were outstretched. Arrows were being shot from the warriors on their backs, burning arrows that embedded themselves in the sides of her drakons.

"Catapults!" she shouted, and at once black granite missiles flew into the sky. Eishoxa's drakon swerved to avoid one. Dragons and riders were knocked out of the sky. She watched as they fell, wounded and broken, onto the armies below.

"Again!" she commanded, and another onslaught flew across towards the enemy lines. She looked back at her generals, the ones commanding the foot soldiers.

"Now?" they asked.

"Now!" A thunderous yell vibrated through the ranks of waiting Empty, a murderous cry that resounded in the mountains. Then they started marching. The catapults attacked for the third time. Eishoxa forced her drakon forward, flying high above her soldiers, her generals right behind her. When she saw the Indocani lines beneath her, Eishoxa dug her heels into her drakon's shoulder bones and stood up. Taking her bow off her back, she fitted an arrow in place.

"Pick off the leaders!" she shouted. Taking aim, she fired. Her drakon flew even lower and she could see the upturned faces of the Indocani. Some of them looked so young. Their faces knew a fear that not even she thought they should know at that age. She remembered the book that she'd seen with Rush, the book that showed the death and blood and terrible fury of war. That was a long time ago. Rush had met death at their hands. They would meet death at hers. She soared over their ranks. There were more than she'd anticipated, but not too many to deal with. She took aim again and again and again. She never missed. But her drakon met death from below. A single arrow felled it, taking them both to the ground. Eishoxa slung her bow over her back and drew her sword. These people were the ones she had laughed with. One dead. Two dead. These people were the ones she had fought alongside. Three dead. Four dead. These people were the ones who had betrayed her. Five dead. Six dead. They wouldn't even know what had hit them.

Fire coursed through the air and snaked along the ground as the Indocani cast their spells. It sped its way through the ranks and burnt the catapults. They crumbled into dust. But as they did so, the monsters that pulled them, the monsters made from chains and rock, lumbered towards the enemy ranks, ploughing through them, throwing them to either side like rag dolls.

"Attack with the drakons!" Eishoxa called. "Keep to the sky!" Something seized her arm and dragged her away from the fighting. She whirled around, but the hand had let go of her as quickly as it had come. It was Ember, looking definitely the worse for wear. She could see where she'd injured him and, from the way he held his sword, he was still in much pain.

"These people are your friends! What are you doing?" he demanded. Eishoxa held her blade before her, a barrier between them. It was a curiously beautiful object, but twisted with the evil that had made it and on which it thrived. In her hands – hands that longed for revenge – it glowed with a violent light. At the sight of it, Eishoxa's heart hardened again. "They are not my friends!" she yelled, spinning on one foot and aiming for Ember's throat. "They lied to me and used me! They are the evil ones!"

Ember, deflecting her sword, was on the defensive, but nevertheless each of his blows shook Eishoxa. Her hands were trembling like dead leaves.

"And what are the Empty doing now?" he asked. "Are they telling you the truth? They are murderers!"

"So are you! I know they're bad, but they keep it in the open. They're not ashamed of their faults."

"Of course they're not ashamed!" He pushed her sword away and, summoning his magic, paralysed her mind with an almighty effort. Unable to move, she could only stand there, helpless before him once again.

"How do you know yourself, when you can't even understand other people?" he asked. "They may have taught you how to control all the elements, but you're still weak! Look at you!" She was stronger than him and he could not hold her for long. Wrenching herself away from him, she held her sword before her. She was so furious the blade was shaking in her hand.

"You destroyed my city. You killed my best friend. You lied to me and led me into trap after trap! I trusted you again! I didn't have to! You killed Rush!" At her last accusation he reeled back and Eishoxa struck again. Reaching down into the black magic that simmered inside her, she sent a giant wave of cold energy at him, a ball of icy wind that blew him back. Advancing on him, she hissed, "I may have loved you once, but that person is long gone. Now, go back and watch as your people die – and learn what power is." She raised her hand. Lightning forked down from the sky and rain poured from the heavens. She sent Ember back in a torrent of driving rain. "Everything I do now," she whispered to herself, "is because of what they have done to me."

She walked out again onto the battlefield. With her sword held high, a whispered word called down lightning and thunder, rain and hail. Fire and rocks answered her call, destroying hundreds below, both friend and foe. Around her, Indocani and Ewdicani were dying. Eishoxa watched emotionless as they fell to the ground, crying and screaming.

She witnessed terrible things, yet did not react. She watched as her hand rose of its own accord and summoned the stone giants, misshapen creations made from rock, that emerged from the mountains wielding huge stone clubs. She looked on as they crashed through the ranks, sweeping Indocani, Ewdicani and Empty alike, through the air and onto the rocks. She ran across the field and jumped onto the back of an abandoned drakon. She rose into the air and wheeled around the battlefield, the drakon cawing its unearthly, screeching cry. She watched an Empty take aim, impeccable aim. The arrow wouldn't miss. Her eyes noted the angle of the shaft and she calculated its trajectory to see its intended victim. Amber. Her brave, fierce friend, fighting with the strength of ten soldiers, her sword raised high above her head and a look of hopeless courage on her face. She would meet instant death. Eishoxa watched and did nothing, simply sat there as the Empty released his arrow. It moved as if in slow motion, parting the air with murderous intent; even the wind and rain didn't touch it. She didn't look to see it find its mark.

"Empty – to me!" she yelled, holding her sword high above her head. There was a long cry from the fighting troops. Some jumped onto waiting drakons and some started to run back to their base. She soared back towards the waiting Empty. Looking back, she saw Nezrax's tent burst into black flames. The Goddess flew out of the rubble and high into the air, streaking towards the fleeing Indocani. Eishoxa watched with dreaded fascination, knowing full well what would happen. With another crash of thunder, a blanket of darkness descended from the sky. The five-pointed symbol of the Pentelement emerged from the darkness, strong and powerful. Nezrax circled high above it, conjuring all the destruction below. Taking the key off from around her neck, she started unlocking the gate of Hell. The black cloud beneath her churned and writhed, like hundreds of snakes. The thunder roared still louder. Eishoxa saw the doors open at the centre of the star and felt a deathly cold wind sweep towards her. The Indocani and the Ewdicani from the battlefield were taken up into the cloud amid desperate wailing. Eishoxa watched as Nezrax drew the cloud through the gate and slammed it shut. The field was deserted, except for a few Empty straggling their way back towards them.

Eishoxa stopped the rain and the lightning, and silence reigned. As the Empty army turned back towards the Sorrowful Mountains, Eishoxa saw a few Indocani creep off the field, the only ones who had survived the battle. She wondered for a moment whether anyone she knew was among the survivors.

CHAPTER 10

EMBER STRUGGLED THROUGH the undergrowth, calling out desperately with his mind for Ferac. He'd seen the black dragon caught in the cloud of darkness that Nezrax had made but could still sense him in the back of his mind.

"Ferac! Ferac!" he shouted, crashing through the bushes. Something moved to his left and he spun around to see who it was. "Rianox," he said with a sigh of relief. He took in the scratches and wounds on Rianox's head and arms and knew he didn't look any better.

"With a war, we can get her out quickly, can we?" Rianox asked.

Ember lowered his head. "Rianox, don't do this now."

"Do you know how many soldiers we took to that war?" Rianox asked, his voice a barely controlled whisper.

"Yes."

"Ten thousand. Two thousand Ewdicani and eight thousand Indocani."

"And do you know how many escaped?"

"No."

"Five hundred. Five hundred, Ember. And for what?" Ember didn't have a reply. With a furious yell, Rianox shoved him backwards and he stumbled, falling over.

"You may once have been a great warrior," Rianox said, looking down at him. "But now you're not. And you were mistaken, in many things – to think that Eishoxa was a traitor, to follow whatever Vera said. You know that Vera despises Eishoxa. Yet you took that risk. Five hundred soldiers, Ember! From fifty thousand." He kicked him in the side before walking away. Ember struggled to his feet again and called after him, "Where are you going?"

Rianox stopped in his tracks. "To the castle. I'm going to try to get her out."

"That's a suicide mission," Ember scoffed, limping towards him.

"And that battle wasn't?" Rianox sneered, turning to face him. Ember had no reply to that. But he said, "I'm coming with you."

"You're too slow. You can't." And he started walking on.

"If you don't let me, then I'll follow and we'll both be killed," Ember called out stubbornly. Rianox paused again, weighing up the situation. "All right," he said. "You can come. My dragon is over there."

Ember nodded and the two of them disappeared into the twilight.

A great celebration was underway at the castle. Eishoxa sat at the top of the table next to Nezrax, in the place of honour. The Goddess had taken her key from around her neck and had laid it in her lap. She was stroking it as one might a dog or cat. Eishoxa looked down at her empty plate and goblet. She never drank or ate anything here. She felt the Goddess's gaze turn on her.

"You won a great victory today," the Goddess said in her purring voice. Eishoxa looked at her out of the corner of her eye. Nezrax was smiling. "I'm sure the Indocani are regretting ever giving you up."

"If they are," Eishoxa reflected, "it's for all the wrong reasons."

"I was wondering," Nezrax said, putting her key back over her head. It hung against her pale white skin, a stark difference between the two. "I was wondering," she continued, "whether you'd given any more thought to the offer I made you." Eishoxa stood up so abruptly that her chair fell over. She didn't want to talk about that now. From the battle today, she'd seen what it meant to be one of the Empty, and deep inside she felt sickened to have led an army of such cold-blooded murderers. The last thing she wanted to do was discuss with this she-devil, cunningly disguised in the body of a child, whether or not she was going to join them.

"May I go hunting?" she asked. Nezrax looked up at her in surprise. "Now?" she asked. Eishoxa nodded. There was a momentary lull in the festivities in the hall and Nezrax looked around. "But we're in the middle of celebrating," she said.

"I know. But may I go?"

"Have you given no thought to my offer?" Nezrax asked in disappointment. Eishoxa shrugged. "I've thought about it. But not a lot." Nezrax gave her a piercing glance. Eishoxa kept her eyes widened innocently until Nezrax nodded. "I suppose so. You may keep guard as well."

Eishoxa pushed her chair back under the table and left the Hall. She could feel the eyes of many Empty following her, including Nezrax. She collected her bow from her room and put it over her back along with her quiver of arrows. She let herself out through her window and headed towards the back of the castle.

Once there she looked around, watching for anything to shoot. The Sorrowful Mountains were surprisingly rich in game, but not the sort she usually hunted. The Indocani shot prey; the Empty shot predators. They tracked beasts hunting their prey through the mountains and at the end took both the hunter and the hunted. For a long time, she didn't see anything. The mountains were deserted, empty of all life, and thick clouds blocked the moonlight, not that the moon was very bright over the Sorrowful Mountains.

As she crept along the edge of a sheer drop, lined with scrubby bushes, the castle's giant spotlight was lit to begin its nightly sweepings of the mountains. She could hear the muted sounds of celebrations going on in the castle. From this distance the noises sounded innocent. She could have been back at the Tree. But all Eishoxa had to do was look back to see that this place knew nothing of innocence. The castle cast bizarre shadows on itself; strange patterns danced across its flanks and ran eerily over the tall battlements. She could see the silhouette of a guard up there on the tower, his bow and arrow in sharp relief. It was strange, she reflected. The white skin of the Ewdicani seemed to blend into the dark of night better than the black skin of the Empty. There was a brief rustling from one of the bushes nearby. Eishoxa crouched, hiding in a shadow, and raised her bow, the poisoned tip of the arrow trained steadily on the quivering leaves. For a long time nothing happened. Then she felt something prickling on

322

her scalp. Putting one hand up, she rubbed her head, but the prickling didn't go away. Then she realised it came from inside her head. Her dulled mind was tingling slightly as if she knew this thing hiding in the leaves. Then someone silently crept out. Eishoxa almost dropped her bow in shock. It was Rianox.

She stood up in his sight. For a long time they stared at each other. Eishoxa saw the flare of delighted hope in Rianox's eyes die out to be replaced with disappointment and guarded caution. Eishoxa knew she had changed. From head to toe she wore black, scaly clothes with large protruding spikes. Her face was keener, sharper, crueler, and her eyes had lost their soft golden hue. They no longer glowed from her copper skin.

"Eishoxa?" he asked and she nodded once. He swept his gaze over her once more and said in a tone of defeat, "What has happened to you?" Eishoxa lowered her bow but did not replace the arrow in her quiver. She shrugged, adopting an air of nonchalance. She couldn't forget how he had smiled at her every day and yet had been lying to her all that time

"Does it matter? I changed. I left you. What are you doing here anyway? If anyone else caught you, they would have killed you."

"But they didn't catch me, and you haven't killed me," he pointed out. Eishoxa gave him a cold, hard look. "Don't push your luck. Tell me what you're doing here and then get off our land."

"Our land?" he echoed. Eishoxa nodded slowly, her hand feeling for the small sharp knife she kept at her belt. His eye followed her motion but he said nothing. Instead, he took a step towards her. "I'm here to ask you to come back. Back to where you belong." Eishoxa stepped back. "No. This is where I am now. This is where I belong."

"Here?"

She could hear exasperation in his voice, as if he were explaining something to a child for the hundredth time. He showed no sign of fear even though, as far as Eishoxa could see, he had no weapon at all.

"Yes," she said. "These people have shown me things; they've taught me how to use fire and water, how to control more than just one element. You restrict yourselves but they don't." Some part of her shuddered to hear her voice, but another part – the greater part – was proud.

"They're evil and you're sick to follow them," he replied bluntly. "You've seen what they do and what they've done. That's not strength. That's weakness." Anger rose in Eishoxa's throat and words spilled out of her mouth, fast and furious.

"Don't you dare come here and talk to me about their faults, about what they've done! I haven't forgotten what you've done to me! You lied to me when I gave you all my trust! You told me you were my friend and were secretly planning the destruction of everything I held dear! And when Ember destroyed Bareth, you treated me coldly. You're just as bad as they are! You and all your people!"

The knife was in her hand. She hadn't forgotten how Rianox had held her back when Ember was killing Rush; she hadn't forgotten his careful lies and little smiles to make her trust him; she hadn't forgotten Ember's arrogance or his merciless actions. They were all rotten, rotten to the core. Rianox bowed his head in sadness. "We had no choice. I am sorry. But now I'm here to beg your forgiveness and ask you to return." His words only made Eishoxa's anger flare up even worse than before. "You murdered my friends and family! You destroyed my country! You don't deserve my help. You and all your people deserve to die. Now get off our land or I'll kill you." The bow was raised again and the arrow pointed at his scarred chest. He raised his eyebrows and folded his arms, holding his ground, meeting her eyes with a challenge. "You won't do that," he said. Eishoxa steadied her aim, refusing to listen to what he was saying. "How do you know? How do you know what I'll do?" she challenged. His gaze was level as he met her eyes but his words stung like arrowheads in her heart. "Because you are weak. This is a pitiful cry for help and attention, not a stand to show your bravery, not a way of proving the injustice done to you. You know what you're doing is wrong and yet you do it still. You want to be like them but your heart isn't in it. The magic you do, the Pentelement – all it does is make you weaker. It eats away at anything and everything that's good in you. We've lost many battles recently, today being only one of them, and we've lost many soldiers. Amber is badly wounded and many of your friends are dead. You saw what they did today. How can you still stay with them? How can you still defend them?"

"I'm not doing this for me," she shouted. "This is for everything you've taken away from me."

"Is it?" he asked. He took another step toward her, his eyes burning with an intensity that matched her own. "We've paid for your losses a hundred times over, a thousand even. Your friend is one life, and we've given countless gallons of blood to pay your price. This turning to Nezrax is for you and your selfish, petty revenge. Because if it were for your friend, you'd know – as I know you do now – that she'd have hated it and you would stop."

The arrow left Eishoxa's bow before she'd even realised it. But she was shaking with pent-up fury and agony and Rianox easily avoided it. She went for another arrow but he was too quick for her. He dived towards her, grabbing her wrist, and twisted her arm. She felt something crack. Searing pain shot through her arm. She tried to pull away, but he wouldn't let go, holding onto her so she could hear the words he was whispering very harshly.

"You cannot control everything, Eishoxa. Look at you – you're disgusting. Does it make them stronger, to try to be the master of everything? No! They rely on poisoned arrows, not the magic that they've been taught." He plucked the arrows from her quiver and held them in his hand. They disappeared in a little flash of orange flames. "See? You're nothing. Nothing compared to what you could have been."

"Nothing?" she hissed. "Did you see what I did today? I brought a great victory!"

"You brought a great massacre. You were responsible for the deaths of thousands of people – and you're proud of that?"

"You used me!"

"If that's what you choose to believe, then I can do nothing to change it," he said simply. "I did wrong. I'm sorry for it. My pride clouded my reason. I have to obey my leader, and my leader is Vera." Eishoxa was saved from replying by the huge searchlight which was sweeping in their direction. Rianox pulled her down into the bushes where he'd been hiding. Eishoxa could feel his mind brushing gently across her own, and pins and needles spread from the place he had touched.

"Little Flame," he said quietly, and Eishoxa started at his use of Rush's name for her. "Come back with me, Little Flame. Come back with me, please! What have you become here? What has happened has happened. I can do nothing to change it. But let me try to make amends."

His heartfelt words penetrated at one level. "I'm a monster," she whispered in horror. In her mind's eye, she could see the awfulness of war, of what she'd inflicted on people. She saw an Indocani lying in the mud of the field, eyes staring; an Ewdicani burnt beyond recognition, small and fine-boned. She was a monster and she belonged with monsters. She steeled her mind against his and felt his consciousness withdraw from hers. "I cannot return. Look at what I did to Ember. If I return, you'll all be in danger. How can I go back knowing that? And knowing …" she stopped, then said so quietly she was surprised Rianox heard, "… knowing Rush is dead?" He still held her broken arm, but he jumped at that.

"Eishoxa, Rush is alive." She looked up at him and froze, shock driving away all pain and making her legs feel weak. "What? But I buried him! He's dead!"

"He's alive!"

"You're lying again, aren't you?" But her voice came out hollowly, grief replacing her anger. Rush was gone.

"No, Eishoxa! No more lies, I promise. He is alive."

She felt one wild leap of hope inside her. "How can you prove it?" Once again his mind carefully brushed against her constructed barriers and for a split second she lowered them. But then she shook her head. That place was gone. "No, Rianox. Not like that. Not anymore."

He took one look at her face and gently pulled her into his arms. She resisted for only a moment. She wanted someone to hold her and love her and tell her that it was all over. That she was waking up from the nightmare she was trudging through. That she would open her eyes and find herself home, wherever that was. And with that one gesture, offered in kindness, her loneliness welled up inside her. She wasn't an Indocani; she wasn't an Ewdicani; right now, she was human – and needed what every human needed and couldn't find in this hell of a castle. She rested her head against his warm chest with its familiar earthy smell. Her cheek felt the uneven ridge of the scar she'd given him. Could she blame him, when she'd done so much against him? He whispered to her in their language, the language of fire and warmth and love, "Oh Eishoxa, what has happened to you here? Where is the Eishoxa we used to know?"

A tear ran down her face; she knew the salty water would sting Rianox, but he didn't flinch. "She's gone, Rianox. I've lost her. She's not coming back. It's too late." She moved his arms off her and stood up. He touched her hand again briefly, but that was to heal her arm. He looked up and Eishoxa saw the pain she was feeling mirrored in his eyes. Stepping back, she whispered, "Goodbye, Rianox. Go back home and don't look for me any more." Then she shouldered her bow, the bowstring knocking against her empty quiver, and headed for the castle.

CHAPTER 11

IT DIDN'T TAKE Rianox long to scramble back down the broken rocks towards their camp. He flashed a little flame once to identify himself and waited for the answering flame, then pushed forward through the bushes. The two of them had made a little place hidden on all sides by large spiky bushes and mounds of rocks.

"Where is she?" hissed Ember as he jumped down. Navaz, crouched in a corner, raised herself slightly as Rianox started to pace. Rianox didn't look at him.

"She wouldn't come. She thinks she belongs there now." He felt, rather than saw, Ember's fist flying towards his head and spun, catching his hand at the last moment. "I tried, Ember! I did! But she's so confused and she doesn't understand anything and she's so ... so different."

"What do you mean?"

"She wears their clothes and carries their weapons and calls this place her land. She really is one of them." Ember pondered this and when he spoke, his voice was barely audible. "You mean, they've Changed her?"

"No, I don't think so. But she's blocked her mind and won't let anyone in. She feels wrong, Ember ... she feels evil." He put his head in his hands and paced up and down the little hollow. He could sense Navaz trying to calm him, but his misery, and the misery he felt in Ember, were too great even for Navaz to soothe. He looked back up. "She hasn't forgiven us, Ember. She said we deserve to die."

Ember turned away. Despair seeped from him like pus from a festering wound.

"We cannot apologise for everything," he murmured. "Some of those things had to be done." His anguish was heavy in the air. Rianox bowed his head. "She is greatly hurt, Ember. There's no denying that." Ember spun around furiously. "I know she's hurt. I can sense it like Ferac can sense Fiera. She once was mine and I was hers. These things don't disappear, Rianox!" Rianox closed his eyes. "I know they don't. But we're nothing to her. The only person she cares about is Rush." Ember looked toward the castle. "I'm going to try to get her out," he said. Rianox grabbed his arm. "What? In your condition? I won't let you go!"

"Amber is dying from wounds inflicted by her best friend and the only person I've loved, or ever will love, is turning into my enemy before my very eyes. If I die trying to make that better, then so be it!" He headed for the side of the slope, but Rianox tugged him back. "Ember, rash action won't put things right, it will just get even more of us killed. Haven't we suffered enough? Listen to me! I'll try again, and try to get into the castle this time. But you must stay here. She won't go with you, and she's a lot stronger than you." As he said the words, the feeling of breaking her weak wasted bone rose to mind again, and he winced inwardly at how easily the lie had slipped off his tongue. "Please, Ember. You'll kill yourself. I shall go again, but you must stay."

Ember looked at him with desperation. His face, once so stern and arrogant, so proud of what he was and what he could do, was now a blank, washed-out canvas from sleepless nights and endless grief and loss. He was only a shell of the man who had been Rianox's ally and rival. Finally, he nodded. "All right, I'll stay. But you must go back tomorrow and you must bring her home. Otherwise I go." Rianox nodded and helped Ember to his blanket. "Sleep now, Ember. Sleep. She will come back." And as Ember's breathing lengthened and the lines of wakefulness on his face smoothed out, Rianox looked up at the black castle towering above them and wondered what would become of the girl he had once loved and the people he had left.

Eishoxa was still shaking as she rested her forehead against the wall of the castle. She'd seen Rianox scramble back down the side of the cliff and disappear into the darkness. And when he'd gone, she'd felt more alone than ever. She tipped her head back and let the wind dry the tears on her cheeks. No crying here. Not inside the castle. Out here, where her only spectators were the night and the rocks, here she could cry. But she didn't allow it. It would be unwise to walk back inside with red eyes and salt drying on her face. Nezrax would immediately suspect something. Eishoxa laid her head back against the wall and let the wind wipe the tears from her cheeks and still her trembling chin.

"Eishoxa?" She turned to see Grimlock walking towards her, not from the castle but from the way she'd just come. As her general he was now under her command; but he had been leader of the army, and he took his subordination to her as a personal insult. When Nezrax had told him that Eishoxa would lead their troops into battle, he'd congratulated her. But she'd not forgotten the look in his eyes, a look of furious, wounded pride. She'd not forgotten how he'd have willingly ordered Respath to kill her. She'd not forgotten his demand of her to kill her defeated opponent. But now she was in charge and, although he frightened her, she refused to let him see it. She straightened from the wall and turned to watch him approach.

He scrutinised her face. "Why are you crying?"

"Is that anyway to address your leader?" she replied coolly, blinking her eyes nonetheless.

He glared at her and barely inclined his head. "General Eishoxa," he muttered and Eishoxa smiled.

"Hello to you as well," she answered, keeping her voice even and neutral. He straightened almost immediately and looked around.

"What are you doing out here?"

"I hardly think that's any of your business," Eishoxa answered. Grimlock surveyed the area once again and turned back to her. "Who were you talking to?" he demanded.

"Who said I was talking to anyone?"

"I heard voices and now you're alone. Who were you talking to?"

"No one. I wasn't talking to anyone."

"You're lying," he said with narrowed eyes.

Eishoxa stood her tallest. "What do you mean by that, Grimlock?"

He took another step towards her. "You may have convinced half the population that you're a gift to the whole world. You may even have convinced Nezrax – but you haven't convinced me. I don't believe that you've left your roots behind you. I don't believe you're truly loyal to us."

"How would you know anything about loyalty?" Eishoxa snapped. "Without me, you would have lost the battle today, and your losses would have been as great as the enemy you've only defeated with my help."

"We had Nezrax," he stated. "We would never have lost."

"She didn't fight," Eishoxa countered. "I can beat Nezrax in a fight and she knows it," she added. "If you don't trust me, you're saying you don't trust Nezrax. Now who's not being loyal?"

He gave her a murderous stare. "Just wait," he threatened. "I'm going to catch you out somehow."

"Looking forward to it," Eishoxa said. She watched him make his way into to the castle before following him.

On entering the castle, Eishoxa was told that she had been summoned by Nezrax to the Star Hall. She hurriedly put her bow and quiver in her room and went. Nezrax was sitting on her chair, alone. She stood as Eishoxa was announced and walked inside. "Eishoxa. Welcome."

Eishoxa nodded to her and crossed the Pentelement star to stand in front of Nezrax. The Goddess gestured towards a smaller chair that was set beside her and they both sat down. "How was your hunting?" Nezrax asked. Eishoxa had a moment of panic. Had Nezrax learned of her meeting with Rianox? Then she remembered that she'd asked permission to hunt in the mountains and shook her head. "Unsuccessful."

"No doubt the game were frightened off by our celebrations." Nezrax sighed. "I've summoned you here this evening, Eishoxa, to congratulate you on your performance today. I was very impressed – and surprised that, even facing your old friends, you didn't veer from the path I can see you walking down. Well done." Eishoxa looked down, unsure how to react. Did Nezrax believe that this was only a game for her, a performance, a play? Did it not occur to Nezrax, with all her intelligence, that today had been one of the worst days of Eishoxa's life: having to look at soldiers she'd killed, wanting to look after their wounded and beg them to let her care for them?

Nezrax continued. "But also, Eishoxa, I must warn you that no matter what you do, you are still one of my soldiers – and I expect the utmost from my soldiers." She stood so that Eishoxa had to look up at her. The Goddess carried on, clasping her hands behind her back in what looked like a thoughtful, pensive gesture. "Soldiers are not in demand, you see. They come daily from the Ewdicani and Indocani and therefore I can afford to dispatch a few now and then. And if soldiers are not completely loyal to me and to the cause, I do not hesitate to get rid of them. I will not tolerate a snake in the grass, do you understand?"

Eishoxa nodded. "Of course."

"And of course – as I'm sure the Indocani would agree – I can't have enemy scouts roaming free on my lands. Any scouts of mine discovered at the Tree are dealt with mercilessly, and I will do the same. Do you understand what I'm saying?" Eishoxa nodded mutely again. "Good," said Nezrax. She came back to her chair and sat down. "Well, I must inform you of evidence that Indocani have been on our mountains recently, Indocani who may be very close to you."

"I assure you—" Eishoxa began hastily, but Nezrax put her hand up.

"I don't want to hear it," she said quietly. "I give no one a second chance, Eishoxa, remember that. I am without mercy for traitors. I will find these scouts. We're preparing a trap for any other Indocani who decides to cross my lands again. I will not have it anymore, do you understand?"

"Yes," Eishoxa said in a whisper.

"Good. Now, don't give me reason to doubt you, Eishoxa. You may go."

Rianox waited for nightfall before attempting to clamber back up to the castle. He didn't have a plan about how to get Eishoxa out, but he assumed she would be sent out again and told to keep guard. He could easily take her from there if she was on her own. If she wasn't, he would have to wait. He didn't think about what Ember would do or say if he came back without her again. Returning to his station of the day before, behind large scrubby bushes, he crouched close to the ground, motionless. He watched as the castle searchlight, blindingly white, swung over him, once, twice and then again. Every time it approached he pressed himself closer to the earth, to be sure they couldn't see him. An hour passed and then another, but no one had come. Rianox told himself he was being foolish to keep waiting, but still he stayed there, praying that she would come out.

The castle was dark and silent tonight, unlike the night before when a strange white light and the sounds of celebration had poured out of it. From the direction of the gates, he could faintly hear the sound of guards and a rumbling as though something were being pushed along the ground. But apart from that, everything was silent. He was about to return to the hollow when he detected something scrambling very fast along the ground towards him. He kept his head down until he could be sure who it was. The shadows from the castle hid the person from view and their mind was carefully closed off – it might have been dead for all the energy radiating from it. The figure paused, looked around and then ran off, further into the mountains, away from the castle.

Rianox couldn't be sure if it was Eishoxa or not. If she came and he wasn't here, then he would miss her. And if that had been Eishoxa, then it would be even easier to take her away. He straightened his bow on his back and crept along the ground, keeping behind the bushes but moving fast. Before long he caught sight of the figure again, crouched as he was, looking every now and then over the top of the rock as though waiting for something. He extended his mind and brushed as gently as he could over what he suspected was the mind of the figure. At first he felt nothing, but then he sensed something like a small spark. Excited, he tried again and thought he felt the little spark brushing back tentatively against his own. It had to be Eishoxa. He looked around, scanning for anyone who might see him. Quietly and carefully, he made his way through the bushes and up towards the person, who still crouched behind the rock. The figure was further away than he'd anticipated and he had to keep dodging from rock to rock to avoid the searchlight. But when he got to the place where he'd seen her, there was no sign of anyone.

"Eishoxa?" he hissed. Where had she gone? He'd seen her just moments before. He peered behind the rock, but no one was there.

"Rianox?" When he heard his name he straightened and turned. Eishoxa was standing on the edge of a rock a few steps behind him, where he'd just been.

"Eishoxa, we have to …" He trailed off as he noticed something. Her feet weren't touching the ground and her limbs moved stiffly, as though controlled by something. The moment he understood was a moment too late. A net dropped over him and he was hoisted into the air upside down. His bow was dislodged and all the arrows slipped out of his quiver. He watched as the shape of Eishoxa disappeared in a cloud of black smoke. Several Empty stepped forward. He closed his eyes briefly, cursing his foolishness. How could he have been so naïve? It had been a trap.

"Well, well, well," came a slimy voice from the shadows. "Look what we have here."

Rianox had not returned and it was getting late. Ember paced up and down the camp alone, wondering where he was.

"He should've let me go," he thought to himself angrily. "I should've been the one to go." He sat down on the ground, then rose to his feet and started pacing again. As the searchlight from the castle swung over, dimly illuminating their camp, Ember ducked low. He wouldn't put it past Nezrax to have Empty patrolling the surrounding mountains, scouring for Indocani and Ewdicani who had escaped. He kindled a small flame and stared at it, flickering in the darkness. Ever since Fiera had abandoned them, the fire hadn't danced as it should have done. And here, in the very heart of darkness, the fire was even dimmer. Ember extinguished it and felt even more alone than ever. His fire had gone, his dragon had gone, his sister was wounded, and the one person he cared about in the world more than anyone – even Amber – was gone … The list went on and on and on. Was there anything left to lose?

"If you don't try," Ember told himself, "you'll never know whether you could have done it." He picked up his quiver of arrows and bow from the ground. Rianox had taken most of the arrows because he needed them more, which left Ember with four. Not many, but he had his sword. It would have to do. Pulling himself up the side of the hollow that the camp was in, he started out for the castle. He kept his bow in his hand, an arrow at the ready, looking around carefully, searching every shadow for any type of enemy. Suddenly, he heard a yell that was cut short.

"Rianox!" he shouted, and his voice echoed through the mountains, loud and clear. Then came another scream, higher, louder and very familiar. "Eishoxa!" he shouted, frantically looking from side to side, trying to distinguish the direction of the scream. He started to run, but before he gone a couple of paces, something swept him up and carried him in the opposite direction. Ember struggled to hold onto the claw that held him.

"Ember!" In the circumstances, Ember couldn't have been more relieved to hear Ferac's voice. Then Eishoxa's scream came again and he shouted at his dragon.

"We have to go back! Rianox and Eishoxa are in trouble!"

"It's you they want! They're trying to draw you in! To trick you! To kill you!"

"Where's Rianox?"

"They took him. I saw them. I was watching. I tried to warn him. We have to go back to the Tree and ask Fiera to help."

Ember looked down at the feet that were wrapped around his middle. Ferac had lost two claws and had bled heavily from gashes on his sturdy legs. Something warm trickled down Ember's shoulder, and when he looked up he saw a deep bleeding wound carved out of Ferac underside.

"You're hurt," Ember said, putting his hand up to touch the dragon's stomach. Ferac growled. "I know. But we must get back. The dragons are going to try to talk to Fiera. Only she can save Eishoxa now."

"And if it doesn't work? The dragon didn't need to say anything. He tossed Ember into the air and soared underneath him so that Ember landed heavily on his back. Then Ferac flew away from the Sorrowful Mountains back towards the ravaged Tree.

CHAPTER 12

S HE COULD FEEL something pounding at her head. A great pain was pulsing through her brain, and when she woke up she was in Fiera's palace. The Goddess was angrier than Eishoxa had ever seen her. Sparks flew uncontrollably from her hands and fingertips and her face was a mask of fury.

"What are you doing?" the Goddess roared and the castle around her trembled. Eishoxa stood. She was once again dressed in the flowing red robes of the Indocani, but beside the vibrant colours her skin looked washed out.

"If I could get my hands on you, I would kill you without mercy. As I hope my sister does! You traitor!" Fiera accused, flying towards Eishoxa in a rage and shaking her violently. "What are doing with Nezrax?"

"What other races have failed to do with me?" She shook off Fiera and the Goddess stepped back. "They've taught me how to harness my powers, they've taught me how to be brave."

"Can you hear yourself?" Fiera demanded. "Look! Look at yourself! This is how you should be." She seized Eishoxa's arm and dragged her towards one of the walls. Eishoxa looked up unwillingly. It was a mural. She could see herself, as she had in the dreams she'd had when she'd fallen in the river. She felt a strong keening pain. She wanted to be that. Above her was a picture of herself. Dark-skinned and beautiful, flying high above an army on her golden dragon, with bow in hand. A fierce girl, a proud girl, a girl arrogant but doing good for her people.

"Look. That is who you should be," Fiera snapped. "That was when you fought for a people you loved and cherished. You don't love these people – a fool could see that. What Rianox said to you made sense! You know it did!"

Eishoxa didn't ask how Fiera knew Rianox had spoken to her. Instead she retorted, "The people I fought for back then gave me something. This people that I've left have given me nothing but misery."

"Do you think that's enough? Do you think that justifies your actions?"

"They killed Maya! She was my friend! She was my only friend!"

"I don't know who killed your friend, Eishoxa, but I wouldn't put it past Nezrax to have made this up, to convince you that the Indocani are to blame."

"What are you talking about? Are you defending them? They killed her!"

"How many times have I had to sacrifice something for my people?" Fiera insisted. "I've given up everything for my people – everything! More than you could possibly imagine. That's what warriors are. They fight to the end, no matter what happens. You've given nothing to this people."

"They destroyed Bareth. Ember blew it up," Eishoxa protested, but her voice sounded weak. Fiera made an exasperated sound and flung her hands in the air. "I didn't give you the powers of fire so that you could waste them on my sister." She turned around suddenly and Eishoxa jumped. "She's clever, I know," Fiera said, taking Eishoxa's shoulders again. "Her words make sense. But at her core she wants you only for her own gain. She'll drag you in the dust and leave you there once she's got everything she wants out of you. When we divided the world, Wella and I gave her power and more power because her words made sense. We see now that we ruined the world because we listened. Learn from us and don't listen to her, Eishoxa."

"And what do you have at your core?" Eishoxa accused. "I know what you did. You abandoned me. You've wreaked war upon many people. Why are you telling me to learn from you?"

"It was necessary," Fiera admitted. "I'm not proud of it. I don't look back on those days and think of glory."

"If you think my powers are so dangerous, why don't you just take them away?"

"I can't," Fiera said, grinding her teeth. "Otherwise, I would have. A long time ago. Other Goddesses have intervened beyond my control. Earth, Air, Rock, Water and Fire – they all belong to you. And while you have control over them, you form a new person. One nobody can touch. That's why Nezrax thinks she's won." Eishoxa said nothing. Fiera, in a surprising gesture of kindness, took her hand. "Listen to me, Eishoxa. You can't let her in. You can't let her win. A single flame will quiver and die. A single droplet of water will dry up. If you lose your people, you lose everything." Fiera pulled her into her arms. Eishoxa did not resist. Fiera rested her cheek against Eishoxa's head and spoke again, "I'm sending you a friend. A friend to help you, a friend you will remember, although not immediately. You're waking up now, Eishoxa. Don't listen to them." Fiera's voice faded and the arms that held Eishoxa melted away until she could feel herself back in her room at the castle.

CHAPTER 13

SHE WAS SHAKEN awake while it was still dark. "Wake up," came a gruff voice. Eishoxa groggily opened her eyes and peered through the darkness. One of her generals stood there. "Nezrax wants you in the Star Hall. Now." And he left the room. She threw her legs over the side of her bed and stood up. She pulled on the tight black clothes and stuck two knives in her belt. Running her hands through her tangled hair, she sorted out most of the knots and left the room in the direction of the hall. Before she got there, she could sense that Nezrax was furious. Even in the dulled state of mind Eishoxa had put herself in, she couldn't help but shiver in fear and pause for a moment. Nezrax was not a forgiving Goddess.

The two guards at the doors pushed them open for her, then shut them quickly behind her. Eishoxa stopped, taking in the scene ahead of her. The star on the ground was blazing. In the fire corner, black flames surrounded the normal orange flames, holding them down. In the water section, a tiny trickle of water cowered between two black boulders. In the rock corner, each rock in a big pile was cracked down the middle. In the earth, small plants were crushed beneath stones of hard granite. Nezrax stood in the air section, stirring up a tempest of wind and lightning such as Eishoxa had never seen before.

"Tell me, are you happy here?" Nezrax asked. Then she shook her head and chuckled darkly before Eishoxa answered. "Of course you aren't. You're still one of them."

"What are you talking about?" Eishoxa enquired, bewildered. Nezrax rose upwards, and the storm she'd made rose with her.

"You dare to lie to me again? I've taught you my knowledge, taught you everything I know, and you betray me as well? As well as your own people?"

"I don't know what you're talking about," Eishoxa replied, casting her mind around desperately for a reason why Nezrax might think this. She'd been careful. She'd not left the castle since the night she'd seen Rianox. She'd let it be known that she was in her room. What had she done? Nezrax swooped back down and landed in front of Eishoxa. Her eyes were wild and furious.

"I warned you I'm not to be trifled with, Eishoxa. You know very well what you've done – and you'll pay for it!" She clapped her hands and the doors at the other end of the Hall opened wide. Two Empty marched through, dragging someone between them. Another Empty followed.

"We found this person. Grimlock told me of his concerns the night of the banquet. He said he didn't think you were loyal. I didn't believe him. I didn't *want* to believe him. I warned you. Now it seems I have no choice but to act." Eishoxa watched as the two Empty hauled the person towards her and dropped him at her feet. It was Rianox.

"So," Nezrax said. "What do you have to say? Eishoxa didn't reply. She looked down at him. He stirred feebly. His arms and legs had been injured by net and his face was swollen and bruised.

"Do you know him?" the Goddess asked. Eishoxa paused for a moment and then nodded. She heard the doors to the Star Hall open.

"Ah, Grimlock," Nezrax called in greeting. "Yes, come in. Is this the one you identified?" Eishoxa didn't look at Grimlock as he came to Nezrax's side. "Yes, that's the one. I believe he and Eishoxa have been talking. As to how many times, I cannot say." Eishoxa shook her head. "Once," she snapped. "We spoke once after the banquet." At the sound of her voice, Rianox lifted his head. Eishoxa looked away from him as his eyes narrowed with recognition. It was the only part of his face that could move without causing pain. "I told him my loyalty had changed."

"That's debatable," Grimlock began, but Nezrax held up her hand and Grimlock was silent. Nezrax said nothing but kept her eyes trained on Rianox, who met her gaze. Eishoxa had the urge to back away but stayed where she was.

"Do you know who I am?" Nezrax asked him. "Do you know where you are?" Rianox nodded. "I know who you are," he croaked. Nezrax smiled. Eishoxa had seen that smile before and knew that it did not bode well. "And yet you enter still?"

"You've stolen something from me and I came merely to take it back," Rianox replied. His voice was stronger and bolder than Eishoxa had ever heard it. Nezrax laughed. "Stolen? Oh, I think not. She came here of her own free will. She chose to leave you."

"No one comes here of their own free will, witch," Rianox countered. Nezrax put out one finger and touched Rianox's forehead. A translucent oval appeared above his head. Eishoxa blinked against the radiance that flooded the Hall. His mind was alive with bright light, light that had not appeared in this Hall for a long time.

"A witch you call me," Nezrax mused, moving her fingers in and out of the oval. Eishoxa's heart twisted as she saw Rianox grit his teeth.

"Yes, I am a witch. I am a sorceress. The Great Sorceress. Yes, I am. I take that as a compliment. What I don't take as a compliment is your thinking you can wander over my land unchecked with impunity. We've caught many more of you here than I would like, and I've sworn to put a stop to it." Eishoxa was watching her out of the corner of her eye with bated breath as she could tell Rianox was. She was transfixed by the sight of his mind. The whole oval was filled with light, more light than she could ever have thought possible. She could see dark undercurrents of other thoughts, other things, but it didn't matter. Deep down, he was good and pure. If she'd had to imagine Rianox's mind, it would not have been this. Nezrax turned away briefly, then turned back with the tiniest of daggers in her hand. Eishoxa anticipated what she intended to do – she'd seen it before. No matter what, she couldn't let that light die, that beautiful, vibrant light, black out as she'd seen. She looked wildly from Rianox to Nezrax again and stepped out in front of him.

"No!" she said. Nezrax's hand was raised, ready to slice right through the oval and destroy all that light in one practiced sweep.

"No?" Nezrax asked. "Are you sure your loyalty has changed to us,

Eishoxa? Are you sure you're not as much a traitor as he is?" Eishoxa had no answer. She could see the triumph on Grimlock's face and knew that he had wanted this, had been hoping for this.

"Stand aside, Eishoxa," Nezrax ordered, her dagger still raised. Eishoxa shook her head. "No," she repeated. Nezrax lowered her dagger and stared at Eishoxa, who was desperately calling to mind all the magic she had been taught. "Do you want this fight, Eishoxa? Because I promise you it will get very nasty, very fast." Eishoxa thought about everything she'd been taught and knew it was nothing compared to what the Goddess could do. Nezrax was not so naive as to reveal everything to her. Nezrax was cleverer than either of her sisters realised.

"You can kill him," Eishoxa said. "But you can't do that. I won't let you." The last words rang out clear and strong throughout the Star Hall. Nezrax's face froze with surprise for a split second, but then she recovered. "Why would you care?" Nezrax asked. She looked down at Rianox on the floor, his face bruised and battered, his skin ravaged and ruined. "Why do you care about what I do to him? Does it mean you're no longer happy with your life here and you are missing the ways of your old life? Our rules are clear. Any traitors are dealt with by me, as I see fit."

"I shall not stand aside," Eishoxa said. "You may kill him and kill me, but not this." That seemed to stop Nezrax. "I gave you my trust, Eishoxa," Nezrax said slowly.

"If Grimlock thinks I've betrayed you, he's mistaken. My loyalty has not changed."

"But you've spoken with the enemy and you've not told anyone that they roamed our lands. If another soldier had done that, I would have killed him. On the spot. We cannot have traitors, Eishoxa. I will not stand traitors." Eishoxa could feel everyone's eyes on her, all daring her to speak, to come up with an excuse. Eishoxa closed her eyes briefly and then felt the words form in her mouth and spill out into the air. They sounded so monotonous, but they stole her existence away.

"I would do anything to prove my loyalty to you and to the Pentelement," she said. Grimlock's eyes widened and she knew that he hadn't been expecting her to say that. Neither had Nezrax. Her face was again frozen in surprise, and then another mask slipped in place to challenge, to dare.

"Even Change?" Nezrax asked. "Would you? Give up your fire and instead claim all five elements as your own?"

Outwardly Eishoxa didn't move, but inwardly her whole body crumpled. She'd known, deep down, that Nezrax would ask for that. Her undying loyalty. Once she Changed, there would be no going back and no possibility of regaining her old self. Her mind would corrupt, decay and disappear and she would become as one of Nezrax's soldiers – brainwashed, without a personal identity or individuality. No longer would that oval hang above her head whenever she looked at her mind. She would have to give that up. That was the price.

"Would you?" Nezrax repeated. "Would you do even that to prove your loyalty to me?"

"Even that." Nezrax laughed. "Well, we have a victory. Another victory. And so soon after the first. Very well, I will grant your request."

"When will the Changing happen?" Grimlock asked Nezrax. The Goddess looked at Eishoxa and said emphatically, "Tomorrow. Before sunrise."

"And what do we do with him?" one of Rianox's guards asked. Eishoxa was not looking at him or Nezrax, although she could feel the Goddess's eyes on her. Rianox had hung his head again. For Eishoxa, that was the ultimate sign of his surrender. "Lock him up," Nezrax ordered. "Post a guard at the door. He dies at dawn."

CHAPTER 14

Eishoxa was left to go free. She returned to her room and shut the door. Leaning back against it, she felt a panicked breath hitch in her throat. She should have just let Nezrax get rid of him. Then she shook her head. No, something had touched her from that glowing oval, something that meant she couldn't watch the destruction of it. She walked to her sword and arrows lying on the bed and the sight of them sickened her. She flung them as hard as she could across the room. Then she screamed aloud and kicked one of the legs of her bed so hard that it broke and the corner slumped. How could she have been so stupid? Nezrax was never going to let Rianox go free. And that meant Eishoxa had given up her life for someone she shouldn't care about, someone who would die the following morning, before dawn. She had forfeited her life for the few hours remaining to an enemy before his death. She put her hands up to her face and lay back on the bed. She had forgotten how to cry and how to feel sad. Instead she felt a consuming anger which coursed through her veins like liquid fury, filling her heart and making her limbs tingle. She placed a hand on her forehead and drew the oval out her mind. The shadows rushed around it, faster and faster the angrier she became. Tension built relentlessly until suddenly it was released and, for the first time since she'd extinguished it all that while ago, a little ball of light appeared in the oval.

She sat up and looked at it: weak and feeble, but it was there. Then she started to feel it pulsing away uncomfortably in her mind. Fiera's words echoed inside her head as well: *"I'm sending you a friend. A friend to help you, a friend you will remember, although not immediately."* The words themselves hovered in the oval, then faded. She retracted her mind and the oval disappeared. She picked up her sword from the floor and slid it into the empty scabbard hanging at her waist.

She walked through the castle until she reached the dungeons. Prisoners had not been kept for a long time, so it was easy to see which cell Rianox was in. It was the one Maya had been in, right at the end. An Empty stood guard at the door. When she saw Eishoxa approach, she straightened and drew her sword.

"Nezrax's orders. No one is to go in."

"I think you can make an exception for me," Eishoxa said. She pushed the Empty to one side and pointed at the lock. "Open it."

"I am not allowed." Eishoxa drew her sword. She could see that the Empty had once been an Ewdicani. When flames started flickering up and down the blade, she stiffened. "Open it," Eishoxa repeated. The Empty paused for just another second and then fumbled for the keys at her waist. "Guard the door. I won't be long." She opened the door and closed it behind her. The guard looked in for a moment and then stood to one side.

"Rianox," Eishoxa said. He sat with his back to her, his arms held above his head by black chains. She moved quietly and stood in front of him for a moment, then lowered herself to the ground.

"Eishoxa." Rianox smiled at her. His face had drained of all colour and the little glint that had been in his eyes had disappeared. "I hoped you would come."

"I told you to stay away. You were stupid to come back," she said hollowly.

"And I told you I would never stay away. Not with you in this place," he declared, smiling at her.

"They were too clever. I knew what they were going to do. Why did you come back?"

"Did they catch Ember as well?"

"Ember?" Eishoxa stiffened. "Is he here too?"

"He's waiting for me. He's been injured," Rianox said.

Eishoxa rose to her feet. "Where is he?"

"Do you think I'd be so reckless as to give his location away?" Rianox asked. "He's well hidden, though he probably won't remain there if I don't return tonight." He shifted on the cold floor and winced as the chains dug into his arms. "I don't suppose you've come here to free me," Rianox said, and then laughed hopelessly.   Eishoxa looked down and shook her head. "I wouldn't even know how. Those chains are made by Nezrax just for this purpose. Only she knows how to break them."

"Then could you light a fire?" he asked. Eishoxa's head jerked up. She hadn't missed the quiver of fear in his voice. She snapped her fingers and her hand burst into flames. Rianox smiled and said, with a sort of chuckle in his voice, "Do you know what I was thinking about? There's a proverb in the Ewdicani teaching: It is good to be great, but it is greater to be good."

"What are you talking about?"

"You are Changing tomorrow. You'll join their ranks. You're choosing to lose your fire and to become one of the Pentelement." Eishoxa nodded dumbly.

"The Indocani look for greatness, Eishoxa, but the Ewdicani look to be good. You are already great. Maybe you should look for goodness."

"Is that what you did?" Eishoxa demanded. Rianox smiled. "What I did doesn't matter. My life is over tomorrow. You still have a choice."

"I chose it for you," Eishoxa snapped. "I defended you! I could tell what she was going to do to you. I've seen it before. Another scout of yours was captured. She cut right through his mind and it disappeared." She took a deep breath, trying to rid her mind of the horror it was revisiting.

"What disappeared?"

"The light," Eishoxa replied. "And your mind was so full of light that I couldn't let that be destroyed. I couldn't do that."

"Why did it matter?" Rianox asked. Eishoxa looked at him, confused. "Why did what matter?"

"Whether the light was destroyed or not? I thought you hated me." She said nothing for a moment, then murmured, "That was not a fate I could wish upon anyone, friend or foe."

"I see." Rianox looked down, then raised his eyes to meet hers. "You could change your mind, you know. They can kill me. I don't care. But you don't deserve to lose your life for something like that."

"I'm a bad person," she said quietly. "I know that. I don't think any words you say now will make me change my mind. Many people have tried."

"You are not a bad person," Rianox replied fiercely. "You are a good person, who has done many bad things."

"If you're trying to make me feel guilty, don't," Eishoxa snapped. "It doesn't work."

"I'm not going to try that," Rianox promised. "If I'd been in your situation, I'd have done the same."

Eishoxa looked puzzled. "Fiera said that any other Indocani would behave differently."

"That's because the Indocani Fiera holds in her head is one of perfection. But that Indocani cannot exist and sometimes she doesn't see that. I'm not asking you anymore to forgive, Eishoxa, but I am asking you to see that this isn't you. What you're doing comes from the command of the personification of pure evil. Nezrax is evil. And she'll do whatever it takes to harm you the most."

"Fiera said that she was going to send me a friend. A friend to help me," Eishoxa said. "Do you know who that might be?"

"No," Rianox replied after a pause. "But maybe you should wait until the friend comes."

"I'm being Changed tomorrow, Rianox, and you are dying tomorrow. These are the facts." He paused again, then whispered, "They are the facts if you make them so."

"Are you trying to get me to release you?" Eishoxa replied just as quietly. He looked into her eyes. "I'm not trying to get you to do anything. I'm just a very frightened person who is waiting to die." Eishoxa nodded. They sat in silence. Rianox was staring at the flames around her hand. "They don't speak anymore," he said sadly.

Eishoxa gazed at the flames. "No," she said. She was going to say "I don't let them speak" but she changed it to "Nezrax doesn't let them speak." Rianox didn't respond.

"Why did you hold me back that day when Ember was beating Rush?" Eishoxa asked. She had to know the answer.

"To protect you," he said it without hesitation.

"From what?" Eishoxa asked. She had not been expecting that response.

"From yourself," Rianox answered. "I knew what Nezrax was doing to you and I knew you would only make things worse. I knew that if you did anything to one of your own people, even Ember, the part of you that was Indocani would be damaged beyond repair. But you were stronger than I expected. Not like now." Disgust flashed in his eyes and Eishoxa had to turn away, to force herself not to be ashamed. She didn't care what he thought. She didn't.

"Rianox," she said. She could feel words on the tip of her tongue, words that she should say. Then her hand twitched and she caught

341

sight of her black snake-skin clothing. She was different now. And talking to him, wanting to talk to him, was traitorous.

"I've got to go," she burst out.

"Eishoxa," Rianox said.

She turned slightly at the door but didn't wait for his next words.

CHAPTER 15

THE NEXT DAY was one of great excitement. It had been a long time since they'd had a Changing. Eishoxa greeted the dawn as the last she would see. She'd made herself a promise the evening before, after returning from Rianox's cell. *It is good to be great, but it is greater to be good.* She had nothing left now that was worth living for here. But not even Nezrax could take away her freedom. She would not live long as an Empty. And speaking with Rianox had taught her something. She had been bowing to Nezrax and to her power, and whenever the good side of her tried to straighten itself, the bad side forced her lower. She'd been prostrated, but now she'd had enough. There was good in this world, but only for those who asked for it.

Eishoxa opened the black shutters of her window and looked out over the courtyard. It was deserted, for the first time in many weeks. Everyone was inside. Eishoxa picked up her knife but then replaced it, instead strapping her sword into her belt. She donned the tight black clothes and shook her hair free of the plait she wore when sleeping. There. She was ready. She left the door open behind her and walked down towards the Star Hall, sensing already the aura of anticipation and bloodlust. She met no one on the journey down, but she could feel the walls and the castle itself coming to life. Today was a day that would make history. Eishoxa allowed herself one smile before rearranging her features into an expressionless mask. She could have no mistakes, not today. Approaching the Star Hall, she was stopped by a guard at the double doors.

"You are not to go in yet," the Empty told her. Eishoxa noticed for the first time that the doors bore the same inscriptions as the Pentelement star. Suddenly three loud booms came from inside the Star Hall. The Empty standing in front of the doors took hold of the handles.

"You may go in now," the other said.

Eishoxa took a deep breath, then walked inside where a wave of whisperings and murmurings greeted her. The Empty were grouped along the walls of the Hall. The Pentelement star was clear in the centre and Nezrax sat in her chair at the top of the Hall. Eishoxa stopped before her feet touched the edge of the star and looked at the Goddess. Nezrax paused before standing. The cloud around her feet was the biggest that Eishoxa had ever seen it. Nezrax appraised Eishoxa for a moment.

"Is your intention the same as it was yesterday?" Nezrax asked finally. The murmurings stopped.

Eishoxa nodded. "It is."

Nezrax walked down the steps, her feet visible through the cloud, touching the ground. It was the first time Eishoxa had seen her walk. The Goddess stopped before reaching the other side of the Pentelement star. They looked at each other over the symbols. Keeping her eyes on Eishoxa, Nezrax clapped her hands. The door at the end of the Hall opened and two Empty dragged Rianox inside. He was no longer chained, but he looked drained of strength. The Empty dropped him at Nezrax's feet. She paid no attention to him. Nezrax stepped into the centre of the Pentelement's circle. The star rippled faintly. Nezrax gestured for Eishoxa to step into the fire section. Eishoxa could not look at Rianox, but his words echoed in her head: *It is good to be great, but it is greater to be good. You are already great. Maybe you should look for goodness.* The symbol beneath her feet started to glow and its heat moved through her body. Somewhere in the midst of the waiting Empty, feet started to stamp. Soon everyone joined in. The noise pounded throughout the hall, growing louder and louder. Nezrax was standing very still with her eyes closed. Suddenly she opened them and the noise stopped immediately. Silence hung over the hall. Nezrax opened her mouth to speak, but another voice spoke, quiet, insistent.

"Eishoxa, I am the friend of a good person." Nezrax spun around. Rianox was staring at Eishoxa. No one spoke. He continued, "No matter what you've done, in your heart you are good." Again no one said anything. Eishoxa held his gaze. His voice, quiet and gentle, reminded her of Rush's voice. Rush ... alive. When Rianox had told her before, it hadn't registered as it might have. But Rush was alive.

"Do you hear me, Eishoxa? If you believe nothing else, believe that. The people around you are bad, but you stand alone as a good person."

"Quiet!" Nezrax commanded. One of the Empty kicked him in the gut and he doubled over. But he lifted his head. Eishoxa had not looked away from him. Something was burning behind her eyes. "Your choices define you. You don't have to do this." His voice was growing louder, stronger even. "Have courage. Somewhere in there is the real you, and that part of you is beautiful." She glanced downwards for a fraction of a second, and in that moment the Empty struck him over the head and he hung limply. Eishoxa looked at her feet.

"Have you changed your mind?" Nezrax asked dangerously. Eishoxa looked past her at Rianox and shook her head. "No," she said. Nezrax smiled. "Good. Let us begin then."

Her eyes closed again and put her hands out in front of her. The cloud around her feet grew and grew. The ground beneath Eishoxa started to shake. The five points of the Pentelement star began to glow and then suddenly the star's perimeter burst into flames. Yellow flames. Real fire. Eishoxa's eyes were blinded by its brightness and her legs seared by its heat. But she didn't move a millimetre.

Nezrax started speaking in a strange chanting voice. Eishoxa understood some of it. The Goddess called on spirits and sprites, creatures of darkness and shadow. She called on beasts of places unknown. As Nezrax went on, the child form she assumed flickered in and out of view. In its place was revealed a terrible thing, something monstrous, which could only have been Nezrax's true form.

As Nezrax continued to chant, the circle within the Pentelement started to glow. Then, of their own accord, her hands moved to point at Eishoxa. She felt something seize her and root her feet to the ground. Her mind was pulled abruptly out of her head. The oval hung suspended between her and Nezrax, a barrier between them. Eishoxa watched as tendrils rose out of the ground and moved towards the oval, circling but not touching it.

"*Eishoxa. I'm coming.*" The voice pierced through the barriers she had placed around her mind as though it belonged there. Eishoxa started and glanced around. Apparently no one else had heard the voice, not even Nezrax, who was still intoning her spell, her eyes half closed, her arms uplifted. The air around the Goddess was humming and buzzing with magic. She had started to twist and shake violently. The ground trembled as though frightened.

Eishoxa looked around, but no one seemed to notice anything. Her eyes fell on Rianox, wondering whether he was aware of anything, but he hung limply, his head still lowered. Nezrax's voice crescendoed. Black smoke rose from the ground around her feet, obscuring her legs and the roof of Hell. Eishoxa then saw the same smoke rise from around her own feet, felt it slowly swallowing her up, taking each part of her into itself and changing it. She was being remade.

Again she heard the voice in her head, more urgent this time. "*Eishoxa, I'm coming! Wait for me!*" Eishoxa looked around again and saw Rianox twitch. His head slowly rose and he locked eyes with her. A short, sharp pain flashed through her, right through her chest. Right where her heart had once been. "*I'm coming.*" The words were reverberating in her head when she heard a cry from outside, loud enough to shake the walls of the castle. Nezrax's eyes opened but she did not break her spell. The thick smoke had reached Eishoxa's waist now. A terrible coldness was spreading through her body. The smoke that was creeping up her body was now spreading along the floor like something alive.

"*I'm here.*" The words had barely finished in Eishoxa's head when something exploded through the wall. A huge flash of gold streaked crossed the hall and with tremendous force picked her up, spun her into the air and threw her onto the stone floor. Winded and bruised, she could only lie there, gasping for air. As the golden streak flew around the room, fire licked up the walls as it passed. Nezrax, incredulous, stood frozen to the spot, her arms still in the air as she stared. Eishoxa watched mesmerised as the streak landed on the central chandelier and she saw what it was: a dragon, the most beautiful she'd had ever seen. It was golden from head to foot, its big yellow-brown eyes flecked with amber. Around its neck was a giant ruff, and two horns crowned its head.

"Fiera," Eishoxa said, knowing it could only be her. "*Yes, I'm here. I've returned for you. Your mother found me and sent me home.*" Nezrax lowered her arms. The dragon growled and leapt down to the ground. With one sweep of her tail, she knocked a crowd of Empty into the wall. Then she opened her mouth and sent a blast of violent yellow flames straight for Nezrax. The Goddess was ready. Before the flames could reach her, she leapt into the air, somersaulting over the fire and landing behind the dragon. The flames collided with Nezrax's smoke with a high-pitched squeal. Dust and debris filled the air. Coughing, she looked around. Fiera was snarling at Nezrax, her ears pinned back, teeth bared, claws scraping against the stone floor. Eishoxa looked around for Rianox but couldn't see him. The rest of the Empty had fled or were unconscious on the floor.

"So this is what my sister sends me!" Nezrax screamed. She snapped her fingers and a ball of black magic appeared around her hand, trained at her beloved dragon. Eishoxa had seen what those things could do. As Nezrax moved, the cloud grew around her feet again, the cloud that showed the roof of Hell. "Such a pity. We were almost done." Fiera held her ground, but Eishoxa could sense her fear.

"I would have sent Fiera something back," Nezrax continued. "But I suppose, given the circumstances—" The Goddess raised her hand and threw the black magic before Eishoxa could call out a warning to Fiera. But Nezrax hadn't thrown it at the dragon. She'd thrown it at Eishoxa.

As the ball of black magic moved deliberately through the air, Eishoxa saw it change shape. Tendrils grew out of it, stretching towards her as though to embrace her. She wouldn't be able to move in time any-way – her magic wouldn't come. Even so, she stretched her hands out towards it. Out of the corner of her eye she noticed something moving towards her, but couldn't make out what it was. The flames hit her just when the ball of magic did. Her body filled with crushing pain, burning like fire, freezing like ice. Nezrax looked smug as Eishoxa fell. A strong and painful tug stabbed through her abdomen and chest, causing her to convulse. But even in her agony she saw the smug look slide off Nezrax's face as Fiera flew towards Eishoxa, her massive bat-like wings buffeting the air. The dragon opened her mouth and bathed her in flames. The pain dissipated, washed away by the fire, and Eishoxa lay on the ground shuddering. Nezrax started forward, shocked. Eishoxa, trembling all over, saw the dragon blink its eyes at her before turning and hissing at Nezrax. The Goddess took one look at the bristling dragon and disappeared in a flurry of smoke and black feathers. Another fit seized Eishoxa, contorting her whole body. As it passed, a little flame, as blue as the depths of the sea, crawled over her fingers and covered her hand with a fiery web. She pushed herself to her feet and watched her hand in wonder. The blue flames spread up her arm and suddenly she felt something crack inside her, as though a dam had just broken. A blazing flood of memories poured through Eishoxa like a fire ravaging dry grass. The barriers she had erected around her mind, forcing it into submission and taking away all feeling and emotion, were swept away like trees in a raging river. Memories poured through her mind and then her dragon's and then hers again, connecting them in a paralysing siege of sights and sounds and smells. Memory after memory flew through her, and fire burned through her mind, even stronger than when it had claimed her, long ago, in Dulcacohefen. Even stronger than the shadow of fire that had grown its evil seed in her mind. This fire was real fire, as it had been the first day it touched Earth. Resilient and fierce and loyal and beautiful.

So very beautiful. It burned away, one by one, each layer of her mind – girl, woman, human, princess of Bareth, daughter of fire, beloved of water, blessed of earth, master of rock and air, Indocani, friend of Ewdicani, bad, good – until there was nothing left. Then a single voice spoke, a quiet little murmur: "*Be yourself. Just be Eishoxa!*" The memories ceased, but only for a second. Then the fire once again roared in her ears and she could feel it in her bones and her blood. Her whole being was consumed by fire. She was the fire princess, the flame that would rage through the land and change everything. She was the Destroyer and the Deliverer, hot and cold, fire and water, earth and rock. She was herself, and for once – for just a moment, a second, a fraction of a second – she understood what that meant.

Finally, the noise ceased. Eishoxa had changed. She looked down at herself through golden eyes. Her desert skin had darkened, and patterns of yellow and orange and red covered her skin. Her senses had sharpened. Her mind was alive with the life all around her, bubbling and fizzing with new scents and sounds. Her legs and arms were longer and stronger and her muscles were filled with the urge to run, to move, to fight, to fly, to live and to be free. And best of all, she could feel the golden dragon, her dragon Fiera, in the back of her head, a constant presence, there now and there forever.

She left the rubble of the castle behind her. Her Changing and Fiera's attack had resulted in an explosion that had almost completely destroyed it. Rianox sat on Fiera's back as well, recovering. They said nothing to each other. Nothing needed to be said. Everything was forgiven. Eishoxa told Fiera where to go and then leaned back against Rianox, resting as well, the fatigue hitting her like a hammer in every inch of her body. Rianox stirred and moved slightly, looking around.

"We're going home?" he asked.

Eishoxa smiled. "Yes. We're going home."

Nothing was solved yet. The Empty would come back, greater and more powerful than before. Nezrax would not be defeated, not by her nor by anyone else. Eishoxa had things to resolve, things to correct. She had lost a friend, a country, a people and a family. But she had gained an identity that belonged to her, gained another people and another family. She thought of Rush and what they would do together, and she had to think of her own people, of Amber and Ash and Ember and Rianox. She glanced back at him. And she had to think of herself. But all that could wait. For now, the low sun heralded a new beginning and its pale light was warming her skin. As she looked out towards the horizon, she smiled. It was going to be a beautiful day.

Amber was resting on the top bough of the Tree. Its foliage had been burned away when Eishoxa had attacked it, so there was nothing protecting her from the cold air as she awaited the dawn. She shivered but could not bring herself to conjure fire. She had lost her childlike delight in the flames she had once believed so beautiful that they could not harm anyone. Now she had only to look around her to see how naïve she had been. She had spent many nights up here, in a sort of desperate penitence, hoping that the horizon would bring good news. Her arm, where she had been shot in battle, was still useless. The archer had been aiming for her heart but she had dodged and, by some miracle, the arrow had pierced her arm instead. Even after some weeks, her arm ached with the pain. The Indocani had suffered in that war. Ember had returned with Ferac but with no sign of Eishoxa and news that Rianox had been captured.

Despite what he had done, Amber feared for her friend and for what Nezrax would do to him. Even though Fiera had abandoned them, Amber waited up here every day, begging the Goddess to send them home safely. Fiera was the only one who could help them now. Amber took out her knife and dug it into the bark of the Tree. Her dragon had also been terribly wounded in the battle and was recovering in the Dragon Forest. Coal, the main healer when the survivors had returned, had forbidden Amber to move from the Tree so she couldn't even go to see if the dragon was all right. She closed her eyes and rested her head back on the cold bark of the Tree. The first rays of sun lit up her face, but even their brightness couldn't lift Amber's dark spirits. Something tickled her back. She shifted but it was still there. Sitting forward, she turned to see what it was and gasped. A little shoot was sprouting from the Tree. Amber looked around. The same thing was happening everywhere. As she watched, the shoots grew and matured, turning into twigs and then branches and then thick boughs. In a matter of minutes, a canopy of fresh leaves had formed over her head. The Tree was repairing itself. Amber stood and peered through the leaves, wondering what on earth was happening. When she looked down, she could see Indocani all over the Tree climbing up towards her, looking around, talking in amazement to one another, as the Tree grew fresh green leaves and new vines curled around its thick trunk. She turned to the horizon, where the sunrise was breaking over the trees of the Black Forest. Suddenly a shout came from below.

"I can see something!" Amber squinted her eyes. In the distance something was coming towards them. Amber climbed onto the bough above, newly grown, and stood leaning out, trying to get a better view. Then she knew who it was. Who could mistake that golden dragon, roaring joyfully? That beautiful golden dragon who had disappeared for so long and now was back, with scales glittering and gleaming in the early light? And, above all, who could mistake the rider, in her true colours at last, her hand held above her, healing the Tree? Eishoxa, their Princess, had finally come home.

Author's Note

Shadows of Fire is the first book of *The Pentelement Trilogy*. I started writing it when I was about ten or eleven, when it was called *The Daughter of the Sun and the Cousin to the Sea*. I stopped writing it when I ran out of ideas and focused instead on another book, *Timeless*. Shortly before that was published, I rediscovered *The Daughter of the Sun and the Cousin to the Sea*. I took the idea apart, changed it slightly, renamed it *Shadows of Fire* and began writing it again. It was completed in about six months.

Why did I want to write this book? Because, quite simply, I am fascinated by the strength of nature. We as a species are capable of doing so much, but nature is stronger than us in many ways. Think of the sea. Think of forest fires. Think of earthquakes. We can repair the damage they do and sometimes harness their power, but we cannot control them. And from the variety and strength that nature has in its elements, I knew I could create interesting characters and exciting storylines.

Secondly, in my own family I see there are both similarities and differences between me and my three siblings. I love to read; we play five different instruments between us; my younger brother is good at sport; my younger sister is very good with animals; my older brother and I have quite short tempers. So I thought it would be intriguing to have a world with two different races and a protagonist who could potentially belong to both.

Finally, there were two recurring themes that I wanted to explore – namely, the difference between good people and bad people, and what makes someone a good or bad person. In a lot of the books I was reading, heroes and heroines seemed capable of sacrificing everything they had, or wanted to serve a greater good. They never followed their own wishes. To me this seemed unrealistic, especially when as humans they had no exceptional powers. I wanted to create a character who was thrown into a world where much was expected of her and she wasn't able to fulfil expectations. I wanted to experiment with this question: does making mistakes and being selfish in your wishes and choices make you a bad person? If it does, the protagonist in Shadows of Fire is neither a heroine nor a good person.

The two main races in Shadows of Fire are the Indocani and the Ewdicani. The Indocani are a very harsh race. Their language is based on the sound of Germanic languages, with a very definite texture. I imagined the Indocani to be like the Vikings, Spartans or Celts, with a reputation for great skill in combat and a primal instinct that made them very animal-like. The character of Vera, their leader, is loosely based on Boadicea.

The Ewdicani, on the other hand, are based on the ancient Greeks and Egyptians. With a great love of learning, they combined science and philosophy to form their moral code. They are a much sweeter race and their language is based on Romance languages. Dulcacohefen was inspired by pictures of old Arabian architecture, with its unique beauty.

After much listening to languages online, I found that the sound of Hebrew was very like the sound I imagined for Düerasgörn, the language of the Indocani. I had gone through several names for my protagonist, but finally created the name Eishoxa based on He-brew (*esh* means fire), adding my own diminutive twist, *-oxa* (little).

About the Author

Clare Ritchie was born in 1999 in south-east London, where she lives with her parents, two brothers and sister. She enjoys reading (particularly Oscar Wilde and Philippa Gregory), debating and playing the piano. Clare has wanted to be a writer since the age of 6 and she completed her first published book, *Timeless*, at the age of 14. *Shadows of Fire* is her second book, the first in a trilogy. Clare is currently attending Trinity Sixth Form in Croydon and plans to read History and Spanish at university.

www.ingramcontent.com/pod-product-compliance
Lightning Source LLC
Chambersburg PA
CBHW062009170626
46813CB00001B/90